Second Chance Love

By

David Johnson

ISBN: 979-8-4198-7307-0

SECOND CHANCE LOVE

CHAPTER ONE

Opening the back door of her mother's car, Megan Charles pitches her quad cane onto the back seat, then slams the door shut. As she moves to get in the front passenger seat, her mother, Grace, takes her arm.

"Let me help."

"Quit hovering!" Megan snaps. "I can do it myself." With difficulty, she gets in and snaps on her seatbelt.

Her mother hurries to the driver's side and slips in. "I was only trying to help."

"I know, I'm sorry I barked at you. I love you, Mother."

Grace pats her arm. "I love you, too, honey. Are you ready to get one of those great breakfasts at the Huddle House? I love their pecan waffles."

"Why do we always have to go to their after my appointments?"

"You don't like the Huddle House? I thought you liked it. It's just that warm syrup they give you. I mean…mmm." She closes her eyes and licks her lips.

"Don't close your eyes when you're driving, Mother," Megan tells her.

During the five-minute drive there, Grace asks, "Did Dr. Scott work with you today?"

"He's not a doctor, Mother, he's a physical therapist. But yes, he worked with me some."

"He's dreamy, don't you think?"

"That's what you say about every man my age. I'm not even sure what it means."

"Yes, you do, you're just being contrary. What do you all say nowadays? Hot? Is that what he is? Is Dr. Scott hot? That doesn't even make sense. What does temperature have to do with how someone looks?"

Megan smiles. "Wasn't your generation the one that started using the word 'cool' to describe everything? Cool jeans, cool music, cool food, cool looking boys and girls."

Pulling into the parking lot of the Huddle House, Grace answers, "Well that was different."

Megan's learned this is her mother's default way of ending an argument she can't win, so she happily lets it go, too.

Especially if it'll help her get off the topic of 'Dr. Scott.'

"Now you sit still, and I'll come help you get out," her mother tells her as she gets out.

"I'm not an invalid," Megan replies as she opens her door before her mom gets there.

"Wait a minute," her mom insists.

Swinging her legs out the door, Megan says, "Scott says I need to be doing things for myself as often as I can, Mother. Just let me do it."

"What does he know? He's not even a doctor," Grace scoffs as she fetches the quad cane out of the back seat.

They enter the diner and are greeted with, "Welcome to Huddle House, ladies," by Teri, the familiar waitress, who's ringing up someone's tab at the cash register. "Your favorite table in the corner is available."

"Thank you, Teri," Grace says.

Turns out it's the only table available. Even the seats at the bar are occupied.

Grace calls several people by their names as she and Megan make their way to the corner.

Megan, though, keeps her focus on maintaining her balance as she walks. She arrives at the table first and sits down.

As soon as she does, Teri calls to her, "You want coffee this morning, Megan? I know your mom does."

Megan feels like everyone in the restaurant swings their attention in her direction. *It's bad enough using a cane causes people to stare at me. Why can't she just walk over here to the table, like a normal waitress does?*

Tamping down her embarrassment and irritation, Megan answers, "Just water, please."

Grace joins her and sits down. "Did you see Carla and John? John's not looking very well. That heart attack really did a number on him. And Carla looks like she's just let herself go. She's stopped coloring her hair and wearing makeup. It's sad."

Megan replies, "I don't know any Carla and John, Mother."

"Yes, you do. Carla used to be married to your daddy's sister, Cindy's, third husband. I think he's now on his fifth wife. It's shameful how he treats his wives, just up and leaves them after a few years. Cindy should have known better, but you never could tell her anything. And John, John used to be the administrator at the Henry County Nursing Home. Bless his heart, he's probably headed back there, but as a patient this time. I think their son, Jeff, is living in Houston, Texas. At least that's the last I heard. Someone told me he's gay, but I don't believe it."

Who needs ancestry-dot-com when I have my mother?

Teri interrupts Grace by placing their drink orders in front of them. "What do we feel like this morning, ladies? Waffles? Pancakes? How was your physical therapy this morning, Megan? Looks to me like you're doing lots better than when you first moved here."

"With me, it's literally one step forward and two steps back some days," Megan answers.

"That's not so," her mom interjects. "She's doing great, Teri. I'm just so proud of her."

Closing her eyes, Teri says, "I'll tell you this, if that Dr. Scott was my physical therapist, I'd do backward cartwheels if he asked me to." She opens her eyes. "And I haven't done cartwheels in…well, let's just say it's been a while."

Megan and her mom give Teri their orders. As she walks away, her mom whispers, "I'd give twenty dollars to see her try to do a cartwheel, backwards or forwards. Lord, has she put on the weight since she quit school and had a baby ten years ago. You know what they say?"

"No, I don't know what they say."

"Nothing puts weight on a woman like quitting school."

"Mother, I've never heard an expression like that in my life. I think you just make these things up sometimes."

Looking indignant, Grace says, "Well, it should be a saying, because it's true. Think about anyone you knew who quit school. Didn't they gain twenty or thirty pounds?"

Megan counters, "Why don't we say anyone who's thirty-eight years old weighs twenty or more pounds than they did when they were in high school, whether they quit school or not?"

Grace looks befuddled.

"Yes, Mother, it's nature; not a social commentary."

"You may be right." Grace reaches for her hip pocket and looks alarmed. "My phone! Where's my phone?!" Standing up, she pats all her pockets and looks on the floor. "Where is it?"

Megan calmly answers, "Maybe you left it in the car."

"The car! Of course! I'll be right back." She scurries out the door.

Megan looks out the window at the redbud trees blooming in front of the motel beside the Huddle House.

Before moving in with Mom, I never paid that much attention to those kinds of things. I guess slowing down gives a person time to look around and notice things that have been there all along.

Grace returns, huffing and puffing, brandishing her rescued phone. "I knew that's where it was." She sets the phone on the table, then in a conspiratorial tone says, "He's here again."

"You know," Megan smiles, "when you start a sentence like that, you sound like an FBI agent on a stakeout. Actually, you should consider coming out of retirement. You've got a skill set I'm sure the FBI could use."

"Now you're making fun of me. Just for that, I'm not going to tell you who it is."

Megan laughs out loud. "Mother, you couldn't stop yourself from telling me even if someone paid you a thousand dollars."

Grace brushes her comment aside. "You're right." She whispers, "It's that man who works for C&B Nursery and Landscaping. I don't know his name or who he is, but he's really nice looking. Check out that cute butt of his."

"Mother!" Megan whispers back. "Just stop it! I don't care who's here or what they look like."

Grace ignores her and takes a quick glance across the diner. "I bet you two are close to the same age. And I don't think he's wearing a wedding ring."

Just then, Teri appears, carrying a plate in each hand. "Here you go, gals. Y'all dig in, and I'll be back with some more water and coffee."

Grace continues, paying no mind to the food, "Just because you say you'll never get married again, doesn't mean you can't enjoy the scenery. I'm not interested in horseback riding, but I sure do admire a good-looking stallion when I see one."

Megan salts and peppers her eggs, trying not to show her irritation. The truth is, she did notice the man as soon as she and her mother walked in; him sitting with the same man he's always with. *It's like the Huddle House is his favorite restaurant, too.*

She's often seen his sad looking eyes and shaved head. But he's never paid much attention to her, as far as she can tell. One time, she and her mom walked right past his table, and he never even glanced her way. She's learned folks around here will at least nod at you if they don't know you, but not him.

Finally, she says to her mother, "Look Mom, even if I was interested in remarrying, what man is going to be interested in a thirty-seven-year-old woman walking around with a cane like she's—" She stops herself.

"Like she's my age," Grace says. "Go ahead and say it. Just push me on over in my grave, and I'll leave you alone."

“Stop it. Quit being that way. You know what I meant. You get around very well for a woman in her seventies. But most people your age don’t.”

“I’m just barely in my seventies.”

“Whatever you say, Mother. Anyway, the only reason a guy would be attracted to someone like me would be because he felt sorry for me and wanted to rescue me, and that’s the last thing I’m interested in.”

CHAPTER TWO

Cross Daniels and his best friend, Buck, exit the Huddle House and walk across the parking lot toward their pickup truck. Hitched to the truck is a flatbed trailer piled high with a load of mulch.

Buck says, "Did you notice she was there again? My goodness, she's a cute thing!"

"Who?" Cross replies, even though he knows exactly who Buck's talking about—the petite woman with chestnut hair and large hazel eyes.

"Don't act like you don't know who I'm talking about. It's that girl we've talked about who comes to the Huddle House regularly."

"You mean the girl *you've* talked about. I haven't been talking about any girl." *But I'd like to know what's the deal with that walking cane.*

"So, her name is Megan," Buck says.

"How do you know?"

"I overheard Teri call her that."

Standing on opposite sides of the hood of the truck, Cross looks at Buck and asks, "Does Betty know you pay so much attention to other women?"

"What's wrong with noticing? I mean, if you and I saw a Lamborghini sitting in the parking lot here, I guarantee you we'd walk over and take a look at it. So, quit trying to act like you're a blind man."

"Lamborghini," Cross mutters as he opens the driver's door and gets in the truck.

Settling into the passenger seat, Buck asks, "How long has it been since you've been with a woman?"

Cross cranks the truck and eases out of the parking lot. "Since the night before Heather was killed."

"Seven years, Cross. It's been seven years! Dang, man, don't you think that's long enough?"

"How many times are we going to have this conversation? I told you, I'm never going to be in a relationship again. And I'm tired of you and my Pop bringing it up all the time. If being single isn't a big deal to me, why should it be such a big deal to y'all?" His tone rises. "I had everything a person could want, the perfect wife, a beautiful child—and I ruined it all!" Blinking back tears, he pounds his fist on the dashboard. "Just shut up about it!"

Buck lays his arm across the back of the seat and rubs Cross's neck. "I've been with you through all the dark times, haven't I, Cross? It's been hard for me, too, like watching a bad dream. I didn't mean to upset you, but I love you, man, and I'm always gonna do what I think is best for you, even if you don't like it. I'll shut up about it for now." Reaching for the dash, he turns on the radio. Immediately, the high tenor voice of Bill Monroe singing "Footprints in the Snow" fills the cab. He punches Cross's arm. "Come on, let's sing it with him." He rolls down his window, sticks out his head, and sings at the top of his lungs.

Cross looks at him and laughs, then turns up the radio and joins in.

Some drivers pass by them and laugh, others look confused, while one older man rolls down his window and sings with them.

"That's it!" Buck yells at him enthusiastically and gives him a round of applause.

When the song ends, the old man gives them a thumbs up and pulls past. Cross and Buck laugh.

"You want to play some music tonight?" Buck asks. "You and Harlon come on over. I'll get Betty to fry us up some pork chops and cook a mess of greens."

"I would, but I've got a meeting to go to tonight, remember?"

"Oh yeah, I forgot," Buck replies. He takes out his phone and taps the screen. "I'm gonna search Facebook for Megan."

"Buck!"

"Hey, I can look for myself, can't I? How many Megans can there be in Paris, Tennessee?"

"You don't even know if she lives here," Cross retorts.

Buck focuses on the screen and ignores Cross's comment. "Bingo, I found her! Last name is Charles, Megan Charles. Hmm…looks like all her info and pictures are private. She has to friend me first. I'm gonna send her a friend request."

"Why would she accept a friend request from you?"

"I guarantee you she's seen me at the Huddle House and is curious to know if a good looking man like me is available."

Cross bursts out laughing.

"Hey, what's so funny about that?" Buck asks.

"I don't know, maybe it's your narcissism or the fact that you're delusional; I'm not sure which. Just be sure and let me know if she accepts your friend request. I'll be there to help you recover from your damaged ego."

"I'll bet you twenty dollars she accepts."

Holding out his hand, Cross says, "That's a bet I'll take."

As they shake hands, Buck says, "You better get ready to say goodbye to that twenty."

Cross brakes the truck for a stoplight up ahead and turns on his left blinker. "I'll be glad when we get finished with this Rhinehart job. I'm tired of planting things and digging them back up because Dr. Rhinehart's wife doesn't like the looks of it."

"Hey, as long as he keeps paying for it, I'll spend all year here. They've got more money than they know what to do with. I heard he made all his money in Memphis and moved here to retire in a few years."

"You're probably right," Cross agrees. "Paris has become an attractive place to retire, I guess. Sure are lots of folks doing it."

Rubbing his hands together, Buck says, "And all those retirees are loaded with money and want pretty yards."

Cross drives them along the winding driveway lined with waist-high juniper trees and thinks about how different it will look ten or fifteen years from now, when the trees are eight to ten feet tall. *It'll feel like you're entering a magical place.*

The three-story brick house with white columns appears, as does an older model pickup truck that seems to have forgotten what color it is. The driver's side door is white, the tailgate is red, and the rest is primer gray.

"Harlon's here!" Buck cheers. "I thought you said your Pop was sleeping in this morning?"

"That's what he told me."

Just then, a smiling older man with a deeply creased face and wearing overalls and a pith safari helmet walks out of the front door, followed by a woman trying to tug closed the gap in the front of her housecoat. She finally gives up, cinches the belt, and ties it in a bow. She attempts to bring order to her uncombed hair that's sticking out in every direction.

As Cross pulls to a stop behind Harlon's truck, he says, "Oh my gosh, what has he been doing?"

Laughing, Buck says, "It looks like the old rooster nailed him a hen. I bet your dad has sex more often than I do. I need to ask him what his secret is."

"It's disgusting. Don't encourage him. Ever since Mom died, he's gone off the rails with this kind of behavior."

"He has developed a reputation," Buck admits.

Grabbing their gloves off the dashboard, they exit the vehicle.

Buck calls out, "Hey, Harlon."

"Morning, Buck."

"What are you doing here, Pop?" Cross asks. "I thought you were—"

Harlon cuts him off. "I decided I needed to get out here early and help you boys unload this mulch before it starts raining." To Mrs. Rhinehart he says, "I give my son lots of technical advice, but he also depends on me to do the heavy lifting sometimes."

Looking at the sky, Cross says, "There's hardly any clouds this morning. I don't think it's going to rain."

"That's because you boys don't pay attention to the signs. The wind's been blowing out of the east for two days." He looks at Mrs. Rhinehart. "This younger generation, I don't know what's going to become of them. All they know how to do is look at their phones to see if it's going to rain."

Blushing, Mrs. Rhinehart speaks to Cross and Buck. "I know I look affright. You boys got here a bit earlier than I expected. Your father and I were just…uh…discussing…uh…" She looks around, then points at some plants. "These nandinas you planted in front of the house."

Harlon hooks his thumbs in the straps of his overalls and puffs out his chest. "Why, yes we were, weren't we?" He winks at Buck. "And what fine nandinas they are."

Buck barely stifles a laugh, but Cross scowls at him. Walking up to the couple, he elbows his father aside and stands between them. "I apologize if my Pop was bothering you, Mrs. Rhinehart. My intention was to get this work done before you woke this morning."

"He was no bother at all," she replies. "It was nice to spend some time with him. I haven't made many friends since we moved here. Seems I'm considered an outsider."

"That's because they haven't got to know you like I have," Harlon says over Cross's shoulder.

Cross snaps, "Buck, why don't you take Pop and start spreading the mulch?"

"Yes, sir." Buck salutes him.

With the clang and clatter of the shovels and wheelbarrow being unloaded behind him, Cross faces Mrs. Rhinehart. "This load of mulch should be the finishing touch to our job. I hope you're satisfied with our work. I think your yard is only going to get more beautiful over time."

"I just so appreciate your expert advice about everything," she replies. "You should be a botanist with all the knowledge you have about plants. And I'm sorry about changing my mind a few times and you having to undo and redo some of your work."

"That's not a problem. The most important thing is, you're happy with the job."

She puts her hand on his forearm. “I’m very happy with it.” Inching closer, whispers, “Can I ask if your father’s married?”

“No, ma’am, he’s not. My mother’s been dead for six years now. Pop says he enjoys the company of women but never intends on marrying again.”

His answer seems to satisfy her, so he says no more.

Pulling an envelope out of his back pocket, he hands it to her. “This is the final bill for the work.”

“Let me run and get my checkbook,” she says.

“Running” isn’t a word that should be used to describe any of Mrs. Rhinehart’s movements. But she manages to return in a few moments, checkbook in hand. She takes the envelope from him, reads the statement inside, and writes him a check.

Handing it to him, she says, “I hope this is satisfactory.”

Without looking, Cross says, “I’m sure it is.” Then he looks at the check and nearly chokes. “Mrs. Rhinehart, you misread the statement. This is twice the amount it should be.” He offers it back to her.

She holds up her hand. “I wrote it for the exact amount I intended to. I want you to be happy with me as a customer, so you’ll do a good job going forward maintaining my yard.”

“Well, I appreciate that offer, but it’s not necessary. We’ll do an excellent job taking care of your yard anyway. Please, it’s too much.”

Turning away from him, she heads back to the house. At the front door, she pauses and says to him, “Tell your father, perhaps we’ll see each other again sometime.” Stepping inside, she closes the door behind her.

Cross heads to where his dad and Buck are working. “Y’all won’t believe this.”

They stop what they’re doing and look at him.

“She paid us twice the amount we charged her.”

“You’re kidding?!” Buck exclaims.

“No, I’m not. She said she wanted us to be happy with her as a customer, so we’ll do a good job maintaining her yard.”

“What did you say?”

“I told her it was too much and tried to make her take it back, but she wouldn’t do it.”

Harlon clears his throat loudly. When they look at him, he points his nose in the air and sniffs. “I suppose you boys can thank me for that. She is a very satisfied customer.”

Buck guffaws.

But Cross gets in Harlon’s face. Through gritted teeth, he says, “Look, you may not care anything about your reputation, but I know how hard it is to outlive a bad reputation in a small town. That’s why I moved back here. Buck and I have this business going and are trying to make it work. You’re not making it easy to win the confidence of people around here. I’m just glad Mom can’t see what you’ve turned into.”

Grabbing a handful of Cross’s shirt, Harlon says, “Don’t you talk to me about your mother.”

Cross shoves him back. “I will if I want to. She’s my mother.”

“Hey, hey, hey, you guys,” Buck says as he steps between them. “Y’all’s problem is, you’re too much alike—hardheaded and quick tempered. Pick up your shovels, and let’s finish up.”

For the next several minutes, they all work in silence.

Finally, Buck says, “Hey Harlon, you know that girl at Huddle House me and Cross are always talking about?”

“*You’re* talking about,” Cross corrects him, “not me.”

“What about her?” Harlon asks.

“We learned her name is Megan Charles.”

“Charles? Is she kin to Grace Charles?”

“All we’ve learned is her name so far. Why?”

Harlon’s tone turns surly. “’Cause if she is, you better stay away from her and keep her away from me!”

CHAPTER THREE

After his meeting that night, Cross's mood is unsettled as flashes of scenes from his past keep bumping into each other. Making a turn off Highway 79 and onto Elkhorn Road, he pauses to let a herd of deer trot across.

"You're safe in the spring," he says to them, "but come fall, you better make yourselves scarce, or you'll be in my freezer."

Ten minutes later, he parks in front of his dad's house. Spotlights on the corners show him the way, but they could have saved their efforts; he could walk the path blindfolded. In his mind, he can still see the tire swing hanging from the white oak tree in the front yard and the small mound in the front yard his dad made for him to practice pitching baseball when he was growing up.

"Memories," he says, with a sigh.

Something cold and wet touches his hand. He looks down and says, "Hey there, Roxie girl, you snuck up on me, didn't you? What have you been up to today?" Reaching down, he scratches her muzzle.

The big Golden Retriever slowly wags her tail.

Squatting in front of her, he holds her head in his hands. "Have I told you lately how much you mean to me? That you accepted me back after I'd been away so long meant the world to me. You help keep me sane, you know that?"

She whines, and he hugs her.

"Come on, let's see what Pop's got going on."

Inside the house, his ears are greeted with the sound of Dean Martin singing "That's Amore."

Roxie leads the way to the living room, where Harlon sits with a record jacket in his hands.

He looks up and says, "Did you know Jerry Lewis paid to have this song written for Dean Martin in hopes it would be a big hit for him? And it received an Academy Award nomination for Best Original Song. How about that?"

Cross smiles at him. "You know what gets me? You love playing bluegrass music with your fiddle, but you're in love with this kind of crooner music."

"I used to not like it, but your mother did. She's the one who taught me to love it. It always reminds me of her. And the only way a person needs to listen to it is on vinyl. I found this copy at the thrift store." Reaching over, he lifts the arm of the record player and turns it off. "So, how was your meeting?"

"It was good. I wanted to ask you about your reaction today when Buck told you about Megan Charles. You bristled up when he mentioned it."

"I don't want to talk about it, because you'll think it's stupid."

Lying down on the couch, Cross says, "I promise I won't. I'm just curious."

"To put it simply," Harlon says, "Grace Charles broke my heart fifty years ago. Maybe this Megan Charles isn't even related."

"Dang, Pop, that must have been some kind of hurt if you still feel it fifty years later. What did she do to you?"

"She was my first real love. I was crazy about her and thought we'd marry one day. But she must not have felt the same about me, because she cheated on me."

"How come I've never heard you talk about her?"

Lifting the record off the turntable and slipping it into the dust cover, Harlon replies, "Because it hurts to remember it, and because I didn't want your mother to think I still had feelings for Grace."

"Did you?"

"Did I what?"

"Still have feelings for Grace when you married Mom?"

Harlon returns the record to its jacket and slides it in with his other albums. Standing up, he says, "I think I'll turn in for the night. I'll see you in the morning."

Well, that was weird, Cross thinks to himself. *Obviously, there's something there he doesn't want to talk about.*

Sitting up, he reaches for the book he's been reading and opens it while raising the foot of the recliner sofa.

****

A driving rain, plus the headlights of oncoming traffic, makes it nearly impossible for Cross to see where he's going. Using his hand, he rubs away the fog on the inside of the windshield.

"Watch where you're going, Cross," his wife, Heather, exclaims, her voice full of tension.

From the back seat, their daughter, Claire, asks, "Are you okay, Daddy? I'm scared."

"I'm fine," Cross replies. "We'll be home in a minute." But a sudden flash of lightning blinds him even further.

"Cross! Look out!" Heather screams.

Cross yells Heather's name as he falls off the couch and lands on his shoulder. He thrashes around for a second before he comes awake with his heart hammering against his chest.

His dad comes lumbering into the living room. "Hey, you okay?"

Sitting on his knees, Cross answers, "Yeah, I'm all right."

"The dream again?"

Cross nods. "Yeah—again." He gets up and goes to the kitchen for a glass of water.

Harlon follows him and pours himself a glass of milk. "Do you need to talk to someone about it? You know, like a counselor or one of those psychiatrists? They might can help you, Cross."

“I don’t want them to help me. I don’t ever want to forget what happened, even if it torments me the rest of my life.”

“Holding on to stuff too long isn’t good for you.”

“Says the man who still holds a grudge against somebody for what happened fifty years ago.”

Harlon stares into his glass. “That’s different.”

“Really? Different how?”

Setting his glass on the counter, Harlon walks away while saying, “It just is.”

Picking up a notepad off the counter, Cross sits down at the table and takes out his phone to listen to voicemails related to his business. All of them but one are from established customers ready for him to start cutting their grass. One, though, is from a nameless person asking him to come look at her yard and come up with a design for improving it. These are the jobs he enjoys the most, because they give him an opportunity to use his imagination and vast knowledge of plants. The address is on Sulphur Well Road, so it’s not that far away from where he lives.

I’ll check it out first thing in the morning before I head to work.

CHAPTER FOUR

Yawning as she carries her miniature schnauzer, Lacy, Megan Charles limps into the living room. Rubbing the sleep out of her eyes, she's surprised to see her mother, Grace, completely dressed and staring at her phone.

"You're up awfully early. Are you feeling okay?"

Ignoring the questions, her mom angrily punches the screen of her phone with her index finger. "Come on! Aargh! This phone makes me so mad!"

Walking to her mom, Megan says, "You know, getting mad at your phone really doesn't help anything. And abusing it the way you do only shortens its lifespan."

"I don't know what you mean by that."

"Uh, what about dropping it in the toilet? Knocking it off tables onto the floor? Dropping it on the concrete driveway? Should I go on?"

"I don't know when you became such a smart butt, but it's not a flattering look. I'm just playing Scrabble with friends, and my phone locked up on me. It drives me crazy. Maybe I need a new phone."

Maybe you need a short course on how to use a phone, Megan thinks but keeps the thought to herself. "Let's go back to my first question: Why are you up and ready so early? Going somewhere?" She goes to the door and lets Lacy out to pee.

Grace says, "It's getting close to time for The World's Biggest Fish Fry and parade. I'm meeting with one of the committees this morning. I moved away from here and married your dad before you were born, so you never got to experience it. When I moved back after he died, I knew I wanted to be involved in planning it. And now you'll get to experience it, too. Maybe one day if you have children, they can experience it, too."

Megan groans. "I've told you, I had my chance for the whole 'husband and kids thing' and blew it. I'm just not very good relationship material. I know it bothers you, but I'm comfortable being single."

“But Meg—”

“Just don’t, Mom.” She walks over to the Keurig and makes herself a cup of coffee.

“Shouldn’t you be using your cane?” Grace asks.

“I just got up; I’ll get it later.” Megan tries to keep the edge out of her tone but is uncertain how successful she is. “Tell me something, since I moved here to live with you, I’ve heard lots of people talk about this World’s Biggest Fish Fry, but is it really?”

“Really what?”

“The *World’s* Biggest Fish Fry? I mean, really, how believable is that?”

Sounding indignant, Grace says, “They serve over six tons of catfish during the event! Does that sound big enough?”

“Okay, okay. I didn’t mean to insult anyone.”

Her mom stands up and says, “It’s time for me to go. Listen, you know how you’ve been wishing we could spruce up the yard here? Well, I contacted a landscape designer, and he might be coming out this morning.”

“When? I’m not even dressed yet.”

“I don’t know. I left a voicemail message on their phone.”

“Well, crap, so much for sitting around and being lazy today. What am I supposed to tell them when they get here?”

“I’ll leave that up to you. Design it any way you want.”

Megan takes a sip of her coffee and heads back down the hallway. “I’m going to jump in the shower. Let Lacy in when you leave.”

“Okay, I will. Have you seen my purse? I had it right here just a second ago.”

Megan stops and turns around. “Is it in your bedroom?”

“No, I had it right here.” Grace wanders into the living room to look.

Megan spots it lying on the couch. “Here it is, Mom.” She holds it up for Grace to see.

“Where was it?”

“On the couch here.”

“Oh, that’s right. I remember setting it down there. Thank you.” She slips it on her shoulder. “Now where’s my phone? I just had it. I think I’m losing my mind.”

“Check your pocket, Mom,” Megan tells her.

Grace pats her back pocket and smiles. “There it is. I don’t know what I’d do without you.” She blows Megan a kiss. “See you later.”

“Love you,” Megan says as Lacy scoots inside just before Grace closes the door.

In the bathroom, Megan slips off her T-shirt and panties but loses her balance and nearly falls. Grabbing the bar on the shower door is all that saves her. She waits for the room to stop spinning, then turns on the shower. While waiting for the water to warm, she looks at her body in the mirror.

When will I completely recover? Will I ***ever*** *completely recover? I’m sick of hearing the physical therapist say, ‘One day at a time.’*

She thinks about when she used to go rock climbing nearly every weekend, the thrill of pushing her body to the limit and the excitement of reaching the top of a cliff. Closing her eyes, she rummages through memories of the vistas she’s enjoyed.

Suddenly, something cold and wet touches her leg, and she cries out. Looking down, she sees Lacy looking up at her.

She smiles and says, “You’ve got to quit sneaking up on me like that.” She pats her on the head. “You know I didn’t mean that, don’t you? You’ve been with me through it all, haven’t you?”

Lacy wags her nub of a tail and licks Megan’s hand.

“I’ve gotta get in the shower. We may have company this morning.”

She turns on the Bluetooth speaker, runs through the playlist on her phone until she finds what she’s looking for, then taps play. As she steps into the shower, “Get Up,” by Shinedown, comes blaring through the speaker. Singing at the top of her lungs, Megan joins in.

Lacy tips her head back and howls.

A few minutes later, Megan is towel drying her hair when she hears someone knocking at the front door.

Lacy explodes into fits of barking and races out of the bathroom.

What in the world?! Don't tell me the landscaper's already here!

Megan grabs her mother's bright pink housecoat, which is twice the size she needs, and pulls it on. She reaches for the belt so she can cinch it around her waist but discovers it's missing.

That's great!

Using her fingers, she tries to bring some order to her hair but sees it's useless, so she crosses the hallway into her bedroom to get her cane just as the knocking on the door becomes more insistent.

Lacy's barking reaches an ear-piercing octave higher.

"I'll be there in a minute!" Megan yells. "Lacy, stop barking!!"

Holding the housecoat closed with one hand and her quad-cane in the other, she makes her way to the door and swings it open.

Standing there, looking back at her, is the bald guy she's always seeing at the Huddle House.

For a moment, all they do is stare at each other.

Being this close to him, Megan sees his eyes are cobalt blue and there's a faint scar across his right cheekbone.

Lacy stops barking and sniffs his shoes and the leg of his jeans.

Finally, the man speaks. "Good morning. I'm Cross Daniels, with C and B Landscaping and Lawn Service. You called me yesterday about coming out and discussing a design for your yard." Looking at her housecoat and wet hair, he asks, "Were you not expecting me?"

"Actually, I wasn't. It was my mother who called you, and she didn't tell me you were coming until a little bit ago."

He rubs his hand over the top of his head. "Oh...so this is her place?"

Megan fears his question is going to lead them to the uncomfortable topic of her living with her mother, which is something she hates to admit to herself and others. *What kind of impression does that give people? That I'm too lazy to work and am leaching off my parent?*

"Yes, yes, it is," she answers.

He shifts his weight and says, “Sooo, should she not have asked me to come out?”

Megan frowns. “What do you mean?”

He averts his eyes from hers. “I mean...does she, like, have dementia or something and isn’t supposed to use the phone, or something like that?”

Chuckling, Megan answers, “No, of course not. But I can’t wait to tell her you asked me that.”

“I’m sorry, I didn’t mean to offend anyone. I just thought maybe you took care of your mother.”

Megan laughs. “Oh, she needs taking care of, but in truth, she’s the one who’s been helping take care of me.” She brandishes her cane.

Shoving a hand into the back pocket of his jeans, Cross says, “Well, I guess we’ve got one thing in common, ’cause I live with my Pop.”

Even though she’s intrigued, Megan asks no questions about his situation, because she doesn’t want to encourage any questions about her own. “If you’ll give me a few minutes to get dressed,” she says, “I’ll come out, and we can walk around the yard together.”

“Oh, yeah, sure, that’ll be fine. I’ll just wait in my truck.”

Megan flirts with the idea of being polite and offering him the option of waiting in the house but doesn’t trust that he won’t get the wrong idea, so she closes the door. Watching him retreat to his truck, she says to herself, *Mom’s right: he does have a cute butt.*

In her bedroom, she finds a pair of jeans and sits on the edge of her bed to put them on.

No more bouncing on one foot while stuffing myself into my pants. At least, no more for right now.

Rummaging through her drawers for her favorite T-shirt, she finally finds the lime green shirt with IMAGINE DRAGONS printed across the front and puts it on. Tennis shoes come on next, then a quick look in the mirror. She grimaces at her makeup-less face and thinks for a second about taking the time to put some on.

Looking at Lacy, she says, “What do I care what this man thinks? If he doesn’t like looking at me, that’s his problem, right?”

Lacy cocks her head and barks.

"I'm glad you agree. Now, let's go outside and see what ideas he has for our yard."

At the words "go outside," Lacy spins in circles, then races to the front door and begins barking.

"Okay, I'm coming," Megan calls. "Just let me get my cane first."

Outside, on the porch, Megan sees Cross sitting in his truck, with his head bowed down.

Looking at his phone, maybe?

The sound of banjo and fiddle music flows out of the open windows on his truck.

Yuck! Who can stand that kind of music?

As she walks toward him, she wishes she could hold her hands over her ears.

And who plays that kind of music that loud?!

She rolls her eyes.

So engrossed is he in whatever he's doing, she's able to walk right up to his door without being detected. When she taps him on his shoulder, he yells and jumps, throwing his phone into the air and bouncing it off the ceiling. He attempts to catch it on the rebound but can only juggle it for a couple seconds before it flies out the window and hits Megan on the nose, ultimately landing on the ground.

"Oh my gosh, I'm sorry!" Cross exclaims as he quickly opens his door.

Megan tries to get out of the way, but the door strikes her, causing her to lose her balance and fall down.

She's only there for an instant before Cross is at her side. "I'm so sorry," he says. "Are you okay? Are you hurt? Can I help you up? I'm such a klutz!" Looking like someone who can't decide which end of a snake to pick up, he reaches for her hand, stops, reaches for her arm, stops, then looks at her helplessly. "I don't know how to help you up. I don't want to injure you or something."

Coming to a sitting position, Megan lies by saying, “I’m not hurt,” because the truth is, she’s for certain one of her hips must have landed on a rock as big as her fist and produced a knot at least as big. “If you’ll stand in front of me and take both my hands and help pull me up, I’ll be fine.”

Cross gets a firm grip on her hands, stands, and lifts her easily to her feet. Then, keeping hold of one of her hands, he reaches with his other hand and picks up her cane. “Here you go,” he says as he hands it to her.

She takes it but also continues to hold his hand. Closing her eyes, she waits for her head to stop spinning.

“Hey,” Cross says, “I don’t think you’re okay. Do I need to take you to the doctor or call an ambulance or something?”

She opens her eyes. “It was just a dizzy spell. I’m fine now. It happens sometimes.” She loosens her grip on his hand, but he still holds tight.

“I think you’re just saying that,” Cross says. “I’m afraid I’ve hurt you.”

Megan glances at his truck and says, “The only thing that’s hurting me right now is that music you’re playing. Could you at least turn it down?”

CHAPTER FIVE

SEVEN YEARS EARLIER

Heather, Cross's wife, reached for the volume control on the car radio and turned it down.

"Do you always have to play it so loud?"

Cross tried to rein in his irritation but couldn't. "Man, I love listening to Tony Rice. He's the best flat-top guitar picker ever. Don't ever turn him down!" Fumbling with the radio, he turned it up even louder.

From the back seat of the car, their daughter, Claire, put her hands over her ears and cried, "It hurts my ears, Daddy."

"Why do you have to be this way, Cross?" Heather asked.

"There's nothing wrong with how I am! Everything'd be fine if you'd just lighten up and enjoy the music. Can't I do anything right? You're always harping about something."

Rain began to pelt the windshield as he cranked the car and pulled out of the parking lot of Jackie's Bar and Grill.

"Where are you going?" Heather asked.

"Home. Where do you think I'm going?"

"Well, you're headed the wrong way."

Cross tried to look at his surroundings, but the dark of night, coupled with the rain, made it impossible. "I am not going the wrong way," he asserted. "Don't you think I'd know if I was going in the wrong direction?"

Heather folded her arms and said nothing for several moments.

About that time, the headlights of the car illuminated a road sign up ahead. Cross leaned forward and squinted his eyes as they approached it. "Cedars of Lebanon State Park? Why are we headed toward the park?"

“I tried to tell you,” Heather responded. “Why don’t you just let me drive?”

“I just got mixed up,” Cross snapped. “I’m fine. I just need to find a place to turn around.”

In the deep recesses of his brain, a tinkle of a warning bell sounded, but neither it nor his wife’s pleas could get past his determination to prove he could drive them home.

A vehicle behind him came so close, its headlights illuminated the inside of the car. The reflection in the rearview mirror nearly blinded Cross. Swearing at the driver of the vehicle, he twisted up the mirror. The vehicle then swung to the left and passed, honking loudly as it did so.

Cross put his lights on bright and sped up. “Let’s see how you like it,” he muttered.

“Quit acting like a child,” Heather told him. “You’re going to get us all killed. I insist you pull over and let me drive.”

Thunder rumbled overhead as the rain reached a deafening roar inside the car.

Cross let his foot off the gas and dimmed his lights. “Man, this rain is crazy.” Switching his wipers on high, he said, “Is there anybody behind me?”

Heather turned around and looked. “No. Why?”

Without warning, Cross made a U-turn in the middle of the highway.

“Cross!” Heather cried.

In the back seat, Claire began to cry. “Mommy, I’m scared.”

“It’s okay, honey,” Cross said. “The thunder and rain are nothing to be afraid of. I’ll have us home soon.”

“That’s not what she’s afraid of,” Heather declared.

CHAPTER SIX

PRESENT DAY

The sting of Megan's criticism of his music makes Cross want to turn it up even louder, but the business side of him doesn't want to make a new customer angry, so he turns off the radio.

Pointing to her shirt, he asks, "What's Imagine Dragons?"

"You've never heard of them? It's a very popular band. I love their music."

He shrugs his shoulders. "Can't say as I have. If you're sure you're not hurt, why don't we get started looking at the yard?" He scans the property with a practiced eye. "This is a really nice place, being tucked away in these pine trees like it is."

"It's a quiet place," Megan agrees. "Why don't we start at the house?"

"You lead the way."

As she walks ahead of him, Cross is careful to keep his pace slow, which is something he'd probably have to do even if she wasn't using a cane because of the one-foot difference in their heights.

Even though he'd never admit it to Buck, he knew who Megan was the instant she opened the door to greet him. Her hair, eyes, and turned up nose were dead giveaways.

"How long has your mother lived here, Megan?" he asks.

Stopping and facing him, she frowns and says, "How do you know my name?"

"At the Huddle House...you know...they called out your name."

Megan rolls her eyes. "Oh yeah, that's true. I didn't know you were paying attention."

Cross feels hemmed in a corner by her assertion. "I don't want it to sound like I've been shadowing you or something like that. I mean, it's a small restaurant, and you can't help noticing the people who are there. You, and I guess it's your mom, have become regular customers there."

I wonder if her mother is the Grace Charles my dad talked about? I've got to figure out a way to ask without it sounding nosey. I'd love to know more from him what that situation was all about.

Megan looks at him for a few seconds, then continues toward the house. "That's my mom's fault; she loves their waffles. To answer your original question—she grew up around here, but she moved away when she was a teenager. Father died five years ago, and Mother wanted to move back. This piece of land was for sale, so she bought it and removed just enough trees to build a house. She's just never done anything with the yard. I love the blanket of pine needles, but I think it would really be pretty to add some color."

"Well, one thing we know is, whatever we plant will have to be acid-loving plants, or at least tolerant of it."

She gives him an uncertain look.

"All these pine needles leech acid into the soil."

"That sounds bad. Is it?"

"Not necessarily. But we won't plant any forsythia, because it won't grow as well as something like azalea or hydrangea." Pointing at the porch, he says, "Azaleas would look really pretty growing along there. You've got some native plants I spotted in the yard area you may want to leave where they are."

"Where?"

"Let me show you." He walks about thirty feet and points to a cluster of green plants. "These are unusual. They're called American Columbo. They come back every year and will do so for years, even decades before they bloom. Then, once they bloom, they die."

"That's kind of sad," Megan remarks. "They finally get a chance to show off, and that's it."

“I hadn’t thought about it, but yeah, you’re right. Plants have all kinds of quirks. Take pokeweed or poke salad. You know what that is, don’t you?”

Megan wrinkles her nose. “My mother cooked some one time and made me eat it. It was disgusting.”

Cross laughs. “Yeah, it’s an acquired taste. Did you know every part of the plant, from roots to stems to leaves to fruit, is poisonous in varying degrees?”

“Are you serious?”

“Yep. Another quirk is, the seeds have to go through the digestive tract of a bird or animal before they’ll germinate.”

“So, it takes going through shit before they can grow? If that was true for humans, I should be full grown and blooming like crazy.”

Cross watches her face closely to see if she’s speaking in hyperbole or being serious. He detects no hint of a smile. “I think that would be true for a lot of us.” Pointing at her cane, he asks, “Do you mind me asking what that’s about?”

Megan pauses before saying, “The simple answer is, I fell. The longer answer is, I had multiple injuries, including a closed-head injury, was in a coma for a while, and when I finally came to, I was paralyzed.”

Cross stares at her. “Oh, my God, I don’t know what to say. I can’t imagine what that must have been like.”

“Here’s the weird thing about it: the coma was easy for me, though devastating for my mom. It wasn’t until I came out of it that things became hard for me.”

Tears pool in her eyes, and Cross quickly says, “Hey, I didn’t mean to upset you. That’s none of my business. I shouldn’t have asked.”

She brushes away her tears. “That’s okay. Don’t worry about it. It’s just not something I talk about very much. But now I get to ask you a question. How come you know so much about plants?”

The question knocks on the door of his private life.

Once I answer this question, I know it’ll lead to other questions I don’t want to answer.

He shifts awkwardly on his feet. "I've always been interested in them, even as a kid, so I majored in botany in college."

In the silence that follows his answer, he can almost hear the follow-up questions lining up in Megan's mind, but she surprises him by simply saying, "That's interesting."

There's stuff in her past she doesn't want to talk about, so I guess she can tell I'm in the same boat. That's pretty cool.

For the next little bit, they stroll around the house, with Cross making suggestions about what to do to make the area more vibrant. Megan has no objections to any of them and seems to be able to visualize it along with him.

"You know," he says, "the project we just got finished with was a real pain in the you-know-what. The woman kept changing her mind, making us dig up things we'd planted and put in something else. If your mom agrees with you about the things I want to do to this yard, it'll be much more enjoyable."

"Oh, she'll agree. If it makes me happy, that's all that matters to her."

"That's pretty special. You two must be pretty close."

"Don't get me wrong, she makes me crazy at times, but she stood by me when I got hurt and has been with me every step of the way since. I really don't know what I would have done without her."

"My Pop's the same way." As soon as the assertion passes through his lips, Cross regrets it.

She's gonna want to know what I mean by that, and then I'll have to make up a story or tell her the truth.

Again, Megan surprises him when she says, "That's nice" but proffers no questions. Looking at his hands, she says, "I noticed you didn't make any notes while walking around. You want to sit on the porch and jot down some things? I'll get you a drink of water if you want one."

He starts to tell her he never makes notes when designing, that he has something like a photographic memory of the details. Instead, though, he surprises himself when he says, "Sure, that'd be great."

They make their way back to the front of the house, and she starts up the stairs.

Cross quickly steps up and takes her elbow. “Can I help?”

Megan’s affable demeanor changes in an instant, and she jerks her elbow out of his hand. “No, I can do it!”

But her sudden movement causes her to lose her balance, and she starts to fall. She cries out, and he catches her and brings her upright. “I’m so sorry,” he says. “That was my fault. I should have left you alone.”

She closes her eyes, and tears leak out. “No, don’t apologize. You were just trying to help. It’s just that I’m tired of having to be helped and want to do things for myself. I shouldn’t have reacted the way I did.” Opening her eyes, she looks at him. “I’m just glad you caught me before I fell. It’s my biggest fear.”

“Not wanting to let people help me is one of my issues, too,” he replies. “Pop got mad at me one time because of a situation I was in, and he told me if I was a goat on a concrete pasture, I wouldn’t ask for a blade of grass.”

Megan laughs. “I’ve never heard that expression, but I like it. I think it’s an apt description of me.”

Just then, a UPS truck comes barreling up the drive and stops suddenly. The driver bounds out of the open doorway, carrying a package. Walking toward them, he says, “I’ve got a package here for Grace Cunningham.”

“That’s my mother,” Megan says. “I’ll take it.”

As the driver returns to his truck, Cross asks, “So, your mother’s last name is Cunningham?”

“Well, it’s a little bit complicated. When she moved back here, she took back her maiden name, but she still gets mail in her married name. Then, when I moved here, I decided I wanted a completely new start for myself, so I created all new profiles on my social media and changed my last name to her maiden name. Maybe I shouldn’t have, but that’s just what I did.”

Scratching his head, Cross says, “That means your mother’s real name is—”

“Grace Charles,” Megan finishes his sentence.

CHAPTER SEVEN

TWELVE MONTHS EARLIER

Lying in the bed of the physical rehab facility, Megan used her left hand to lift her right hand onto her stomach. Then she forced a tennis ball into the palm of her right hand and concentrated on squeezing it.

"Come on, you can do it," Donna, the physical therapist assistant, told her. "Get that brain of yours busy making some new neuropathways."

In slow motion, Megan's hand began to close but stopped short of gripping the ball. The effort to make that small movement was enough to make beads of sweat appear above her lip.

"You're doing great. Good job," Donna cheered. "Now, can you open your hand one finger at a time?"

Max, Megan's husband, entered the room and stood at the foot of her bed, watching. Speaking to Donna, he asked, "Has she made any progress today?"

"For sure she has. Look at her holding that tennis ball."

"She's not really holding it," he replied. "I mean, a two-year-old could knock it out of her hand."

Megan heard the disdain in his tone.

Taking the ball out of Megan's hand, Donna said, "That's enough for today, Megan. I'll see you tomorrow morning." She gave Max a hard look, then left the room.

He remained at the foot of the bed and crossed his arms.

"I haven't seen you this week," Megan remarked. Then she made up an excuse for him. "I guess you've been busy with work," she said, an excuse not even she believed. It was a game they played for the past year or so as their lives slowly drifted apart.

He played his role by saying, "Yeah, this new project is taking lots of time." Then, as he'd been doing since she awoke from her coma, he added a stinging remark. "Besides, I'm the only one bringing in money right now. I can't just lie around all day."

Megan accepted the dig in silence, even though she knew money had nothing to do with it. Between his job as an architect and her job as a Farm Bureau insurance agent, they'd always had more than enough money to do whatever they wished, and they had a bulging savings account, too.

Before her injuries, she'd been wondering if money contributed to the unwinding of their marriage. Everything came too easy for them. They could pursue whatever interested them. It was just that their pursuits never coincided. Gambling was his thing, while hiking and rock climbing were hers.

At first, Max complained about her being gone all the time with her hobby and even plainly said, "I feel like we're losing each other." They might have turned things around if she'd listened to him, but she was having too much fun.

The point of no return came when she had a brief affair with a man who was a member of the rock-climbing club she'd started. Max found out about it, she immediately ended it, and they both swept it under the rug, never bringing up the subject again.

She looked at him fiddling with his phone at the foot of her bed and said, "Maybe if I could've had children, things would be different between us." When he didn't respond, she spoke a little louder. "I'm sorry, Max."

Looking up from his phone, he said, "I was texting Jerry at the office. What'd you say?"

"I said I'm sorry."

"Sorry for what?"

"Lots of things. That I couldn't have children, that I had an affair, that I wasn't a good wife, that I was selfish."

"Yeah…well, things just happen sometimes."

"Maybe when I'm better, we could go to counseling or something and try to put the pieces back together again. Or better yet, start over again, maybe renew our vows."

He averted his eyes from her. "The doctors are saying this is going to be a long process, that you'll require lots of help whenever you get to leave here. I just don't know, Megan…" His voice trailed off.

“What are you not saying?” she asked.

“I’m not cut out to be a caregiver. I could barely stand to visit my dad when he was dying from ALS, much less take my turn staying with him.”

“We could hire a private duty nurse,” Megan countered.

“That’s one idea,” Max mumbled. “I guess we can talk about it when the time comes to get you out of this place.” He waved his phone at her. “Look, there’s things going on at work I need to attend to. I’ll come back by when I get a chance. Take care.”

As she watched him rush out the door without so much as a perfunctory goodbye kiss, Megan’s slim hopes of saving their marriage grew even slimmer.

CHAPTER EIGHT

PRESENT DAY

Music fills the living room of Buck and Betty's house as he plays "Foggy Mountain Breakdown" on his banjo and Cross and Harlon try to keep up on their guitar and fiddle. Loose ends of broken horse hairs dance on the end of Harlon's bow. Each musician focuses on the neck of his instrument, making sure their fingers press the correct string on the right fret. The end of Cross's tongue presses against his upper lip.

Buck increases the tempo to a feverish pace and finishes the song with a flourish. His red face beams as he wipes sweat from his forehead. "Whoo-eee, boys, that's some fine playing!"

Sitting down heavily in a ladderback chair, Harlon exclaims, "Are you trying to kill this old man? I about had a heart attack keeping up with you."

"You could have quit playing anytime, old man," Buck teases him.

"Hrmph! The day you can outplay me is the day they put me in a casket."

Betty and Cross laugh.

Moving toward the kitchen, Betty says, "Time for some cookies and something to drink. Who wants a glass of iced tea?"

All three men answer, "Me!"

Harlon fine tunes his fiddle as Buck lays down his banjo and flexes his fingers. Blowing on his hand, Buck says, "I hope my hand doesn't get any stiffer, or it'll be the devil to play this thing."

Harlon laughs. "Well, don't let me discourage you, but you've got a stiffer time a'coming to you."

Cross interjects, "Hey, Buck, maybe that stiffer time will help you out with your problems in the bedroom."

"What's this?" Harlon asks. "Buck, you got trouble with Mr. Johnson?"

Both Harlon and Cross laugh.

"Oh, shut up!" Buck replies. To Cross, he says, "Do you have to tell everything you know?"

Betty walks in, carrying a tray with cookies and glasses of tea on it. "What are you boys laughing at?"

"It's nothing," Buck quickly says. "They're just poking fun."

"At who?"

"We're poking fun at Buck," Harlon answers, "because it seems he can't, uh, let's say rise to the occasion in the bedroom like he used to."

Cross doubles over with laughter.

Betty laughs as she passes around the refreshments. Sitting down, she says, "Did he tell you about his latest effort to be romantic?"

"We're all ears!" Cross encourages her.

"Betty!" Buck snaps. "You don't have to tell."

"It's sweet," Betty answers, "and funny, too. And a little painful as well."

"Oh, I got to hear this," Harlon says.

"Well, you know we have one of those big Jacuzzi bathtubs," Betty begins.

"Here," Buck huffs, "let me tell it. I read how women like hot baths and candles. So, the other day before she got home from work, I ran her a tub full. I lit a dozen candles I'd bought. Then I saw this jar of those little round smelly balls she keeps in a jar by the tub, so I poured a bunch of them in."

Betty can't constrain herself. "He was so sweet when I got home. Took me in the bathroom and told me to take my time, that he was going to fix us some supper while I relaxed in the tub. But when I got undressed and into the tub, I discovered the bottom of the tub was covered in marbles."

"Marbles?" Cross asks.

“Yeah, that jar of fragrance beads was actually a jar of decorative marbles. My bottom’s going to be bruised for a week from sitting on them.”

Harlon roars with laughter.

“How was I supposed to know?” Buck asks defensively.

“Did you not think to smell them?” Cross asks, then dies laughing.

Walking over and sitting on Buck’s knee, Betty kisses him and says, “I love you for trying, sweetie. Maybe next time, you should ask a friend for some advice.”

“Ha! All I do is work around these two goats, one who’s as celibate as a priest, and the other who’s some kind of Don Juan and can get women in bed with him without even trying. Anyway, I wouldn’t believe anything either of them told me.”

This elicits howls of laughter from Cross and Harlon, until Cross is wiping away tears.

After everyone settles down and catches their breath, they drink some tea and take a bite of the cookies.

“Mmm, mmm,” Harlon moans, “Betty, these cookies melt in my mouth. I love that lemon flavor. What kind are they?”

“Actually, they’re called lemon cookies. They’ve got lemon juice and lemon zest in them.”

“Well, I love them.”

“Thank you.”

“Hey, guys,” Cross begins, “I went and checked out this new job we’ve been asked to do. I think we can really make a dramatic change in how the yard looks. There’s some natural features we can keep and highlight, plus add our own touch to things.” He looks at his dad to see if he’s listening.

Harlon frowns. “Is it that Charles family you were talking about?”

“Yes, Pop.”

“What’s their name?”

“It’s Grace Charles and her daughter, Megan, who lives with her. They seem like nice people.”

"Well, I'll tell you one thing: don't expect me to do any work over there."

"Aw, come on, Harlon," Buck says, "can't you leave the past in the past?"

Setting down his glass of tea, Harlon snatches up his fiddle and places it in its case. As he buckles it shut, he says, "Thank you for the snacks, Betty. Cross, I'll be out in the truck whenever you get ready to leave." Without giving any opportunity for rebuttal, he walks out the door into the night.

CHAPTER NINE

FIFTY YEARS AGO

The music of Three Dog Night singing "Find Someone To Love" blared through the 8-track stereo of Harlon's 1968 2-door Chevy Malibu as he and Grace lay on the back seat. Her breath came in gasps as the two of them climaxed together.

"Oh, Harlon," she whispered in his ear.

"I love you, Grace," he whispered back.

"I love you, too."

"Like the song says, will you always be in my corner?"

"Always," she affirmed.

They lay quietly for a few moments.

"I can't believe we just did that," Grace said.

Sitting up and fastening his pants, Harlon said, "Yeah, me either. Did I hurt you?"

She sat up and rearranged her clothes. "A little at first, but it was good at the end. My dad will kill me if he ever finds out, and he'll kill you, too."

"Yeah, I know. I swear, I'll never tell anybody."

"Guys like to brag."

"I'm telling you, Grace, this will stay locked away in my heart. No one's ever going to know. I won't even tell my best friend, Tom."

"What if I get pregnant?"

"Can that happen after just one time?"

"Mama says it can. I would die if I got pregnant."

The possibility settled heavily on Harlon's shoulders. "I never thought about that. You're lucky you've got parents who talk to you about those kinds of things. You know I don't have parents and live in an orphans' home. I don't deserve somebody like you. I'm from the wrong side of the tracks."

Putting her finger on his lips, she told him, "Don't say that. I don't care what people say about you." She crawled onto his lap and faced him. "You're a good person, Harlon, an amazing person. You had three strikes against you from the start, but you didn't let that define you. That's what makes you more than amazing." She paused and touched his cheek. "Why are you crying?"

"When I'm with you, you make me feel like anything's possible. You're the best thing that's ever happened to me. But I'm scared I'm going to lose you."

Leaning in, she gave him a long kiss. When she pulled away, he took a deep breath.

"You're never going to lose me—never." She moved off his lap and said, "Let's get out of the car and walk down to the lake."

He pushed forward the back of the seat in front of him and stretched to reach the handle of the oversized door. Pushing the door open, he got out, then reached back to help her. "I'll tell you one thing, two-door cars weren't made for going out parking."

She gave an easy laugh. "I won't argue with that."

Holding hands, they made their way down the moonlit path leading to Kentucky Lake, as whippoorwills, tree frogs, bullfrogs, owls, and nighthawks serenaded them. It was a scene of the innocence of youth cast against the ancient sounds of nature.

As boys have done since the beginning of time, Harlon picked up a flat rock and skipped it across the smooth surface of the water.

"Wow, seven skips," Grace commented. "That's really good."

"One time I did eight skips, but no one was with me when I did it, so nobody believes me when I tell it."

"I believe you."

He smiled at her and saw the moonlight dancing in her eyes. "You're beautiful."

Snuggling against him, she said, “And you’re handsome.”

“I love this spot on the lake, but it also makes me kind of sad.”

“Why’s that?” she asked.

“I think about all the people who lost their homes and land when they flooded this area to make the lake. They’d lived there for generations and had their own family cemeteries, but now all their history is under water.”

“That right there,” Grace said, “that’s one of the reasons I love you. You’re such a deep thinker. You think about things most people don’t pay attention to.”

Her praise made his heart sing. “And one of the reasons I love you is because you’re so kind and thoughtful toward others. You’re not mean and spiteful, like most of the girls in our class.”

Just then, way off in the distance, they heard a tugboat pushing a load of barges in the area of the lake where the channel of the Tennessee River lay. Its powerful spotlight swept across the silent waters and darkened shoreline.

Harlon said, “I always thought that’d be a cool job. I want to be the captain of a tugboat.”

“Don’t they live on the water? How do they manage having a family?”

“That’s what Johnny Parker’s dad does. He says he’s gone from home a month at a time but home for a month at a time. The only problem is, when his dad’s gone, his mom runs the house the way she wants to, but when his dad comes home, he wants to run the house his way. Johnny says they argue a lot about that.”

Sitting down on a piece of driftwood, Grace said, “It sounds complicated.”

Harlon sat beside her. “If you don’t want me to do that, I can do something else. Besides, I may end up getting drafted to go to Viet Nam.”

Grace shivered.

“Are you cold?”

"No. It just scares me to think about you going to Viet Nam. That war is so messed up, so many boys are getting killed. You heard about Luke Simpson, didn't you? He was only there for a few months and got killed. They say he drowned in a rice patty." Squeezing his arm, she said, "I don't want you to go."

"I can't say as I'm eager to go myself, but the draft is the draft. I don't come from a rich and powerful family that can influence the draft board. If my number gets drawn, I'll have to go."

CHAPTER TEN

PRESENT DAY

Megan eases out the front door and into the pre-dawn gray before the sun has shown its face and the world looks like a black-and-white photo. It's mostly quiet, as only a couple of songbirds have started singing.

This is Megan's favorite time of day, listening to and watching nature awaken. Not until her climbing accident and ultimate move to her mother's house in the country, during which time she had no choice but to slow the frenetic pace of her life, did she learn about the beauty in simple things like this time of the morning. It's not that she'd never started her day early; it's just that those early mornings were all about starting out on a rock climb, where her singular focus was on conquering the rock, looking for handholds and footholds.

As quietly as she can, while still using her cane, she walks across the yard and sits down underneath a large dogwood tree whose flower buds are swollen and within days of making a snowy display underneath the canopy of towering pines. Thirty feet away hangs the bird feeder her mother keeps filled with seed. Opening her copy of *Peterson Field Guide to Eastern Birds*, Megan watches and waits.

For a little while, the birds that show up to eat either on the feeder or on the ground underneath it are ones she's already made note of in the book: Cardinals; Dark-Eyed Juncos; House Wrens; Rufous-Sided Towhees; Tufted Titmouse; Downy Woodpeckers; Red Breasted Nuthatches.

In her periphery, there's a movement. She turns her head, scans the ground and tree trunks, but sees nothing.

I know I saw something. It was black and white.

Suddenly, a splash of red appears on the side of one of the pine trees. Megan holds her breath and stares as a bird three times bigger than a blue jay makes its way around the trunk while clinging to it. Bright red feathers adorn the top of its head, while its back is black. White streaks are on its face and neck.

I've never seen anything like you. What kind of bird are you?

With minimal movement, Megan opens the bird book and turns through the pages as she tries at the same time to keep an eye on this unknown visitor.

Suddenly, the sound of a twig snapping startles both bird and birdwatcher. Megan jumps, and the bird spreads its nearly three-foot wingspan and flies away.

"Oh, my," Megan's mother says, "was that a Pileated Woodpecker? I'm sorry, I didn't mean to scare it away."

Megan flips through the pages of her book. "What did you call it?"

"A Pileated Woodpecker."

"It was beautiful! And so big!"

Grace joins her. "And unusual to spot around here, because they're so elusive."

"I found it!" Megan says, pointing to a page in the book. Taking a pen, she writes down the day's date and location, like her mom suggested she do when she needed to find a hobby to occupy her time. Then she looks at Grace. "How come you know so much about birds? I don't remember you hardly ever talking about them while I was growing up."

"I kind of let that hobby go when we started living in the city. But when I was in school, I had a boyfriend who knew the name of every bird around." Getting a distant look in her eyes, she softly says, "Those were fun years."

Getting to her feet, Megan asks, "Why did you come looking for me?"

Grace gives her a blank look. She blinks her eyes a few times before saying, "I don't remember. Why would I have come out here?"

Rather than throw out possible answers, Megan has learned to be quiet and let her mom sift through her thoughts. Sometimes it helps, and sometimes it doesn't.

Grace claps her hands together. "Oh, I know! Do you know where my phone is? I've looked everywhere for it and can't find it."

“My gosh, Mother, why don’t you use that watch I bought you that helps you find your phone?”

Looking at the ground, Grace says, “I can’t find it. I think I lost it. I’m so stupid! I can’t keep up with anything. You might as well put me in a nursing home.”

Megan hugs her. “Now, don’t exaggerate things and play ‘poor me.’ I’ll go with you to the house and help you find them both. Come on.”

As they head toward the house, Megan says, “What’re the pen and notebook for?”

Waving the notebook, Grace says, “Oh my gosh, I’m in charge of putting together downtown entertainment during Fish Fry Week. It’s a very important job, and everyone’s expecting me to hit a homerun with my selections. That’s a lot of pressure.”

“What do you have so far?”

Referring to her notes, Grace says, “The Flash Back Band, from McKenzie. They play music from the fifties to the nineties. They’re a relatively new group, and people really love them. The King Beez come from B.B. King’s Blues Club, and they’re fabulous. Of course, we must have The Barons, who’ve been a staple around here for fifty years. They do rock-and-roll, and even big band music. Then I’m going to check out Derek Fields, who performs and writes his own music. He comes highly recommended.”

“Wow, it sounds like you’ve already taken care of everything, Mom. So why are you stressed?”

“Well, I just want to have something for everybody, and I think I need to add a bluegrass band to the lineup.”

Megan makes a face. “Bluegrass? My gosh, I hate bluegrass. It’s like fingernails on a chalkboard to me.”

“Seriously?”

“Seriously.”

They walk inside the house, and Megan starts looking between the couch cushions for Grace’s phone.

"If you're looking for my phone, I've looked there," Grace informs her. "And I have to disagree with you about bluegrass. There's an earthy authenticity about it."

Megan's arm disappears up to her elbow as she digs deeper in the sofa. Suddenly, she jerks it out and holds a phone in the air. "Ta-da!"

Snatching it from her, Grace says, "Let me see that." She examines it and exclaims, "This is the phone I lost and had to replace with the one I have now. I can't believe you found it; I looked everywhere for it."

Megan looks at her and starts to chastise her. Instead, though, she smiles and gives her a hug. "You're a peach, Mother; you're a peach."

"That's what your father used to tell me; I just don't know why."

Megan laughs. "I do. Now, we still have to find your new phone."

"Maybe I could just activate this old one, it's still practically new. Eventually, we'll find the other one and be surprised and excited by it. Are you ready for some breakfast?"

"Sure. By the way, it was awfully sneaky of you to hire the guys we see at Huddle House to do the landscaping job. You could have told me that's who was coming."

Grace's eyes dance with excitement. "You didn't tell me he came."

"I forgot."

"How was he? Was he nice? Is he as good looking up close as he is from a distance? Is he married? Is he seeing someone? Did you like him?"

"He was wonderful and amazing. It was love at first sight. We're getting married next week."

From the kitchen counter, where she's putting a bagel in the toaster, Grace throws a dish towel at her. "Quit! You're just making fun of me now."

"Well, you need to quit trying to play matchmaker. I've told you until I'm blue in the face—I'm never getting in a relationship again, and for sure never marrying. Just accept it and move on, please."

"My father used to say, 'Never say never.' You don't know what the future holds, Megan."

Megan ignores her comment. "One thing you'd like about this man is, he loves bluegrass. He had it blaring over his radio."

Grace frowns. "Were you ugly to him about it? You know you don't have to say everything you think."

Smiling at her, Megan says, "Says the woman who has no filter."

"Well, what's his name?"

"Cross. Cross Daniels."

Grace stops what she's doing and stares at her.

"What? Is there something wrong with that?"

"Is his father Harlon Daniels?"

"I don't know. Does it matter? Who's Harlon Daniels?"

Grace's eyes grow red. "It has to be him. I had no idea."

"What's the matter? Is there a problem?"

Grace turns her back to Megan and dabs at her eyes.

Megan moves beside her and puts her arm around her. "What's going on, Mother? Tell me."

"Have you ever made a mistake you've regretted and felt guilty about for fifty years?"

CHAPTER ELEVEN

FIFTY YEARS EARLIER

The air was thick with the sweet smell of cotton candy as Harlon and Grace strolled along the midway of the carnival during Fish Fry week. The voices of carnival barkers rang through the air as they enticed people to try their games of chance.

One close by yelled, “Come on, fella, win your girl a stuffed teddy bear!”

Harlon looked his way and saw him holding a huge bear in one hand and a baseball in the other.

“Come on, give it a try,” the barker told him.

Pointing at the bear, Grace exclaimed “Look how cute!” Then she whispered, “That guy doesn’t know you pitch for the high school team. It’ll be easy for you.”

A brief tug-of-war took place in Harlon between his certainty the game was rigged and his desire to make Grace happy. As is usually the case in matters of the heart, logic lost.

“Yes, sir, step right up,” the barker cried as Harlon and Grace headed in his direction. “It’s easy as pie. Just knock over the six bottles with one throw, and you win the bear.”

Harlon looked at the bottles stacked on each other, three-two-one, in the shape of a triangle, and hefted a baseball in his hand. The weight of the ball felt the same as what he was used to, though it did feel a little softer than normal.

“The more balls you have to throw to knock all the bottles down, the smaller the prize,” the barker explained.

“Let me feel one of the bottles,” Harlon said.

“You got you a smart one there,” the barker said to Grace. “Checks things out first, is careful how he spends his money. Yes, sir, a smart boy.”

When the barker made no move to retrieve a bottle, Harlon repeated, “A bottle, please.”

Laughing, the barker walked toward the target. “I’m sorry, I get carried away with this job sometimes and don’t pay attention. I apologize.” He strode back, carrying a bottle. “Here you go, check it out. Just a plain old milk bottle.”

Harlon looked it over and tapped it with his fingernail, to be certain it was glass.

“Satisfied?” the barker asked.

“I guess so,” Harlon replied.

The barker yelled, “Gather ’round, folks, and see if this young man can win a prize for his girl. Yes, sir, gather ’round, everybody, and cheer him on.”

Immediately, people detoured from meandering through the carnival and made a beeline to see what was going to happen.

Harlon frowned at the barker, who ignored him. To Grace, he said, “I don’t like a bunch of people staring at me.”

“Why not? It happens all the time at your baseball games.”

“Yeah, but I’m in a zone during a game and don’t even notice the people, especially since they’re a hundred feet away in the stands.”

“Come on, just pretend you’re pitching in a baseball game.”

“Hey, it’s Harlon,” somebody in the crowd says.

Harlon turns and sees it’s Tom.

“Come on, man,” Tom called to him, “this’ll be easy for you, like shooting fish in a barrel. I bet the guy doesn’t know you pitch for the baseball team.”

“Hey, hey, hey,” the barker cried, “seems we have a town hero up to pitch. Anybody want to bet whether or not he can knock the bottles down with one pitch?”

Several men took out their billfolds, under the disapproving scowls of their wives, and handed over money, all betting Harlon would do it.

Harlon’s heart galloped, and his throat felt tight as he looked at the wad of five and ten-dollar bills clutched in the barker’s fist.

The crowd began to clap in rhythm and call his name. "Har-lon, Har-lon, Har-lon." Faster and faster, they called and clapped.

"One dollar gets you three balls," the barker told him as he stepped back out of the way.

"I'm only throwing one," Harlon replied.

"The boy wants the bear!" the barker played to the crowd. "One ball, one pitch. Can he do it?"

Everyone cheered, Grace loudest of all.

Nothing about the setting felt natural to Harlon—no glove, no pitcher's mound, no warm-up pitches, no catcher's mitt to aim at, and people crowded so close, he couldn't swing his arms.

"Give me some room," he told those around him.

"Step back," somebody said. "Give the boy some room. He's fixing to throw."

The announcement silenced the crowd. The only sound was the calliope playing in another area of the carnival.

Harlon windmilled his arms to loosen them up and did a few squats.

"I think the boy's ready," the barker declared.

Harlon looked at Grace. Her face was filled with excitement, and she clasped her hands under her chin.

"You can do it," she mouthed at him.

Maybe at a ball game. But here? Like this? I'm not too sure.

He shook his pitching arm, then stared at the bottles. With deliberate and practiced motion, he reared back, stepped toward the bottles, and threw the ball.

The distance was so short and speed so great, afterwards people would declare they couldn't even see the ball. The bottles fell like pins in a bowling alley, twirling in every direction. Five landed on the ground, leaving the sixth one teetering back and forth.

Everyone held their breath. What was only a couple of seconds felt like twenty as they pulled for the bottle to tumble over.

But Harlon wasn't watching. His eyes were on Grace, because he knew she'd reveal the results first.

He wasn't disappointed, as suddenly she leaped into the air, screaming with excitement. A millisecond later, the crowd joined her with their own cheers.

The barker's face collapsed on itself as he reached underneath a shelf and pulled out his moneybox.

"Give him the bear," someone called out.

Handing the stuffed toy to Harlon, the barker offered an unenthusiastic, "Good job."

Everyone shook Harlon's hand and offered congratulations before dispersing, until only Grace was left.

She threw her arms around his neck and kissed him. "You were amazing! It was like something out of a movie. Did you hear all those people cheering for you?"

He smiled at her and offered her the bear.

Burying her face in it, she snuggled it for a second, then said, "I will keep this forever, and every time I see it, I'll think of you."

Harlon offered her his hand and said, "Let's go ride the Ferris wheel."

As they walked hand-in-hand toward the ride, random people pointed at them or called out Harlon's name, congratulating him.

"You're famous," Grace told him.

Grinning at her, he said, "For one night anyway."

They got in the back of the line to ride the Ferris wheel until some of those ahead urged them to go to the front of the line.

When Harlon declined their offer, they physically took him and Grace by the arm and marched them forward.

The man in charge of the ride looked at the couple, then pointed at the bear and said, "So you're the ones who won the bear." He held open the bar on the next empty passenger car of the Ferris wheel, and, in an exaggerated manner, bowed low. "Behold, the king and queen of the fair."

Harlon and Grace settled in, her arm linked in his.

"Has there ever been a more perfect night?" Grace asked. "I feel like I'm in a fairy tale and you're my Prince Charming."

"Everybody's making too big a deal out of what I did," Harlon told her. "It's embarrassing."

"Maybe they are, but just enjoy it and have fun."

Suddenly, the Ferris wheel whisked them in the air, causing Grace to squeal.

Harlon closed his eyes and enjoyed the wind on his face.

"Hey, look, there's Tom and Jane," Grace told him.

Opening his eyes, he saw his friend and date standing far below, waving at them. He and Grace waved back.

After a few minutes, the Ferris wheel began stopping to let off some of the riders. One stop left Harlon and Grace at the very top of the ride.

"I don't want to ruin tonight," Harlon began, "but I've got to tell you something."

All the glee deserted Grace's face, and concern creased her features. "What's wrong?" she asked.

"I've been drafted."

She squeezed his hand. "No, it can't be true. I don't want you to go."

"I'm not too excited about it either, but I'm going whether I want to or not."

"Maybe you won't have to go to Viet Nam. Maybe they'll send you somewhere else."

Slowly shaking his head, Harlon said, "You and I both know where they'll send me. But instead of them putting me in the army, I'm going to go sign up for the Marines. I think they'll do a better job of training me for what I'll be facing over there."

"Oh, Harlon," Grace cried, and she buried her face in his chest. "Please, please don't go. I can't stand to think about it. I'll be worried every minute of every day while you're gone. It'll be miserable."

He tilted her chin toward him and looked into her eyes. "Tell me this: will you wait for me until I come home? I want to marry you, but I'm not going to do like some guys and marry you one day and then ship overseas the next. I don't think that's fair. But if I come home, I want us to start our life together."

Striking him on the chest with one hand, she replied, "Don't say it that way! Don't say *if* you come home, because you *are* coming home. You hear me? You are! And yes, when you come back, I'll be the first person to greet you. I love you, Harlon Daniels, and I want to be your wife."

"I love you, too, Grace Charles, and one day I'm going to marry you."

CHAPTER TWELVE

PRESENT DAY

Sitting in the Huddle House, Cross drains the last bit of coffee from his cup and says to Buck, "You ready to go?"

"I could eat another one of those pecan waffles, and maybe some more sausage," Buck replies, "but I'm going to be a good boy and resist."

They rise from the table and head to the counter to pay for their breakfast.

"Wonder why we don't see Megan and her mom here like we used to?"

Cross shrugs his shoulders. "Couldn't say." Laughing, he says, "Why don't you message her on Facebook and see?"

"Yeah, that's exactly what Betty needs to find on my phone, me messaging strange women. She'd cut my balls off with a dull knife."

The young girl at the cash register gives the two of them a startled and uncertain look.

"Don't pay any attention to him," Cross tells her. "He's just joking around."

"I am not," Buck contradicts him. "Betty's not a woman to mess around with, you know that. Ever since I—"

"Just pay the woman," Cross interjects. "She's not interested in your life story. Come on, we've got work to do."

They finish up and head outside to the parking lot.

Once they get in the truck, Cross says, "Watch for me as I pull out of this parking lot. We've got the twenty-four-foot trailer hitched to the truck, and I sometimes forget how much room it takes to make a turn or turn around."

“Gotcha covered,” Buck replies and turns around to look out the back window at the shrubbery and flower-laden trailer. “We’ve got some really pretty stuff. I bet Megan and her mom are really going to like it. Have you met her mother yet?”

Cross eases past a car. “Am I good on that side?”

“You’ve got plenty of room. Go ahead.”

Pulling onto the highway, Cross says, “No, I haven’t met the mom. I’ve only dealt with Megan.”

“What’s she like?”

“She seems nice enough.”

“Nice enough to ask out?”

“I don’t know. I don’t think like that anymore.”

Buck grunts. “She’s nice, she’s definitely good looking, what else do you want? What else do you know about her? Why does she use a cane? Has she been married?”

“Good grief, you’re as bad as a woman wanting to know details. I’ve told you all I know. Oh yeah, there’s one other thing: she doesn’t like bluegrass.”

“What?! Well, mark her off the list. You don’t need to be with anybody who doesn’t like bluegrass.”

“First of all, Buck, there is no list. And secondly, everybody has a right to have their own musical tastes.”

“All I’m saying is, don’t waste your time with this one. She’s not the one for you. How could you be married to someone who wouldn’t enjoy hearing us play? That’s what made Heather so perfect for you.”

Cross steals a look at him, then turns his attention back to the road and squeezes the steering wheel.

“I’m sorry,” Buck says. “I shouldn’t have mentioned Heather. That was wrong of me. I’m just going to shut up.”

After driving in prickly silence for a couple miles, Cross says, “That’s okay. What you said about Heather is correct—she was perfect. And that’s why I’m never marrying again. Anybody who destroys something that’s perfect doesn’t deserve a second chance.”

“I’ll agree that’s your opinion, but that’s all I’ll agree to. I’ll shut up about it—for now. Just know I reserve the right to bring it up in the future.”

“Whatever,” Cross mutters.

He turns off the highway and heads toward the Charles’ house.

“I guess it’s just you and me working this job, after what your Pop said.”

“Yeah, I think so. He’s dead set on how he feels about the woman.”

“Do you know the full backstory to all that?”

Cross shakes his head. “Nope. He won’t talk about it.”

A bit later, they pull to a stop in front of the house and get out. Megan’s dog, Lacy, comes tearing out of the front door as it opens and races toward them, barking every step of the way.

“That’s Megan’s dog,” Cross explains.

“Aha, so she’s a dog person,” Buck says. Sucking his teeth, he adds, “That’s definitely a point in her favor. Just not sure if it cancels out not liking bluegrass.”

Megan and her mom step off the porch and meet Cross and Buck.

Lacy smells Cross’s leg and finally stops barking. He reaches down, picks her up, and scratches behind her ears.

“That’s unusual,” Megan comments. “Lacy usually doesn’t take up with strangers so easily.”

Smiling broadly, Buck says, “Cross here is a natural with dogs. Kind of like a dog whisperer.”

“Really?” Megan asks.

“No,” Cross replies. “You’ll have to be careful believing what my partner, Buck, says. He’s been known to stretch a foot of truth and turn it into a mile.”

Grace speaks up. “Introduce me to these fine looking boys, Megan.”

“This is Cross Daniels, the one who came out the first day to talk about landscape designs.” She looks at Buck and says, “I’m sorry, but I don’t know who…wait a minute. Did you send me a friend request on Facebook last week, or something like that? You *are* the one! I recognize you now.”

Buck’s face turns beet red. “Look, I’m sorry about that. I’d just seen you both at the Huddle House and wondered—”

“Wondered what? If I want to hook up with you?”

Cross studies her face and sees a hint of a smile playing at the corners of her eyes. “I’m sorry, Megan, Buck here has a problem he needs to get help for. He’s just in denial about it.”

Buck stares at him, mouth agape. “What? You? Listen here, I’m not a stalker, and I’m not interested in a hookup.”

Megan bears down on him. “Oh, so I’m not pretty enough. It’s the cane, isn’t it? Are you prejudiced against people with handicaps? Are you one of those kinds of people?”

Cross can hold it in no longer and bursts into laughter, followed quickly by Megan.

“Man, did she have you going!” Cross tells him. “I wish I’d taken a picture of your face. It was priceless.”

Buck looks at Megan. “You mean you were just kidding with me?”

“Yes, yes,” Megan answers between ripples of laughter.

“This,” Cross says, “is Buck, my best friend and business partner.”

Grace extends her hand to Cross. As he shakes it, she says, “I’m Grace Charles. I’m pleased to meet you.”

“Did you grow up around here?” Cross asks her.

“Sure did. Some of the best years of my life were spent in Henry County. Your last name is Cross.” She hesitates, then asks, “You wouldn’t be related to Harlon Cross, would you?”

Cross and Buck exchange a quick look.

“Yeah, he’s my dad.”

Grace stares at him, and her eyes grow red.

Just then, a cell phone rings, but no one makes a move to answer theirs.

Grace looks around at them as the ringing continues until Megan says, "Mother, it's your phone."

"Oh, my goodness. I…I didn't realize it was mine." She fishes it out of her back pocket and answers, "Hello." She listens for a moment, then says, "Yes, yes, I've been working on that." She continues talking as she walks toward the house.

CHAPTER THIRTEEN

PRESENT DAY

The three of them watch Grace walk away, then Megan says, "I apologize for my mom's sudden departure. She and her phone are a story all to themselves. I'm going to get out of your way and let you start working. If you need anything, just let me know."

When they're alone, Buck looks at Cross and says, "Man, did you see how her mother looked when you told her you were Harlon's son?"

"Yeah, it was hard to miss."

"There's some kind of story there between the two of them, and you need to find out what it is."

Turning away and heading to the truck, Cross says, "You know as much as I know."

They begin unloading shovels and wheelbarrows.

Buck says, "I'm going to try and find out some details."

"Better be careful, Pop will bite your head off. He clearly doesn't want to talk about it."

"We'll see." Hefting some shrubs into a wheelbarrow, he says, "I see what you meant when you said this is a nice place. It's tucked away into these pine trees like some kind of secret cottage."

"I know. And it's going to be nice doing this job mostly in the shade rather than out in the hot sun, like the Rhinehart job."

"This Russian sage will look really nice alongside the pink coneflowers you chose."

"And I think the white roses mixed with lavender will really stand out."

"You know we sound like a couple of gay guys, don't you?" Speaking in a higher tone, he says, "I'm enamored by your choice of colors. However do you do it?"

Laughing, Cross says, “Oh, shut up before the politically correct police arrest you.”

~~~~~~~~~~~

After a few hours, Buck says, “Hey, did you hear about Tony Koslinski?”

“No, what happened?”

“Betty says they found him dead in his trailer with a needle and syringe sticking out of his arm. Had been dead a few days.”

Cross stops in mid-motion, with a shovelful of dirt. The next second, he throws his shovel to the ground. “Damn!”

“What’s the matter?” Buck asks.

“I talked to him two nights ago, and he looked and sounded fine. Addiction is such a cruel disease. I hate it!”

Buck sets down the two azaleas he’s carrying. “I’m sorry. I didn’t know you guys were still friends. I haven’t talked to Tony in I don’t know when, which I guess is bad on me. We were all pretty close when we played ball in high school. Ever since he ran off the rails and began dealing drugs, though, I’ve stayed away from him.”

Cross retrieves his shovel and resumes digging. “This ground has so much clay in it, it’s as hard as a rock. We’re going to need to amend the soil some, or these plants won’t thrive.” He grunts and strains to pry loose a shovelful of dirt until the handle makes a loud cracking sound. Kicking at the handle, he swears and says, “Well, that’s just great! Who bought these shovels, with their pencil-thin handles?”

“Hey, hey, hey, buddy, it’s just a shovel; we can buy another one. What’s the matter with you?”

“Addiction! It takes people farther than they ever meant to go and costs them more than they ever meant to pay. And you did what most people do, and what I used to do, when they find out someone has an addiction—they desert and marginalize them. A man can cheat on his wife, gamble, or cheat on his taxes, and he won’t lose any friends. But you let him start using drugs, and suddenly he’s a pariah. It’s not right, Buck. It’s just not right.”
~~~~~~~~~~~

Squatting down and absentmindedly picking up some pine needles, Buck says, "Well, what are we supposed to do, Cross, hang around them while they're using? Go with them to get drugs? Man, I want to stay as far away from that scene as I can."

"Of course not. But how about continuing to be their friend by calling them, letting them know you care, telling them how sad it makes you to see them traveling the path they're on, inviting them to your house if they'll come sober? You see, they know they're lost, even if they deny it to your face." Pointing to his chest, he continues. "In here, they know the truth. They feel lost and powerless to do anything about it. What they need is hope."

Buck looks up at him. "You're right. I just never thought about it that way."

Cross is about to say more when a movement in his periphery catches his attention. Turning his head, he sees Megan slowly walking toward them with a heavy looking plastic shopping bag in each hand.

"Hey," she says, "I thought you all could take a break and have a snack."

Buck jumps up and goes to help her. "Where's your cane?"

"I get so tired of lugging it around. I'm getting better and don't think I need it all the time."

"What does your physical therapist say about that?" Cross asks.

Smiling, Megan says, "He's entitled to his opinion, and I'm entitled to mine."

Buck takes the bags from her and opens one of them. "Is that homemade sausage and biscuits I see?" He hands the other bag to Cross and reaches inside the one he's holding. "I've got what I want."

Megan laughs.

Cross opens his bag and sees a six-pack of beer bottles, with condensation clinging to them. Setting the bag on the ground, he says to Buck, "Give me one of those before you eat them all."

With biscuit crumbs falling from his mouth, Buck obliges him.

Cross takes a bite. "Mmm, these are delicious. Are these homemade biscuits?"

"Yes, but not by me," Megan answers. "Cooking's not my gift. Mother thought your breakfast from the Huddle House might be burned off by now."

"How come we don't see you two there anymore?" Buck asks.

"I don't have to go to physical therapy as often, and my appointments have been changed from morning to afternoon."

"Well, we've been missing you, haven't we, Cross?"

With his mouth full of food, Cross looks at him in surprise, then nods his head.

"Hey, what's in your sack?" Buck asks him.

Cross swallows and says, "Cold beer."

Buck utters a disappointed, "Oh."

"I didn't have anything else I could carry down here," Megan explains. "I know sausage and biscuits and beer is a weird combination, but I thought you'd like something cold to drink."

Cross puzzles over how to turn down her thoughtfulness without hurting her feelings or making her uncomfortable.

I could open a bottle, pretend to take a drink, and hope she doesn't notice. Or I could take the shortest route and just be honest.

Instead, he chooses to lie. "Thanks, but I'm not thirsty right now."

Megan's face tells him she doesn't believe him, but she says nothing and lets the lie hang in the air, suspended by the southern grace of not being pushy.

An awkward silence ensues for a few moments until Megan points at his hand and says, "I see you're married. Do you have any children?"

Cross feels as if he's suddenly been thrown on his back and pinned by a wrestler. He looks down at his wedding ring and rubs it between his finger and thumb. "My wife and daughter were killed by a drunk driver. I've just not been able to take off my ring."

Megan gasps. “Oh, I’m so, so sorry. I apologize for asking. I can’t imagine how devastating that was for you.”

“Don’t apologize. It’s a normal question.”

“But that makes sense.”

“What do you mean?”

“That’s why you don’t drink, isn’t it? Losing loved ones because of the thoughtlessness of a drunk driver would be enough to make me quit drinking, too.”

Cross’s truth hangs in the air between them. He sees her staring at him with compassionate eyes, then he looks away and says, “Yeah, you’re right; it turned me completely against drinking.”

The bitter taste of his lying words nauseates him, and for a moment he thinks he’s going to throw up.

CHAPTER FOURTEEN

FOUR YEARS EARLIER

Cross put his hands over his ears to block out the perpetual din of noise for a moment. It was one of the things he hated the most about being in prison.

Why won't everybody just shut up?!

Pete, an old man who'd been there for over twenty years and become somewhat of a friend to Cross, answered the question one day. "What else is there to do here? You do what you can, whenever you can, or this place will destroy you. Always remember, the most dangerous prison is the one between your ears."

Those last words resonated with Cross. Ever since his wife and daughter were killed in the wreck, he'd lived in self-imposed solitary confinement within a prison whose four walls were made of resentment, regret, anger, and self-loathing. Daily, he tortured himself with questions that began with, "Why didn't I..."

"There were so many choices I could have made that night," he told Pete one time, "that might have kept them from being killed."

"Of course there were," Pete agreed, "but you only see those choices because of hindsight, which we both know is twenty-twenty. Everybody in this prison can play that game, because we're all here because of choices we've made—all of them bad ones. The thing is, no matter how many times you play the game, nothing changes; you're still here."

Sitting on the edge of his bottom bunk bed, he took his hands off his ears and let in the sounds of what had been his home for the past three years: the Northwest Tennessee Correctional Facility.

Bella, the Golden Retriever service dog he was responsible for training, sat within arm's reach on the concrete floor, staring at him with her amber-colored eyes.

Cross stroked the side of her face. “You know I’m going to miss you when you’re gone, don’t you? When they offered this training job to me, I eagerly accepted. Doing something useful has helped pass the time.”

Bella’s tail slowly swept across the floor.

“You remind me of my Golden Retriever, Roxie. You think she’ll still remember me when I finally get out of here?”

Suddenly, the door of his cell slid open, and a burly guard appeared. “Get up, and come with me, Daniels. We need you for suicide watch. Billy Wayne tried to kill himself again.”

“I pulled a shift with someone last week,” Cross replied. “Can’t you get someone else this time?”

“This isn’t a request. Besides, you’re the one who signed up for this job. Come on, let’s go.”

Looking at Bella, Cross said to her, “I’ll be back later.”

He and the guard passed through several checkpoints, including the ritual of a strip search, before arriving at their destination. On the way, Cross asked how Billy Wayne had tried to kill himself, but the guard ignored him.

Instead of sitting in the plastic chair outside the cell, Cross looked through the thick plexiglass window.

Billy Wayne, wearing the safety smock, a heavy, quilted garment that can’t be torn or wrapped into a ligature to hang himself, was seated on the mattress lying on the concrete floor. Other than a stainless steel toilet, nothing else was in the cell.

During a previous time Cross had sat with him, Billy Wayne said he was twenty-seven years old, but in Cross’s opinion he looked closer to seventeen. Being tall and thin, with a pitiful attempt at growing a mustache and goatee, coupled with his naturally high-pitched voice, made him a constant target of ridicule by fellow inmates.

Cross, though, felt sorry for him. He reminded him of students he used to teach in high school who had every disadvantage working against them, were constantly in trouble, and didn't care. Those were the kids Cross worked hardest to reach, to try to make a difference in their lives by showing them they could succeed if they just applied themselves. Often, he stayed after school with students, trying to help them catch up on the work they missed or failed.

Speaking through the opening in the plexiglass where food could be passed to inmates, Cross said, "Hey, Billy."

The young man turned his head to see who was speaking to him and immediately recognized Cross. "I'm glad they let you come."

"I am, too. Want to tell me what happened?"

"Nothing more than what always goes on here. I just can't take it. I try to do what you've told me before and focus on one day at a time, but every day I'm here is just hell, and there's no reason to believe it'll ever change. I'm not strong minded like you are. I can't quit thinking about how much longer I've got to be in here. Tell me again how you do it."

Cross searched his mind for another way to explain it to Billy that would be different from the ways he'd told him in the past. "I've never told you why I'm here, have I?"

Standing up, Billy walked to the plexiglass. "No, you haven't."

"I killed my wife and daughter."

Billy swore at this revelation. "You're kidding me?! You murdered them?"

"Not in the way you're thinking, but I'm the reason they're dead. You know I used to be an alcoholic."

"That's why you attend the AA meetings in here."

"Right. Well, one night I took my wife and daughter out to eat. I'd already drunk some before we left the house, then drank more while we ate. Just as we were heading home, a big thunderstorm hit, not that that's an excuse for what happened. I shouldn't have been driving anyway."

Even though Cross had told his story several times during AA meetings and gotten to where he could tell it without breaking down into tears, the sting of regret hit him hard as he told it to Billy.

In a voice choked with emotion, he declared, “We hit another car head-on. I was driving in the wrong lane. My wife and daughter were killed instantly.” He swiped away a tear rolling down his cheek. “So, being in prison is okay with me, because I deserve to be here.”

Billy Wayne was quiet for a moment, then said, “Nobody deserves to live in this hellhole and be turned into an animal. It’s like living in a jungle where wild animals attack the weak. What’s the point of prisons and jails? What do people think is going to happen when you throw criminals together and make them live together for years or decades? Do they really think we’ll walk out of here a better human being? A reformed person?”

Cross shrugged his shoulders. “I’ve got no answers for that. I just know, for me, it’s given me time to reevaluate my life and realize what kind of person I’d become. I believed the mirage I was living was real. I was what people call a functioning alcoholic, which is maybe the most dangerous kind, because it made me believe I didn’t have a problem.”

They both fell silent.

With his back against a wall, Billy slowly slid to the floor and sat there cross-legged, while Cross relived the images of the wreck.

CHAPTER FIFTEEN

PRESENT DAY

The pain and sadness on Cross's face as he tells Megan about the drunk driver killing his wife and daughter awaken every sympathetic bone in her body.

"Well, I hope they threw that drunk driver under the jail!" she snaps. "People like that don't deserve to live."

"Hey, now," Buck quickly interjects, "that's an awfully judgmental thing to say."

The suddenness of his statement and fervor in his tone catch her by surprise, as does Cross's silent reaction to it. She says to Buck, "I would have thought you'd be the first person to agree with me. I mean, your best friend's life was destroyed by the thoughtless actions of a drunk."

He looks at Cross as if he expects him to say something, but Cross is looking at the ground, seemingly lost in thought. Buck responds to her, "People make mistakes; no one's perfect. I'm sure that driver carries around the weight of the world on his heart and shoulders because of what happened. I can just imagine how guilty he feels."

Megan is again surprised as tears well up in Buck's eyes. "I just don't understand," she says.

Cross suddenly says, "Hey, can we just change the subject?"

"I've just got to say one more thing," Megan replies. "Life's about choices, and choices have consequences."

"That's well-said," Cross agrees.

Grace wonders where Cross's anger is about what happened to his family and why Buck sounds like he's defending the driver. *There must be more to the story than what they're telling me.*

Just then, Grace returns to the group and says, "Did you two enjoy your snack?"

“Mmm, mmm,” Buck answers, “these biscuits melt in your mouth. You need to give me your recipe so my wife, Betty, can try it.”

Grace laughs. “I wouldn’t have any idea how to write it down. I don’t even measure the ingredients anymore. I just learned by watching my mother when I was growing up.”

“Well, you learned it well. My compliments to you.”

“What’s your last name, Buck?” she asks.

“Uh oh,” Megan says, “you better look out. Miss Ancestry-Dot-Com is fixing to climb your family tree.”

Buck says, “My last name is Cordell. I’ve always been called ‘Buck,’ but my real name is Thomas Cordell the Second.”

Grace stares at him. “You’re not Tom Cordell’s son, are you?”

“Yes, ma’am, I am. Not that it’s anything to be proud of, if you knew him and how he died.”

Megan notices her mother turning pale. “Mother, are you all right? Do you need to sit down?”

Buck and Cross hurry to her side and take hold of both of Grace’s arms.

“Sit down here, and lean against this pine tree,” Cross instructs her.

Grace doesn’t argue and lets them help her to the ground.

“Did you take all your medicine this morning?” Megan asks.

“Yes, yes,” Grace answers, sounding irritated. “You always ask me that.”

“That’s because sometimes you forget. Do I need to go get you a drink of water or something?”

“I’ll be fine. Maybe I need to eat one of those sausage and biscuits; it might be my blood sugar.”

Cross finds the plastic bag, takes one out, and brings it to her. “Here you go.”

“Thank you.” She takes a bite and chews it for a moment. Looking at Buck, she says, “Tom Cordell…I haven’t thought about him in a long time. We were in school together, but I moved away after graduation and lost track of him.”

“He died when I was a baby, so I never knew him,” Buck explains. “The story I’ve been told is that he was a bad alcoholic and died of alcohol poisoning when he was twenty-seven, or something like that.”

“Wow,” Megan says, “your dad drank himself to death, and Cross’s family died because of a drunk driver. Talk about weird coincidences.”

Wiping tears from her eyes, Grace says, “I’m really sad to hear about Tom. He was such a good boy when I knew him. We were quite close.” She looks at Cross. “So, you’re Harlon Cross’s son, and your best friend here is Tom Cordell’s son. It’s really hard to believe.”

Cross and Buck look at each other and shrug.

“What’s so odd about that?” Megan asks.

Grace ignores the question and asks Cross, “Who is your mother?”

“She passed away six years ago,” Cross answers. “Her name was Darlene Sanders, and she grew up over in Camden.”

“I’m sorry for your loss. But Harlon’s still living?”

“Yes, he is.”

“How’s his health?”

“He’s actually in really good health. Oftentimes, he helps me and Buck with our landscaping business, and we play music together, too.”

“He’s probably in better health than I am,” Buck inserts. “And he’s become quite the ladies’ man.”

“Really?”

“Yes, ma’am.”

Looking at her mother, Megan asks, “Did you know him, too?”

Grace opens her mouth to speak, but nothing comes out. She puts her fist to her mouth and closes her eyes. Silver tears cling to her eyelashes as she bumps her fist against her mouth. In a hoarse voice, she says, “Yes, I knew Harlon. He and Tom and I were…” her voices catches, then she finishes her sentence with, “good friends.”

Questions flood Megan’s mind as she tries to make sense out of the entire conversation.

I’ve never heard Mother mention either of those names. It’s like someone suddenly opened a door to a room in her past she’s kept secret for years. I don’t think prodding her with questions in front of Cross and Buck is a good idea, but she’s definitely going to tell me later what this is all about.

Opening her eyes, Grace says, “Help me up, please.”

Cross and Buck give her a helping hand.

“I’m sorry for getting emotional,” Grace says. “It’s just been so long since I’ve seen either of them.” Looking at Cross, she asks, “Do you think Harlon might be coming here with you one day? I’d love to see him.”

Cross hesitates and gives Buck a quick glance. “Well, it’s…uh…hard to say. He kinda does what he wants, when he wants. I really never know when he might show up.”

“I understand,” she replies.

The sound of a notification on someone’s cell phone interrupts the group.

Cross and Buck give their phones a quick look, then tuck them back away.

“Wasn’t me,” Buck says.

“Me either.”

They look at Megan and Grace.

“My phone’s at the house,” Megan says. “Mother, check your phone.”

Grace dutifully obeys and stares at her phone for a few moments. "It's Margaret. She's wanting to know about the live music for Fish Fry week. Hey! You two boys mentioned you and Harlon play music. Does he still play the fiddle?"

"Does he ever!" Buck answers her. "He's probably the best fiddle player around these parts."

"What kind of music do you all play?"

"Bluegrass," Cross explains. Looking at Megan, he adds, "It's an acquired taste. Not everybody likes it."

Megan wrinkles her face.

"How good are you?" Grace asks.

"People tell us we're pretty good," Buck says.

Cross adds, "We perform for different kinds of events, like the bluegrass festival in Holladay, Tennessee. Even played at the Tennessee State Fair one time."

Shaking his head, Buck says, "Man, that state fair gig was a nightmare. On one side of us was a man using a chainsaw to make sculptures of bears out of logs, and behind us was a stock car race on the Nashville Speedway. People could hardly hear us playing."

Megan laughs. "Oh my gosh, that's the most redneck thing I've ever heard."

Grace gives her a withering look and says, "You two will have to excuse my daughter. She didn't grow up here and doesn't have an appreciation for some of our traditions." Turning her attention to the men, she says, "I was wondering if you all have ever played during the Fish Fry?"

"We did a few years ago," Cross answers, "but my Pop and the woman in charge of organizing it kinda got crossways with each other, and she sort of blackballed us after that."

Buck laughs. "Yeah, she thought the two of them were a thing until she found out about him sleeping with another woman. Man, she got as mad as a wet hen."

"Well, I'm in charge this year," Grace tells them. "Would you be willing to play again?"

“Absolutely!” Buck says.

Holding up his hand, Cross says, “Hold on a minute. We really appreciate you asking, but I think we better ask Pop what he thinks about it first.”

CHAPTER SIXTEEN

After watching Megan and Grace return to their house, Cross grabs his shovel and starts digging.

Joining him with his own shovel, Buck says, "I'll tell you one thing, you can mark Megan Charles off your list. She's an insensitive, conceited smart-ass who thinks she's better than everybody else. Did you see the face she made when you said we played bluegrass? And her comment about drunk drivers was way out of line. What a jerk! Don't be discouraged, though, there's a woman out there somewhere for you, and we'll find her."

"I agree, even though she was never on any list of mine. But what she said about drunk drivers—"

Buck cuts him off. "Don't even say it, not a word. I know how you feel about it, but just because you feel that way, don't make it so. When are you ever going to forgive yourself?"

Resting his foot on the shovel, Cross replies, "My guess is, never."

"You know what? I get tired of talking to you about it," Buck says sharply.

"Then shut up. I'm tired of you talking about it, too," Cross snaps.

Buck pushes his shovel into the ground with his boot, then lifts and pitches the dirt to one side. In a kinder tone, he says, "You know I'm not going to quit talking to you about it, don't you?"

Cross sighs. "Yeah, I do. And it's okay, I know you only do it because you love me."

"Shut up talking like that, or somebody's going to make a TV show about us and call it 'Queer Eye for the Landscaping Guy.'"

Cross bursts out laughing, drops his shovel, and bull rushes his friend. Bear hugging him, he says, "Come here, you big ox, you know you love me."

Buck pushes him away and backs up. "Now cut that out! Megan and her mom are probably looking out the window at us. No telling what they think." He brushes himself off like he's trying to get rid of ticks or mosquitos.

Cross keeps laughing. "I don't care what they think." Then he gets quiet and picks up his shovel. "One thing I learned from everything I went through is, if you love somebody, you need to tell them every chance you get, because one day they might be gone."

In a somber tone, Buck says, "Yeah, you're right."

They resume working, but in silence.

After a couple of minutes, Buck says, "You still miss her, don't you?"

"Every day. I miss them both every day. I still have dreams about them and wake up and think all that horribleness was just a nightmare."

"I'd do anything to make it that way for you," Buck tells him.

"Thanks. I know you would. I'll tell you one thing, though, changing the subject, I'm going to talk to Pop about him, Grace, and your dad. There's got to be some whale of a story there."

Nodding, Buck says, "Boy, ain't that the truth! Did you see how she reacted to learning who our dads are? It's surprising to me, knowing how much Pop likes to tell tales, we've never heard a single word about it."

Pulling a red bandana out of his back pocket and wiping the sweat off his face, Cross says, "Don't worry. I'm going to pin him down this evening and make him tell the story."

"Good. And while you're at it, ask him about playing music for the Fish Fry."

~~~~~~~~

Late that afternoon, Cross pulls to a stop in front of his house and smiles as Roxie bounds off the porch and comes running to greet him. When he doesn't immediately open his door, she begins barking at him, insisting he get out.

Smiling, Cross gets out and kneels on one knee.
~~~~~~~~

Roxie wriggles all over while licking his face and neck.

"Hey, hey," Cross protests, "you don't have to give me a bath; I'll take my own shower later. You need to sit and calm down."

At the word "sit," Roxie immediately restrains herself and sits down, but her eyes still dance with excitement.

He scratches her muzzle and strokes the side of her face. "Why do I need a woman in my life when I've got you? You're always glad to see me, you don't hold grudges, and you keep me warm at night." Laughing, he says, "What more could a guy need?"

She raises a front leg and rests her paw on his chest.

"I'm glad you agree. Now, let's go inside and see what Pop's been up to today."

Walking through the front door, the aroma of fish frying greets them. Immediately, Cross's stomach growls. In the kitchen, he finds his dad standing in front of the stove, wearing a grease-stained chef's apron.

"Man, that smells delicious! Catfish or crappie?"

Harlon keeps his focus on the slotted spoon in his hand and lifts a piece of fish out of the bubbling oil. "Tennessee River blue-channel catfish, the best there is."

"Some of those we caught last summer?"

"Yep."

"What can I do to help?"

"You can pour the tea if you want. This is the last piece of fish."

Cross puts ice in two wide-mouth quart jars and pours tea out of a blue, gallon-sized plastic pitcher. The ice crackles as the dark liquid runs over it.

"Plates are over here," Harlon says. "Come help yourself."

After setting their tea on the table, Cross joins him. "Man, this looks delicious."

He spoons a helping of white beans out of a pot and onto his plate, making sure to get a piece of the ham cooked in it. Using some tongs, he gets a helping of French fries and two catfish filets. On one edge of his plate, he puts a couple of green onions with bulbs the size of a silver dollar and balances three hushpuppies next to them.

"You sure that's enough?" Harlon kids him.

"Ha, this is just the first go around," Cross answers. "You know me, I can eat my weight in catfish and the trimmings."

Taking a seat at the table, he waits for Harlon to join him.

As Harlon pulls out a chair, he says, "What are you waiting on? Dig in!"

"I'd like us to say a prayer tonight, before we eat."

"Sure thing. What's going on?"

"I found out today Tony Koslinski died of a drug overdose. He'd been dead a while before someone found him."

Harlon's face sags at the news. "I'm sorry. I hate to hear that. Addiction is an s.o.b., isn't it?"

"Yes, it is, Pop."

Harlon folds his hands in front of him and bows his head. "Go ahead."

Cross bows and says, "Holy Father, I don't talk to You as often as I should, but I think about You every day. It's because of You I found my way out of the bottle. Right now, though, I'm thinking about Tony. First of all, if there was something I could have done or said to save him, please forgive me. But secondly, I'm really sad for his family. Help them find a way to deal with his death in a way that won't make them feel guilty. What he did was his choice; there's no one to blame." He pauses for a second, then says, "Help us all to be more caring, especially toward those who are hard to love. Amen."

Harlon keeps his head bowed and adds, "And thank You for saving my son and bringing him home to me." Grabbing a handkerchief out of his back pocket, he blows his nose and wipes his eyes.

Cross takes a gulp of tea to try and wash down the lump in his throat.

For the next few minutes, they eat in silence, with the only sound being their crunching on the hushpuppies and crisp cornmeal batter on the fish.

Cross's thoughts turn to the happenings that day at the Charles's, and how he's going to get his dad to open up about that chapter of his past. "I want us to try fishing for catfish again on the rocks along the banks of Paris Landing Bridge during their spawning, like we did last year. That was fun!"

Smiling, Harlon says, "That surely was! We couldn't haul them in fast enough."

"You're right. We'll take Buck with us this time."

"Buck's too loud to be a good fisherman. He scares off all the fish."

Cross laughs. "You're right, but he's a lot of fun to have around."

"He's a good boy who means well. He sure was a good friend to you when you needed one."

"That's for sure." Taking a knife, Cross cuts a hushpuppy in half and uses the soft side to sop up what's left of the bean juice on his plate, then puts it in his mouth. After he finishes it, he says, "You know, you've really never talked about Buck's dad. I know you knew him, but that's about it. And all Buck really knows is how his dad died. What kind of person was he?"

Harlon eyes him suspiciously. "What's brought this on? Why're you asking me about this now?

Cross hears the tension in his voice. "I'm just making conversation with you. Just wondering, that's all."

Harlon purposely drops his fork on his plate. "What'd she say?" he asks sharply.

"Gee, Pop, why are you getting mad? What did who say? What do you mean?"

Scooting his chair back, Harlon gets up and carries his plate to the sink. "I'm done talking about it."

Cross turns halfway in his chair and says, “You can’t be done talking about something you’ve not even started talking about.” He hesitates, then adds, “She said you and she and Tom, Buck’s dad, used to be good friends. Is that true?”

Harlon stops what he’s doing and rests his hands on the side of the sink. Without turning around, he says, “Yes, that’s true.”

“Then tell me, Pop, what in the world happened?”

CHAPTER SEVENTEEN

FORTY-EIGHT YEARS EARLIER

July 22, 1973

Dear Grace,

I haven't heard from you in a while, and it makes me worry something's wrong with you. But then again, I know the mail service here sucks. Some guys in my unit get four or five letters at a time from the same person, with dates ranging from five or six weeks or more. So, I'm hoping any day now I'll get a bundle of letters from you.

I've got to be honest with you, when I signed up to do a second tour here in Nam, I thought I was doing the right thing for my country. I thought this war was making a difference for the people, but I don't believe that anymore.

The United States has been fighting here for nearly twenty years—twenty years! And nothing seems to have changed. I've decided you can't change what people believe by killing their friends and family. You just make the survivors angry and resentful and bent on revenge for generations. Edwin Starr's song, "War," sums up my feelings about war in general: it's good for nothing.

That's why the news I have for you today is so sweet: my tour is about to wind up, and I'll be coming home in a couple of weeks! I just hope I survive that long. B.J., the guy I've made friends with I've written you about, was killed yesterday. He was shot in the leg and drowned before I could get to him. That was hard to take.

I can't wait for you to hold me in your arms and tell me everything's going to be okay. I feel like I'm going to go crazy over here. The only thing that keeps me sane is memories of you. You're all I've got to go home to. I mean, I'll probably visit the orphanage where I grew up, but that's not a real home. What I want more than anything is for us to get married as soon as I get home so we can start making our own home and family.

I love you more than anything in this world!

I'm coming home!

With all the love in the world,

Harlon

~ ~ ~ ~ ~ ~ ~

Seven weeks later, Harlon stood with his duffle bag over his shoulder at the front door of Grace's house, staring at her mother.

"What do you mean she moved away? Where did she go? Why did she leave? How long is she going to be gone?"

Dabbing tears with a tissue, she said, "Harlon, I'm so sorry. I promised Grace I wouldn't tell. Just know I'm very sad about it all. She hasn't been the same since you went away. You don't know how hard war is on the people who stay behind."

The duffle bag slipped off his shoulder and landed beside him with a thud. Tears filled his eyes as he said, "What am I supposed to do? Where am I supposed to go?"

"I'm sure the orphanage will let you stay there until you can figure things out, won't they?"

"Yeah, probably, but that's not the way it's supposed to be, not the way Grace promised me. I mean, we were supposed to get married. You hear me? Grace and I were going to get married!"

"I know, I know. This is awful for you, and I hate it." She looked away for a moment, then said, "Maybe I shouldn't suggest this, but why don't you talk to Tom? Maybe he'll give you some answers to your questions."

Cocking his head to one side, Harlon said, "Tom? What's Tom got to do with this?"

She began closing the door while saying, "I've said too much. I wish you the best, Harlon."

~ ~ ~ ~ ~ ~ ~

Lying on his back on the floor, Tom tried to cover his face with his arms as Harlon pummeled him with his fists.

A stream of cuss words spewed from Harlon's mouth. "She was mine! How could you have sex with her? I'm going to kill you!"

"It wasn't something we planned, Harlon. It just sort of happened."

Harlon pulled Tom's arms away from his face and pinned them on the floor with his knees. "Do you hear how stupid and pathetic you sound? What kind of best friend are you?"

"The worst kind," Tom admitted. "I'll regret what happened for the rest of my life. Go ahead, beat me to death. I deserve it."

Harlon shoved his face, then rolled off him. Sitting on his knees, he said, "You're not worth killing. Tell me this: why did you let her leave?"

Tom sat up and spat a mouthful of blood onto his T-shirt. "We had sex one time; I promise. Of course, I didn't use a rubber because I wasn't intending to do anything like that. And when Grace turned up pregnant, we both felt like our worlds were crashing down. I felt sorry for her, and for you. She said she just couldn't face you because she knew how bad you'd be hurt. She was so ashamed and knew her reputation around here would be ruined. I mean, having sex with your boyfriend's best friend while he's fighting a war? People would never let her forget it. That's why she ran off."

"Where did she go? What's her plan?"

"That, she didn't tell me. My guess is, she went to a home for unwed mothers way off somewhere. Did you ask her mom about it?"

"Yeah, but she's not going to tell me anything."

Harlon sat back and hung his head. "What am I going to do? My life is over just when I thought it was about to begin. It would've been easier if I'd gotten killed in Viet Nam."

"Harlon," Tom said, "I'm not going to ask you to forgive me, because I don't deserve it. But I want to somehow make up for it. What that'll be, I don't know. Just know you can always call on me for anything, anytime, and I'll be there. For the rest of my life, I'm going to try to make things right between us."

Standing up, Harlon squinted his eyes at him. Through gritted teeth, he said, "You'll never be able to do that, because you're dead to me. Don't ever let me see you again!"

Turning away, he stormed out of the house, slamming the door behind him.

CHAPTER EIGHTEEN

PRESENT DAY

Cross stares in disbelief as Harlon finishes his story. "Oh my God, Pop, why have you never told me this? Did Mom know?"

Harlon shakes his head. "I didn't see any reason to tell her. What would be the point?"

"I'll tell you one thing, it helps me understand why Buck's dad turned out like he did, and why you've always treated Buck like a son."

Returning to the table, Harlon sits down. "I guess it's been my way of making up for me being so hateful and unforgiving toward Tom. I was stupid and prideful back then and held tightly to my grudge against him."

"I can see why," Cross says. "He ruined two lives—yours and Grace's."

"No!" Harlon snaps. "She ruined my life, and I ruined Tom's by turning my back on my best friend. I knew he'd become an alcoholic and in some twisted way was glad of it. But when he died, leaving his wife and Buck behind, I was filled with regret for not forgiving him and trying to help. That's why I befriended her and made every effort to be involved in Buck's life. Of all the things that make life hard, living with regret is one of the worst."

A thought strikes Cross. "How come Buck doesn't know this story? Why didn't his mom tell him?"

"I'm guessing Tom never told her. She wasn't from around here; I think she lived in Dover. So, she wouldn't have learned about it from anybody. I thought about telling her after Tom died, to help her make sense out of his self-destructive life, but then again, I thought, what difference would it make? Plus, I was too ashamed to tell her. Are you going to tell Buck?"

Leaning his chair on the back two legs, Cross takes a big breath and lets it out slowly. "Oh man, I don't know. Don't you think he deserves to know?"

"Maybe, but I'm afraid it'll change how he feels about me. You know I couldn't love him more if he was your brother." Two big tears roll down his creased face.

Cross puts a hand on top of one of his dad's. "Years ago it might have changed things, but Buck's a grown man. I think he'll understand." He watches Harlon nod his head in agreement, then asks, "I've got to say something else. You've been holding a grudge and hating Megan's mom for nearly fifty years. You hear that? Fifty years! Tell me, what good has that done you?"

Harlon pulls his hand away from him. "You have no idea how bad what she did hurt me!"

"You're right, I don't. But again, how has feeling this way about her helped you? How has it benefited you? Are you a better person because of it?"

Harlon studies him for a moment. "I get what you're driving at. You think I should forgive her, don't you? Well, she doesn't deserve to be forgiven."

"Maybe she does, maybe she doesn't. That's not for me to say, but I'll tell you one thing, what I saw in prison was this: the men who held on to grudges and resentments were the unhappiest and most discontent, but those who practiced forgiveness were better able to live life one day at a time. I even heard one of them say one time, 'Holding a grudge is like putting poison in your enemy's coffee and you drinking it.' You regret not forgiving Tom, but you refuse to forgive Grace. Have you ever thought about the fact that it's possible Grace has lived with regret ever since all that happened? You might help her unload that burden if you told her you forgive her."

Getting up from his chair, Harlon says, "You're awful wordy this evening, chock full of advice. But the man who tells me I need to practice forgiveness won't even forgive himself." He walks away and starts clearing the pots and pans off the stove.

Harlon's words strike the steel wall of Cross's heart and bounce off, having no effect.

He doesn't understand anything. He's never done something that got someone killed.

CHAPTER NINETEEN

PRESENT DAY

Sobbing uncontrollably, Grace says, "I'm so ashamed of running away. I hurt so many people."

Megan holds her mother in her arms and rocks her gently as she tries to process everything she's just learned about Harlon, Tom, and her mom.

"Are you telling me I've got a sibling I never knew about?"

Grace sits back up and wipes her tears. "No. The baby was stillborn. At least that's what they told me. I never saw it."

"I don't understand why you didn't stay home and have the baby and raise it with Granny."

"Dear, things were so different back then. If you got pregnant, you were looked down on as an immoral and promiscuous person. Homes for unwed mothers were everywhere, some of which were very unscrupulous. You probably never heard of the Tennessee Children's Home Society, run by Georgia Tann. She was a little before my time, but she made millions of dollars stealing and selling babies and children under the guise of trying to help them."

Megan gasps. "You're kidding?!"

"No, I'm not. You can check it out."

"Mom…do you think it's possible…I mean, I don't even want to say it out loud. But could it be your baby wasn't stillborn, but born alive and given to someone? You never saw the baby, so how can you be sure?"

All the blood drains from Grace's face, and her lips begin to tremble. "I never thought about that," she whispers. "The truth is…" She turns her face away from Megan.

"What? The truth is what?"

"It's shameful. So shameful, I don't want to say it out loud for fear God will strike me dead."

“My God, Mother, what could be worse than what you’ve already told me?”

Grace takes a breath, and her shoulders shudder. Keeping her face turned away from her daughter, she says, “When they told me the baby was stillborn, I was relieved. I wasn’t ready to be a mother, at least not to Tom’s child. I was afraid the child would be a constant reminder to me of how I’d ruined things with Harlon. No child deserves to be viewed as a mistake. I can see now how wrong that was of me, how selfish it was.”

Slowly shaking her head, Megan says, “The person you’re describing is so different from the person I’ve known my whole life. I don’t even recognize that person. It feels like you’re making this all up, even though I know you’re not.”

“I know, but that’s who I was. The unwed mothers home I was living at was in Indianapolis, Indiana. Mother drove me up there, let me out, and drove home. Neither she nor my father made any contact with me the whole time I was there. It was the most miserable time in my life. I felt so alone, besides being crushed with guilt over how I’d wronged Harlon. He was a good boy and deserved better.”

Standing up, Megan stretches and massages her leg that’s grown stiff. “So that’s the real truth about how you came to meet my father in Indiana.”

Grace nods. “Yes. Two days after the baby was born, they told me I had to leave the home. I got a job as a secretary in a large insurance agency where your father worked. That’s where we met.”

“Did he know your story?”

“Heavens, no! I couldn’t tell him, or he’d have had nothing to do with me. And the longer we were married, it seemed less and less important he know.”

Megan flops back down beside her. “And you never communicated with Tom or Harlon after that?”

“I wanted to but could never find the words to say to either of them, plus I didn’t figure they wanted anything to do with me.”

“You know what I think?”

“No, what?”

"I think you need to talk to Harlon and make things right between you two, or at least try."

Wringing her hands, Grace says, "Oh, I don't know, Megan. I don't know if I could. I mean, I'd like to, but what would I say? How do you apologize for a devastating choice you made over fifty years ago? A choice that changed the trajectory of at least three lives?"

Megan stills her mother's hands with her own and holds them in her lap. "I just think he deserves to hear your side of things, all the emotions you were having, the daily fear of being told he'd died fighting in Viet Nam, and your friendship with Tom filling the void Harlon left in your heart. Mom, you were only eighteen years old, just a kid, living in a world very different from today's. Don't be so hard on yourself."

Grace looks at her, and Megan notices the red lines crisscrossing the whites of her mother's eyes.

"Thank you," Grace says.

"For what?"

"For asking me about that time in my life. Carrying a secret for so long is exhausting. I feel better now that I've set it free." Leaning forward, she kisses Megan on the cheek. "I love you."

Megan's heart swells with emotion. "You know what's interesting? If I hadn't come to live with you and we'd gotten closer, I don't think this conversation would have ever happened. Even though I didn't see it at the time, something good came out of my accident and Max leaving me."

Grace tells her how disappointed she was in what Max did, but Megan says she can understand why he did it.

"I don't blame him, mother. I wasn't giving him the love and attention he deserved long before my accident. I didn't put the work into our marriage it deserved and needed. It's so easy to see now, looking back on things, how selfish I was."

Grace eyes her. "So, if you could go back in time, you'd do things differently, right? You'd be a better wife?"

"Absolutely."

“You know,” Grace says slowly, “that Cross Daniels is a really good looking man and seems really nice. You should—”

“Stop right there,” Megan cuts her off. “I keep telling you, I’m not going to ruin another man’s life like I ruined Max’s.”

CHAPTER TWENTY

PRESENT DAY

Helping her mother load the dishwasher with their breakfast dishes, Megan says, "Don't forget, I have an appointment at the suboxone clinic this morning."

"How long are you going to have to take that medicine?"

"I don't know the answer to that. I guess as long as I think I need it. My doctor and my therapist say that decision is up to me; they don't dictate to people when they should get off it."

Grace furrows her eyebrows but doesn't say anything.

"What's that look for?" Megan asks.

"Nothing."

"Yes, it is. Tell me what's bothering you."

"Well, I've read on Facebook people who use suboxone are just swapping one drug for another, that they're still addicts."

Putting her hands on her hips, Megan replies, "Well, by all means, let's use Facebook as the authority! What's interesting to me is how many people who know nothing about addiction think they know everything about addiction. What matters the most to me is, this medicine helped save me from destroying my life."

"Okay, okay, I'm sorry," Grace says. "I just don't want you to head down the wrong path again. I guess I need to trust you know what you're doing."

~~~~~~~~~

At the suboxone clinic, Megan and seven other patients take a seat in the circle of chairs in one of the therapy rooms.

Lauren, the therapist, is already seated. Smiling, she says, "Good morning, everyone. Let's go around the circle and have you share your first name, how long you've been coming to our clinic, and how your addiction got started in the first place. Terrance, why don't you start?"
~~~~~~~~~

A large Black man with sad eyes says, "I'm Terrance, and I've been coming here for about seventeen months, I think. Doing pills came easy for me, because my mama used to give me and my brother pills to make us sleep so she could do her partying and drugging at the house. First time I remember her doing it, we were seven and eight years old. She said they were vitamins, but looking back now and knowing what I know, they were probably pieces of Xanax. I was somewhere in my teens when I discovered opiates, and man, they took over my life."

To his left, a frail looking grey-haired woman gives everyone a weak smile. "My name is Sandy. I've been here five years. I guess you could say my addiction got started when I was really little and my daddy would put beer in my milk bottle so I'd quit crying, at least that's what I've been told. I was an alcoholic in high school but kept it hidden by making good grades. My senior year, I hurt my knee while doing a stunt as a cheerleader, and the doctor gave me hydrocodone. They quickly took over my life. I tried to quit many times but couldn't stand the physical withdrawal. It wasn't until I discovered suboxone that I was finally able to kick the habit."

The person beside her nods in agreement. "My name is Donna. I was shooting meth with my mama when I was fourteen. I was eighteen when I went to prison for six years, and that's where I was introduced to heroin. It gave me a high like nothing I'd ever done. When I got out, I started dealing while working at a strip club. Eventually got busted and sent back to prison. It finally dawned on me I was living what people call insanity, doing the same thing over and over and expecting a different result. But like Sandy, I couldn't deal with the withdrawals. One day, though, somebody gave me a piece of a suboxone, and suddenly I felt normal again. Not high, because suboxone doesn't make you high. As soon as I got out of prison, I came straight here and have been here for six years. My life has never been better. I've got a great job, bought a car, and am about to buy a house."

A grizzled-looking man beside her says, "You're right. It don't make you high. I wish people who still think we're addicts would understand that."

Everyone mutters agreement with him.

“I’m Carl,” he says. “I’ve been here nine years. I grew up in a good home with good parents, so I can’t blame them for what I did. I never did any kind of drugs until I fell off a scaffold and broke my back. The doctors started loading me up with Percocet and oxycodone. I took them just like they told me to, and they kept giving me more. I had no idea I was becoming an addict until a year later, when the pain management doctor I was seeing got busted for running a pill mill, and I got sicker than I’ve ever been in my life. I was so ignorant, I didn’t know it was withdrawal. The only way I could get relief was to buy opiates on the street or steal them from people I knew. And that’s what I did for about fifteen years, spending all the money I was making on pills. Then someone told me about suboxone, so I tried it. It was like a miracle drug. It stopped those awful withdrawals and took away my cravings. It saved my life.”

“Let me make a comment about that,” Lauren says, “because it’s a comment I hear often around here. You all need to remember, suboxone doesn’t make you make better choices, doesn’t make you say no to drugs, doesn’t change you. Those things happened because you did the work of rebuilding your lives. You need to take credit for the changes you’ve made and feel proud of yourselves.”

Smiles crease the faces of the members of the group.

“Moon, why don’t you continue?” Lauren directs.

A morbidly obese woman with short-cropped hair says, "I'm Moon, and I've been here two months. My dad sexually abused me while I was growing up. I told my mom about it, but she didn't believe me. When I got to be a teenager, he started giving me pills to help me get in the mood. What a liar! What the pills did was help numb me out so I didn't have to deal with what was happening. When I was seventeen, I ran off with my boyfriend, who I didn't know was a meth cooker. He'd beat on me when he was high. Opiates helped me deal with that. You know how it is—you can put up with a lot of crap when you're high all the time. He finally got busted, though, and was sent off. If that hadn't happened, I guess I'd have stayed with him till he killed me. Being pregnant's the best thing to happen to me." She rubs her abdomen. "As soon as I found out, I told myself I wasn't going to screw this kid's life up like mine was. I got in here as soon as I could. So far, it's going real good. I'm glad I'm here, and glad to be clean."

The next person, an athletic looking young man, says, "Hey, I'm Donnie, and I'm here for the third time to try and make it work. I've been kicked out twice for failing drug screens, which is what they should have done to me. Where I got on the wrong track was when I got my leg messed up playing football in college. I kept playing on it for a little while, even after it got injured. I just took a handful of hydrocodone and played through the pain. But finally, I had to have surgery on it, and that's when my life spun out of control. Percocet, that became like the Holy Grail to me. It's what got me up in the mornings and kept me going during the day. I couldn't function without it. The problem is, I keep lying to myself that I don't have a problem, I can still take an opiate here and there. But the truth is, I have a serious problem. I'm thankful for another chance here, and I promise to do it right this time, Lauren."

Smiling, Lauren says, "Just do the right thing one day at a time, Donnie. Keep it simple. I think you can do it."

Next to Donnie sits a hard looking woman with a scowl on her face. "I'm Scarlett. Been here maybe three or four years; I don't keep up with it. So, if you grow up in a house full of addicts, with your mom and dad shooting up every day, grandparents getting drunk, and people coming in and out all hours of the night buying and selling drugs, what do you grow up and do? You'd think a person would be smart enough to tell themselves to stay away from that life, and I did for a while. But I had a car wreck and messed my back and hip up, and they gave me pills. Man, I couldn't take them fast enough. I was an addict within six months, and, stupid me number two, I married an addict. Ten years ago, he died of an overdose with oxy and Xanax. That should have been a wakeup call for me, but it wasn't. I got with another man who constantly cheated on me. I didn't care because he kept me supplied with pills. The final straw, though, was when I caught him molesting my little girl. I contacted Child Protective Services, and he got arrested. But they drug screened me and took my daughter away from me and put her in foster care."

Suddenly, her scowl melts away, and she begins to cry.

"That's what motivated me to come here and clean up my life. It took me over a year, but I got my daughter back. I've got a job now and am taking care of her. I'm not in a relationship, and not interested in one. My daughter's all I need."

Megan glances around the group, then says, "My name is Megan, and I've been here three months, I think. I'm like Carl in that I had good parents growing up. I was an only child and got anything I wanted. I did well in school, went to college, and married a good man. Everything looked perfect, except for me being selfish and narcissistic. My hobbies were rock climbing and hiking. Really, they were more than hobbies; they were obsessions. I wasn't mean to my husband, but I wasn't good to him either. Then I had a fall when hiking, got broken up pretty bad, had a closed-head injury, and was in a coma. When I finally came to, I had a morphine IV drip connected to my arm, steel rods and screws holding my leg together, and I was paralyzed. That's when my husband left me, but as long as I could take pills, I didn't have to deal with that pain. So I kept taking more and more. I would steal them from other patients in the physical rehab place I was staying in. One of the nurses got fired because they thought she was stealing medicine. I'm just glad I learned about suboxone before I ended up in trouble. But I keep asking myself, have I just traded one drug for another and I'm still an addict?"

The attention of the group swings to Lauren as Megan's unanswered question hangs in the air.

"That's an easy one to answer," Lauren says. "Some of the criteria that are required to fit the diagnosis of having an addiction are that the person is always craving and searching for more of whatever it is they're taking. They also take increasing levels of the drug, even though they know it's harmful to them. Their life becomes unmanageable, out of control. None of that is true when you're taking suboxone, is it?"

Everyone shakes their heads.

"What you have to realize and accept," she continues, "is that there will always be people who say you're still an addict. Some of those may even be your friends and family. I encourage you to quit trying to convince them differently. You have no control over what they think, so let them think what they want. In most cases, what will convince them is your changed life. That's what you need to focus on—you working on you, making better choices, reclaiming and rebuilding your life. Even then, though, there will be some who will always say you're an addict. Just accept it, and keep moving forward."

After group is over, Megan thinks about what Lauren said and wonders if her mother will be one of those persons who never believes. Sadness seeps into her heart at that thought.

She's the only person whose opinion I really care about. Please God, open her mind and heart so she can see who I am, rather than who I was.

CHAPTER TWENTY-ONE

PRESENT DAY

Leaning his ear closer to the banjo hanging around his neck, Buck raises his voice and says, “Will you all be quiet for a second? I’ve got a string out of tune.”

Harlon untucks his fiddle from his neck and sets the base of it on his knee. “If you wouldn’t buy new strings every time we practice, we wouldn’t have to go through this. Put them on a week or two ahead, so they’ll get stretched out and stay in tune.”

Buck nods like he agrees, but it’s clear the only thing he’s listening to is the strings of his banjo as he plucks each one and twists the tuning keys.

“Is that a new bass, Glynn?” Cross asks a man standing beside him.

Smiling, Glynn answers, “Yeah. I dropped by Chandler Music, over in McKenzie, the other day and found it. They made me a deal I couldn’t refuse.”

The other man in the quintet gathered on Harlon’s front porch strums his guitar and says, “If you boys would invest in a good instrument, you wouldn’t have to buy any more.”

Cross and Glynn laugh.

“How old is that Martin guitar, Randy?” Harlon asks the man.

Randy looks in the G-hole of the guitar and proudly says, “Made in nineteen forty-seven. It’s a classic.”

“You’re not fooling anybody here,” Cross says. “We all know the only reason you haven’t bought another guitar is because you’re too cheap.”

The loud sound of Buck strumming a G chord interrupts them. “Got it! I’m ready now. What were we working on?”

“‘Blue Moon of Kentucky,’” Glynn answers.

Harlon points his bow at Cross. “Count us off.”

All sense of joking among the men disappears as Cross counts to four.

Immediately, and in perfect time, everyone jumps into the introduction of the song. Then, in a thin, nasal voice, Cross begins singing. At the chorus, Glynn and Randy join him, singing harmony. Harlon plays the break, making his bow dance across the strings like the feet of someone clogging.

Two-and-a-half minutes later, the song ends, but the music echoes among the trees for a few more seconds.

"Whooee!" Glynn exclaims. "Mighty fine, mighty fine."

Randy says, "I don't know how you make yourself sound like Bill Monroe, Cross, but man, you've got it right on the money."

Cross smiles. "Randy, let's do 'I Wonder How the Old Folks Are at Home.' You kick it off, Buck."

Without hesitation, Buck plays a verse of the song, then Randy closes his eyes and begins singing.

For the next thirty or forty minutes, that's the way it goes, from one song to another, first one of them taking the lead, and then another, one singing melody and the others singing harmony.

"Before we take a break," Randy says, "I want to hear 'Duelin' Banjos,' Cross and Buck."

"We haven't done that in a while," Cross says. "You up to giving it a try, Buck?"

Fiddling with his tuning pegs, Buck says, "Let me make sure I'm in tune." After a couple moments, he says, "Okay, I'm ready."

The two of them turn and face each other. The beginning starts out painfully slow but gradually picks up speed until their hands and fingers are a blur.

Glynn and Randy clap and stomp in time to the music.

Harlon grins and twirls his bow in the air.

Buck finally ends the song with a flair but misses the last note by a half-step. Immediately, he inches his finger up a fret and plays the right note.

Everyone laughs.

"Doggone it!" Buck exclaims. "I'll have to work on that. Don't worry, I'll have it down by the time we play the Fish Fry."

They set aside their instruments and take a seat in cane-bottom, ladder back chairs.

Using his foot, Cross nudges a cooler into the circle and lifts the lid. "Y'all get something to drink."

Each of them, except Buck, grabs an ice cold can of their favorite non-alcoholic drink.

"You not thirsty, Buck?" Cross asks.

"Oh, yeah, I'm thirsty, but Betty says I gotta start drinking more water and losing some weight. She says I'm mashing all the air out of her when we have sex."

Dr. Pepper spews out of Glynn's mouth, and Randy gets choked on his drink. Cross and Harlon laugh so hard, their faces turn red.

"This is serious," Buck says, with a straight face. "She says I can't have sex until I lose fifteen pounds."

His comment has the effect of throwing gas on the fire of his friends' laughter.

It takes several minutes before everyone calms down and catches their breath.

Cross rubs his cheeks on his sleeves to dry his tears. "You know Betty will kill you if she finds out what you told us."

A look of surprise takes over Buck's face. "Y'all aren't going to tell, are you?

In an overly dramatic way, they all promise never to tell.

"Every one of you aren't nothing but a you-know-what!" Buck tells them. "And you can put any low-down, sorry word you want in that blank, because it'll be true."

"Hey, when is the Fish Fry?" Randy asks. "Two weeks?"

"Yes," Cross answers. "Which means we've got to get some more practices in in a hurry."

“How did this invite come about anyway?” Glynn asks. “I thought we got blackballed because of a certain member of our little group?” He nods his head toward Harlon.

“That wasn’t my fault,” Harlon asserts. “I have no control over what other people think.”

“Buck and I started a new landscaping job,” Cross explains, “and it turns out the woman who owns the place is in charge of procuring entertainment for the week. We were having a conversation with her and her daughter, and the next thing I knew, Buck was agreeing to us performing.”

Smiling, Glynn says, “Harlon, will you please keep your pants zipped up around this woman, at least until we play for the Fish Fry? Don’t use her to put another notch on your belt.”

In an instant, Harlon jumps up, swears at Glynn, and charges toward him. “You shut your mouth, you smart-ass weasel!” He hits both of Glynn’s shoulders with the palms of his hands, knocking him backward.

As the chair topples over, and Glynn with it, Cross jumps out of his chair and gets in front of Harlon. Putting his hand on Harlon’s chest and pushing him back a step, he yells, “Pop! What are you doing?!”

Harlon jabs his finger toward Glynn. “You tell him to keep his mouth shut!”

“He was just joking with you. Get ahold of yourself!”

Randy and Buck help Glynn to his feet.

“Are you hurt?” Buck asks him.

Rubbing the back of his head, Glynn answers, “No, I’m all right.” Eyeing Harlon, he says, “What’s got into you? We joke about this all the time.”

Harlon knocks away Cross’s hand, returns to his chair, and packs up his fiddle. “Screw all of you, screw this music, and screw playing at the Fish Fry!” Stomping across the porch, he enters the house and slams the door behind him.

The four friends stare in stunned silence at the closed door.

Cross turns to Glynn. "I'm really sorry, Glynn. I've never seen him lose his temper like that."

"I didn't mean anything by it," Glynn replies. "I was just joking."

"I know, we all know, you were just having fun."

"That was crazy, Cross," Buck tells him. "Harlon looked like he wanted to kill Glynn. What's going on with him?"

Cross thinks about the recent conversation with his dad about what happened years ago between him and Grace and Tom. "He's had a lot on his mind lately," he explains to Buck, "but that's still no excuse for him acting that way."

"What are we going to do about playing for the Fish Fry?" Randy asks. "There's no way we can get another fiddle player at this late date."

"Let me talk to him," Cross answers. "I think when he calms down, he'll feel really bad about what he did and apologize to all of us."

Later, after the guys have gone home, Cross picks up his guitar and goes inside the house. Walking to his dad's bedroom, he pauses at the open door and looks at him sitting on the edge of the bed, with his head in his hands.

Without looking up, Harlon mumbles, "Don't say it."

Cross joins him on the side of his bed and puts his arm around his shoulders.

"Has everybody left?" Harlon asks.

"Yeah."

"What an ass I made of myself! I don't know what came over me. I just saw red."

"Like you did when you confronted Tom?"

Harlon's head snaps up, and he looks at Cross. "I guess maybe it was. I haven't felt like that in a long, long time. After that happened with Tom, I promised myself I'd never get that angry again. Then Glynn makes a joking remark toward me, and I lose it. What's going on?"

A few moments of silence pass between them, the way it does when men are thinking.

Cross chews the inside of his cheek, then says, “I can tell you the common denominator between both incidents.”

“What’s that?”

“Grace Charles.”

CHAPTER TWENTY-TWO

The next morning, Cross finishes getting dressed for work by tying on his work boots. Walking through the kitchen, he speaks to Harlon, who's sitting at the table, staring blankly into space.

"Are sure you're okay this morning? You're awfully quiet."

Harlon looks at him. "I guess I'm still a little sleepy. Didn't sleep well last night. I kept reliving what happened with Glynn. How am I going to make things right with him?"

"That'll be easy—just apologize. Glynn's not one to hold a grudge. He probably hasn't given it another thought. You want his phone number?"

"Yeah, give it to me."

Cross searches through his phone and gives the number to Harlon, who writes it down on a piece of scratch paper.

"You and Buck need any help today?" Harlon asks.

"We're glad for you to help anytime you want to. We're about to finish up over at the Charles' place. You need to come see it anyway. I'm pleased with how it's turned out."

"I might do that."

Roxie rises from the floor, where she's been watching and listening to the proceedings. Walking over to Cross, she nudges his hand with her muzzle.

"You want to go with me today?" Cross asks her.

She wags her tail and smiles.

"I think that's a 'Yes,'" Harlon tells him.

"See you later, Pop."

"Yeah, see you later."

Cross opens the back door to let Roxie out first. "Get in the truck," he tells her.

She runs across the yard and leaps into the bed of the pickup truck.

After droving over to Buck's house to pick him up, Buck climbs in and says, "Morning."

"Morning."

"Man, am I ready for a big Huddle House breakfast! This diet Betty has me on makes me hungry all the time."

Cross laughs. "She's got you on a short leash, doesn't she? But what about no sex until you lose fifteen pounds?"

"Sex won't matter if I'm dead from starvation!"

"Okay, okay, I'm going to rush you to the Huddle House before you keel over. Should I turn on my flashers and drive like an ambulance driver?"

"If you're willing to, yes!"

Laughing, Cross pulls out of the driveway and heads to town.

After a few moments, Buck asks, "What in the world got into Harlon last night? I've never seen him act that way."

"Honestly, I never have either. He felt awful afterwards, so bad it kept him awake most of the night."

Is now the time for me to tell Buck the whole story? Does it really matter one way or the other if he knows?

He thinks about something he read in some of his Alcoholics Anonymous material that said amends should be made with those who've been harmed by our actions as long as it doesn't harm them.

Could telling Buck do more harm than good?

Buck interrupts his thoughts by saying, "I just don't understand why he got so mad. Do you?"

"There's some things from Pop's past that still upset him, some things I never knew until just recently."

"Like stuff that happened over in Viet Nam? I know that war left a lot of men scarred."

"Kind of. It was during that time, but it was more about what happened here while he was there and how he dealt with it when he came back."

In the restaurant parking lot, Cross pulls to a stop, turns off the truck, and sits in silence.

Buck says, "It seems like whatever he told you is bothering you, too. You want to talk about it? Or is it none of my business?"

His friend's last question clears up Cross's uncertainty. Turning to him, he says, "It's very much your business. Let's go in, and I'll tell you about it."

The time and setting for telling the truth can't always be scripted, so in the middle of the hustle and bustle of a busy restaurant, Cross unzips the story of his father, Buck's father, and Grace Charles and lets it tumble onto the table. Their order of food and coffee sits untouched as the story winds its way through their hearts.

Buck's face grows slack at the beginning, then turns red with anger until sadness takes over and tears fill his eyes at the end.

Cross waits, wondering if what he's just shared will result in any changes to his relationship with his best friend, or if it'll drive a wedge between his dad and Buck.

Buck says, "Why have I never heard about any of this?"

"I felt the same way," Cross answers. "But the more I thought about it, I thought about how hard it would be to tell. I guess Pop thought it would hurt people who didn't deserve to be hurt. And maybe he was afraid it would change how I thought of him, or how you'd think of him."

"So, the reason he was so good to me growing up was because he felt guilty? I was his scapegoat to make him feel better about how he treated my dad? That's messed up, Cross."

Cross notices the waitress heading toward them, carrying a coffee pot. He holds up his hand to stop her and shakes his head. She immediately pivots left and refills a tableful of customers' cups.

Turning his attention back to Buck, Cross says, "That may have been how things started between Pop and you, but I think it became something else. I think he loved you because of you. He enjoyed you and felt like he had two sons instead of one."

Sitting back in his chair, Buck pushes up the bill of his cap and says, "One thing's for sure, if he hadn't taken such an interest in me, you and I wouldn't have the lifelong friendship we have. That kind of makes it all worthwhile, doesn't it?"

"I think it does. I can't imagine where I'd be today without your friendship."

"Stop right there. If you say you love me, I'm getting up and walking out. Just leave it where it is—we're close friends."

Smiling, Cross says, "I love you, Buck."

Buck slaps him with his cap and leaves the table. "I'll be in the truck, waiting on you."

Cross laughs.

When he goes to the register to pay for their food, Teri asks, "What's up with you and Buck this morning? You didn't eat a bite of your food. It looked like a pretty intense conversation going on between you."

Yes, and you'd like nothing better than for me to tell you what it was about so you could spread your own version of it to everybody.

"We were just discussing what a good looking woman you are and why some man hasn't snatched you up."

Putting her hands on her hips, she gives him a flat stare. "If you're not going to tell me what you were talking about, just say so. You don't have to make up a stupid story."

Winking at her, he hands her his debit card.

Once he's in the truck, Buck says, "You know, the story you told me explains why Grace and Harlon have had such strong reactions in hearing each other's names."

"Yeah, it does, doesn't it? Are you going to talk to Pop about all that?"

"The longer I sit with the truth, the less upsetting it is. I mean, my dad did sleep with Pop's girlfriend and got her pregnant. I probably would have reacted the same way Harlon did. And he didn't have to step in and make up for what happened to my dad. Dad's drinking was Dad's choice; Harlon didn't make him drink."

Cross nods. "I don't know which of the three of them I feel the sorriest for. It's like this bomb blew up in the middle of them and threw them in completely different directions. It changed the trajectory of everyone's life. It's sad they couldn't have worked things out and at least remained friends. Good friends are hard to come by."

"Amen to all of that," Buck agrees.

At the Charles' property, they pile out of the truck and head toward the wheelbarrows and shovels sitting beside a trailer loaded with mulch.

Rubbing his stomach, Buck says, "I'm going to regret not eating breakfast."

"Me, too. Maybe Megan will bring us some of those sausage and biscuits."

"Let's lay here on the ground like we're passed out so she'll come and see about us. Then we'll tell her our blood sugar dropped because we missed breakfast and ask her to please give us something to eat."

Pushing his shovel into the mulch, then dropping a shovelful into his wheelbarrow, Cross says, "If you want to make a fool of yourself, go ahead. But I'm going to try and finish this job."

"All right," Buck growls and begins filling his wheelbarrow.

An hour later, they pause as Megan approaches.

"Good morning," she says, with a smile. Looking around the yard, she says, "I can't tell you how beautiful you've made this place look. The transformation is just amazing."

"Thank you," Cross replies.

The unmistakable sound of Buck's stomach growling makes her and Cross look at him.

“Sorry,” Buck says as he puts his hand on his belly.

“You’re not hungry already, are you?” Megan asks. “Because I know you all always eat that big breakfast at the Huddle House.”

“Well,” Cross says, “we had our breakfast interrupted this morning and didn’t get to finish it.”

“Finish it?” Buck interjects. “We didn’t eat a bite of it.”

“You want me to make some sausage and biscuits for you?” Megan asks.

“That’s too much trouble. You don’t have to do that,” Cross tells her.

“But would you, please?” Buck begs. “I’m starving.”

“I’ll be glad to,” Megan replies. She pivots to return to the house, but her leg crumples, and she falls to the ground.

Cross is at her side in a second. He places his hands on her shoulders and looks at her. For a second he sees the face of his wife, but he shakes his head to chase away the memory. “Don’t try to get up yet. Are you okay? Are you hurting anywhere?”

“I’m okay. I just tried to turn around too quickly. I’ve got to remember to make that kind of move slowly.”

He looks at her legs and notices for the first time she’s dressed in Levi jeans and cowboy boots. “You ever worn cowboy boots before?”

Her face turns red. “No, but I decided I need to try and fit in around here. Maybe I need to stick to tennis shoes for a while longer. Will you help me up?”

Cross takes her hands and pulls, while Buck puts his hands under her arms and lifts.

She continues to hold Cross’s hands while taking a few cautious steps.

He’s surprised at the strength of her grip. “You’re really strong,” he comments.

“It’s all that physical therapy,” Megan explains and lets go of him. “Thank you.”

"Sure thing. You didn't twist your ankle or anything, did you?"

"No, I'll be fine."

They stare at each other for a moment, then she says, "You'll have to settle for canned biscuits with your sausage this morning, because Mother left out early this morning, going somewhere important. At least it seemed important because she put on makeup and perfume."

"Canned biscuits'll be great," Buck says, with a smile. "I can't wait." They watch her head toward the house, then he says, "What was that look about?"

"What look?"

"That look you and her shared a second or two ago. It was like you both got lost for a moment. Did something happen right then, like a feeling or something? I mean, if there was, I can overlook that she doesn't like bluegrass."

"Just shut up, and let's get some more of this mulch put down on the side of the house."

But inside, Cross ponders, *I did feel something, but what? Was it because I had that fleeting memory of Heather? What was she thinking when she was staring at me?*

About that time, the sound of a vehicle approaching draws their attention.

"Looks like Pop's going to help us out," Cross says.

They both watch as he gets out of his truck, sporting tan Dickie pants, a white short-sleeved shirt, and a bolo tie.

The two friends share a look of astonishment before looking back at Harlon walking up the sidewalk to the front door.

Harlon knocks and waits.

In a moment, Megan opens the door, and they exchange some words, but Cross and Buck are too far away to distinguish them.

Then Harlon turns on his heel and stomps back to the truck as he jerks off his bolo tie and throws it in the cab.

Buck sniffs the air. "Do you smell that?"

Cross sniffs. “Yeah, that’s Pop’s Brut cologne. I haven’t smelled that since before Mama died.”

Scratching his head, Buck asks, “What in the world just happened? Why did he come out here? Because it for sure wasn’t to help us work.”

The front door opens again, and Megan rejoins them and has a look of consternation on her face. Looking at Cross, she says, “Your dad…” She glances at him driving away. “Your dad was asking to speak to my mom, but when I told him she wasn’t here, he acted all mad and stomped off. I hope I didn’t do anything to upset him.”

A look of understanding passes between Cross and Buck.

“It’s okay,” Cross tells her. “You didn’t do anything wrong. Pop’s just trying to find his way.”

CHAPTER TWENTY-THREE

EARLIER THAT MORNING

Sitting up on the edge of her bed, Grace lets out a heavy sigh, the kind of sigh that carries with it the weight of years of unresolved feelings. She looks at the alarm clock by her bed. Neon red lights tell her it's not yet four in the morning.

The covers on her bed are a tangled mess—a perfect metaphor for the thoughts that have kept her awake most of the night.

Putting on her glasses, she pads over to her closet and turns on the light, then gets down on her knees and rummages through shoeboxes. She sticks one particular box under her arm and uses the door knob to help herself stand up. Clicking off the light, she returns to her bed, climbs onto it, and leans back against the headboard.

From under her pillow, she pulls out a penlight and switches it on. A soft, yellow glow encircles her as she lifts the lid off the box sitting between her legs. Inside it is a small stack of odd-sized and soiled envelopes held together by a yellow ribbon. Carefully, like an archaeologist opening a sarcophagus, she unties the ribbon and takes the envelopes out one at a time, pausing and reading her name on each one, handwritten by the same person. All of them have a postmark with APO, noting the military postal service.

Finally, she has twenty envelopes lined up in chronological order, staring at her.

Fishing around under her covers, she finds her phone, opens a playlist titled HARLON, and pushes "play."

Immediately, the smooth voice of James Taylor comes on, singing "You've Got A Friend."

Nothing can transport you to a time and place more quickly than a song.

Memories come rushing at Grace with such force, she struggles to get a breath. Placing her hand on her chest, she feels her heart pulsing against it. She smiles at the memory of Harlon winning the bear for her at the county fair.

With each song on her playlist, a memory attached to it sends her spiraling backwards into a place of innocence and passion, joy and bliss, until she thinks about the heartbreaking event when Harlon left to go to war. Not until a tear drips onto her hand does she realize she's been crying. She squeezes her eyes shut, hoping she can stop this journey down the past, because she knows what's coming.

The blessing and curse of memory is that you don't get to choose what you remember, and you don't get to choose what you forget.

As the images of her and Tom flicker through her memory, all her pleasant feelings evaporate in the face of the heat from her regret and self-loathing.

Squeezing her hands into fists, she says out loud, "Why was I so stupid?! I ruined everything—my life, Tom's life, Harlon's life. If I could have seen how much damage one stupid decision would cause…"

She doesn't finish the sentence. "What's the point?" she sighs. "Nothing can change the past."

She thinks about her conversation with Megan.

Should I try to talk to Harlon? Would he even see me, or would he send me on my way? What can I say? How can I undo the hurt? And maybe I just need to let him get mad and cuss me out, say all the things he's wanted to say for fifty years. Maybe that can be my gift to him, to let him get it all out.

Looking up, she says, "Lord, what should I do?"

As clear as if He was standing beside her bed, she hears, "You should go to him."

Grace jumps and drops her penlight. Grabbing it up, she shines it in the area beside her, but it only travels three feet before being swallowed by the darkness.

"Was that really You?" she asks.

Silence is the only reply she receives.

Well, I know what I heard, and if what I heard was Who I think it was, I'm definitely not going to ignore the message.

She reassembles the envelopes in the box just as they were and returns the box to the closet. Then she heads to the bathroom, turns on the shower, and gets out her curling iron.

If I'm going to climb this mountain, I'm at least going to look good doing it.

After showering and changing clothes a dozen times, she fixes her hair and puts on her makeup. Staring into the mirror, she says, "I just need to remember he's not going to look like he did fifty years ago, so neither can I."

The smell of bacon cooking draws her to the kitchen, where Megan is cooking. Her daughter's hair looks like it hasn't seen a brush or comb in ages, even though it's only been since yesterday. She's wearing an oversized Tennessee Titans T-shirt and shorts.

"Good morning," Grace says.

Megan keeps her back to her and says sleepily, "Morning." Then she stops and turns around. Sniffing, she says, "Do you have on perfume? And what are you doing all dressed up in the middle of the week, much less this early in the morning?"

"Uh…we've got a Fish Fry meeting this morning," Grace lies.

"You didn't say anything about it last night."

"I forgot. I got a reminder on my phone this morning."

Putting one hand on her hip while turning the bacon with her other, Megan says, "So, you pay attention to reminders, but it takes you two days to reply to a text message from me?"

"It does not! I always reply."

Megan laughs. "Yes, you do. But by the time you reply, whatever I was wanting from you doesn't matter."

Grace's agitation rises.

Arguing with Megan is not what I wanted to be doing before heading over to Harlon's.

"Well, I'm sorry I can't be perfect like you."

"Oh, calm down. Have a seat, and let's eat breakfast. Let me start this conversation over: You look really nice this morning."

Grace smiles and relaxes. “Thank you. I’ll fix us a cup of coffee.”

“That’ll be great.”

Grace goes to the Keurig, brews two cups, and carries them to the table. Sitting down, she picks up her cup to take a sip and notices her hand trembling.

Will you calm down, old woman? You’re silly for being so nervous.

She sips her coffee, but it feels like it gets stuck in her throat. The same thing happens when she chews and swallows a bite of bacon.

As Megan sits down, Grace stands up. “I’m not really hungry this morning. I better run. I’ll catch up with you later.”

Megan stares at her. “Are you feeling okay? Have you had all your medicine this morning?”

Walking away, Grace says, “I’m fine, I’m fine. See you later.”

On the drive over to Harlon’s, she tries rehearsing what she’ll say, but all that does is produce a dozen different ways of saying what she wants to say.

Which one’s the right one to use?

As she pulls to a stop at his house, her palms are sweaty, and she’s having difficulty breathing.

Lord have mercy, I’m going to have a stroke!

With fear begging her to go back home, she gets out of the car and walks to the front door.

She knocks and waits.

Please don’t be home. Please don’t be home.

After a moment, she knocks again and listens for sounds of footsteps inside but can hear nothing.

Don’t tell me I got all fixed up and came over here and he’s not going to be home!

One more time, she knocks and waits. This time, when nothing happens, she heads back to her car.

If I needed a sign that coming over here was a bad idea, I’d say this is a clear sign. I was stupid to think about doing it anyway.

CHAPTER TWENTY-FOUR

THAT SAME DAY

Grace turns her car around and starts down Harlon's driveway when suddenly she's met by someone driving a pickup truck. She pulls halfway off the lane and stops to let them pass, but the driver stops when he gets beside her and rolls down his window. She reciprocates by rolling down hers.

With a scowl on his face, the man asks, "You looking for somebody?"

"Yes, but no one's at home."

She lets her foot off the brake and eases forward until something clicks in her memory. The man's voice has a familiar ring to it, and something about the tilt of his head reminds her of…

Looking in her rearview mirror, she sees the truck still sitting there. She jerks to a stop.

Could it be?

Still gazing at her mirror, the man gets out of his truck and stands there, looking in her direction.

Something like the feeling of a dream comes over her, and she turns off her car and gets out.

The two of them stand there, thirty feet and fifty years apart, gazing at each other. Without a word, they slowly walk toward each other.

Grace's heart races as she peels away the creases from the man's face, as if she was removing the makeup from a clown's face. Her knees feel weak as Harlon Daniels appears.

Six feet apart from each other, they stop.

"Harlon?"

"Grace?"

Familiarity knocks on the door of her heart and begs her to open it, but uncertainty makes her hold onto the door knob.

He stuffs his hands in his pockets exactly the way she remembers, and she smiles.

"I just came from your house," he says.

Surprised, she says, "Really? You don't look dressed to help your son. Why were you there?"

"Why are you here?" he retorts.

A soft breeze carries the scent of his cologne to her, and she's whisked away to the back seat of his Chevy Malibu, and the passion and heat of being in his arms.

An overwhelming urge to rush to him engulfs her.

But is he still angry and resentful about the past? Is that why he went to my house, to unload all the hurt I caused him?

She tries to read his face to learn his intent but finds it impossible.

"Can we talk?" she asks.

"Uh…sure, we can do that." He nods in the direction of his house and asks, "Why don't we go to the house, where we can sit down?"

His offer gives her hope and tamps down her fear a bit. "I'd like that," she replies.

"You want me to turn your car around for you?"

"No, I can manage."

They negotiate Harlon's driveway and pull to a stop beside each other in front of his house.

She's unbuckling her seatbelt when her door opens and Harlon offers her his hand. "Can I help you out?"

Taking his hand, she says, "You always were the chivalrous one."

"Back then, it was drilled into us boys at the orphanage. I don't see men doing it anymore; I guess it's gone out of style."

"Sadly, it's true."

Once they're inside the house, Harlon offers her a seat on the couch, and he sits in a leather recliner sitting at a ninety-degree angle to it.

Suddenly, he stands back up. "You want something to drink?"

“Not right now, thank you.”

She looks around the room, taking in the masculine ambiance created by Terry Redlin paintings of outdoor hunting scenes hanging on the walls accompanied by a massive, mounted deer head and a Canadian goose posed in full flight. “You always enjoyed hunting, didn’t you?”

“Yeah, there haven’t been many animals in these parts I haven’t hunted.”

Her eyes return to gaze at his face. They’re quiet for a moment, then she sighs, “It’s been a long time.”

Returning her gaze, he replies, “Yes, it has. When I think about how long it’s been, it seems like forever, but when I look at your face, it seems like only yesterday.”

“Through the years, I’ve had dreams about this moment,” Grace tells him. “Sometimes they were very sweet dreams, and other times they were nightmares. I’ve thought about what I’d say to you if you gave me the chance.” Her chest grows tighter, and a lump in her throat threatens to prevent her from speaking. She swallows hard and says, “Have you ever done something you’ve hated yourself for for nearly all your life?”

Harlon looks down and folds his hands in his lap. “Yes…yes, I have.”

His answer surprises her, and she wonders what he’s thinking about. Taking a deep breath, she says, “Regret is a very poor bed partner because it never sleeps. It tortures your mind with unending accusations and blocks every avenue of escape from it.”

He raises his head and looks at her with sad eyes. In a voice choked with emotion, he says, “That is so, so true.”

For a second, she thinks about questioning him about his regret and his story, because that would be easier than laying bare her heart to him and exposing all the hurt that lies there.

No, I’ve got to do this, because I may never have another chance.

Leaning forward, she says, "Harlon, I have wished a thousand times—no, ten thousand times that what happened between me and Tom hadn't happened. I'm not going to make any excuses, because there aren't any. I can tell you I'm sorry for how I wronged you, but that won't take away the pain I caused you. What I do want to do is try to explain what was going on with me back then.

"I have no idea what it was like for you in Viet Nam, but you have no idea what it was like for me, not knowing day-to-day if word was going to come you'd been killed. Days and weeks would go by without hearing any news of any kind. That may have been the worst, because then my imagination would take over, and I would assume the worst.

"And you know what? It was the same for Tom. You don't know how much you meant to him, how much he looked up to you. It was like he was lost without you. I felt sorry for him; he felt sorry for me. And we'd spend time together either crying or trying to cheer each other up."

A sudden movement by Harlon stops her. Reaching in his hip pocket, he pulls out a red bandana and wipes his eyes with it, then blows his nose. She waits to see if he wants to say something, but instead he motions with his hand for her to continue.

Turning her eyes away from him, she says, "The sex thing? I don't know what to say about it. I'll tell you it only happened one time—one time, I promise. We'd had a few beers and were down at the lake, and it just happened. Immediately afterward, we both regretted it and promised it would never happen again. And like I said, it didn't. What we never dreamed would happen is me getting pregnant."

She looks back at him. "You remember how things were back then. If a girl got pregnant, she may just as well be branded with a scarlet letter. My parents made me go to a home for unwed mothers, and I cut myself off from everyone and everything back here in Paris. My shame would never let me return. There was no way I could face you. What do people say nowadays, 'I didn't have the balls to face you?' And then, the baby was stillborn."

The memory is too much for her, and she breaks down crying.

CHAPTER TWENTY-FIVE

As Harlon listens to Grace, all the signs of age evaporate from her, and all he can see is how she used to look and act. The ice castle he built around his heart, related to his feelings about her, melts due to the pathos of her story.

He's flooded by alternating memories of good times with her and good times with Tom. But his heart breaks in two when she talks about how Tom felt about him. Everything in him wants her to stop and leave, but he reins himself in, knowing this is what he needs to hear, all of it, if he's ever going to let go of the horror of that fateful time in his life.

Pulling out his bandana, he wipes his tears and blows his nose. Emotions have made him mute, so he motions for her to continue.

At the end, when she tells him what happened to her baby and begins to cry, it's more than he can stand. He moves beside her, puts his arm around her, and pulls her to him.

She buries her face into his chest, and they weep together.

Sometimes, tears are the only words sorrow can find to express itself.

Eventually, they both take a deep breath and pull back.

Brushing the front of his shirt, Grace says, "Oh my goodness, I made a mess on your shirt. I'm so sorry."

Looking down, Harlon sees the dampness caused by her tears mixed with smudges of her makeup. "I think it's beautiful."

She smiles. "You're sweet. You always were."

"You've made me realize something."

"What's that?"

"I've wasted decades by holding on to resentment and regret. What a fool I've been." He wags his head. "I'm sorry for all the bad thoughts I've had about you. I should have known better than to believe you were trying to hurt me. And look what I did to Tom. I ruined his life, turned my back on him, and he was my best friend! It's shameful. I'll never be able to fix it."

Grace lays her hand on his forearm. "Can we agree that between the two of us, we've carried enough regret for a hundred people?"

Harlon nods. "For sure."

"There's only one thing I want…need from you."

"What's that?"

"Will you forgive me for what I did?"

He looks at her and smiles. "You know what? That's going to be the easiest thing I've ever done. Which is crazy, because for a long time I didn't think it was possible. I absolutely forgive you."

Squeezing his arm, she says, "Thank you." She clears her throat. "I believe I'll have something to drink now."

"Good idea. I've got tea, coffee, lemonade, water. What do you want?"

"A nice glass of iced tea sounds good."

"You used to like half-tea and half-lemonade. Do you still?"

She laughs. "You still remember that?"

"I remember everything about you."

"Well, I'd love some."

In the kitchen, Harlon touches his arm where Grace squeezed it.

How could something like that make me feel like I'm eighteen years old again?

Carrying the drinks into the living room, he hands one to Grace, then sits down in his recliner.

She takes a sip and sits back. "Ooo, that's good. I haven't had this since way back then. I stayed in Indiana after the baby died, and people up there made fun of me for always drinking iced tea. When I put lemonade in it, they thought I was crazy."

"Well, that's Yankees for you," Harlon comments. Crossing his legs and taking a gulp of his drink, he says, "So, tell me about your life since we last met."

"Honestly, there's not a lot to tell. When I had to leave the home for unwed mothers, I got a job, met a man where I worked, and married him. He was a decent man, and he found ways to make me happy and help me forget the past. He died a few years ago from lung cancer."

"So, he helped you forget the past?"

"I guess the more truthful way to say it is, he helped me pretend like I forgot about it. He never asked about my past, and I never told him that chapter of it. But clearly," she waves her hand, "I never forgot it. I never forgot you."

Tugging at his shirt collar, Harlon says, "I don't know whether it should or not, but that makes me happy, because I sure never forgot about you and about us. Did you ever hear that Joe Tex song, 'I Think I'm Gonna Make It'? It was about a soldier trying to survive the Viet Nam war and wanting to go home."

Grace's eyes light up. "Yes, I do! I used to imagine you singing it." Sadness takes over her eyes, and she looks at the floor. "But after what happened with Tom, it broke my heart to hear it."

"I'm not trying to make you feel bad. I just bring it up because it was the only thing that kept me believing I would survive that crazy war. When I got home and learned what had happened, I went a little crazy for a year, drinking heavily, probably was an alcoholic. But I met someone from McKenzie, and she helped me climb out of the bottle. I loved her, and we had a good marriage. She died of a heart attack. The best thing we did was produce Cross, who you've met."

Grace gives a small laugh. "Can you believe of all the people I might have asked to do my landscaping, I selected someone who turned out to be your son? What are the chances?"

“Yeah, I’ve thought about that. And here we are, sitting together, talking about old times.”

They’re quiet for a moment, then Grace says, “Cross seems like a good boy.”

“Oh, he is. He’s one of the best. I couldn’t be prouder of him. There’s only one thing I wish he’d do, and that’s get over losing his wife and daughter in an accident. It’s been several years now, but he refuses to even consider finding another woman and remarrying. He says he doesn’t deserve a second chance. ‘When you ruin a perfect chance, you don’t deserve another,’ is what he always tells me.”

Shaking her head, Grace says, “That is unbelievable. The best thing to come out of my marriage is my daughter, Megan. She, too, lost her marriage, but through divorce. She blames herself for what happened, claiming she deserved to be divorced because she wasn’t a good wife. And now, just like your son, she refuses to give herself another chance. I’ve tried everything to convince her otherwise, but she’s very stubborn.”

Harlon uncrosses his legs, letting his foot land with a thud. “I can’t believe how parallel our worlds have been. After all these years, my son and your daughter find themselves in similar places in their lives.” A thought strikes him. “Hey, do you think we could nudge them in each other’s direction?”

Grace considers the idea. “We’d have to be really careful, because if Megan got any hint of what we’re trying, she would throw up those iron walls of hers, and nobody would be able to penetrate them.”

“Same thing with Cross,” he replies. “We’d have to tiptoe around it.”

“Let me ask you this: does Cross know our story?”

Nodding, Harlon replies, “Yeah, I’ve told him. It’s really because of him I decided to come to you and try and make things right between us.”

She laughs. “Now that’s funny, because the only reason I came here was because Megan convinced me I needed to.”

Harlon laughs with her. “They think they’re pretty smart, don’t they?”

"What about this? Why don't I invite you and Cross to our house for supper? The excuse could be because we want them to see we've buried the hatchet between us, and we want to thank them together."

"I like that!"

"What about the day after tomorrow? Could you all do that?"

"Absolutely. What time?"

"Let's say six o'clock."

"We'll be there."

CHAPTER TWENTY-SIX

TWO DAYS LATER

Carrying a large bowl of mashed potatoes out of the kitchen and toward the dining table, Megan says to her mother, "I don't know why you're making such a big deal out of this. I mean, don't get me wrong, I think it's great you and Harlon made peace with each other, but why invite him *and* Cross over for a meal?"

And why did I feel like I needed to dress up and put on makeup?

Grace stands at the table, with the silverware in her hands. "I can't remember what goes on which side of the plate. Why can't I remember that? I've known it since I was a girl."

"Don't worry about it. As long as we've got Google, we don't have to remember anything anymore, right?"

"Of course! I can Google it." She sets the silverware down and scoots into the kitchen. From in there, she calls, "Megan, where's my phone? Have you seen my phone? I just had it a minute ago."

Megan rolls her eyes and sighs. Walking into the kitchen, she asks, "Where did you use it last?"

"Well, if I knew the answer to that, I'd know where it is, wouldn't I? That's not helpful. I think I'm getting dementia. I bet there's a test for dementia online. I'm going to look that up tonight." She picks up a potholder off the counter and exclaims, "Here it is! I found it."

Suddenly, the doorbell rings.

Grace jumps and drops her phone.

Megan tells her, "I'll pick up your phone for you. You go answer the door."

Picking up her mother's phone, she opens it, touches the camera app, and flips it so she can see herself and check her hair. A stray strand of hair needs tucking behind her ear. Satisfied, she turns off the phone, sets it on the stove, and heads to the living room, where she hears Cross's voice.

“Thanks for having us over,” Cross is saying as she walks into the room.

She isn’t prepared for how different he looks not wearing his usual work clothes. His bald head gleams, and he’s wearing a long-sleeved cotton shirt that’s the same blue color as his eyes. Khaki pants that are tight, but not too tight, and leather sandals round out his outfit.

He’s a good looking man.

Turning his attention to her, he smiles. “Hi, Megan. I’d like you to meet my Pop.”

Harlon is wearing what appears to be a brand-new pair of pressed overalls and long-sleeved white dress shirt. His slicked back gray hair is long enough to cover his ears.

I’ve never seen someone look dressed up while wearing overalls, but he really pulls it off. And it’s clear to see where Cross gets those blue eyes of his.

Harlon takes a step toward her and sticks out his hand. “It’s very nice to meet you.”

She takes his hand and is surprised at how warm and gentle yet firm it is. “I’m glad to meet you, too. Mother and I couldn’t be more pleased with the work Cross and Buck have done with the yard. Did you notice it?”

Hooking his thumbs in the straps of his overalls, Harlon puffs out his chest and says, “Yeah, I taught them boys everything they know about landscaping.”

Cross gives an exaggerated cough and says, “Excuse me, but I think I got choked on something.”

Harlon looks surprised. “Choked on what?”

“Maybe it was that big ol’ lie you just told.”

Megan picks up on the joke and moves to Harlon’s side. Hooking her arm in his and looking at Cross, she says, “Well, I think you should be more respectful of your elders, even if they do exaggerate the truth sometimes.”

Cross laughs. "Sometimes?! Oh my, Megan, you've got a lot to learn about my Pop. He's well-known around here for spinning yarns. The one sure way to tell if he's telling a lie is if he opens his mouth."

Harlon gives a hearty laugh, and Megan and Grace join in.

"I just like to entertain people," Harlon explains. "What's the harm in that?"

"Yeah, what's the harm in that?" Megan agrees.

Holding up his hands, Cross says, "Clearly, I'm outnumbered here. I give up." He turns his attention to Grace. "Thank you for the invitation to come. Whatever you've been cooking smells delicious."

Her eyes brighten. "Thank you. It's just plain country cooking: fried pork chops, mashed potatoes, green beans, black-eyed peas, and cornbread. Nothing special."

He closes his eyes. "Mmm, mmm, mmm! That sounds wonderful."

"We were just setting it on the table," she says, "so why don't we go on into the dining room, and we'll get started. Megan, you lead the way."

Megan pulls Harlon by his hand and leaves Cross to follow, while Grace heads toward the kitchen.

"I feel like the lamb being led to the slaughter," Harlon jokes.

Megan suddenly realizes she and her mother didn't discuss seating arrangements for their circular table. "Uh...why don't you and Cross sit beside each other?"

They're about to take their seats when Grace walks in, carrying glasses of iced tea on a tray.

"Oh, no, no," she says, setting the platter on the table. "Let's sit boy-girl-boy-girl."

"You go ahead, Pop," Cross says, motioning for him to sit down. "I'll scoot over a seat."

Megan moves to the chair he was about to sit in, and he slides it out for her. "Thank you," she says as he slips it under her.

"Isn't that nice," Grace says. "Look what a gentleman he is."

Harlon looks a little startled and starts getting up. "Uh, here, Grace, let me help you."

She stops him by putting her hand on his shoulder. "If you get up and down every time I do, you'll become exhausted. I'll be up and down taking care of things. But thank you for being willing. Here, let's pass the tea around."

They take turns passing the glasses to one another.

Grace sits down, then exclaims, "The cornbread! I forgot the cornbread."

"You stay, Mother," Megan tells her. "I'll get it."

"You need any help?" Cross asks.

His question startles her, and she mumbles, "No, thanks."

Why the heck do I need help bringing in a plate of cornbread? Because he thinks I can't manage it because of my leg?

She remembers her embarrassing fall the other day.

Of course that's it. He's seen Miss Klutz in action. If only he could see how agile I used to be.

Once she returns with the cornbread and takes her seat, Grace says, "Harlon, would you mind offering grace for our meal?"

Immediately, his cheeks turn pink, and he fumbles with his napkin. "Uh…well, uh…sure…sure I will."

Megan pays no attention to what he says, because she's trying to understand his reaction to the request. She takes a quick peek at Cross and sees his head bowed, but his eyes are open.

What's going on with these two? Is it possible they've escaped the religious leanings of everyone else in the Bible Belt?

Not until she began living on her own in Tennessee did Megan realize how much of her former life was devoid of God and religion because her mother and dad rarely, if ever, took her to church. She'd never seen so many churches as there are in Tennessee.

"Megan, will you pass the cornbread, please?"

Megan looks up and realizes the prayer is over and people are filling their plates. "Oh, sorry." She takes a piece of cornbread and passes it to Cross. For the briefest of moments, it looks like he's asking her a question with his eyes. But just as quickly, he turns his attention to her mother and passes the bread to her.

"I love me some cornbread," he says to her.

"This was cooked in my mother's cast iron skillet," Grace brags. "Nothing makes cornbread like well-seasoned cast iron."

"Very true," Harlon agrees. "You know, your mother never was too crazy about me. I was an orphan, so I might come from a bad seed." Looking at Megan, he grins and says, "She had to sneak out to see me."

"I never heard about that, Mother," Megan says. "I bet there's lots of things Harlon can tell me you've never told me."

"Did she ever tell you about the time she got caught toilet papering our English teacher's house?"

"That was *your* fault," Grace asserts. "You do know, don't you, you don't have to tell everything you know. There're a few stories I might tell Cross about some of your shenanigans. Like the time you and Tom got caught skinny dipping in the clay pits."

"Ho, ho!" Cross speaks up. "Tell me more." To Megan he says, "You and I are going to be well-rewarded because of these two being friends again."

Harlon slides his open palm across the table to Grace. "We are friends again, aren't we?"

Taking his hand, she replies, "Yes, once again."

CHAPTER TWENTY-SEVEN

THAT SAME NIGHT

Letting his spoon clatter into his empty bowl, Harlon says, "That was the best peach cobbler I believe I ever ate. What do you say, Cross?"

Cross pats his stomach. "I agree one hundred percent. That was the best *meal* I've had since…" he considers what he was about to say, thinks better of it, then says, "well, in a long time. Thank you for having us over, Grace."

"We're delighted you came," Grace tells him. "Aren't we, Megan?"

"Yes. It was a lot more entertaining than I expected it to be. I'll have to spend some more time with Harlon to catch up on what a character my mother was when she was growing up."

Everyone laughs.

Grace stands up. "Now, Harlon and I are going to do these dishes. Why don't you two kids go sit on the front porch and visit a while?"

Everyone looks surprised, especially Harlon.

"Uh…well…" he stammers.

Nudging his shoulder with her elbow, Grace says, "Oh come on, old man, get up and help me."

He gives Cross a questioning look, then shrugs his shoulders and scoots back his chair. To Grace, he says, "I'll wash, and you dry."

"Deal," she replies.

Cross and Megan offer to carry their dishes to the kitchen, but Grace shoos them away.

So, they amble into the living room.

Cross feels like he should say something but doesn't know what.

"What do you want to do?" Megan asks. "You don't have to go out on the porch with me. I'll turn on the TV if you want and let you find something you're interested in."

There's a coldness in her tone and body language that are abruptly different from what they were at the table. "Are you okay? Did I do something wrong?"

"No, it's not you. I just don't like Mother trying to coerce someone into doing something they might not want to do."

Cross frowns. "As in…?"

Waving toward the front door, she answers, "You going out on the front porch with me, like you don't have a choice. I just don't like that, that's all."

"Well, what if I don't mind going out on the porch with you? Is it okay if we do?"

"Uh, sure, that's fine, but only if you want to."

Nodding toward the door, he says, "You lead the way."

He notices the slight, lingering limp in her gate but is still impressed with how far she's come since he first noticed her at the Huddle House.

"I love how deep this porch is," he tells her. "Most porches are just there for looks, but they're not big enough to serve the purpose they used to. You know, so people can sit outside like it's an extra room. And of course, you guys have the porch swing, which is essential."

"And we have the Adirondack chairs as an option," Megan responds. "Where do you prefer to sit?"

The chairs might be harder for her to get in and out of.

"Why don't we use the swing?" He winks at her. "I promise not to make it go too high."

"Don't worry, I used to be an adrenaline junkie. The scarier and riskier, the better."

They settle into the swing, with just a few inches separating them.

Tree frogs and crickets are beginning to sing, and moths are flitting at the windows as the day draws to a close.

Cross eases the swing back and releases it, letting their weight carry it forward. "I know this isn't as exhilarating as rock climbing, but it'll have to do for now."

Keeping her attention on something in the distance, Megan says, "One of these days, I'm going to be back climbing. One day."

"It must be hard not being able to do something you loved so much."

"You have no idea."

He thinks about his teaching career, which he loved. "I might."

What am I going to do if she asks me what I mean? If I tell her I used to be a teacher, that'll just trigger more and more questions.

"Everybody has a history, don't they?" she asks.

"Very true. Just like our parents. I've never heard him talk about his time with your mom, not until just the other day."

She twists around and looks at him. "Same here. And I thought I knew everything about my mom. I just didn't realize there was this three-year hole in the timeline of her life she always bypassed. Did you notice how they were looking at each other tonight?"

"How could I miss it? It's almost like they were flirting with each other."

"Yes, absolutely. How did it make you feel?"

"Honestly? Kinda weird. My dad has developed a certain reputation since Mom died."

"What do you mean?"

"Since she died, it's almost like he's trying to have sex with as many women as he can before he dies. I find it disgusting and shameful, and embarrassing, too."

"Oh, my God! I bet Mother doesn't know."

"I don't see how she couldn't. I mean, small town equals small town gossips." He shrugs his shoulders. "She's bound to have heard something."

"You think that's why he tried to patch things up with her? So she'd have sex with him?"

"No. This is different, I'm certain of that. This was about healing old wounds and coming to grips with himself. And he was different in there than he usually is with other women. He listened when she was speaking. He didn't brag about himself. You know, his star didn't have to shine brighter than hers. I've never seen him act like that around any other woman except my mom."

Megan raises her eyebrows and sits back in the swing. "That's good to hear. I was afraid I was going to go inside and find them on the floor, doing God knows what." She shudders.

Cross laughs. "I think your mother's safe."

They fall quiet and settle into an easy rhythm with the swing.

After a little bit, Megan says, "I used to not be able to do that."

"Do what?"

"Just be quiet and let the quiet speak its own language. I always felt like I had to fill up the silence, usually with noise."

"'Quiet speak its own language.' I like that because it's true. I, too, have learned to be comfortable with silence. There are times I actually enjoy it."

"Can I ask you something?"

"Sure."

"I noticed your dad had a funny reaction when Mother asked him to lead a prayer at supper, and I noticed you didn't appear to be paying attention when he said it."

Tilting his head and giving her a sideways glance, he says, "Was someone peeking?"

"I might have been. I'm sorry."

"I was just teasing." He stops pushing the swing with his foot and lets it slowly come to a stop. "When I was growing up, Dad said a prayer at every meal. We went to church regularly, and I gave my life to Christ when I was twelve years old. It was a big part of our life. What about you?"

“It was never an important part of our life. My dad was probably agnostic, if I was going to guess. It’s not a topic that was ever discussed in our home. I went to church some with my girlfriends and found it interesting. What’s curious is, ever since my dad died and mother moved back here, she’s gone to church faithfully. I’m not sure what that’s about and haven’t asked her, but I’ve gone with her some and found it enjoyable. I just don’t understand a lot of what’s said. What happened with you and with your dad?”

Cross holds her question in his hands and thinks about it.

How do I explain without telling everything? Do I care if she knows? Should I care if she does? I’ve told it in AA meetings, so why am I hesitant to tell her?

“Wow, you’ve run inside a cave on that, haven’t you?” Megan asks. “Look, it’s none of my business. Forget it; it doesn’t matter.”

“I’m sorry. I didn’t realize I was quiet for so long. Look Megan, my life, my adult life, has been complicated, complicated because I made it that way. You don’t know me or what all I’ve done. I really don’t want to get into it tonight. As far as the God-thing goes, I grew up being told and believing God was loving and forgiving, that He’s a God of second chances.”

Leaning forward, he puts his elbows on his knees. “But I did something, something unforgivable, and because of that, I don’t feel like I deserve God. He’s too good for me. Pop and I argued back and forth about it for a while, until I told him I don’t want it brought back up again or I’d move out.” Sitting up straight, he says, “I’m sure that’s a lot more than you wanted to hear.”

“No, no, it’s not. I appreciate you being honest with me. It sounds like you’re in a complicated place in here.” She taps her chest.

Nodding, Cross says, “That’s a good way to explain it: complicated.”

“Your past is none of my business, but I’m still curious about it. Maybe someday you can tell it to me, and I’ll tell you about mine, which isn’t squeaky clean either.”

A movement in Cross’s periphery catches his attention, and he looks at the window beside the swing. Pointing, he says, “Look.”

Megan looks where he's pointing and cries out, "Oh, my God! Are you two spying on us?!"

From inside comes the sound of someone being startled, followed by the sound of something breaking.

Cross bursts into laughter. "I feel like I'm fifteen years old and my dad wants to be my chaperone."

Megan's scowl turns into laughter. "They're both pitiful. And really poor at being sneaky."

Standing up, Cross takes her hand and lifts her from the swing. "We better go inside and see what else is broken besides their pride."

CHAPTER TWENTY-EIGHT

THE NEXT WEEK

Friday morning, Megan awakens to the sound of silence in the house. At first, she wonders if her mother is sick and in bed, but then she remembers:

This is the start of Fish Fry week, and 'the big parade' is today. I don't understand what the big deal is and why everyone gets so excited.

Rolling onto her side, she pulls the bed pillow over her head with one hand, snuggles Lacy to her chest with the other, and falls back asleep.

Her ringtone of Imagine Dragons singing "Thunder" rouses her out of Dreamland. Grabbing for the phone on her bedside table, she knocks it onto the floor, and it goes skittering underneath the bed. She reaches under the bed as far as she can but feels nothing. Suddenly, though, she loses her balance on the edge of the bed, and she and Lacy fall onto the floor with a thud.

"Well, crap!" she says as the phone keeps ringing. "I'm sorry, Lacy. Are you okay?"

Lacy does a cat-stretch, then walks over to her food and water dishes and laps up some water.

Megan lies on her belly, looking for her phone. She spots it, stretches her arm, and grabs it. Without first looking to see who it is, she answers, "Hello?" in an agitated tone. But the caller has hung up.

She checks to see who the caller was, but all it says is "Unknown."

Another number I can add to my blocked list.

Opening the Hiya app, she's just about to block the number when the phone rings again. It's the same number calling.

Out of simple curiosity, she answers it. "Hello?"

"Oh, hey, you answered."

The male voice is familiar, but she doesn't immediately connect it with a name or face.

Clearly, they know me, so I'll play along for a second until I figure out who it is.

"Yeah, my phone was under the bed, so it took me a minute to find it."

The man laughs.

Cross!

"What's so funny?" she asks him as she rolls onto her back.

"You might think about keeping your phone somewhere else other than under your bed."

"You're really funny," she says sarcastically. "You should perform at a comedy club."

He seems to ignore her dig as he says, "What kind of plans do you have today?"

"To do as little as possible. Why do you ask?"

"Ever been to the Fish Fry parade?"

"I'll have to say I've never had the pleasure, or even wanted the pleasure, really."

"Oh."

The phone goes silent, and for a moment she thinks he's hung up on her or the call has dropped. "Are you still there?"

"Yeah. Uh…Pop had this idea that you might like to go to the parade, but that's all right. I'll talk to you later."

This time, the line does go dead.

Megan stares at her phone.

Was he going to ask me to go to the parade? Why would he do that? Because his father told him to? Did my mother tell Harlon to tell Cross to ask me? As she sits up, another voice in her head says, *You know, Megan, he just might be being nice. Quit spinning things in a negative light all the time.*

So, should I call him back and agree to go after I've told him I'm not interested? How will I explain my change of mind?

Without a plan in place, she taps redial on her phone and waits.

Before the first ring finishes, Cross answers. "Hello?"

"Hey, it's Megan. Were you going to ask me to go to the parade?"

"Yeah, but you're not interested."

"Tell me, did my mother have anything to do with you asking me?"

"Your mother? No. Why do you ask?"

Getting up off the floor and sitting on the edge of the bed, Megan answers, "My mother is obsessed with hooking me up with a man. I've told her how much it irritates me, but she doesn't seem to care. And I don't want to be someone's sympathy date. You know, the cripple girl with the cane and all that."

As she's speaking, Lacy trots back to her, sits down, and gives her an expectant look. Megan strokes her head and mouths the words, "In a minute."

"Whoa, slow down there," Cross cuts in. "And I thought I had an active imagination. Listen, this is nothing more than me asking if you want to go watch the parade. There's no big, elaborate scheme going on. If you want to go, that'd be great; if you don't want to go, that'll be fine, too."

Megan closes her eyes and lets out her breath. "I sound like a crazy woman, don't I? Can we pretend the last couple of minutes never happened and I've just now answered the phone for the first time?"

Chuckling, Cross says, "Hi, Megan, this is Cross. Would you like to go to the Fish Fry parade?"

She replies, "I'm so glad you asked. I'd love to go."

"Great. We need to get there early so we can find a place to park and get a good place to watch from. Can you be ready in an hour?"

"Uh…sure. I'll be ready."

"We'll probably be in the sun, so dress cool."

"Thanks for the tip."

The call ends, and Lacy barks at the same time.

"You have to pee? Well, I've got to jump in the shower."

After letting Lacy outside, she heads to the bathroom. She looks at herself in the mirror and pulls a brush through her long hair.

No time to wash and dry this mess. I'll wear it up today.

Once she's finished showering, she walks to the living room with a towel around her and lets Lacy back in and picks her up. "Oh my goodness, your beard and skirt are wet. There must have been a heavy dew this morning."

Lacy's pink tongue flashes, and she kisses Megan on the cheek.

"No time for cuddles," Megan says, setting her on the floor. "I've got to get dressed."

In her bedroom, she opens the closet and stares.

Dress cool, he says. So maybe a T-shirt?

She flips through the hangers as if they were files in a file cabinet and finally settles on a pink one with flowers and butterflies on the back. Pulling it on, she steps over to a full-length mirror and tugs at the shirt.

This fits tighter than it used to.

Turning sideways, she sees the small "muffin top" her stomach has become since her injury. She sucks it in and tightens her muscles.

I've got to get in shape and lose some weight.

Stepping over to her chest-of-drawers, she pulls out a pair of jeans and holds them up.

I'll never squeeze into these.

Tossing them on the floor, she rifles through other options until she settles on the same pair she wore the day she stumbled and Cross had to help her up.

Will he notice they're the same pair? Probably not. We girls are the only ones who obsess about that kind of thing. It's a pain in the ass being a female.

Suddenly, she hears a knock on her door. Lacy explodes into fits of barking and races to it.

Who in the world?!

Squeezing herself into her jeans, she goes into the living room. Through the bay window, she sees Cross's truck.

He said he'd be here in an hour, not thirty minutes! I don't have any makeup on!

With agitation rising, she walks to the door. Without opening it, she yells, "You said you'd be here in an hour. I'm not ready yet."

"I know," Cross yells back. "But I had an idea we could run by the Huddle House and eat breakfast before going to the parade."

"Why didn't you call and tell me?"

"I didn't think it'd matter." He remains silent for a moment, then adds, "Or maybe, I didn't think, would be the more accurate thing to say. I'm sorry. You take your time and finish getting ready. I'll just sit and wait out here on the porch."

Megan says to herself, *Oh, what do I care if he sees me without makeup?*

Opening the door, she waves at her face and says, "Okay, so this is me without my face on. That's why you're going to have to wait. And Huddle House sounds good."

An easy smile spreads across his face, and his eyes twinkle. "I don't see anything wrong with the face I'm looking at."

Despite herself, she blushes. "Well, thank you for being nice, but I'm not sure the rest of the world would agree. You can come inside and wait if you want to."

Winking at her, he says, "That's okay; I'll sit out here and admire your yard." Bending down, he scoops Lacy into his arms. "Lacy and I will spend time getting better acquainted." She licks him on the chin.

Megan relaxes a bit. Smiling at him, she says, "I'll hurry up," then heads back to the bathroom, where she puts on her makeup.

Once she's finished, she slips on a pair of sandals and heads outside, where she finds Cross sitting on the porch swing, with Lacy asleep on his lap.

Smiling, she says, "Lacy is such a lap dog."

At the sound of her voice, Lacy stands and stretches.

Pointing to her own face, Megan says, "Don't you think this is better?"

"Yeah, I see what you're saying, but you've got the kind of face that doesn't need much makeup. Not every woman has that kind of face. Some really need to put a heavy coat of paint on the barn door."

Megan laughs out loud. "I've never heard that expression. So, our faces are barn doors?"

Shrugging, Cross answers, "Well, you get the point."

Lacy bounds off the swing and trots to Megan's side.

"Come on, girl," Megan tells her, "you've got to go inside. I'll be back later." She lets her in, then faces Cross. "I think we're ready."

He hesitates for a second, then says, "Do you need your cane? We might have to walk a ways from where we park to where the parade will pass."

"You don't mind being seen with someone with a cane?"

He frowns at her. "No, why should I?"

"I guess it's really more about me and how I feel having to use a cane and wondering what people are thinking. The last thing I want is for people to feel sorry for me."

"Let them think what they want. You've got no control over that. People probably think about us a lot less often than we think they do."

"That's what my mother tells me. She says, 'When I was in my twenties, I worried what people thought about me. When I was in my forties, I didn't care what people thought about me. And when I reached my sixties, I found out people weren't thinking about me anyway.'" Turning to go inside, she says, "Give me a second."

Walking to her bedroom, she notices her nervousness has evaporated.

He's got a way of making a person feel relaxed. And how thoughtful to think of me needing my cane.

Back outside, she says, "Now we're definitely ready to go."

As they walk down the flagstone sidewalk towards his truck, she notices for the first time how tall his truck is.

This'll be interesting.

Apparently, it dawns on Cross at the same time. "I should have driven the car instead of the truck."

Megan gives a wave of her hand. "Oh, don't worry. We can do this. You'll just have to help."

"How tall are you, exactly?"

"Five feet, two and one-quarter inches. And the one-quarter matters."

Cross laughs. "I'll try to remember that." Opening her door, he says, "Now, you're going to have to tell me how best to help you."

She considers her options. "Well, if you lift me up to where I can grab that handle on the inside there and then put your hand on my butt and give me a push, I think I can swing onto the seat."

In moves so effortless and swift, Megan finds herself sitting comfortably on the seat before she knows it.

My goodness! His hand is as big as my butt cheek.

For a second, she lets herself think about how nice it felt to have a man's hands on her but quickly brushes aside those thoughts.

Single I am, and single I'll be.

A new thought pushes its way forward.

But does that mean I can't enjoy having sex with a man?

Knowing how aghast her mother would be at such a thought, she laughs out loud.

"What's so funny?" Cross asks.

"Oh, nothing. I'm just having random thoughts over here." Fastening her seatbelt, she says, "Let's go. I'm starving."

CHAPTER TWENTY-NINE

As Cross pulls into the parking lot of the Huddle House, he says, "You know this is going to start the gossip mill, don't you?"

"What do you mean?"

"If Terri's working, as soon as she sees us, her wheels are going to start spinning, making up all sorts of stories about us, then she'll start texting everyone she knows about it. And before the end of the day, you and I will be married with two children."

"Wow, you're serious, aren't you?"

"Absolutely. That's the only thing some people live for, to tell people what they think they know."

"Well then, why don't we give her something to really talk about?"

He gives her a confused look.

Unbuckling her seatbelt, she says, "Come help me out, and I'll show you."

Cross comes around to her side of the truck, scoops her out of her seat, and stands her up. While he's leaned toward her, she throws her arms around his neck, kisses him on the mouth, then lets go.

He stumbles backwards, his eyes wide and mouth open.

Reaching for his hand, Megan tells him, "Don't act so surprised, or you'll ruin everything." She glances toward the restaurant. "I'll guarantee you she saw what just happened and she's turned her radar on. You and I are going to give her an Academy Award-winning performance when we get inside."

Cross smiles, and his eyes twinkle. "You've got a little devil in you, don't you? That's an awesome idea." He puts his hands on her waist, lifts her so they're facing each other, and gives her a kiss.

"That's the idea!" Megan says as he sets her back down.

I just hope my face isn't as red as it feels. My goodness, he's strong.

Holding hands, they stroll across the parking lot and into the Huddle House.

Teri stares at them as they enter.

When she doesn't greet them, Cross says, "You want us to just pick an empty table, Teri?"

His question brings her out of her dazed state. "Uh, sure…yes, just pick a table."

When they're seated, Megan whispers without moving her mouth, "Did you see the look on her face? Oh my God, it was priceless."

Cross responds in the same manner, "It's the only time I've ever known her to be speechless."

Megan puts her hands in the middle of the table, and Cross takes ahold of them.

"Let's make dove eyes at each other," Megan says.

"What the heck is that?"

"Just look at me as if I'm an angel and you can't believe how lucky you are to be with me."

Cross laughs but quickly covers it by turning it into a cough.

Teri arrives at their table and sets two glasses of water on it. "Well, don't you two look cute? Is there something I should know? I didn't even know you two knew each other. You've been in here before at the same time and never said a word to each other."

Megan speaks breathlessly, "It all happened so fast, we can't believe it ourselves. One day we're strangers, and the next—" She pulls his hand to her mouth and kisses it.

"It's both unbelievable and magical," Cross adds, and he kisses both her hands. "I'm just the luckiest guy in the world."

In a flat tone, Teri says, "Well, good for both of you. What do you want for breakfast?"

After they place their order and Teri walks away, Megan says, "I'm going to fall on the floor laughing. Did you see how she looked at you? I didn't know she had a thing for you."

"Well, she doesn't."

"Oh, yes, she does. She looked like she'd lost her best friend when you said you were the luckiest guy in the world to have me, and she shot daggers in my direction."

"You're crazy. I didn't see any of that."

"Of course not. You men are blind to everything. If we didn't show you the way, you'd get lost in your own houses. You wait and see, she'll bring my coffee, but she'll spill some of it on the table."

"I think you're the one making things up now."

Raising her eyebrows, Megan says, "We'll see. Let's just stare at each other until our food gets here. It'll make her crazy."

"Okay. You're the director of this movie. I'll do what you say."

What Megan wasn't expecting was how hard it is to stare at him and not let her mind wander. The memory of his hand on her butt just won't go away, and she worries her face is turning pink.

I just wonder what he's thinking about. I know men say they don't think about anything, but could that really be true? Does their brain really go into neutral most of the time?

All of a sudden, she hears a question in her head coming out of her mouth. "What are you thinking about?" She quickly puts up her hand. "Wait. Did I just say what I think I said? I know I was thinking it, but I didn't mean to say it out loud."

"You women really are curious about that subject, aren't you?" Cross replies. "It's really pretty simple. We're usually thinking about sports or hunting and fishing or buying a new boat or car. That's about it."

"Not sex?"

Oh my God, I can't believe I just said that.

"I thought you all were always thinking about sex, too." She cringes inside at what he must think of her.

Pursing his lips, he answers, "For sure. From the time we're a teen for the next twenty years or so, it's on our minds a lot. And I mean a lot. But when my wife died, it's like that part of me died, too." He shakes his head. "I really can't explain it."

To have their conversation make a sudden shift from play-acting to private, inner thoughts catches Megan off guard, and she's unsure of what to do or say next.

Teri saves her when she shows up with two coffee cups and a pot. "Here you guys go. Your food will be right up."

She pours Cross's almost to the rim, then points the pot at Megan's cup but tilts it too much so it pours too fast and splashes out onto the table. "Oh, I'm so sorry," she says as she sets down the pot and reaches for a rag in her apron. "Did I get any on you?" she asks Megan.

"No, I'm fine. Don't worry about it. Waitressing is a hard and thankless job sometimes."

Teri looks at her differently. "You can say that again, sister."

This time, she carefully pours the coffee. Pointing at Cross, she says, "You be good to her." Then she walks away.

Megan gives him a triumphant look.

"Okay, okay," he says, "you were right. And how cool that you were able to make her an ally and me the villain in, like, two seconds."

Megan laughs. "Yeah, at first the story she was going to tell is how you were stuck with some poor, crippled girl, and now her story's going to be how you're not good enough for me."

"Yes, exactly! I never got thrown under the bus so fast in all my life."

****

An hour and a half later, Cross and Megan are standing on the crowd-choked sidewalks of Wood Street, in Paris. Toddlers are perched on the necks of men, craning to see another approaching marching band. Young girls stand in front of their mothers and imitate the moves of the majorettes twirling their batons.

A shiny red convertible with its top down slowly rolls past. Sitting in the back seat is a smiling young man with Down's Syndrome. He waves at everyone as they cheer and clap for him.

"Who is that?" Megan asks Cross.

"That's Jordan St. John. He's the Grand Marshal of the parade this year. His family are remarkable people who created a business where special needs adults can work. It's called Sweet Jordan's. You need to go there sometime. They sell cookies, ice cream, and sandwiches. Every time I eat there, I leave with a smile on my face and a good feeling about the world."

Yelling so she can be heard above the marching band, Megan says, "It sounds like an amazing place. I'll make sure I go sometime."

Next up in the parade is a group of older men wearing fezzes and riding tiny motor cars, driving in circles, smiling, and waving at the children.

Shielding her eyes against the sun, Megan looks up at Cross just as he looks down at her.

"You don't know who they are, do you?" Cross asks.

"No."

"Ever hear of the Shriners Children's Hospitals?"

"Yes. I had a friend who went to one in Dayton, Ohio."

Pointing at the men, Cross says, "Well, those are Shriners."

"What's a Shriner?"

"I don't know much about them. Somebody said they're members of the Masonic Lodge."

"Really? My father was a Freemason."

"That's interesting. I don't know anybody who's a Mason, at least I don't think I do. It's such a secretive organization. Did your dad talk about it much?"

Megan shakes her head. "Not at all. I asked Mother about it one time, and she told me not to talk about it, that Daddy would get mad if I did. It was very hush-hush, which is weird, isn't it?"

Cross shrugs. "Maybe a little. We men just have a thing for being a member of a club or a team."

The blaring sound of sirens interrupts them as four state troopers driving massive motorcycles roll past the crowd.

Interspersed between the nearly twenty marching bands are scores of floats of every size and description — Cub Scouts and Brownies, churches, winners from area beauty pageants, a daycare, and the local Lion's Club and Rotary Club.

By the time the parade ends, Megan feels sweat rolling down her back as she fans herself with one of the paper fans representatives of a funeral home were passing out to the crowd.

I bet my nose looks like Rudolph the Red Nose Reindeer's.

Her leg has been aching for the last thirty minutes, and a part of her wishes she had a wheelchair to ride in back to Cross's truck.

"Well, what did you think of the parade?" Cross asks as they turn to leave.

"I was surprised at how big it was, and how many people came to see it."

"If you live in northwest Tennessee, you have to see the Fish Fry parade at least once in your lifetime. It's a tradition. The other big parade is in Humboldt, where they have the Strawberry Festival. It's as big a parade as this one."

"What are other local traditions around here I've missed out on?"

"Well, let's see. I'd say eating fried catfish underneath the big tent during Fish Fry week is one. Going skinny dipping in Kentucky Lake is another. Everybody needs to try the barbeque from Trolinger's Meat Market, and on Veteran's Day there's a program outside the courthouse that used to be a big deal, but the crowd seems to get smaller every year. I go to honor my Pop, even though he doesn't attend it."

Megan cocks her head to one side. "Why doesn't he?"

"You and I really don't know what things were like in our country back then. It's nothing like it is today, where anyone wearing a service uniform is treated with respect and honor. Pop says when his plane landed in California on his way back home, people spit on him and his buddies and called them baby killers and told them they weren't welcome back here. I think that's a wound that'll never heal for him."

“That is so sad! It’s hard to even imagine them being treated that way. It makes me mad. Don’t you think it would make him feel better if he’d attend the Veteran’s Day ceremony and be treated with the honor and respect he deserves?”

“I do,” Cross replies. “But Pop is really hard headed sometimes. Last time I tried to talk to him about it, he got mad and told me to never bring it up again.”

Without warning, Megan’s leg buckles on her, and she nearly falls to the ground if not for Cross catching her.

“Whoa, careful there!” he exclaims.

A woman behind them cries out in surprise.

Megan grits her teeth against the sharp pains going through her leg.

Several people gather around them as Cross helps her stand up.

“Hold on to me,” he tells her.

“Do I need to call an ambulance?” someone asks.

“I live close by and have a wheelchair I can run and get,” someone else says.

Another person hands a water bottle to Megan. “Do you need some water? Maybe you got too hot.”

Embarrassed by all the attention, Megan grips Cross’s arm and says, “Thank you, but I’ll be okay. I’ve just got a bum leg, and it gave out on me.”

Cross whispers in her ear, “Why don’t you wait here, and I’ll go get my truck.” Pointing, he adds, “You can sit in the Subway store and get a cold drink.”

Giving in to her leg is the last thing Megan wants to do, but it hurts so bad, she’s not sure she can walk the rest of the way. She heaves a sigh and says, “Okay.”

She turns toward the store and starts to take a step in that direction, but Cross says, “Uh uh, not like that.” With seemingly little effort, he sweeps her off her feet and into his arms. “I’ll carry you there.”

CHAPTER THIRTY

The next morning, her mother's scream jerks Megan awake.

Before she can get out of bed, her mother bursts through the door.

"Tell me about you and Cross!" Grace exclaims, her face a picture of excitement.

Sitting up in bed, Megan replies, "What?"

"I just heard you and Cross are dating, or whatever young people call it nowadays. Why didn't you tell me? How did it happen? I'm so happy."

Adrenalin mixed with irritation courses through Megan at being scared out of her sleep, so she decides to return the favor. "It's been magical, Mother, like a fairy tale. It just sort of grabbed me and Cross at the same time. We're getting married next weekend."

Grace's eyes grow wide, and she holds her hand on her chest. "Thank you, Lord Jesus, for answering my prayers."

Megan begins laughing. "Oh my gosh, Mother, I'm joking. Cross and I aren't seeing each other or getting married."

Looking confused, Grace says, "But Alice said Margaret told her you two were making out in the middle of the Huddle House, that you were practically having sex in front of everybody."

Megan howls. "Oh my God, that is hilarious! So, who did this Margaret person hear it from?"

Grace purses her lips. "I don't know. Why does that matter?"

"Cross was right. The rumor mill is alive and well in Paris. Listen to me, me and Cross decided we'd play a trick on that waitress, Teri, who works the morning shift at Huddle House, just to see how fast and far the rumor would go."

"You weren't kissing and holding hands?"

"Yes, we did, but it was only part of the scheme to make her believe something was going on between us."

"And you're not getting married?"

"No, Mother. You know better than to believe something like that. I've told you many times how I feel about that subject."

Grace folds her arms across her chest. In a flat tone, she says, "Well, I don't think this is funny at all. You get people all stirred up, telling all sorts of tales, and nearly give me a heart attack. It's a mean thing to do."

Megan reaches for her mother and motions for her to take her hand. "I'm sorry you're upset. We thought it would be funny."

Grace turns away from her. "Well, it might be funny tomorrow, but right now it's not." As she walks out of the bedroom, she says, "Don't forget, we're going to Music on the Square tonight. Cross and Buck's bluegrass band is playing. I'm sure you and Cross will want to put on another show for the crowd." She slams the door behind her.

Despite her mother's indignation, Megan can't help chuckling.

I hope Cross hears how perfectly our plan worked.

Falling back onto her pillow and staring at the ceiling, she wonders how he felt about their kiss and if he had any dreams about it last night, like she did.

How do actors and actresses deal with those kinds of things, making out, or even making love with someone? I'd think you'd have to be dead if you didn't feel something, even if it is just a job. Sitting back up, she thinks, *I hope he didn't read more into it than intended. What if he's thinking he wants to start seeing me? I mean, he's easy to be around, but I don't want him to get the wrong idea. It was just a game; we were just play-acting. But if that's all it was, then why did I have those dreams about him and I being together? Dreams don't mean anything; they're just dreams. Then why did I wake up in the middle of the night, having an orgasm? I have no control over what my body does when I'm sleeping. Maybe it's a good sign, since it's the first one I've had since my accident. It's just another part of my body, a really nice part of my body, waking up. So, it's not about Cross at all. Is it?*

She groans in frustration and pulls the extra bed pillow over her face.

And this is why we women can't imagine a man thinking about nothing, because our brains run non-stop, connecting dots of unrelated things and creating multiple crazy scenarios and believing all of them are real. Ugh!

~~~~~~~~~

Later, as the sun is setting, Megan and Grace get out of the car and join others walking toward the court square.

"How long are you going to stay mad at me?" Megan asks.

Grace waves at someone and calls to them, "Evening, Carla. Nice night for a concert, isn't it?"

"Beautiful," Carla replies.

In a half-voice, Grace says to Megan, "I haven't made up my mind. Maybe forever."

"It was just a joke, Mother. Why can't you see the humor in it?"

"Hi, Grace," a woman calls out.

"Oh, hi, Mary," Grace answers.

"I know you're thrilled to death," Mary says. "Congratulations to you, and to you, too, Megan. Cross is a fine catch."

Grace turns on Megan. Through clenched teeth, she says, "That's why I don't see the humor in it! You can't unring a bell. That rumor will likely outlive me."

Megan turns her head to hide her smile and shifts the lawn chair she's carrying to her other arm. To change the direction of the conversation, she says, "Are you supposed to introduce the band or emcee the show?"

A panicked look takes over Grace's features. "I hope not! I hadn't even thought about that. What if I'm supposed to? What will I do?"

"Mother, if there's one thing you're good at, it's talking. Just be yourself, welcome everyone and thank them for coming out, then ask everybody to give a big round of applause for the band. Thirty seconds, that's all it'll take. You can easily do that."
~~~~~~~~~

“I hope I don’t have to. Don’t forget to remind me I’m supposed to take pictures for the Fish Fry Facebook page. I did remember to bring my phone, didn’t I?”

“I saw you put it in your purse. Try to relax and enjoy the evening. I just hope I can find something in one of their songs I like.”

Just then, they turn a corner and get a view of the courthouse lawn, which is thick with people. Some are unfurling quilts in the air, letting them float to the ground, where family members can sit. There are so many colors, collectively they make their own patchwork quilt. Other people are setting up lawn chairs and settling into them. Everyone is either smiling at, waving to, or greeting familiar faces and old friends.

Emotions she can’t immediately identify stir in Megan, and she blinks back tears. “This is really beautiful,” she says, to no one in particular.

I guess this is what sets small towns apart, everyone being connected in some way or another and enjoying shared experiences.

As she and her mother help each other over the high curb, she says, “I’m glad you insisted I come. I needed to see this.”

“See what?”

“Never mind, it doesn’t matter.”

The squeal of feedback from a sound system draws their attention to a four-foot-high stage, where Cross and Buck and the rest of the band are tuning their instruments and doing a soundcheck.

A man in the audience yells out, “Get that banjo tuned, Buck. We’re ready for some music!”

Laughter and a smattering of applause follow his admonition.

Megan tells her mom, “You run on, Mother, and find out what you’re supposed to do, if anything. I’ll set up our chairs and wait for you here.”

Unfolding the chairs, she positions them on a level place and sits down. It strikes her she’s probably the only person here who doesn’t know anybody.

That's not true. Quit being so pessimistic. I know Buck, Cross, and Harlon. And I know the people at my physical therapist's office.

Behind her, she overhears two women talking.

"Is that Cross Daniels up there? Harlon's son?"

"Yes, I think so."

"I hear he's getting married."

Megan nearly falls out of her chair while stifling her laughter. The next comment, though, sends an icy chill through her veins.

"I hope the woman knows what she's getting—a murderer and an ex-con."

Grace's voice comes across the P.A. system. "Welcome, welcome, welcome! I'm so excited to see so many people coming out to support our local musicians. Let's give a big welcome to these boys, who call themselves 'Long Time Comin'."

The music starts, and everyone claps in rhythm.

But Megan hears none of it. Her mind has seized up because of the woman's description of Cross.

CHAPTER THIRTY-ONE

As the band plays, Grace meanders through the crowd back to her chair, speaking to everyone and taking in their congratulations on bringing a bluegrass group to the square. She feels her heart and head might burst with pride and a sense of relief because of the chance she took in hiring the group to play. But when she looks at Megan, alarm bells go off in her head.

She hurries to her and sits down. Keeping her voice low, she says, "Megan, what's wrong? You look like you've seen a ghost."

When Megan doesn't reply, Grace takes her hand and squeezes it. "Megan, look at me. Are you okay?"

Slowly, Megan turns her head and looks in Grace's direction, but her eyes seem unfocused.

"Megan!" Graces says sharply.

This time, Megan looks at her and frowns.

"Are you feeling sick?" Grace asks. "Do I need to take you home?"

Shaking her head, Megan says, "No. I'll be alright. I just need to catch my breath." Waggling her phone, she adds, "I just read a rather shocking news story. I'll talk to you about it later. Turn and listen to the music. I'm going to get something to eat from one of the food trucks. You want something?"

Grace isn't completely convinced by Megan's explanation but knows there's no point in pressing the issue.

She'll talk about it when she wants to.

"Just bring me back something to drink," Grace tells her.

The sharp sounds of a fiddle turn her attention to the stage, where Harlon, dressed in overalls, is playing The Orange Blossom Special. He bobs and weaves at the waist and bounces from one foot to the other as the tempo continually increases until it reaches a frenetic pace. Some of the horse's hairs on his bow break and do their own dance as he strokes the strings of his fiddle.

The crowd goes wild, whooping and hollering and clapping. An old man teeters his way through the crowd and surprises everyone when he turns around and starts buck dancing in front of the stage, looking every bit like a lumberjack toy.

When the song ends, Harlon and the band receive a standing ovation.

Two or three more songs pass before Grace thinks about Megan. She looks around for her and finally sees her making her way toward her, carrying her food and drinks. Seeing she's struggling, she goes to her.

"I'm sorry," she says, "I should have thought about how difficult it would be to carry an extra drink with you." She takes the drinks from her.

"I didn't think it'd be too hard," Megan replies, "but keeping my balance is still a challenge. Any extra weight can throw me off."

Seated back at their chairs, Grace asks, "What did you get?"

"Well, of course I got you your Diet Coke."

Grace smiles and takes a long sip through the straw.

"And I got a lemonade and barbeque sandwich." She laughs. "I can't believe how much my diet has changed since I moved here. My friends back in Nashville would laugh if they saw how I eat. No Starbucks coffee, no tofu. No Vietnamese or Thai food, which I love. And I used to rarely eat meat."

"Honey, it's not a meal if there's not meat in it," Grace replies.

"Exactly my point," Megan says, with a smile. Nodding at the stage, she adds, "Looks like you did the right thing having them play during Fish Fry. The crowd is loving it."

"Oh, I know! I'm so relieved and excited, too. They're much better than I expected. Actually, they're really, really good. Harlon is the biggest surprise. He was all into rock music when we dated—had the long hair and sideburns to go along with it."

Talking with her mouth full of barbeque, Megan asks, "Do you like this music?"

"It has an old, ancient feeling attached to it, or it does for me. It's stripped down, without electrical sound effects to distort what they're playing or drums to drown it out." Cocking her head, Grace says, "You know, you seem to be in a totally different mood than you were a moment ago. What happened? What were you upset about?"

"It's nothing. I thought it was something, but really, it has nothing to do with me. Why should I care anyway?"

Grace stares at her a second. "Well, that doesn't make any sense. What in the world are you talking about?"

Megan takes another bite of her sandwich, shakes her head at Grace, then turns her attention to the stage and nods.

"Next time," Grace says, "just slam the door in my face when you don't want to talk to me. Really, Megan."

An hour later, Cross tells the crowd, "We're gonna take a break right now and wet our whistles. Y'all be sure and visit these food trucks here and tell them we appreciate them setting up for these concerts."

Grace tells Megan, "I'm going to go speak to the band and tell them how much I appreciate them performing. Want to come with me?"

Shaking her head, Megan says, "No, not really. I'll just sit here, or I might go get something more to drink. You go on."

"Don't you want to speak to Cross?"

Megan's face turns stony. "Absolutely not."

Grace meets the band as they're stepping off the stage. "You guys are terrific! I hope you can tell how much the crowd is enjoying you."

"We're the ones having a good time," Cross replies. "But to tell you the truth, we didn't expect to see more than a dozen or so people show up."

Buck speaks up. "It's nice to know there's still an appetite in people for this kind of music."

"Who are these other boys in the band?" Grace asks.

"I'm Glynn."

“And I’m Randy. Thank you for inviting us to play.”

Grace gives a broad grin. “Thank you for being as good as you are.” Pointing at Harlon as he approaches, she says, “And who’s this big guy who’s lucky his fiddle didn’t catch on fire during ‘Orange Blossom Special?’”

Harlon shoulders his way through the group and steps up to Grace. Giving an exaggerated bow toward her, he then stands erect and says, “Harlon Daniels, Madame, the best fiddle player you ever dated. At least I’m assuming I am.”

“As a matter of fact, you are,” Grace replies, “because you’re the only fiddle player I’ve ever dated.”

Cross, Buck, Glynn, and Randy all laugh.

Harlon laughs with them. “You don’t have to worry about her; she’s always had my number.”

“We’re going to hit the food trucks,” Cross tells him. “You want us to bring you something?”

“Bring me a bag of fried pork rinds, the spicy kind, and some water to wash ’em down.”

As they move off, Mrs. Rhinehart walks up to Harlon and kisses him on the cheek. “You are one amazing man. Who would have thought you’d have so much talent? I wish you’d drop by the house sometime. I’ve got some ideas on changes to the yard. I’d like your input on them.”

Harlon’s face turns red. “Oh…uh…well…well, that might be hard to do. I’m really busy helping Cross and Buck, you know.” He shoots a sidelong glance at Grace.

Grace folds her arms and raises her eyebrows at him.

To Mrs. Rhinehart, he says, “I was just going to get something to eat with Mrs. Charles, if you don’t mind excusing us.”

Grace feels Mrs. Rhinehart giving her an appraising stare.

Harlon takes ahold of Grace’s elbow and begins moving her through the crowd with him. All along the way, they’re stopped by people wanting to brag on Harlon.

Eventually, she asks him, “You know what this reminds me of?”

“No, what?”

“You remember that time you won the pitching game at the county fair? You knocked over all the bottles.”

“Oh, wow, I haven’t thought about that in forever.”

“Remember? You won me that giant stuffed bear.”

“My gosh, I’d forgotten that detail. What I remember from that night is the ride on the Ferris wheel. I thought about it all the time when I was in Viet Nam.”

“Would you believe I still have the bear?”

He gives her a look of astonishment. “You’re not serious!”

“Yes, I am. I’ve kept it all these years. Sometimes I’d take it out and relive the memories of that time in my life. I’m sorry I messed things up and ruined everything.”

Holding up his hand, Harlon says, “Stop right there. I thought we’d agreed we weren’t going to keep apologizing about the past? There’s plenty of blame to go around.”

“But you’re just being nice when you say that. If I’d just—”

He covers her mouth with his hand. “If you’re going to keep talking like that, I’m going back onstage to wait for my pork skins and water.”

Grace purses her lips and kisses his hand.

“Hey, Pop, what’s going on?” Cross asks as he joins them.

Grace’s eyes are locked on Harlon’s, and she can’t tear herself away from his gaze.

Waving his hand between their faces, Cross asks, “Is this a staring contest of some kind?”

Finally, Harlon blinks and looks at Cross. “You get what I wanted?”

Cross hands over a large, clear plastic bag filled with fried pork rinds.

Taking it, Harlon says, “Oh yeah, baby, this is going to be good.”

Cross turns to Grace. “Didn’t I see Megan here with you? I found where you both were sitting, but there’s only one empty chair there now.”

“She’s been acting strange this evening,” Grace answers him. “I have no idea where she is.”

CHAPTER THIRTY-TWO

Cross and Harlon place their guitar and fiddle cases on the back seat of his pickup truck, then climb into the front.

"Man, that was fun, wasn't it?!" Harlon says.

Cranking the truck and turning the air conditioner on high, Cross answers, "Yes, it was." He turns the air vent so it blows directly on him. "That may have been the most fun I've had since I got out of prison. The applause from the crowd was almost like a drug. I can see how professional performers get addicted to their careers."

"I agree. Hey, swing by Sonic. I want to get one of their large sweet teas."

Cross flips on his blinker and turns off Veterans Drive onto Tyson Avenue.

When he stops in one of the Sonic's parking stalls, he says, "I wonder if the Sonics up north have sweet tea. I hear most people up there don't even know what sweet tea really is."

"Your new girlfriend might know the answer to that," Harlon says. "Why don't you ask her?"

Pushing the button to place an order, Cross says to Harlon, "What are you talking about?"

A young-sounding female voice says, "Can I have your order, please?"

"Two large sweet teas," Cross answers her.

"Is that all?"

"Yes."

"We'll have it right out."

To keep the cool air inside, he raises his window. "Now, what were you saying about me and a girlfriend?"

“You and Megan Charles. I heard what happened at the Huddle House. I’m really happy for you, but I can’t believe you didn’t let me in on what’s going on between you two.”

A hearty laugh rolls out of Cross. “Pop, none of what you heard is true, except for what people saw. Me and Megan decided to play a trick on Teri, so we acted like we were a couple, and she swallowed it hook, line, and sinker.”

“So, you really didn’t make out in the parking lot?”

“We kissed and hugged, but it was all fake. We were play-acting, like actors and actresses do.”

“You’re telling me you put your lips on hers and held her body against you and didn’t feel anything?”

Cross hesitates before answering.

“That’s what I thought,” Harlon says. “I’d have accused you of lying if you denied it.”

“I admit, it felt good. It reminded me of how I used to feel when Heather and I were together. But that’s all it was, just my body reacting to being close to a woman. It was just for fun and didn’t mean anything.”

“Mmmhmm. Whatever you say. I just know you got everybody in town stirred up over your little escapade. Teri made sure of that.” He chuckles. “But I kind of like what you did, getting Teri all stirred up. I bet her eyes were bugged out and her blood pressure was sky high.”

Cross laughs. “It worked perfectly. She took it in completely.” Taking a sip of his drink, he asks, “You and Mrs. Rhinehart got a meeting set up?”

Harlon looks at him. “What are you talking about?”

“I saw her come up to you and give you a kiss. I wondered how Megan’s mom felt about that.”

Clearing his throat, Harlon replies, “That woman was as bold as sunshine. It was embarrassing. But I’ll tell you what I did then and there: I made a decision to change my ways. I’m through sleeping with all these women around here.”

"Wow, Pop, am I ever glad to hear that. I'll be honest with you, it's been embarrassing how you've acted since Mama died. Why do you think you started doing that?"

Harlon shrugs his shoulders. "I don't know. Because I was stupid, because I was hurting, because I was bored—you pick one, or maybe all of them. I'll admit, it fed my ego. But it made sex cheap. I suspect your generation looks at sex as just something to do and you give it no thought. That's not how it should be, though. It should mean something. It's a way of speaking to someone when there're no words to describe how you feel about them. Sex is a language all its own." He drains the rest of his drink and rolls down his window to dump the ice in the parking lot.

Cross pulls out his phone and messages Megan.

HEY THERE. MISSED GETTING TO SEE YOU TONIGHT. HOPE UR OK.

He adds a smiling emoji and presses "send."

"You know, Pop, I think you and Grace are the ones who are getting close to each other. You all seem to be a good fit."

"She's a nice lady, just like she always was. I remember one time when we rode the same bus to school. I guess we were, like, eleven or twelve years old. There was this little kid in kindergarten who cried every morning when he got on the bus. Poor little fella was homesick, I'm sure. Some kids made fun of him, but Grace made it a point to get up and go sit beside him. And then one time he stood up to get off the bus at school, and he dropped some kind of papers he'd made. Kids walked right past him, stepping on the papers. He started bawling. Grace, though, jumped up and yelled at everybody to sit back down until she could help him get everything picked up. And even though several of the kids were older than her, they did what she said. That's just the kind of effect she had on people."

Cross's phone dings with a notification alert. He looks at it, expecting to see a reply from Megan, but it's only a notification she's read his message.

"Do you have feelings for Grace, Pop?"

"Yeah. I'm just not sure what kind. Are they the feelings from fifty years ago that have resurfaced like a dream? Are they based on then, or now? What's real, and what's my imagination? I can't figure it out."

"That sounds like a complicated place to be, Pop. I don't know what to tell you except give yourself some time."

He checks his phone again. Still nothing.

"Why do you keep checking your phone?" Harlon asks.

"I texted Megan I missed getting to speak to her tonight and hope she's okay, but she hasn't replied."

Rubbing his chin, Harlon says, "If you two aren't a couple or nothing like that, why are you texting her you missed speaking to her? Sounds like you may have feelings for her."

Cross wants to reply but doesn't know what to say.

Why do I care if I spoke to her or not? And why should she care? Maybe she hasn't replied because she's weirded out by my text. I thought we had fun going to the parade and then tricking Teri. Why can't my texting her just be a friend texting another friend? But are we friends? We're friendly towards each other, at least it seems like it, so I'd say we're kinda like friends. Would she say the same?

"Hey there," Harlon's voice breaks into his musings. "You want me to throw you a rope and pull you out of whatever hole you've fallen into? What in the world are you thinking about?"

"I'm trying to figure out how to answer your question. Would you say Megan and I are friends?"

"When two people have funny stories to tell about things they've done together, I think that makes them friends. And you two will always remember messing with Teri's head and the rumors it triggered."

Cross snaps his fingers. "That's it! Maybe the rumors are bigger and worse than what Megan expected. Maybe she's upset about it and regrets doing it. She's like a turtle retreating into its shell and isn't going to have anything else to do with me."

"Would you be okay with that?"

"Sure I would. Why should I care one way or the other?"

Starting the truck, Cross pulls out of Sonic and heads home.

After several moments, Harlon says, "I think it was Shakespeare who wrote, 'Methinks thou doth protest too much.'"

"What's that supposed to mean?"

Shrugging his shoulders, Harlon replies, "I'll let you figure it out."

CHAPTER THIRTY-THREE

The next morning, Megan awakens to the sound of her mother singing one of the songs from last night's concert on the square.

"Good ol' Rocky Top. Rocky Top, Tennessee."

After taking the time to pee, Megan pads into the living room, where she finds Grace placing a stuffed bear on the couch.

"Oh my gosh, that's my bear!" Megan squeals. Hurrying to the couch, she sits down, picks it up, and hugs it. "I didn't know you still had it. I slept with it every night and told it all my troubles." She runs her fingers over its worn face and touches the place where one of its eyes is missing. "I remember when it lost this eye. I was so upset and looked everywhere for it. Remember?"

Grace smiles. "Yes, I remember."

"What made you decide to get it out and bring it in here?"

"Well, you don't know the story about how this bear came to be yours. You see, it was my bear at first." She joins Megan on the couch.

"Yours? You never told me that."

"That's because if I'd told the truth, your father would have thrown the bear away."

Frowning, Megan says, "Now I'm really confused. You need to explain."

"Let's go into the kitchen, and I'll tell you while I fix us some breakfast."

With her head full of questions, Megan follows her mother and takes a seat at the table.

For the next little bit, Grace tells her about what happened at the county fair all those years ago. As she finishes, she sets two plates of French toast and sausage on the table and sits down.

Megan takes Grace's hand. "That's the sweetest story, Mother; I love it! Why haven't you ever told me?"

"Your father was a very jealous man and wouldn't have understood me holding on to a memento from an earlier relationship, so I always kept the story to myself."

Taking a bite of sausage, Megan says, "I can see Father being a jealous person. I think that's why he was so controlling. But why have you brought the bear out now? Is it because you and Harlon are a thing?" She punctuates her question with a wink and smile.

"I'd all but forgotten about the bear until last night. Everyone's reaction to Harlon's music reminded me of that night at the fair, and he and I reminisced about it." She laughs. "He was shocked to know I still had the bear. He probably thinks I'm some kind of hoarder now."

"You didn't answer my question, Mother."

"What question is that?"

"You know exactly what question: Are you and Harlon a thing now?"

Grace forks a bite of French toast, dips it in a small bowl of maple syrup, and puts it in her mouth, giving Megan no indication of an answer. When Grace reaches for her coffee cup, Megan stops her hand.

"Quit playing around with me, and answer the question."

Pulling her hand away from Megan's, Grace says, "If you'll let me get a sip of coffee, I'll tell you."

Megan mirrors her mother's move and takes a sip of her own coffee.

"I'm not sure what being 'a thing' means," Grace answers. "A part of me wants to say we've never *not* been a thing. You know the sayings, 'Your first love never dies' or 'The first candle never goes out?' I think that's true for me. Or maybe I'm just remembering how it used to be and reliving those feelings. For certain, I've never forgotten the time I had with Harlon. It was the most perfect time in my life…until it wasn't."

Megan wrestles with whether or not to say what's on her mind. "Can I say something about you and Harlon?"

"Of course you can."

“There’s no doubt you and Harlon had something special, and I hate things didn’t work out. The thing is, you don’t know anything about him now and what kind of person he’s become. People change, you know. He might have become somebody very different from the boy you loved.”

Grace cocks her head and looks at her thoughtfully. “I get the feeling you’re trying to tell me something without telling me. Is there anything going on I need to know about?”

The dread of telling her mother something that might be hurtful tugs on Megan. Picking at the food on her plate, she says, “Since Harlon’s wife died, he’s become somewhat of a Casanova, having sex with multiple women around here. I just don’t want him to view you as another of his conquests.”

Grace’s back stiffens. In an icy tone, she says, “And how would you know anything about something like that? You don’t know anybody around here, and you don’t get out. Are you just making it up because you don’t want to lose me to a man?”

“Oh my God, Mother, no! That’s not it at all. I want nothing more than for you to be happy, whatever it is that brings you happiness. So, I’m not making this up. Cross is the one who told me about it. He’s really embarrassed by his father’s behavior. He told me so. He says he believes Harlon’s intentions with you are different, but how can he be certain? I’m sorry to tell you, but I thought you deserved to know. Please don’t be mad at me.”

Watching her mother turn pale and tears fill her eyes breaks Megan’s heart. “Oh, Mother.” She gets out of her chair and moves to embrace her, but Grace avoids her by standing up and carrying her plate to the sink.

Megan follows her. “Would it be better if I hadn’t said anything to you about it?”

Grace’s shoulders sag. “No. I needed to know. I just wish…” Her voice trails off.

Megan then tells her what she heard about Cross last night on the square.

Grace replies, “Well, how do you know it’s true?”

“Mother, why would someone make something like that up? I mean, people tell tales on people, but to start a rumor that someone’s a murderer? I just don’t think someone would do that. Do you?”

Slowly shaking her head, Grace says, “No, but I just find it hard to believe. A murderer? Does he seem like that kind of person to you? And if he is, why isn’t he still in prison? And what about Buck? He doesn’t seem like the kind of person who’d be in business with a murderer. It just doesn’t make any sense.”

An unpleasant silence fills the space between them.

After a moment, Grace says, “That’s why you started acting weird last night, wasn’t it?”

“Yes. It was such a shock, I didn’t know what to think or believe. He texted me last night, but I ignored him. I expect he’ll try to message me today. Maybe I need to block his number.”

“Why don’t you ask him about what you heard? Give him a chance to deny it or explain it, one way or the other.”

Putting her hands on her hips, Megan counters, “Are you going to ask Harlon about his philandering ways?”

“I see what you’re saying. That’d be awkward, wouldn’t it?” She hesitates, then adds, “But you know what? I think that’s exactly what I’m going to do. I’m going to confront him and see how he reacts, and what he says. After fifty years, I think he deserves at least that much.”

“Well, I don’t have that kind of history with Cross. I don’t think I owe him that chance.”

Suddenly, Grace winces and doubles over.

Grabbing her, Megan says, “Mother? What’s wrong?”

“Just give me a second,” Grace answers. Eventually, she straightens up and says, “I’m fine.”

“You are not fine,” Megan replies.

“It’s nothing. Probably just gas.”

“Has it happened before?”

“I’m fine, I’m fine.”

"It *has* happened before, hasn't it? I've noticed recently you've lost some weight, too. When's the last time you had a good checkup?"

Brushing past her, Grace heads out of the kitchen, saying, "Quit your worrying. I'll be fine."

Calling after her, Megan says, "What would you say to me if the roles were reversed? You know exactly what you'd say."

From deeper in the house, Grace can be heard launching into her own rendition of "Rocky Top."

CHAPTER THIRTY-FOUR

TWO YEARS AGO

Lying awake in bed, as he'd been all night, Cross heard the familiar shuffling footsteps of Harold, the prison guard, approaching his cell.

"Rise and shine, Daniels," the guard announced before reaching the cell, "this is your last day here."

Not that Cross needed reminding. It was all he'd focused on for the last week, being careful to avoid a confrontation with another inmate intent on getting him in trouble to cause a delay in his release. It was an attitude among inmates he never understood. They didn't celebrate a fellow inmate's release. Instead, they resented and hated that they weren't getting out.

The cell door opened, and Harold's body filled the space. "You got everything packed up you want to take with you?"

"I'm not taking anything with me. Do what you want to with it."

"Not your radio or books or nothing?"

"No. I'm ready for this chapter of my life to end and to get started writing another chapter."

Pitching a package toward Cross, Harold said, "Here's you a set of clothes to wear. It ain't much, but it's better than that pair of overalls you're wearing."

Cross opened the package, zipped off the overalls, and put on the clothes.

"Come on," Harold said, "we've got to go to the admin office. You've got papers to sign."

Harold backed out of the way so Cross could go first.

"So, how does it feel, getting out?" Harold asked as they walked down the corridor.

"I guess I feel glad to be leaving the monotony and drama of this place, but I also feel guilty because I don't deserve to be getting out. For what I did, I should never get out."

"That's where you're different from most of the guys in here. None of them believe they should be here, it's everybody else's fault but theirs: judges, lawyers, police, juries, their girlfriend, the phase of the moon. I mean, you've heard them talk. It's ridiculous. But you gotta be careful about keeping yourself in a prison in your head. Forgive yourself, and move on; that's my advice."

Cross was impressed with the guard's insights into human nature and sound advice. "I hear what you're saying," he replied. "But yourself is the hardest one to forgive."

"Can't deny that," Harold replied. "No, sir, can't deny that."

Cross stopped at a closed door, and Harold reached beside him and swiped his keycard. The door latch buzzed, and Cross pushed through.

Inside were three desks, with officers sitting behind them. One of them motioned to a table with a solitary chair. "Your papers are there. Be sure you read them and sign everywhere there's an X."

Having already familiarized himself via the prison library with what he'd be signing, Cross flipped through the pages and signed where required.

A door in the corner of the room opened, and the warden stepped in. Walking across the room, he shook Cross's hand.

"Daniels," he said, "you've been an exemplary inmate during your time with us. I appreciate that, as do all the guards here. Now, your debt to society has been paid. It's time to re-enter the real world and resume the productive life you once had. All of us here wish you well."

Cross nodded at him but said nothing.

"This way," Harold said and walked him through another door.

Next stop was to have what he wore when he entered prison returned to him.

Cross poured the contents of the bag onto the counter. He dug through and pushed aside the shirt, pants, socks, underwear, and shoes. "Give these to somebody else." Then he spotted what he was looking for: His wedding ring. Slipping it onto his finger, he massaged it with the finger and thumb of his other hand.

Harold then led him through a series of locked gates.

After passing through each one, Cross felt a part of prison life, and who he'd had to become in order to survive, peel away.

When the last one led to the outside, Cross used his hand to shield his eyes against the bright morning sunrise.

"Good luck," Harold told him and closed the gate behind him.

Across the parking lot, Cross spotted Harlon getting out of a pickup truck and walking toward him. Memories of other momentous occasions when his dad had been present washed over him: Graduations from high school and college; helping him move into his first apartment; his wedding; the birth of his daughter. So many emotions filled his chest, he felt as if it might burst.

Tears streamed down Harlon's face as he reached for him and bearhugged him, lifting him off the ground.

The familiarity of his father's strong arms and smell of his aftershave unlocked the torrent of tears Cross had been holding back ever since he entered prison five years ago and put on a face of indifference to the world. His body convulsed with grief and regret.

"Let it out," Harlon whispered in his ear. "Let it all out. I've got you. I love you, son."

Eventually, Cross cried himself out and was able to draw a deep breath. Taking a step back from Harlon, he said, "Whew! I didn't see that coming."

Harlon wiped his tears with a red bandana and blew his nose. Shoving it into his back pocket, he said, "You've probably needed to do that for a while."

As they turned and headed toward the truck, Cross said, "I think you're right."

After they climbed inside and shut the doors, Harlon asked, "Where do you want to go first? Maybe get a good breakfast somewhere?"

"I want to go to Heather and Claire's graves," Cross answered. "I never had the chance to apologize to them."

“Cross, you don’t have to do it that way. I know you’ve done that in your heart a thousand times. Going to their graves will be…you know…”

“Hard,” Cross filled in the blank. “Yes, it’ll be hard, but it’s what I want to do. We can stop at a Cracker Barrel on the way there and get that good breakfast, too.”

Cranking the truck, Harlon said, “Okay, whatever you want. It’ll take a few hours to get there, so why don’t you just close your eyes and rest?”

Three hours later, they walked out of the Cracker Barrel just off Interstate 40 at the Lebanon, Tennessee, exit.

Harlon rubbed his stomach. “That was a fine meal!”

“Best I’ve had in a long time,” Cross agreed. “I don’t remember how far the cemetery is from here.”

“It’s only about thirty minutes or less.”

Thirty minutes later, Harlon eased through the entrance to Wilson County Memorial Park and wound his way through the cemetery until he pulled to a stop. Pointing, he said, “It’s just beyond that old cedar tree there. Heather’s parents bought a really nice headstone for her and Claire.”

They got out of the truck and made their way past headstones, old and new, till they stopped in front of the graves.

The engraving on the heart-shaped, oversized stone read, “Heather and Claire, mother and daughter, at rest with Jesus.”

“It made me mad they didn’t put your last name on their or mention she was your wife,” Harlon said, “but what could I do about it? They’re the ones who paid for it.”

“It’s okay, Pop. I don’t blame them. My name doesn’t deserve to be mentioned. You got your pocket knife with you?”

“Uh, sure. Why?”

“I need it for a second.”

Harlon fished his pocket knife out and handed it to him.

In a split second, Cross opened the blade and sliced open his palm.

“Cross!” Harlon yelled as he grabbed for him.

Jerking away, Cross said, “Leave me alone.” He held his hand up over the graves and let the blood drip onto them. “Blood for blood, Heather and Claire. I’ll never be able to take back what I did, but I swear on my blood I’ll never make the same mistakes I made when we were together. And I’ll carry this scar on my hand as a constant reminder of this promise, of my love for you, and of how my selfishness took your lives.”

Holding out his bandana toward Cross, Harlon said, “Here, use this.”

Cross swapped the knife for the bandana and wrapped it around his hand.

“I’m guessing you won’t let me take you to the hospital to get that sewed up.”

“You’re right. I want it to heal badly so the scar will always be visible.”

Harlon swiped a tear off his cheek. “What now?”

“There’s nothing left for me here in Lebanon. The news of what I did has ruined my reputation here, because I’ll guarantee you people haven’t forgotten, and they shouldn’t. I’m going home with you and will try and figure out how to rebuild my life.”

In a hoarse voice, Harlon told him, “I love you, son.”

“Thanks, Pop, because that’s the only anchor I have right now. It’ll have to be enough.”

CHAPTER THIRTY-FIVE

<u>*PRESENT DAY*</u>

Sitting in the parking lot of Blues Landing, Grace watches people entering the restaurant and notices most of them are half her age or younger. Even with her windows rolled up, she can hear the faint sounds of live music coming from within. "Good food and good music" are the comments she's read on Facebook about the place and the reason she suggested it as a place for Harlon to meet her.

It's been a week since Megan told her about Harlon's scandalous reputation. Since then, she's been trying to weigh out her desire to confront him about it versus if she has any right to do so.

Why is it so important for me to know anyway? We haven't known each other for fifty years. Who is he to me besides an old flame? Are we more than old friends?

She finally decided she'd talk to him about the rumors, mainly because they were the opposite of the boy she used to love, the boy who treated everyone with respect and kindness, who cared about his reputation.

If no one's confronted him about it, someone should.

She had to wait until she finished all the activities associated with Fish Fry week before she had the time and energy to meet with him, but when she called him and asked if he'd meet her tonight, he sounded both shocked and pleased.

"Well, yeah, I'd be happy to meet you there," he'd said, "but I'll be glad to come and pick you up, if you'd like."

She'd declined his offer because she didn't want to have him drive her back home if the conversation at the restaurant didn't go well.

Suddenly, she spots his truck parking underneath one of the outdoor lights. She waits for a moment to be certain it's him.

She's surprised, and maybe a little relieved, to see him dressed in something besides overalls. The blue shirt and khaki pants give him a striking appearance, and she can't help smiling.

Getting out of her car, she calls to him.

His head turns, and when he spots her, a broad smile lights up his face.

When they meet, he offers her his elbow, and in a move as natural and familiar as it was fifty years ago, she slips her arm through his without thinking.

"You look nice," he says.

"So do you." She gives a little laugh. "To tell you the truth, I wasn't sure if you wore anything but overalls anymore."

"Normally, I don't. But I remembered this was a look you used to like, so I made a run to Walmart. What was the name of that men's clothing store that used to be on the square in town?"

"Wasn't it called Five Seasons?"

"Yes, that's it. It was *the* place to go if you wanted to dress to impress."

Entering the restaurant, Harlon tells the hostess they need a table for two. Once seated, the band starts playing a high-energy version of "Footloose," led by a vivacious blonde woman belting out the song.

"Wow," Harlon says, "that gal's got a voice-and-a-half, doesn't she?"

"She does! I've never heard them before, have you?"

"Just heard *of* them," Harlon replies.

They listen appreciatively for a couple minutes until the server shows up.

"I'm sorry, honey," Grace says, "we haven't even looked at the menus. We were just enjoying the music."

"That's fine," the server tells her. "What would you like me to bring you to drink?"

"Just water for me," Harlon says.

"Me, too," Grace agrees.

The server walks away, and they turn their attention to the menus.

"It all sounds delicious," Grace comments.

"Yes, it does. I think I'm going to go Italian and try their lasagna. I haven't had good lasagna in a while."

"Megan says I make a really good homemade lasagna. I need to make it for you sometime." Grace immediately regrets not thinking before speaking.

I don't want to give him the wrong impression. Especially if I don't get the answers I want tonight and this is our last meal together.

She hears the voice of Megan in her head, chastising her to "use a filter, Mother."

"I'd love that," Harlon replies. "Homemade lasagna sounds impressive. But your mother was a good cook. I remember that. I've never tasted a pecan pie as good as hers."

Grace barely stops herself from saying she can make one just as good. Instead, she says, "It's a good recipe, for sure."

The server returns with their drinks, and they place their order.

Grace feels her heart rate increase as she works up the courage to confront Harlon about what she's heard.

As she mulls over her choice of words, Harlon says, "Can I talk to you about something?"

Relieved at having a reprieve, she gushes, "Of course you can."

Sliding his water glass in front of him, Harlon stares into it while slowly turning it in a circle with his fingertips. Without looking up, he begins, "If you haven't heard it yet, you will eventually. I've developed somewhat of a reputation around here, and the sad part, or maybe pitiful part, about that is, it's a reputation I deserve. After my wife died, I don't know what happened to me." There's a catch in his voice. "I think I lost my way, Grace. I didn't know what to do with myself, being alone. I felt empty. Cross was away…doing his own thing and not around anymore." He looks up at Grace and asks, "You know what I mean?"

Nodding, Grace says, "Yes, Harlon, I do. Being alone in an empty house can sometimes feel like a prison. At least for me it was that way. I guess some people are suited to that, but I'm not one of them."

Harlon looks back down. “Well, what I did to fill that emptiness was…uh…I started seeing other women. It kind of turned into a game for me, like going hunting used to be. I wanted to see how many I could bag. Oh my God, that sounds awful! That’s the first time I’ve said it out loud.”

Grace feels as if there’s a tornado in her brain, scattering her thoughts in a thousand directions. She can’t believe Harlon brought up the very topic she wanted to discuss with him and wonders why he’d choose to talk about something that makes him look so bad. She’s afraid to say anything for fear of saying the wrong thing.

Taking a long drink of water, Harlon sets the glass back down and pushes it aside. Looking at her, he says, “I’m ashamed and embarrassed about my behavior. It’s a disrespectful way to treat a woman, and I’m going to change. No more roaming around like a tomcat. I’m done with it. It’ll just be hard to live down my reputation.”

Without having a clue what she’s stepping into, the server shows up with a warm loaf of sourdough bread. She sets a saucer in front of each of them, pours olive oil into them, and then sprinkles Italian seasonings on top.

Grace and Harlon sit back in their chairs and take a mental breath until the server leaves.

Ignoring the bread, Harlon says, “The reason I brought this up is, I didn’t want you to hear about it and think that’s how I was going to treat you.” He leans forward and rests his forearms on the edge of the table. “I would never,” he stops and shakes his head as tears well up in his eyes, “never treat you in a dishonorable manner, Grace Charles. Never.” He dabs his eyes with a napkin and clears his throat.

There is a knowing that comes when two hearts are in tune with each other; it brings clarity to the conscience, and certainty to confusion. This is what comes to Grace and makes her heart sing. She wants to get up from her chair and hug Harlon’s neck, but she fears her knees are too weak with emotion to hold her up.

The band starts playing “Shallow,” and electric sparks run up and down Grace’s spine.

They watch and listen as a man sings Bradley Cooper's part, then the woman sings Lady Gaga's.

When the song hits the chorus, Harlon starts slicing the bread. "I bet this is the last thing you thought we'd be talking about tonight."

Reaching out, she stills his hands. "Look at me," she says.

He fastens his eyes on hers.

"I don't know what's going on between us. To use a line from a commercial only people our age will remember, 'Is it real, or is it Memorex?' I just know it feels good. It feels good to be around you, to be here with you. And I just want to enjoy it. Is that okay with you?"

Smiling, he says, "It's more than okay with me. I think, for me, it's not about 'Where is this going?' It's 'Where is it right now?', because now is all we have."

She takes his hand and touches it to her lips. "That's very well-said."

They sit like that until the end of the song, then join the other customers in applauding.

As the applause dies down, the server appears with their lasagna. Setting the plates in front of them, she says, "I've just got to say this to you two. I watched you during that song, and whatever kind of magic you have between you, that's what I hope I find one day."

Grace smiles at her.

Harlon says, "Then always keep your eyes open to possibilities, because sometimes instead of you finding love, love finds you."

"I'll remember that," the server replies.

After eating a few bites of their meal, Harlon says, "Why did you want to meet tonight? What was on your mind?"

Grace quickly casts aside the truthful answer for fear it'll break whatever spell has fallen upon them. Instead, she says, "I want to know what we're going to do about our children? How are we going to convince them they deserve to remarry?"

"I've been trying to nudge Cross in that direction until I'm just about nudged out. He gets mad whenever I bring it up."

Should I bring up what Megan heard about Cross? It sounds so unbelievable; how will Harlon react?

Harlon interrupts her thoughts. “Hey, what’s going on in that pretty head of yours? Go ahead, spit it out.”

Taking a deep breath, Grace says, “Megan heard something about Cross that really upset her. I told her to quit listening to rumors, but she won’t let it go.”

He raises his eyebrows. “What’d she hear?”

“She heard he’s a murderer and an ex-convict.”

Sadness settles on Harlon’s face as he says, “Well, there’s truth behind that rumor.”

CHAPTER THIRTY-SIX

ONE WEEK LATER

Sitting on the bow of Buck's bass boat as it bobs up and down on the dark, storm-tossed waters of Kentucky Lake, Cross switches on his LED headband flashlight.

"We should be getting close," he tells Buck. "Let's ease over to our right."

Buck shifts the idling boat motor into gear, and they ease in that direction.

Suddenly, the bow of the boat dips sharply into a swell, and water splashes onto Cross's lap.

"Sorry," Buck says. "You okay? It's so dark out here, I can't see anything. That storm really has the water stirred up."

"Yeah, I'm okay; just soaked. Maybe the storm will have made the catfish bite."

"Or it could have blown all our jugs onto the shore or downriver to who knows where."

Buck turns on a handheld spotlight and sweeps it across the water. Bugs dart in and out of the bright beam.

"There!" Cross cries out. "Straight ahead."

"I see it," Buck replies and switches off his light.

Cross keeps his light fixed on a milk jug floating in front of the boat.

As they get closer, the jug is jerked halfway underwater and starts moving away.

Excitement surges through Cross as he puts on a pair of nitrile gloves. "We've got a big one!"

Buck pivots the boat to follow the bouncing jug.

Shifting to a kneeling position, Cross leans over the side and grabs the jug. But as soon as he begins pulling, it jerks out of his grip and scoots faster across the water.

"What happened?" Buck calls out.

"I lost it! It is a *big* fish! I've got my light on it. Can you still see it?"

Bumping the throttle forward, Buck answers, "Yes, I see it. This time, you better hold on to it, or I'm going to push you overboard."

Cross laughs. "Yeah, you and what army?"

One more time, Cross leans over and snags the jug with two hands. He pulls it far enough out of the water to get ahold of the cotton fishing line and wraps it once around his hand.

"I've got it this time. Hopefully, the fish is worn out and won't give us any trouble."

Buck cuts off the boat motor and joins Cross on the bow. Switching on his own headlamp, he asks, "Have you gotten a look at it yet?"

"Not yet."

Without warning, the fishing line jerks so tight, Cross cries out in pain while at the same time losing his balance and falling overboard.

Just before he lands in the water, Buck grabs the waistband of his jeans and begins pulling. "I've got you! Just don't lose that fish!"

Overhead, a bolt of lightning streaks across the sky, followed a second later by a clap of thunder.

"That was close!" Buck says. "We need to get off the water."

Cross grits his teeth against the knifing pain of the fishing line and grabs it with his other hand. "Not before we haul this fish in! I'm telling you, Buck, this is going to be the biggest fish we've ever caught."

Buck lifts him back onto the boat. "Do I need to help pull?"

Getting to his feet, Cross sets himself and pulls with both hands, but nothing gives. "Man, it's like the line is anchored to the bottom. Put your gloves on. You're gonna have to help me."

The wind picks up and swirls around them.

"It's fixing to start pouring rain," Buck says.

"Let it rain. Come on, let's get this fish in the boat."

Buck's words are prophetic, and a driving rain begins lashing against them.

Standing side-by-side, they both grasp the fishing line and begin to pull.

"I feel like Santiago in *The Old Man and the Sea*," Cross grunts.

"I have no idea who that is, but I wish he was here helping us," Buck replies.

Little by little, they pull the fish toward the boat. The light from their headlamps gives the murky water a yellow cast, but no sign of the fish.

Suddenly, something like a dark shadow passes through the light and disappears under the boat.

"Did you see that?" Buck yells.

"Yes!" Cross yells back. "Was that our fish?"

"It had to be. But my gosh, it looked like it was six feet long."

Rain stings Cross's face as he answers. "All we need now is the theme song from *Jaws* to start playing. I don't know what we're going to do with the thing if and when we haul it into the boat."

"We're going to take pictures of ourselves with it and then turn it loose. It won't be fit to eat."

Minutes pass and muscles burn as they battle the monstrous fish until finally its mouth and head break the surface of the water.

"Look at that thing!" Buck exclaims.

"Its mouth looks three feet wide! How in the world are we going to get it on board?"

At that moment, the loud blast of an air horn pierces the night, and their entire boat is bathed in light.

"That's a damn tugboat pushing barges!" Cross shouts. "We must be lying in its path."

"How come we didn't hear its engine?"

"They must have cut it off and are just using the current until they get ready to pass under the bridge."

The light goes off, plunging everything back into darkness.

Cross pears in the direction the light came from and sees the small green and red lights on the tugboat and its barges. “We’ve still got time to get this fish in, if we hurry.”

Buck replies, “You’re going to have to put your arm in its mouth and through its gills to get a grip on it. I’ll hold on to you, and we’ll drag that joker on board.”

Without an argument, Cross pushes his hand into the fish’s mouth and threads it through its gills until nearly his whole arm is inside the fish. “Thank goodness catfish don’t have teeth like a gar.”

“You’re right about that,” Buck agrees. “You ready for me to pull?”

Biting his tongue in concentration, Cross answers, “Yes.”

As if it, too, wants to observe the conclusion to this dramatic scene, Nature shuts off the rain and wind, leaving only the turbulence in the water. Then the rumbling sound of the tug starting its engines rolls across the water.

Buck grabs Cross’s free hand and arm and pulls.

For a moment, nothing happens, and Cross feels as if he’s being drawn and quartered. Then Buck gives out a roar as he pulls harder and Cross and the fish are hauled on board.

Cross frees his arm, and he and Buck stand there, staring at the exhausted behemoth.

Panting, Cross asks, “Have you ever?”

“Never.”

From the distant tugboat comes the voice of the captain over a loudspeaker. “Congratulations, men. Now get out of my way!”

“Quick,” Buck says, “let’s take pictures.”

Once they’ve snapped the pictures, Cross removes the hook from the fish, and they roll the fish back into the lake.

Climbing into their seats on the boat, Buck fires up the engine and gives it full throttle. With a deafening roar, they race across the lake toward their tent at Piney Campground. Even though they can’t even hear themselves, they let out a victorious yell.

After they change into dry clothes, they lie down on top of their sleeping bags and turn off all the lights.

Folding his arms under the back of his head, Cross lets out a sigh. "Man, I'm not ever going to forget this night. The fish, the storm, and then the barge—there's not an ounce of adrenalin left in my body. I'm exhausted."

"I know what you mean," Buck agrees. "I'm not so sure, but I might've torn something in my shoulder when I had to pull you into the boat. In lots of ways, we're lucky the night didn't turn out badly. It's a miracle we didn't get struck by lightning or you didn't fall in and drown, or the barge didn't smash our boat to pieces. You know what I'm going to say, don't you?"

"Yeah. You're going to say it wasn't luck, that it was God who saved us."

"Exactly."

"Sometimes I wish I had a faith like yours, Buck."

"I do, too."

They fall silent, and Cross reflects on all the conversations he and his friend have had on this topic through the years.

He always makes it sound so simple, but I just can't get my head wrapped around all of it.

After a few minutes, Buck says, "You know, Betty and I were talking the other day about our business. She says we need to open up a store at the nursery, where we can sell things women like to buy for their yards, like wind chimes, all kinds of planters and decorative things. She says that's a big business nowadays."

"Do you agree with her?"

"Yeah, I think I do. How does it sound to you?"

"I like the way it sounds, but we don't have time to run it. We'd have to hire somebody."

"Oh, for sure. And I think it ought to be a woman, don't you?"

"Yes, but who would we hire?"

“I was thinking about Megan Charles. She’s got a good personality and is easy to talk to. And I think it would help her, maybe make her feel better. She’s been through a lot, you know, learning how to walk again and everything.”

Leaning up on one elbow, Cross says, “This wouldn’t have anything to do with you and Betty trying to play matchmaker, would it?”

“I told Betty that’s what you’d say. But really, it’s just an idea we had to help our business and help another person along the way. What’s wrong with that?”

Cross lays back down and mulls over Buck’s idea and tries to envision Megan interacting with customers. After a minute, he says, “I guess I can see Megan doing that and being good at it. She knows how to make sales, worked as an insurance agent, you know.”

“Really? I don’t think I knew that, or if I did, I forgot. That sort of clinches it, doesn’t it? I’m going to call Betty right now. She’ll be excited to hear.”

“Just a minute,” Cross says. “Will you let me have a couple of days to think it over? I just want to think about it.”

“Sure, sure, that’ll be fine. Just know I’m onboard with the idea, and as soon as you agree, you can go talk to Megan about it.”

“Why should I be the one? It’s your idea; you can talk to her. That is, if I come around to your way of thinking.”

“Noooo,” Buck drawls, “that would fall under your skill set. I’m not good at that. Besides, you’ve definitely had more conversations with her than I have.”

“Maybe so, but not recently. I can’t get her to reply to any of my text messages. I think she’s upset with me about something, but I don’t know what.”

CHAPTER THIRTY-SEVEN

TWO DAYS LATER

Sitting in his recliner, Cross reads the same paragraph in his copy of *Smithsonian Magazine* for the fourth time.

"This is stupid," he says aloud as he tosses the magazine on the floor.

The ancient Seth Thomas clock that belonged to his great-grandfather strikes ten times.

"And it's ten o'clock," Cross says impatiently.

He walks to the front window and peers into the night.

Just then, headlights sweep across the driveway as Harlon pulls up and parks in front of the house.

Opening the front door, Cross steps onto the porch and waits.

When Harlon gets out of his truck, he stretches his arms, then pats his stomach. He whistles the tune "Pig in a Pen" as he dances up the sidewalk.

"Well, I'm glad one of us is in a good mood," Cross says.

His voice startles Harlon, who comes to a stop. "You scared me to death. What are you doing out here?"

"Waiting on you to come home. You've been out every night this week. Don't you think you need to take a break and rest?"

Harlon brushes past him while saying, "I'm a grown-ass man, I can do what I want to."

Cross follows him inside and shuts the door.

"I'm just worried about you, Pop. I know you're enjoying Grace's company, but—"

"No, you don't know," Harlon cuts him off. "You really don't know anything. You're too young and wouldn't get it. What's gotten into you anyway? You're acting like a mother hen."

The sting of Harlon's tone and words stops Cross, and he sits back down in his recliner. Rubbing his temples, he says, "Honestly, I don't know. I'm sorry for talking to you like that. What you do is your business, and I know that. Maybe I miss us sitting here together in the evening, watching TV, or just quietly reading or napping. That sounds silly and crazy, doesn't it?"

Harlon sits on the couch and takes off his shoes. "Actually, it does make sense. You went from having a family to being thrown into prison, and then you landed here because you didn't know what else to do with yourself. Now, though, you've gotten comfortable with the rhythm and routine of our life together. But since I've started seeing Grace, things haven't been the same. You don't like the change."

He puts his hand on Cross's knee. "Here's what you need to understand: When you're young, you search for love until you find it, and you cling to it like a drowning man holding on to a life preserver. But life is cruel and can snatch that love away from you, either by death or divorce, and you realize you've had your chance at love. So, you resign yourself to living out the rest of your days alone." He pauses, then adds, "However, there are rare times when love comes looking for you when you least expect it. You question if it's possible, if it's real, if you deserve a second chance at love. That's exactly where I am with Grace; I'm trying to find the answers to those questions."

As his father is talking, Cross's chest grows tight, and his throat fills with emotion.

Harlon lets go of his knee and sits back. "Does that make sense?"

Clearing his throat, Cross answers, "It does, Pop. It makes all kinds of sense. I want you to enjoy being with Grace and whatever that becomes. I'm sorry for being small-minded and selfish. Forgive me?"

Harlon waves him off. "There's nothing to forgive."

He reaches for the *Paris Post Intelligencer* lying beside him and looks at the front page. "What's going on in Paris now that the Fish Fry has passed?"

"I need to ask you about something else, Pop."

Still looking at the newspaper, Harlon says, “Go ahead.”

“Buck pitched an idea to me the other day about expanding our business and having a store that sells yard decorations, flowerpots, and stuff like that, kind of like a gift store. What do you think about that?”

Harlon folds up the paper and lays it aside. “I think that’s a really good idea. Y’all have built a good reputation with your landscaping and are getting so busy you need to hire some seasonal help with the mowing. Adding a retail store seems like a natural expansion of what you’re doing. I bet people will really like it.”

“I’m thinking so, too,” Cross agrees. “It’s kind of scary thinking about taking out a loan to get it going, but I think it’ll turn a profit pretty quickly.”

“Don’t take out a loan; let me pay for it.”

“No, not a chance. Buck and I need to make it on our own.”

“I figured that’s what you’d say. Why is it so hard for you to let me help you?”

Smiling, Cross says, “Because I’m just like you.”

Harlon laughs. “Fair enough. I’ll say no more about it.”

“Buck said we ought to ask Megan Charles to run the store. What do you think about that?”

Harlon claps his hands together, and his eyes light up. “Man, I think that’s a great idea, don’t you?”

“Part of me does, but another part makes me hesitate. I don’t want her to get the wrong idea. She and I both know you and her mother want us to get together. I don’t want her to think this job is about me making a move on her. And besides that, she’s not speaking to me. I’ve texted her and left a voicemail, but she’s ignoring me. I’m not sure what’s going on.”

Picking the newspaper back up, Harlon says, “You need to go talk to her.”

Frowning, Cross asks, “What makes you say that? Do you know something I don’t?”

"Aw, man," Harlon says as he looks at the paper, "Jerry Flowers passed away. I hadn't heard about that. He was a year ahead of me in school. A really good guy."

Cross pitches a couch pillow at Harlon, knocking the paper out of his hand. "Quit ignoring me, and tell me what you know about Megan."

"It's not my place to tell, Cross. You just need to go talk to her."

~~~~~~~~~~

The next morning, Cross texts Buck:

YOU GO AHEAD AND GET THE MORNING STARTED WITHOUT ME. I'LL JOIN YOU A LITTLE LATER. I'M GOING TO GO TALK TO MEGAN ABOUT THE GIFT SHOP JOB.

After a moment, Buck replies:

GLAD TO HEAR IT. HOPE ALL GOES WELL.

On the drive to Megan's house, Cross plays out a dozen different ways he can begin his conversation with her and how the conversation might flow afterward.

Do I just jump right in the middle of what I want to ask her, or should I start casual and ease into it? Maybe I can gauge what kind of mood she's in and then decide what to do.

Pulling to a stop in front of her house, he wipes his sweaty palms on his jeans.

Why am I so nervous? What difference does it make what she thinks? What is she to me that I should care?

He pauses at the front door, then lifts his hand to knock, and the door suddenly opens.

Megan stands there, dressed in a rumpled T-shirt and shorts, holding a steaming cup of coffee in her hand. It's her hair that tells Cross she's not been up very long, and he now wishes he'd called first to make sure she was up.

"I saw you coming up the walk," she tells him. "What do you want?"

It's not so much her words as it is her tone that tells him she's on edge. "I want to talk to you."
~~~~~~~~~~

She focuses on her coffee and takes a sip. Without looking at him, she says, "About what?"

So much for easing into the conversation.

"To begin with, about why you won't answer my texts or phone calls. Have I done something that's upset you?"

"Wait here," she replies and closes the door.

Her action startles Cross.

She won't even let me in the house? There's definitely something going on.

She's gone long enough that he wonders if she's coming back, and for a second he thinks about walking away. But then the door opens.

Megan has put on a pair of jeans and bulky sweater over her T-shirt, and she's brushed her hair. This time, she's holding two cups of coffee. Handing one of them to him, she points toward the Adirondack chairs on the porch and says, "Let's sit out here. Black, right?"

"Huh?"

"Your coffee, you like it black, right?"

Walking across the porch, Cross sits in one of the chairs. "Uh, yeah, but how did you know?"

In a matter-of-fact tone, Megan replies, "I noticed at the Huddle House."

He tries to break the tension in the air by laughing and saying, "Boy, we really fooled Teri that time, didn't we?"

But Megan's demeanor doesn't change. Setting her cup on the arm of her chair, she looks him squarely in the face, leans forward, and says, "I heard you were a murderer and an ex-con."

Her directness and the truth in her words strap Cross in his chair as if he's a condemned man about to be electrocuted. With no options of skirting around the truth, he returns her gaze and says, "It's true."

Megan sags back in her chair and stares at her coffee cup.

Taking a deep breath, Cross says, “I used to be an alcoholic, and if it’s true that once an alcoholic, always an alcoholic, then I’m still one. I told you about my wife and daughter being killed by a drunk driver, but what I didn’t tell you was, I was that drunk driver. I was convicted of vehicular homicide, which I should have been, and sent to prison. I served five years of my sentence and was paroled out, but that’s not what was warranted. They should have kept me there for the rest of my life. That, or executed me, because that’s what I deserved.”

CHAPTER THIRTY-EIGHT

Stunned by Cross's confession, Megan doesn't reply. Despite hearing the rumor, she'd hoped it was just that—an ugly rumor and wouldn't be true, couldn't be true. And yet his explanation gave an unexpected twist to the truth.

Looking at him and his sad eyes, she senses he's still in prison, held there by guilt.

"That's not what I expected to hear," she tells him. "I mean, murder, to me, indicates intentionality, plotting how to kill someone. What happened to your wife and daughter was clearly not what you wanted to happen."

"Yeah, but they died because of my choices, my selfish choices," Cross replies.

"I understand why you'd say that, and I have no idea what it would be like to carry that kind of guilt around, but don't you think it's time to practice forgiveness with yourself?"

Bowing his head, Cross answers, "I don't deserve forgiveness."

"That's true, you don't. None of us do. That's what makes forgiveness so difficult, and so beautiful at the same time. You know, step seven of the Twelve Steps says we ask God to remove our shortcomings."

Cross's head snaps up, and his eyes are wide. "How do you know the Twelve Steps?"

"Because I'm an addict. After my accident, I got hooked on opiates. I couldn't function without them and was spiraling out of control. Now, I'm going to a Suboxone clinic, and I go to Narcotics Anonymous meetings. It's not only helped me beat my addiction, it's also helped me figure myself out. It's really saved me." She takes a deep breath and lets it out before adding, "And I can't believe I just told you that."

Running his hand over his head, Cross says, "I never would've imagined you had an addiction."

"And I never would've imagined you were an alcoholic and responsible for your wife and daughter's deaths."

They sit there, minds spinning, staring at their newly discovered truths.

Finally, Cross speaks up. "You know, here's a funny thing: When I attend my A.A. meetings, I'm completely honest and transparent about myself, but any other time I'm guarded and avoid sharing the truth. Why is that?"

Shaking her head, Megan answers, "Me, too. That's just one reason I enjoy the meetings, because pretending and hiding the truth is exhausting."

"Isn't it, though? Having to tiptoe around the truth and trying to remember what story you told this person or half-truth you told that person. Why do we do that?"

"I think it's because we're afraid of being judged. In Twelve Step meetings, there's no judgment; only acceptance of a person's truth and where they currently are in their journey. We're all there to encourage each other and build each other up, like fellow travelers should be with each other."

Tapping the arm of his chair with his finger, Cross says, "What if churches were more like that? I bet you couldn't keep people away."

"Think what the world would be like if everyone was that way."

Suddenly, a thought dawns on Megan. Snapping her fingers, she says, "That's why you turned down a beer back when you and Buck were working on our yard, isn't it? Gosh, I never thought about that. I'm so sorry I tempted you."

"Hey, don't worry about that," Cross replies. "It wasn't a big deal at all. I never think about drinking anymore. I think I'm past all that. I'm curious about something, though. You take Suboxone every day for your addiction, right?"

She nods.

"Then how can you say you're clean and sober?"

"I know there are people who judge those of us who take Suboxone, but I look at it the same way a diabetic looks at their insulin. It's a maintenance medication for me. As long as I take it, I'll be less likely to use an opiate. It doesn't make me high; I just feel normal."

"If it doesn't make you high, then why do people abuse it and buy and sell it on the streets?"

Megan chuckles. "People abuse it because that's what addicts do. Think about all the stupid things you've heard about people doing in an attempt to get high. Some people sell their Suboxone because they're not interested in living a sober life. They sell it so they can buy pills."

"That makes a lot of sense," Cross replies. "I've just never known anyone personally who takes Suboxone and explained it the way you have. Of course, there're going to be people who are hard core A.A. and will never agree with taking a drug to stay sober."

"I know that, and that's okay. Everyone's entitled to their opinion. Focusing on me and my sobriety is a full-time job. I don't have time to worry about proving myself to others."

Without warning, the front door opens, and Grace walks onto the porch. Upon seeing Cross, she pulls together the front of her housecoat and cinches the belt. Fussing with her hair that's yet to be brushed, she says, "Excuse me, I didn't know we had company. Good morning, Cross."

"Good morning."

Megan sees worry at the edges of her mother's eyes. "What's wrong, Mother?"

"Will you call my phone for me? I can't find it anywhere."

"I don't have my phone out here." Looking at Cross, Megan says, "Excuse me while I go inside."

"Sure, sure, that's fine," he replies. "I can run along if I need to."

"No, stay. I'll be right back."

Megan escorts her mother back inside.

"I'm sorry I bothered you," Grace whispers. "What's he doing here so early in the morning? Is anything wrong?"

“Everything’s fine. I’ll tell you all about it later.”

Walking into the kitchen with Grace trailing behind her, Megan picks up her mother’s phone off the stove. Handing it to her, she says, “Here you go. I saw it when I was making coffee this morning.”

Grace kisses her on the cheek. “Thank you! I thought I’d already looked in here.” She opens her phone and punches in a number. Putting the phone to her ear, she says, “This is Grace Charles. Can I get in to see Dr. Norman this morning? Yes, yes, I can. I’ll hurry and get dressed and be right there.”

Frowning, Megan says, “What’s wrong? Are you sick? You didn’t tell me you were sick.”

“This nagging pain in my back kept me awake all night last night. I think I may have a kidney infection or something. It’s nothing big. Don’t worry.”

“You want me to go with you?”

“Of course not. You go back out on the porch with Cross.” As she heads out of the kitchen, she adds, “Ask him to marry you.”

“Mother!” Megan exclaims.

When she returns to the porch, Cross asks, “Is everything all right?”

“Yes. Just Mother and her phone. At least once a day, she can’t find it. The other thing, though, is, she’s not feeling very well and going to see the doctor this morning. She thinks she may have a kidney infection.”

With a voice of concern, Cross says, “I hope she’ll be okay.”

“She’ll be fine. They’ll just give her an antibiotic, which should clear it up pretty quick.”

Crossing his legs, he asks, “So, do you have any more questions about what we were talking about before? Now that the cork’s been pulled out of that bottle, I want to be sure everything’s clear in your mind about my past.”

Megan holds her hand on her heart and says, “I’m touched and honored you were willing to be so transparent with me. And I apologize for the tone I used in bringing the subject up. I guess I felt like I’d been lied to or deceived by you in the sense that you were hiding things from me, which doesn’t make any sense, because it’s not like we’re in a relationship or something and you owe me the truth. So, I’m sorry if I offended you.”

“No, no, there’s no need for you to apologize. You’ve helped me see I need to be more willing to be transparent with people, that people all around us are walking around, carrying some type of secret sorrow or regret, when what they really want to do is unburden themselves of it, like taking off a heavy backpack, and tell it to someone. Because even though, like you said, you and I aren’t in a relationship, I feel closer to you because we shared with each other.”

A warm feeling spreads through Megan’s body as she listens to him, but it scares her. So, she tries to shift the conversation in a different direction. “Why did you come here this morning? I don’t think it was to talk about all this stuff.”

He laughs. “You’re right. I came here to talk to you about a plan Buck and I have.”

He explains to her their idea behind the gift shop, then says, “And we wondered if you’d like a job running the store.”

Megan shakes her head in surprise. “Really? You want me to manage it? Why me?”

“I knew you’d wonder about that. And honestly, that’s what made me reluctant to ask you. I don’t want you to get the wrong idea that this is some sort of way for you and me to be thrown together where we’d fall in love and get married, like both our parents want us to.”

Laughing, she replies, “Well, you’ve got nothing to be worried about there. I’m not crossing that bridge again. I’ve accepted the truth that I’m not relationship material.”

“Whew, I’m glad to hear that, because I’m not interested either. I blew my chance at marriage and don’t deserve a second chance. So, what do you think? You want the job? Do you need to think about it?”

“I want it! It’ll be the perfect opportunity for me to get my feet wet working again and see how my body holds up. My mind’s already racing, thinking of different items to sell. I’ll even let Mother help me pick things out. if that’s okay with you.”

Shrugging his shoulders, Cross says, “That’s up to you. You run it however you choose to. We’ll give you a budget to work with. But we need to talk about how much you want to be paid. There’s no way we can compete with how much you used to make.”

Megan thinks for a moment, then says, “I’ll tell you what, you all pay me whatever you think you can to get things started, and if the business is successful, we can revisit that later. I trust you to be fair with me.”

He raises his eyebrows. “Are you sure about that?”

“Absolutely.”

Reaching his hand toward her, he says, “Then let’s shake on it.”

Megan takes his hand and squeezes it.

For a moment they stare at each other, then they quickly pull their hands away.

CHAPTER THIRTY-NINE

THREE WEEKS LATER

Using a box cutter, Megan opens yet another box to see what new item has arrived for the store she's been stocking for Cross and Buck. She lifts out a two-foot tall flower pot painted with a Mayan motif.

"Oh, yes!" she exclaims, with a smile. "Just what I hoped for!"

The tinkling sound of the tiny wind chime she placed on the door to the store tells her someone has just entered. Setting the pot aside, she goes to greet them.

As she turns the corner, she sees Buck and Betty gazing around the store. "Hey, you two," she says.

"Megan," Betty says, "you have done an amazing job with this place, and in such a short period of time. I just love it!"

Megan beams. "I've loved doing it. I just hope we can draw customers in, and they'll love it, too."

Buck comments, "Well, I think what's going to happen is, we're going to wish we'd done this a long time ago. I bet keeping the store stocked will be your biggest problem."

"I hope so." She looks toward the front door. "I haven't seen much of Cross lately. I guess he's extra busy with the landscaping side of things. But I've been wondering if something's going on with him I don't know about. When I send him a text with questions about the store, he always tells me to check with you, Buck." Focusing her attention on Buck, she asks, "Is he unhappy with how I'm setting up the store?"

"Aw, heck no!" Buck answers. "He loves it."

"How would he know? He's never even seen it."

"He comes in after work some days, then he'll tell me about it the next day."

Betty turns to him and says, "Do you know how silly that sounds? What are you trying to hide? I can tell when you're lying."

Suddenly, a thought strikes Megan. "Please don't tell me he's started drinking again."

"No, no, no," Buck tells her. "It's not that, not at all." He glances at Betty.

Poking him with her finger, Betty says, "Spit it out. What's going on?"

Sighing, he says, "Sometimes Cross overthinks stuff and gets lost in his head."

"What in the world is that supposed to mean?" Betty asks.

"Look, you two, I'm not supposed to tell," Buck explains. "Megan, you need to ask him yourself."

"How am I supposed to do that when I never see him and he won't respond to my texts or phone calls?"

"I'll tell him about this conversation and for him to get his head out of his ass and come and talk to you about it."

~~~~~~~~~~

For the rest of the day, Megan tries to focus only on the store instead of chasing theories about what's going on with Cross, but it's hard not to think about him.

Is it me? Is it him? Is it Harlon? Is it my mother? Has she said something I don't know about? Why is it such a big secret, Buck wouldn't tell me?

She pulls up the memory of the last time they talked when they were on her front porch, being open and vulnerable and how much she enjoyed it.

Maybe that's it. Maybe he feels I'm a threat to his sobriety. Maybe he disagrees with my taking Suboxone.

Chewing on her bottom lip, she says, "It's really a waste of time to wonder. I'll just wait until he stops by."

"Until who stops by?" Cross's voice startles her, and she looks at him in surprise.
~~~~~~~~~~

"How long have you been standing there? And how did you come through the door without me hearing you?" She tries to read his expression but can't decide what kind of mood he's in.

"I've only been here for a moment, and the wind chime did sound when I came in. You must have been so lost in thought, you didn't hear it. But I'm here to try and help you with that."

Folding himself up, he sits cross-legged on the floor and pats the floor in front of him. "Have a seat, and let's talk."

Megan sits facing him, with her legs in front of her. Pointing at his legs, she says, "I'm still not able to bend my legs like that yet."

He makes a move to get up. "I'm sorry. You want me to find us some chairs?"

She motions for him to sit back down. "No, no. This is fine."

Despite her efforts to stay calm, her heart is in her throat.

Cross begins, "You scare me, Megan."

She opens her mouth to reply, but he stops her.

"Just let me say what I need to say, then I'll listen to you."

Megan nods.

"Since my wife and daughter died, I've never even had a conversation with another woman, unless it was related to landscaping their yard. I'd made up my mind that was the best way to make certain I wouldn't fall in love with someone and risk hurting them. Don't misunderstand me. I'm not saying I'm falling in love with you. I just enjoy being around you too much. A few weeks ago, when we were on your front porch and opened up to each other, it stirred feelings I haven't had in a long time, the kinds of feelings you have when you get to know who someone is behind the mask they wear. You feel closer to them and want to spend more time with them and get to know them even better. That's what scares me. And I haven't figured out what to do about it. That's why I've been avoiding you."

He takes a big breath and blows it out. "Whew! That was a mouthful. Now, it's your turn."

“That’s a lot to digest,” Megan replies. “I guess the first thing I’ll say is, thank you for finally telling me. Learning the truth is always better than having your head filled with questions and theories that just go ’round and ’round. It bothered me that you were avoiding me, and I had to ask myself why it bothered me. Why should I care one way or the other? The answer I found is, I’ve come to enjoy being around you. At first I didn’t like you at all—you and your bluegrass music.”

They both laugh.

“After that night you’re talking about, I felt like we’d become friends, which made me realize I’ve not made any friends since moving here. And we both know living isolated is a threat to sobriety. My question to you is, can’t we just be friends? Can’t a man and woman be friends without it meaning they’re going to get married or live together? We’ve both made clear to each other our position on ever getting married again, so that’s our boundary. I’ll maintain my boundary, and you’ll do the same with yours. Won’t that make it safe to be friends?”

Rubbing his hand across his scalp, Cross answers, “That makes a lot of sense. But what if one of us starts wanting more out of our friendship? You know, wants it to move to the next level?”

“Well, I say they need to be honest and let it be known. Can we agree to do that?”

Smiling, he replies, “Honesty—that’s a novel idea, isn’t it? I agree. Now, let me help you stand up.”

After standing her up, he tells her goodbye.

Watching him leave the store, Megan gets a notification of a message on her phone. Pulling it out of her back pocket, she unlocks it and opens the message.

HEY THERE, MEGAN. THIS IS MAX. I KNOW I'M THE LAST PERSON IN THE WORLD YOU WANT TO HEAR FROM, AND YOU MIGHT DELETE THIS MESSAGE BEFORE YOU READ ALL OF IT. BUT PLEASE HEAR ME OUT. I DON'T BLAME YOU FOR HATING ME. WHAT I DID IN RUNNING OUT ON YOU WAS SHAMEFUL, AND I'VE HATED MYSELF FOR DOING IT. WHAT I WANT IS A SECOND CHANCE, A CHANCE TO MAKE IT UP TO YOU. I CAN BE A BETTER HUSBAND. I WILL BE A BETTER HUSBAND, IF YOU'LL LET ME TRY. EVEN THOUGH I DID WHAT I DID, I'VE NEVER STOPPED LOVING YOU. PLEASE GIVE ME A CALL AND LET'S TALK.

CHAPTER FORTY

The next morning, Harlon rises from bed and shuffles into the kitchen to start the coffee brewing. Yawning and stretching, he looks out the window over the sink and sees his Harley-Davidson motorcycle sitting just how he left it last night after washing and waxing it. The morning sun glances off its chrome features, making them look ablaze.

He smiles with satisfaction.

At the sound of Cross entering the kitchen, he turns to face him. "Morning."

"Morning. You're up kinda early. You working with me and Buck today?"

Shaking his head, Harlon answers, "Nope, not today. Got more important things to do."

Cross looks past him and spies the motorcycle. "You brought Black Betty out of mothballs? What's the occasion?"

"I'm picking up Grace, and we're going to ride The Trace at Land Between the Lakes. Might eat up there at Patti's Eighteen-eighties Settlement in Grand Rivers, get me one of those three-inch pork chops." He smacks his lips.

"That sounds like fun. It's been some years since you've ridden, hasn't it?"

"I probably haven't ridden it since you went to prison. Just sort of lost interest in it, and other things, too, while you were there."

"Since it's been a while, don't you think you need to ease back into it? Take some short practice runs before you take such a long trip?"

Laughing, Harlon says, "You think your old man's over the hill, don't you? You don't have to mother me like I live in a nursing home or something. I can take care of myself."

Cross holds up his hands. "Okay, okay."

As Harlon pours a cup of coffee, Cross says, "You'll be interested in knowing Megan and I had a good talk yesterday and figured some things out between us. We agreed to be friends and keep it there, not let it get complicated by moving into complicated areas. I feel a lot better about it since we talked."

"I'm glad to hear it. You guys can be good for each other, don't you think? You've both got a complicated history and are still trying to deal with past mistakes. It'll be good for both of you to have someone you can talk to who'll understand where you're coming from. That's something everybody needs."

"Well, listen at you, Dr. Phil, handing out sage advice on relationships."

"Pshaw! I wouldn't give you two cents for anything Dr. Phil says. I got more sense and more experience than he does." Moving toward the pantry, he takes out a box of Raisin Bran and carries it to the counter.

"Hey," Cross says, "you care if I make you and Grace some sandwiches for your trip? You can carry them in your saddlebags."

As he pours cereal into a bowl, Harlon answers, "That'd be really nice. Just do ham and cheese, with mustard and mayo on mine, and mayo only on Grace's."

"How do you know she just wants mayo?"

"She was always that way."

"How can you remember what a person liked on their sandwich fifty years ago, but you can't remember to take your medicine every day?"

Tapping the side of his head with his finger, Harlon says, "You live long enough, you'll understand, son…you'll understand."

~~~~~~~~~~

An hour later, Harlon rolls to a stop in front of Grace's house and takes off his helmet. He halfway expected her to be on the porch waiting, but since she's not, he walks to the front door and knocks twice.
~~~~~~~~~~

Inside, there's a small cry of alarm, followed by hurried footsteps. Concerned something's wrong, he reaches for the door knob and is about to go inside when it's jerked out of his hand.

Grace stands there, with a look of alarm on her face. "Oh, I'm sorry, Harlon! I started playing a game on my phone and completely lost track of time." Putting her hands on her head, she exclaims, "Don't look at my hair! I haven't done a thing with it yet. And I haven't put on any makeup either. I'm sorry. I'll hurry and be right out."

"Whoa, whoa there," Harlon says. "It's okay. We're not on anybody's clock but our own. I'm going to suggest you leave your hair alone. We'll both be wearing helmets, and it'll make a mess out of whatever you're planning to do to it, so just don't worry about it." Smiling, he adds, "And I think you look great."

"Helmets? We're wearing helmets? You said you had a surprise for me, but I didn't think we'd need helmets."

He backs out of the way and points to the motorcycle. "That's our chariot for today."

Throwing her arms around him, she says, "How exciting! I haven't ridden a motorcycle since…oh my, since you and I rode in high school. This is going to be fun! I'll be right back." She turns and heads back inside.

As he watches her retreat, Megan appears in an opening, scratching her head. "What's all the commotion around here?" When she turns and sees him, she swears and darts back to wherever she came from. He hears her yell, "Why didn't you tell me we had company, Mother?!"

Chuckling, Harlon pulls the door shut.

A little bit later, Grace comes bustling out the door, wearing a bright red sweatshirt with cardinals printed on the front.

Pointing at her, he says, "I love cardinals. They're so commonplace around here, I think we take their beauty for granted."

Smiling, Grace says, "They're my favorite." Reaching her hand toward his, she says, "Come show me this shiny motorcycle you're driving."

Harlon takes her hand, and they walk down the sidewalk together. "I call her Black Betty, after that song by Ram Jam. I used to love that song."

"I don't think I've ever heard it. Is it a new song?"

"No, it came out in nineteen seventy-seven, I think."

Pulling her hand free, Grace slowly circles the Harley. "It's exquisite, Harlon."

"Thank you. Hey, I hope I didn't embarrass Megan when you went inside to change. She wasn't quite dressed when I saw her."

"Don't worry about it. I don't know what's going on with her anyway. When she came home from work yesterday, she didn't eat supper or take a shower. Just went straight to her room and shut the door."

"Is she sick?"

"Maybe in the head. But no, if she'd been sick, she'd have said something or taken some medicine. Something's going on, but I've learned there's no point in trying to push her, because the harder I push, the tighter she shuts down."

Laughing, Harlon says, "My Cross is exactly the same way. He said he and Megan had a good talk yesterday and came to an understanding between them, so I don't think what's going on with her has anything to do with work."

Cocking her head, Grace asks, "So, what's this understanding they've come to?"

"They're going to be friends and just keep it that way, with no plans to take things more seriously." He rolls his eyes. "Whatever that's supposed to mean. I don't know why they won't relax and just let nature take its course, let whatever happens happen, whether that means just being friends or letting it become more than that."

"I don't either," Grace agrees. Pointing to the motorcycle, she says, "So, where's Black Betty taking us?"

"I thought we'd ride up The Trace through LBL. It's a real pretty drive." Reaching in one of the saddlebags, he pulls something out. "I brought you a leather jacket so you won't get cold. It may be a little big, but that won't matter."

Grace slips it on and has to push the sleeves up to find her hands so she can zip it. She laughs. “A perfect fit.”

In an exaggerated tone, Harlon says, “And to complete your ensemble, Madam, we have this beautiful hat for you to wear.” He lifts the extra helmet resting on the sissy bar of the rear seat and carefully lowers it onto Grace’s head. “How does it feel?”

“It feels okay, but I can barely hear you.”

He pulls on his helmet and says, “They’re equipped with a microphone and internal headset.”

“Oh, wow, how nice! I love it. Let’s go!”

After helping her onto the motorcycle, he gets onboard, turns the key to start it, and the engine growls.

Laughing, Grace says, “Ooo, I like the way that vibrating feels. You might not get me off here.”

“You can lean back against your backrest while we ride, or you can—”

Before he can finish, Grace wraps her arms around him and rests her body against his. “Or I can do this.”

Her move makes him smile. “If you ride like that, you may not get *me* off here.”

They laugh together, producing the kind of song that has no words or tune but still has the power to lift the soul.

Easing down the driveway, Harlon then follows the road that intersects with Highway 79. Once there, he turns north and opens the throttle of his Harley. Both of them are pushed back by the G-force, and Grace squeals with delight.

“Oh, Harlon, this is so much fun!”

“Of all the things I’ve forgotten through the years,” he tells her, “I’ve *never* forgotten the sound of your voice. It always reminded me of what creek water running over rocks sounds like: light and clear and bright. I’m glad it still sounds the same.”

“And I’ve never forgotten how much you like to tease and laugh and tell stories. I used to love listening to you talk.”

As they cross the Tennessee River Bridge, he says, "Look how blue the sky and lake are. I don't think there's a cloud in the sky."

"It's a perfect day already, and it's just started," Grace responds.

A few miles later, Harlon turns off the highway and onto the road that goes past Piney Campground and on toward the Southern Welcome Center of LBL. As it twists and turns underneath the canopy of trees, he gently leans the Harley left, then right to accommodate the curves.

Suddenly, an open meadow appears on the right.

Patting him rapidly on the shoulder, Grace exclaims, "Oh, Harlon, look! Can we stop?"

A quick glance in his mirror assures him no one's behind him, so he squeezes the brake lever and stops in the middle of the road.

"Aren't they beautiful?" Grace whispers.

In the middle of the meadow is a doe with her twin fawns. She looks at Grace and Harlon and twitches her ears, while the fawns graze beside her.

A movement along the tree line catches Harlon's attention. "Look to the right, where the trees start."

"I don't see anything," Grace replies.

"Keep watching."

After a moment, another doe eases into the meadow, then another, and another, until finally there's a herd of fifteen grazing peacefully. Occasionally, one stops and looks toward the tourists on the road, but none of them appears afraid.

"It's too beautiful for words," Grace whispers.

"See what you've missed by moving away from here? Deer have become very plentiful around here since when we were kids."

"You don't have to rub it in. I've missed a lot more than seeing deer."

"Seen enough? Ready to move along?"

"Yeah, go ahead."

An hour later, Harlon pulls off the road and into a picnic area at Cedar Pond. Turning off the engine, he says, "Let's stretch our legs a little."

"Well, you may have to help me off, or I'm liable to fall."

With lots of grunting and near falls, coupled with laughs at themselves, they manage to disembark and stand beside the motorcycle, where they take off their helmets.

"That was harder than I expected," Harlon says.

"Uh, for sure. We're a few years older than the last time we rode together."

"I've got some drinks. You want something?"

"Sure, anything'll be fine."

From the compact cooler in a saddlebag, he pulls out a couple of Cokes and hands her one.

They walk to the bank of the pond, whose surface is as flat as a mirror.

Harlon turns to say something to her but catches her wiping tears from her cheeks. "Grace? Are you okay?"

"I'm just a crybaby. Everything is so perfect, I don't want it to ever end, but I know it's going to."

He looks at her curiously. "What do you mean? I can tell there's more behind this than just a fun motorcycle ride."

She sighs. "Oh, Harlon, I don't want to ruin the day. Please don't press me about it."

Ignoring her plea, he asks, "Is Megan okay?"

"Yes, yes, she's fine. It has nothing to do with her. She doesn't know anything about it yet."

He gently tilts her face toward his, but she averts her eyes. "Grace, let's not play games. Tell me what's going on."

Putting her hand on his wrist, she says, "I've got cancer, Harlon. Pancreatic cancer, and the prognosis isn't good."

CHAPTER FORTY-ONE

That same morning, Megan looks through the window and watches her mother ride off with Harlon on his motorcycle.

Shaking her head, she mutters, "What do they think they are, a couple of teenagers? Two seventy-year-olds on a motorcycle sounds like a recipe for disaster. But what do I know?"

Heading back to her bedroom, her mind immediately picks up the thread of thoughts that kept her awake most of the night—Max! She fishes her phone out from the tangle of bedcovers and opens it to the place where it's stayed since receiving his message. She rereads his text for the umpteenth time and then stares at the pulsing cursor begging for a reply.

What should I do? What's the right thing? What do I really want to do?

The unanswered questions circle her like witches around a bubbling cauldron, since giving a wrong answer would be tantamount to taking a fatal potion.

She busies herself getting ready to go to work at the nursery, then goes to the kitchen to get some breakfast. In her mind, she ticks off all her options, but none strikes her. Suddenly, the memory of the Huddle House's pecan waffles comes to her, making her mouth water.

Who's to say I can't go there by myself without Mother?

So, she gets in her car and heads that way.

Inside, she spots Betty, Buck's wife, sitting at a table by herself.

Walking to her, she asks, "Hey, Betty, are you with someone, or waiting for someone?"

Betty looks up in surprise, then smiles warmly. "No, no, not at all. Please join me. This is me giving myself a treat and having someone cook for me and clean up their own mess."

Laughing, Megan sits down. "I just thought about their waffles this morning and couldn't resist coming and getting an order. It's good to see you."

"It's good to see you, too, Megan."

A waitress appears, and Megan orders the pecan waffles with whipped cream and strawberries on top and sausage on the side, plus coffee to drink.

As the waitress walks off, Betty says, "How do you stay so slim and eat like that?"

"Trust me, if I ate like that all the time, I'd be as big as a cow. Like you, I'm just giving myself a treat and am going to eat without feeling guilty about how unhealthy it is. I'm going to enjoy every bite."

"Yes! Preach on, girl! I'm right there with you. I'm through chasing that so-called girlish figure, whatever the heck that is. Especially since I only have one leg to show."

Megan is stunned. "What?"

"I only have one leg. Have you not noticed?" Sticking one leg out from under the table, Betty pulls up the pant leg and reveals an artificial foot attached to what looks like a stainless steel rod. "It goes up to just below my knee. Lost it in a car wreck when I was fifteen."

"I'm floored," Megan exclaims. "I had no idea. I can't believe I haven't noticed. I guess that indicates how well you've adapted. It feels like I should apologize for being so oblivious, or maybe so self-absorbed. The truth is, I don't know you very well at all, and that's my fault for not trying to get to know you. This past year, I've been so focused on me and getting my health back, I've kind of been living in a cave. And that's not a healthy way to live. I'm going to start trying to do better."

She leans back as the waitress appears with her food and sets it in front of her.

Betty tells her to dig in while she finishes her ham and biscuit.

For a few moments, they eat in silence, then Betty says, “I only know you by looking through the eyes of Buck and what he tells me about you. What I’m most curious to know about you is, how do you feel about Cross?”

The question catches Megan just as she’s swallowing a bite of sausage. It catches in her throat, and she nearly chokes. Reaching for her coffee, she takes a swallow to try and wash it down.

“You okay?” Betty asks. “Need a pat on the back?”

Taking a deep breath, Megan answers, “No, I’ll be all right. You just caught me off guard with your question.”

“Well, we could talk about your favorite color, or the kind of music you like, or your favorite recipe, but I think we should talk about things that really matter to us, and Cross matters to me. He and Buck are best friends, and what happens to one affects the other. That’s why I want to know how you feel about Cross.”

“I think he’s a really nice guy, and I enjoy being around him. He’s lived with a lot of pain and been through things I can’t even imagine. He loves Buck, and he loves his father.”

“Wait,” Betty interrupts her, “I didn’t ask you to tell me about Cross; I already know him. I want you to tell me about you.”

Megan feels her face growing warm and knows she’s blushing.

Pointing at her, Betty says, “What does that mean, the fact that you’re blushing?”

The question tugs on one of the strings of Megan’s heart, encouraging her to open up and be honest with this woman she doesn’t really know. But fear and caution warn her to be careful of getting hurt, of being embarrassed, of not being understood. Then she remembers someone in group saying one time, “Transparency in recovery can transform your life, if you let it.”

Resting her fork on her plate, she looks at Betty and says, “Okay, I’m going to be direct with you, because I need somebody’s help in figuring something out. First of all, I like Cross. I didn’t at first, but he’s kind of grown on me. We’ve talked about it and agreed we’d like to be friends and do things together. It’s what we’re both comfortable with right now. But here’s where things get complicated. I got a text last night from my ex-husband, apologizing for deserting me and basically asking for another chance. He said he’s grown a lot and believes we should try again.”

Pushing her own plate out of the way, Betty rests her elbows on the table. “Wow, what did you tell him?”

“That’s just it. I haven’t replied.”

“You haven’t replied, and it’s been nearly twelve hours? What’s that about?”

“That’s what I need you to help me figure out. It doesn’t make sense, does it? All I’ve got to do is say either yes or no. Simple. But I’ve gotten used to my single life and enjoy the freedom it gives me. Plus, I’ve come to believe I’m too narcissistic to be in a relationship. I’m not good relationship material. I mean, there was a time when things with me and Max were good, like in the first years we were together. It just didn’t last.”

“Is that all?” Betty asks. “Is that all that makes this complicated for you?”

“Well, there is Cross. I don’t want to give up that budding friendship. I don’t know how he’d feel about us if I went back to Max and tried to work things out. But why should I care what he thinks one way or the other?”

“Well, first, if you were a narcissist, Cross and Buck wouldn’t have asked you to set up and run a store for them. They’re both pretty sharp when it comes to sizing people up. Maybe you tell yourself that so you’ll have an excuse for not dealing with having a relationship and risking getting hurt. I mean, relationships are risky things, complicated things, and take a lot of work and effort. Lord knows being married to Buck is like that. He says things without thinking, and they sometimes hurt.”

“Sounds like my mother,” Megan comments.

"I also think you're curious to see where things go with you and Cross," Betty continues. "I don't know how much you know about him, but he has a history."

"He's told me about the wreck, him being drunk and his wife and daughter getting killed, and about going to prison."

Betty looks surprised. "Really? He told you that story? That's a surprise, because he doesn't talk about it with just anybody. All of that changed Cross, made him more closed off and more serious about everything. He used to be outgoing and funny."

"That's interesting. I used to be the same way, but now I'm more cautious and concerned because of what people might say about me if they saw what my leg looked like under my pants." As soon as she says the words, she claps her hand over her mouth. "Oh my God, Betty, I'm so sorry. I shouldn't have said that. I mean, you—"

Betty stops her. "It's okay, I know you didn't mean anything by it, and trust me, I know exactly how you feel about how you might look to others."

"I feel really small right now," Megan tells her. "Small and petty. I've got no right to complain about my situation. At least I didn't lose my leg in my accident. I need to get over it and quit feeling sorry for myself and worrying about what other people think."

"You'll be lots happier if you can do that. It took me a while to get there, being in high school when I lost mine made it harder. You know, those years of insecurity and trying to fit in. It was a real struggle. I'm so glad I'm not back there anymore."

"Oh my, me, too! Stressing if my hair wasn't perfect, or if I had a pimple on my face, or if my clothes didn't look right. It was exhausting!"

They both laugh.

Their waitress appears, carrying a coffee pot, and points at Megan's plate. "Was there something wrong with your food? You only ate a few bites."

"No, no, it's fine," Megan replies. "We just got involved in a deep conversation, and I suddenly wasn't hungry anymore."

"Y'all want me to warm your coffee up?"

"Yes, that'd be nice," Betty says as she pushes her cup toward the waitress.

Once they're alone again, they take a few sips of coffee.

Then Betty says, "I'll tell you this: I don't know a better man than Cross Daniels, even if I include my Buck. The question for you to answer is if you think your ex and you deserve a second chance, or maybe if you owe him a second chance. You might talk to Cross about it and see what he thinks."

"Really?"

"You said you're friends, didn't you? Isn't that what friends do, talk to each other about their problems?"

Letting out a big sigh, Megan says, "I'm so glad you were here this morning and we had time to talk. This has been so helpful. And I'm glad I've gotten to know you better. We need to do it again sometime."

"You got anything planned this Saturday?"

"Saturday? Uh, no, not that I can think of. It'll probably be the last Saturday that way, because the grand opening of the store is the next Saturday, and I expect weekends will be the busiest time at the store."

"Buck and I are taking our pontoon boat out on the lake. Why don't you and Cross join us? We'll just relax and have some fun."

"Oh, that sounds wonderful! I'd love to! And I'm going to let Max know something today."

"What are you going to tell him?"

"I'm not sure. But I'm going to talk to Cross about it first."

CHAPTER FORTY-TWO

Late that afternoon, Harlon sits with bowed head on his porch swing as still as a statue, his feet anchored to the floor. Grace's news has saturated him with a heaviness that makes it impossible to think or move.

A blue-tailed skink suddenly appears from between two planks, darts across Harlon's field of vision, and disappears through a crack.

Suddenly, Roxie, who's lying in front of him, raises her head and looks at the driveway. Her ears perk up, and her tail swishes the porch like a broom.

A moment later, the sound of an approaching vehicle pulls Harlon far enough out of his sorrow to look and see who's coming.

At the same time, Roxie bounds off the porch to meet Cross as his truck drives into view.

Harlon watches as his son pulls to a stop and cuts off the engine.

Roxie barks and turns circles beside the driver's door.

When Cross exits, he kneels and greets her, then they head to the house.

"Hey there, Pop, I can't wait to hear about your motorcycle trip with Grace. Did y'all have fun?"

The thought of putting into words what Grace told him that day proves too much for Harlon, and he begins to weep.

Cross rushes across the porch. "Pop, what's the matter?! What's happened?" Squatting in front of him, he says, "Talk to me, Pop."

Harlon wipes his face on his sleeve and says, "If I tell you, you have to swear you'll not tell a soul, because that's the way she wants it for now."

"Who?"

"Grace."

"Okay, I swear I won't tell."

“Grace has cancer.” In Harlon’s ears, the three words sound foreign and disconnected from what’s real.

“No, Pop!” Cross exclaims. “Please tell me it’s not true.”

Heaving a sigh, Harlon says, “It’s pancreatic cancer, and there’s nothing that can be done for her except help manage the pain.”

Cross takes a seat beside him. “I don’t understand. Megan and I talked today, and she didn’t say a word about it.”

“Grace hasn’t told her yet. That’s why you can’t tell anybody.”

“She hasn’t told her?! Why not?”

“What she told me is, Megan’s had such a difficult year and now is doing better than ever, both physically and mentally, so Grace doesn’t want to do anything that’ll send her in a tailspin. I disagree with the decision and told her so, but this is the way she wants things for now. She says she knows she’ll eventually have to tell her, but not now.”

Roxie approaches them and rests her head between them.

Petting her, Harlon says, “I think this is the smartest dog I’ve ever known. She can tell we’re upset. A while ago, she knew you were coming before you could be seen; must’ve heard your truck, I guess.”

Roxie lifts a front leg and sets her paw on Cross’s knee.

Cross responds by scratching her ear. Then he puts his arm around Harlon’s shoulders.

For several moments, they sit in silence.

Finally, Cross says, “I’m so sorry, Pop. I know this is the last thing you wanted to hear.”

Taking a deep breath and blowing it out, Harlon replies, “It’s just another example of how unfair life can be. Sometimes, it feels like that’s all I’ve had for the past several years, one blow after another of life trying to knock me to my knees. Your mother, then the wreck and Heather and Claire dying, your trial and conviction, then you in prison, and now this. My heart is so battered and worn, I just feel like giving up. The battle is too much; I don’t want to deal with it. The mistake I made was letting myself start caring for Grace. I was beginning to think maybe I deserved a second chance at love. I should have just kept living my life of decadence.”

“Listen, Pop,” Cross retorts, “you can’t think that way. Grace is going to need you to be there for her. She loves you and trusts you.”

“What makes you say that?”

“Because she shared with you the most intimate thing in her life right now, shared it with you before she told her own daughter. She and Megan are very close. This news is going to devastate her.”

“Here’s the thing,” Harlon begins, “I don’t want to experience the pain of losing someone else, but I also want to be by Grace’s side every step of the way. And Megan’s going to need you to be there for her, you know it?”

Nodding, Cross says, “I hear you, but there’s another curveball in this picture. Megan’s ex-husband, Max, reached out to her and said he wants them to try and repair their relationship. That’s what she talked to me about this afternoon. She asked what I thought she should do.”

Pushing back with his feet, Harlon forces the swing into a gentle sway. “Sounds like someone cares about you, too, or she wouldn’t have bothered to get your opinion. What did you tell her?”

“I told her she should give it a shot. At one time they had a good marriage, at least that’s what she’s told me. Maybe they can recapture those early years. I know if I had a chance at a do-over with Heather, I’d do things differently.”

"Of course you would. But don't you think everyone thinks that way when they look at their past, that they'd do things differently? Hindsight's always twenty-twenty. There are things I'd do differently with your mother, even though we had a good marriage. I can see where I could have been a better husband to her." He pauses for a second, then asks, "What do you hope Megan does?"

The question hems Cross in a corner, the same corner he's been in since Megan told him about hearing from Max. What he wants to happen stands in opposition to what he's been telling himself ever since the wreck, and to say that makes him uncomfortable is an understatement.

He refuses to say the truth out loud. Instead, he says, "What difference does it make?" Telling Harlon he's going to make some supper, he disappears into the house.

Roxie watches Cross, then looks up at Harlon.

"You're right, girl," Harlon says to her, "he's stirred up inside, and he doesn't like it. It's up to you and me to help him." Grunting, he gets out of the swing and follows Cross inside.

In the kitchen, he finds him washing his hands, so he pulls out a chair from the table and sits down.

"How about a big chef's salad?" Cross asks him.

"That sounds good."

"We've still got that head of lettuce in the fridge, don't we?"

"I think so. You want me to help?"

"Yeah. Why don't you fry two or three pieces of bacon we can put in it?"

"I wish you'd asked me before I sat down here. Sitting down is easy; getting up is what's hard." Using the table and back of the chair, he stands up and retrieves the cast iron skillet from out of the oven and clangs it onto an eye of the stove. "Hand me the bacon," he tells Cross.

Cross obeys, then retrieves the head of lettuce, along with a bag of carrots, container of mushrooms, and jar of olives.

Harlon lets a couple minutes pass before saying, “Can I ask you a question?”

“Sure, Pop.”

“Do you know how you feel about Megan? The only reason I ask is because our conversation on the porch seemed to upset you. I was just wondering if maybe you’ve developed feelings for her you’re uncomfortable with. I mean, you’re a red-blooded male, and she’s a red-blooded female, and it’d be natural if you all felt something. You know what I mean?”

Slamming the head of lettuce against the counter, Cross then removes the core and begins washing the leaves. “I’ll admit, I enjoy being around Megan. We have more things in common than I realized when we first met. Now that I think about it, I guess she’s the first woman since I got out of prison I’ve let get close enough to me to call a friend, and it feels nice. You know how careful I am about letting people into my circle, but I believe I can be real with her. You asked me what I wanted to happen between her and Max. Whatever happens between them, I just don’t want it to get in the way of our friendship.”

Placing some strips of thick-sliced bacon into the skillet, Harlon waits to see if Cross has finished what he wants to say about him and Megan, then he says, “It makes me feel good to know you’re opening yourself up to her. You used to be open with everybody and made friends easily. I’ve missed seeing that part of you. One thing I’ve learned since Grace and I have started seeing each other is, just because you spend time with someone, like I’ve done with all the women I’ve been sleeping with, it doesn’t fill you up here.” He taps the wooden handle of the meat fork against his chest.

Unexpected tears spring up in his eyes, and his vision blurs. In a hoarse voice, he says, “A relationship without intimacy is nothing more than an acquaintance. Life can be so cruel sometimes. I’ve just now figured out what’s important, and Grace and I have something going between us, and it’s going to be snatched away from me.”

CHAPTER FORTY-THREE

Standing in front of her full-length mirror, dressed in bra and panties, Megan stares at her injured leg.

Why in the world did I agree to go out on a pontoon boat?! There's no way to hide that scar, or the fact that one leg is still smaller than the other.

"And don't worry about your leg," Betty had told her when she called her to ask what she was wearing. "Nobody will notice your leg when they've got mine to stare at. I've learned to ignore all that stuff. Just focus on having fun with me and Buck and Cross."

I envy her ability to do that. And it makes me feel petty when I complain about the leg I still have when she doesn't have one anymore.

Walking to her bed, she picks up a plastic shopping bag and pulls out the black one-piece bathing suit she finally settled on buying yesterday. She removes her underwear, slips on the swimsuit, and returns to the mirror.

My skin is so white, it's going to blind everybody.

After putting on her swimsuit coverup, she proceeds to the living room, where she can watch for Cross, who's coming to pick her up.

Grace looks up from watching a rerun of "Family Feud" with Steve Harvey and says, "Don't you look cute? You'll be the prettiest woman on the lake today."

"I doubt that," Megan responds. "How come you've not gotten dressed yet? You usually don't lie around in your pajamas."

"I just feel like being lazy today. I'm old enough, I think I can be lazy if I want to."

"Of course you are. It's just not like you." Frowning, she asks, "Are you sure you're feeling all right?"

"I'm fine."

Suddenly, Lacy starts barking and runs to the door.

Looking outside, Megan says, “Cross is here. I’m going to run on. I’ve got my phone with me, so call if you need anything.”

“I won’t need a thing. You guys go on and have fun. I’ll be eager to hear all about it when you return home. Come here and give me a kiss.”

An inexplicable, uneasy feeling comes over Megan, and she looks intently at her mother’s face.

“What?” Grace says. “Why are you looking at me like that?”

“Something doesn’t feel right.”

“Maybe it’s because you’re fixing to spend the day on the lake with Cross, and tomorrow you’re going to be meeting with Max. That probably feels a little weird.”

Leaning down to kiss her mother, Megan says, “Maybe…” Before walking out the door, she says, “I love you.”

“I love you, too, Megan.”

The sight of Cross walking to meet her wearing bright, Hawaiian-themed swimming trunks, flip flops, a sleeveless T-shirt, and a wide-brimmed straw hat sweeps her uneasy feelings to the side.

Holding his hands out to the side, he asks, “What do you think?”

She can’t help laughing. “I’m not positive, but your legs might be whiter than mine, which is saying a lot.” It pleases her to notice he doesn’t look at her leg.

He chuckles. “Just wait until I take off my shirt and you get a look at my farmer’s tan.”

“You’ll look like a certifiable redneck, won’t you?”

“Ab-so-lutely! But you look great.”

“Don’t even pretend with me. I looked in a mirror and know exactly what I look like: a middle-age, slightly overweight, and out of shape woman with two mismatched legs.”

Pulling off his sunglasses, Cross says, “I’ll tell you what, you focus on what you want to, and I’ll focus on what I want to. What I see looks great.”

Blushing, Megan says, “Thank you, I appreciate it.”

In the truck, Cross pushes "play" on his CD player. "Listen to this song, 'More Behind the Picture than the Wall,' by Doyle Lawson. It'll tear your heart out."

Megan listens intently to the singer's plaintive voice as he sings the song and finds herself swept up in the bittersweet story. Her chest hurts, and the need to cry overwhelms her. She bursts into tears despite her best efforts to contain them.

Cross brakes hard and pulls off onto the shoulder of the road. "Megan, what's wrong?"

"Why did you play that song? It's so sad!"

"I'm sorry. I discovered it last night and couldn't believe how beautiful and powerful it is. I just wanted to share it with someone. I didn't mean to upset you so much." Reaching in front of her, he opens the glove compartment and takes out some napkins and hands them to her. "Here, use these."

She snatches them out of his hand, wipes her face, and blows her nose as her tears begin to fade. "I shouldn't have snapped at you like that. I hate crying in front of people. I've felt emotional all morning, being nervous about today and wanting it to go well. And I'm going to meet Max tomorrow, which has my emotions all up in the air. Then this morning, Mother didn't seem right."

"What do you mean, didn't seem right?"

"Well, she's always up and at 'em every morning, but this morning she was just sitting around, watching TV. Said she felt fine, that she just wanted to be lazy today. But my mother doesn't have a lazy bone in her body."

Turning on his blinker and pulling back onto the road, Cross says, "Did she look okay to you?"

"I guess so. I think she's lost some weight. I don't know…." She shakes her head. "It just gave me an uneasy feeling. I know the time will come when I have to say goodbye to her, but I'm nowhere near ready for that. I still need her."

When Cross doesn't say anything, she looks over at him and sees a solitary tear creeping down the side of his cheek, leaving a silver trail in its wake. Putting her hand on his shoulder, she says, "Hey, I'm sorry for getting so upset. This is supposed to be a fun day, and here I am, dumping clouds and rain on it. We need to lighten up this conversation."

He clears his throat and says, "You got it." He touches some buttons on the stereo, and Ricky Skaggs starts singing "Fox on the Run." Halfway through the verse, Cross throws his head back and joins in singing.

The joy on his face and fervor in his voice chase away Megan's somber mood.

Gosh, I wish I felt that kind of freedom to sing at the top of my lungs and not care what people around me thought.

Just before the chorus of the song comes around, he glances at her and says, "Come on, sing with me!"

"I can't sing."

"Yes, you can. Everybody can sing. Don't worry what it sounds like, just open yourself up, and let the song take over. Here we go—"

For reasons she can't explain, Megan's trepidation evaporates, and suddenly she's singing along with Cross and the stereo. She feels as if an ancient vault inside her has opened and let loose feelings held there since childhood, feelings her stern father would never let her express. Her heart soars.

When the song finishes, Cross says, "You've got a great voice! That was awesome!"

Laughter bubbles around her words as she says, "Don't say that. We agreed to be honest with each other, remember?"

"I am being honest. Did you sing in high school or college?"

"No, no. I used to be painfully shy, even though I was a cheerleader."

"Maybe that's why you have such a strong voice," Cross remarks. "It reminds me of some of Pop's Patsy Cline records. You ever heard of her?"

“I’m afraid not.”

Shaking his head, Cross says, “Oh my, we’ve got a lot of work to do educating you on the great singers who brought country music out of the backwoods and made it universally popular. I’m going to sic Pop on you, so just be prepared.”

As he turns off the highway onto a rural road, Megan says, “I have to admit, I’m warming up to bluegrass. There’s a complex simplicity about it, which sounds like an oxymoron, but it’s true. The stories they tell are timeless, and the voices are pure and unaffected.”

“Now you’re talking,” he replies. Pointing, he says, “There’s the lake. We’re here.”

CHAPTER FORTY-FOUR

They drive underneath a big sign announcing Buchanan Resort and Marina, and hundreds of covered boat slips come into view. Just beyond the marina, jet skis and boats crisscross a large bay of water.

Once they park and get out of the truck, Cross says, “Follow me.”

“I didn’t bring anything with me,” Megan tells him. “Betty told me I wouldn’t need anything.”

“It’s true. Because they’ve never had children, Buck and Betty like to do things for their friends, kind of like they’re their kids. I guarantee you, Betty will have everything we need.”

As they walk single file along the floating dock, tied-up boats on either side of them bob up and down, as if they’re eager to be turned loose to race each other. Small waves slap the sides of the boats, sounding like hands clapping.

“Hey, hey, hey, there they are!” Buck’s voice echoes against the marina’s metal covering. “It’s going to be a beautiful day out there today.”

Megan sees Buck hurrying toward them. He’s wearing an identical straw hat to Cross’s and a T-shirt trying its hardest to contain his girth. It takes her a minute to read the saying on the front: “It took me forty years to look this good.”

Pointing at the shirt, Cross says, “Well, let’s hope the next forty years improve on what the previous forty years failed at.”

Buck poses with his nose in the air. “Envy doesn’t look good on you, Cross. You just wish you looked half as good as I do.”

They give each other a good-natured punch, then start wrestling.

“I’m going to throw you off here,” Cross grunts.

“You and who else?” Buck replies.

At first Megan laughs at them acting like a couple of boys, but then she grows concerned when they keep after each other.

They break apart, grinning and panting.

“You ready to give up?” Cross says.

Kicking off his flip flops, Buck says, “Not a chance.”

Megan notices Betty carrying a towel and coming up quietly behind her husband. She dips one corner of the towel into the water, lifts it out, and cracks it like a whip against Buck’s behind.

“Yeow!” he cries, grabbing his butt and turning around.

In a tone befitting a drill sergeant, Betty says, “You boys behave yourselves, and get on the boat!”

Rubbing the spot where the towel struck him, Buck eases past her. “Dang, Betty, I’m going to have a bruise. That hurt!”

“It was supposed to.”

Cross does a poor job of looking contrite and holds his hand over his smile as he walks toward the boat.

“Come here,” Betty says to Megan. “You’re going to see another side of these two today. When they’re working, they’re all about work, but when it’s playtime, they turn into twelve-year-olds. Now, let’s go ahead and look at each other so we won’t have to pretend we’re not looking.”

Megan’s face grows warm. “You’re just so upfront about things. I like it; I’m just not used to it.”

Pointing at Megan’s leg, Betty says, “Whoever did your surgery could have done a better job of it. I’m surprised the scar still shows.”

Megan stares at Betty’s prosthetic rod and foot and how it fastens to her leg. “That’s just amazing. Is there anything you can’t do with it?”

“Not really. I can still water ski if I want to.”

“You’re kidding?! You’re my new hero.”

Waving Megan to follow her, Betty says, “Now that we’ve gotten that out of the way, let’s go have some fun.”

After they board and are seated, Buck starts the motor, and Cross unties the boat from the cleats and helps ease it out of the slip before jumping onboard at the last second. Buck maneuvers his way through the no-wake zone, then opens the throttle.

Betty pulls out a couple bottles of suntan lotion. Talking loud over the roar of the motor, she says, "Everybody better lather up those white legs, arms, and noses, or you'll get blistered."

Laughing, Megan says, "Pitch me the strongest one you've got. These legs haven't seen the sunshine in a while!"

Cross and Buck peel off their T-shirts.

"Ladies and gentlemen," Buck says, "I present to you, a farmer's tan."

He and Cross stand and make a slow turn for everyone to see.

"I should have brought darker sunglasses," Megan says, with a smile.

"Well, she does have a sense of humor," Buck comments. "I haven't seen that yet. But can you take it as well as dish it out?"

Feeling like she's just been invited inside this circle of friends, Megan answers, "The question is, can you take what I dish out?"

Cross hoots. "Better be careful, Buck, this one's got a sharp tongue and wit."

Bowing to her, Buck says, "I accept the challenge."

As they leave the bay and head into open water, Megan turns her head to face the wind and closes her eyes as it fingers through her hair.

This feels wonderful!

When she opens her eyes, she sees Cross sitting on the other side of the boat, trying to put suntan lotion on his back. Without thinking, she asks, "You want me to help you? You really have to be a contortionist to be able to cover your own back."

He seems to hesitate for an instant, and she's about to retract her offer when he smiles and says, "You're right, it is impossible." He crosses to her side and sits down with his back toward her. "I would appreciate it."

Taking the bottle from him, she squirts some in her hand and rubs it on his back. A sudden and unexpected thrill runs through her as she realizes she hasn't touched another man since Max left her. Cross's skin is warm, and his taut muscles ripple underneath her fingers. The urge to continue rubbing his back, coupled with a forgotten warmth filling her loins, nearly takes over her.

Clapping him on the back, she says, "All done. You should be well-protected now."

Turning to face her, he says, "Thank you. You know what? That's the first time I've had a woman touch me in that way since the wreck. Even though I know you didn't have any thoughts besides just putting suntan lotion on me, it stirred something deep inside me, and it scared me."

"I'm sorry, I didn't mean to—"

"No, it's not you, you didn't do anything wrong. It's just what's going on with me. I just don't want…"

"Hey, you two," Betty calls to them from the back of the boat. "That looks like an awfully serious conversation you're having." Opening a cooler, she says, "Why don't you come back here and get a snack and something to drink before we jump in the water and swim?"

A part of Megan is relieved and another frustrated at the interruption. "I wonder what she brought?" she asks Cross as they both stand up.

"Hopefully, some of her famous oatmeal raisin cookies and her white grape peach tea."

"That sounds delicious!"

~~~~~~~~~~

By the time they glide back into Buchannan Marina, the setting sun is kissing the horizon and filling the sky with orange and red streaks. Pink noses and shoulders are abundant among the crew onboard, as are sore muscles from skiing and riding a skibob.

Megan looks at everyone and says, "I can't remember when I've had such a good time you all. Everything was perfect. Thank you so much for inviting me."

"What was your favorite part?" Buck asks.
~~~~~~~~~~

"I think it was when the ski rope broke when you were trying to ski."

Betty and Cross howl with laughter.

"Next time, we'll use a cable," Cross tells her.

"She just doesn't quit, does she?" Buck pleads with Cross.

"Hey, you're the one who started it by asking if she could dish it and take it."

Buck gives her a gentle smile. "We're really glad you came, Megan. I enjoyed getting to know you better."

The boat comes to a rest in the slip, and Cross jumps out to tie it off.

Betty approaches Megan and gives her a hug. "I'm like Buck, I'm really glad I got to know you better. You're a real gem. The boys are lucky to have you running their store."

"You're the one who's a gem, Betty. I just love you. What I can't figure out is how Buck tricked you into marrying him."

Another chorus of laughter erupts as Buck says, "I give up! You win, you win."

Offering Megan his hand, Cross helps her off the boat. "We'll see you guys later," he says as he leads her along the pier.

Once they're in the truck, she says, "Goodness! I'm going to be sore tomorrow. I'm worn out."

He nods in agreement.

Silence fills the cab as he heads toward Megan's house, and she begins thinking about her meeting with Max tomorrow.

Spending today on the lake with such an authentic group of people, around whom she could relax and be herself, was something she could never do with Max. He was more concerned about himself and impressing others and somewhat forced her to be the same way.

I just don't want to go back to living that kind of life.

She tells Cross she's having second thoughts about meeting with Max, hoping Cross will tell her he doesn't want her to go.

Instead, he says, "I think you owe it to him, to give him a chance to show you if he's become more like the man you want him to be, or if he matches who you've become. Doesn't he deserve a second chance? I know if I'd had a second chance with Heather, I'd do things differently."

"But I thought we'd agreed neither of us believe we deserve a second chance, didn't we? I'm not good relationship material, and you screwed up your chance."

Pulling to a stop in front of her house, Cross puts the truck in park, then turns sideways in his seat. "I'm going to stop you there. You're excellent relationship material. Anybody would be lucky to have you."

Megan is glad the cab is dark, so he can't see how red her face is. "It's easy for a person to be pleasant and fun for a day, Cross, but that doesn't tell you what they'd be like to live with."

"Look, Megan," he tells her, "you've made me rethink a lot of things, and I don't like it. I had my world all figured out, how I'd live and act in it. It was simple. Now I feel like it's complicated. I really don't want you to go meet Max, because I'm afraid you'll move away, and I'd hate to lose you as a friend." He turns his head and looks at the house. "And I want to be there for you, to help you get through some hard times."

With her heart beating at the pace of a sprinter's, Megan struggles to get a breath as she tries to process everything Cross has said.

Lucky to have you; lose you as a friend; help you through hard times. What's he saying?

He opens his door, and the interior lights momentarily blind her. Before he can get out, she grabs his arm. "Just a minute. I want to say something. The last thing I want to happen is for us to lose this friendship we have. I know it's new and fresh, but I think it's worth hanging on to. I promise I'm not going to let that happen. So there's that. But what did you mean when you said you wanted to help me get through some hard times?"

Putting his hand on one of hers, Cross replies, "I just mean, you know, life can be hard sometimes, it throws us curves. I just want to be there for you when that happens to you."

Frowning, Megan takes her other hand and lifts his face toward hers. "You sound awfully serious. Is there something going on you need to tell me?"

"It's just that life is fragile, that's all."

Without warning, he pulls her to him and hugs her to his chest.

With her breasts pressed against him, she feels his heart beating and wonders if he feels hers. But more than anything, she feels a sadness in him, so she hugs him tightly and says, "It's going to be all right."

CHAPTER FORTY-FIVE

Megan hears Lacy barking from inside the front door before she reaches the porch. She opens the door just enough to let her out, picks her up in her arms, and is rewarded with a hundred kisses.

"Did you miss me? I missed you."

Lacy sniffs her way through the tangle of Megan's hair.

"Lots of new smells there, huh? No, you've never been where I was today, but I think you would've had a good time. Did you take care of Mother today? What did you all do?"

Instead of going inside, she sits down on the edge of the porch and sets Lacy on her lap.

Lacy promptly turns in a circle twice, then curls up.

Megan enjoys the warmth of her body and slowly strokes her back, which elicits a pleasant groan from Lacy.

Tiny spots of pale blue decorate the ground of the front yard as moonlight finds its way through the canopy of trees. Tree frogs sing a syncopated rhythm, and a Chuck-will's-widow begins its nightly song from somewhere deeper in the surrounding woods.

"I had a really great time today," she says to Lacy. "More fun than I expected. Betty and Buck have the sweetest relationship and are easy to be around. She's just amazing. I could learn a lot from her about accepting my shortcomings and not worrying about what other people are thinking about me. None of them gave my leg a second look, because none of them cared."

Lacy tries to snuggle deeper into her lap.

Just then, the front door opens, and Grace steps onto the porch wearing the same thing she had on when Megan left that morning.

"What are you two up to?" Grace asks. "Don't you want to come inside?"

"I just felt like sitting out here for a little bit. Want to join me?"

"Sure, but I think I'll sit in the swing instead of trying to sit down beside you and have to deal with the struggle to get back up again." She plops down on the swing, causing the chains holding it to jingle. "Did you have fun today?"

"Oh Mother, I had the absolute best time, the best time I've had in a long time."

"How was Cross? What was it like spending the day with him?"

"Cross was good…very good…maybe too good."

"How can a person be too good?"

"He made me rethink a lot of things, things I'd had settled in my mind, things I didn't have to worry about because I'd made up my mind about them."

"Mmhmm. Tell me more."

"I didn't realize how much I'd missed touching a man or having one touch me. Don't get excited, now; we didn't have sex, if that's what you're thinking. We just put suntan lotion on each other's back. Simple, nothing to it, right? But boy, did it get me stirred up. And it made me think about if I'd like to be married again, if maybe I could be better at it the second time around. And of course, that made me think about Max and my meeting with him tomorrow and if he's the person I'd like to try marriage again with, because I think that's what he's going to ask me to do. I really don't think I want to, not with him. I don't want to return to that life. Just today, I realized I've grown to like life here, living in a small town, and especially living with you. When I first had to move in here, I hated it and couldn't wait until I could leave. But now I don't want to leave you, Mother. I bet you're surprised to hear that."

She turns to give Grace a smile and sees her chin is resting on her chest, and she's quietly snoring.

~~~~~~~~~~

The next morning, Megan leaves while Grace is still asleep and drives the two hours to Nashville to meet Max at Opry Mills Mall. It seemed like the least intimate setting to start their conversation, especially since he pressed for her to meet him at his apartment to talk.
~~~~~~~~~~

“I don’t think I’m ready for that,” she told him. “Let’s just start easy and see how it goes. It doesn’t mean we’ll spend the day at the mall. We can always leave from there and go someplace else if we decide to.”

Max’s tone was disappointed, even though his words said he wasn’t.

Turning into the massive parking lot of the mall, she makes her way toward the entrance that leads to the movie theatre, where they’d agreed to meet, and finds a place to park.

Before she gets out, she checks her makeup in the mirror, then takes a few breaths to try and calm her nerves.

Don’t put pressure on yourself; just let it play out however it plays out. Trust your instincts.

This is the mantra she’d finally decided on during the drive to Nashville, after she’d tried to play out scores of different conversations in her mind.

As she approaches the glass front doors of the mall, she sees her reflection and wonders what Max is going to think about her wearing jeans, cowboy boots, and a pink T-shirt with a picture of the Eiffel Tower with the saying, “Come see our Eiffel Tower, Paris, TN.”

Grasping the handle to the glass, mall door, she plasters a fake smile on her face and enters. Immediately, she sees Max forty feet away, facing the doors, dressed in a steel-gray three-piece suit, white shirt, and teal-colored tie, with a matching, teal-colored handkerchief expertly folded and tucked into the front pocket of the jacket.

Megan thinks of the children’s story about the country mouse meeting the city mouse. At first she regrets what she’s wearing, but then she tells herself this is who Max was and apparently still is: *Dress to impress.*

When he spots her, he breaks into a wide smile and walks to meet her.

She’d already decided she was going to avoid the awkward “should we hug, or should we kiss?” greeting, so she holds out her hand to shake his just as he’s opening his arms to hug her.

He stops and looks at her uncertainly, then quickly smiles and shakes her hand. “Hi, Megan. It’s great to see you.”

She notices some gray hairs have crept into the temples of his brown hair since she last saw him. “It’s good to see you, too,” she tells him.

Still holding her hand, he steps back a bit and gives her an appraising look. “And look at you! You look amazing! But cowboy boots? I never thought you were a cowboy boot kind of girl.”

Pulling her hand free, Megan says, “Well, I really like them.”

“Oh, I’m not saying they don’t look good,” he responds quickly as the tops of his cheeks turn pink. “They look fantastic.”

“It’s okay if you don’t like them. Just be honest and say you don’t. Let’s not tiptoe around each other. That’s one thing I’ve learned since we’ve been apart: I wasn’t always honest with you about how I felt, and I don’t think you were with me either.”

“Wow, we’re going to jump right into things, huh? No warm-up or preamble? I can adjust to that. Can we window shop while we talk? Or do you want to go to a restaurant and sit and talk?”

“Let’s just walk around. I’m a little tired of sitting after my drive here.”

Turning together, they begin strolling down the thoroughfare, maintaining that awkward distance between themselves of people who are vigilant about any slight body language that can send the wrong message or be misconstrued.

Megan decides to let Max be the first to start a thread of conversation and is surprised at how long it takes him to do so because he was never one to be comfortable with silence.

“I’ve got to say,” he finally begins, “how amazing you are doing physically. No wheelchair or crutches, not even a walking cane. That says a lot about your grit and determination—two traits that were always a part of who you are.”

“It’s been a long road for sure,” she replies. “And I still need to build up some strength in the leg, but that’ll come with time, the physical therapist tells me.”

“The first thing I want to tell you, Megan, is how ashamed I am over how I deserted you after you got hurt. It was a cowardly and mean thing to do.”

“Yes, it was.”

"I deserve that. What I don't deserve, but I'm asking for, is your forgiveness. My therapist tells me I shouldn't expect you to forgive me, because I don't deserve to be forgiven, but I can at least express what I want."

Stopping and looking at him, Megan says, "You've got a therapist?"

"Yeah. Started seeing someone about four months ago. It's not been easy, because she's challenged to look at myself and my life. She says I have narcissistic traits."

Megan resumes walking as she says, "I think we've both been guilty of that, especially me. But at least we're both willing to admit it. That's a positive step, isn't it?"

Smiling, he answers, "I'd say yes, for sure."

Megan likes this honest exchange and feels her wall of resistance to him lowering a bit.

Just then, they pass in front of a music store with a sign saying, "Get Doyle Lawson's latest today!"

She makes a sharp turn to go inside while saying, "Let's check this out."

She walks straight to the section marked "Bluegrass" and starts flipping through the available CDs.

"Bluegrass?" Max says. "You're looking for bluegrass? You can't stand bluegrass, a bunch of thin-voiced people singing through their noses and picking a banjo. It's hardly worth calling it music."

Without looking at him, Megan snaps, "That's because it's too deep for you. It's some of the most complex music and subject matter ever sung. It's more real than anything else out there."

Unbuttoning his coat and putting one hand on his hip, he replies, "You're being serious, aren't you?"

She pauses her browsing to look at him. "Yes, I am. I used to be like you and just made fun of it. But someone turned me on to it, and I really heard it for the first time. It'll have you clapping and dancing one moment and crying the next. You ought to try it."

"You've really bought into the whole rural life experience, haven't you? I just never figured you for that."

“I didn’t figure myself for it either, but I’ve grown to really enjoy it. Things move slower, and the people are goodhearted.”

She pulls out the new Doyle Lawson CD and proceeds to the checkout counter.

When they resume their stroll, Max says, “You’ve really changed. Don’t you miss working, and the people you used to rock climb with, and going out to nice restaurants? You used to love those things.”

Megan replies, “Uh…no, a little, and no. You’re right, I have changed…changed into someone I’m beginning to like and enjoy. Isn’t that what we should all be striving to evolve into? I’ve got a job working at a nursery, running a gift shop, and I love it. I make people smile and feel good with what I do. I probably will go rock climbing again someday, just to prove to myself I can still do it. And nowadays, the restaurant I frequent the most is Huddle House.”

Max laughs, but Megan notes a tone of disdain in it. She pivots to face him. “This. This right here is what I’m talking about. The idea that the life you and I used to live is somehow superior to the life I’m living now. I both despise and resent that attitude. Your three-piece suit and tie are nice looking, Max, but they don’t impress me or move me one bit. Those things just don’t matter to me anymore. And I’m not saying there’s anything wrong with you still liking and wanting that life, I’m really not. If it works for you, that’s what you need to pursue. But I’ve gotten off that train and don’t intend to get back on it.”

A look of resignation comes over Max’s face as he says, “There’s someone else, isn’t there? You’re with someone, aren’t you?”

She hesitates for a split second as images of Cross fill her head. Then she says, “Not really. I’ve not even had a date with anyone, so that’s not what this is about. I haven’t changed to make somebody like me, or to please them. Who I am is who I want to be, and that might not be enough for you.”

A movement to her right catches Megan’s attention, and she looks to see an older couple standing perhaps ten feet away, looking intently at her and Max.

Shaking a bony finger at Max, the woman says, "Listen to what she's saying. You need to decide right now if you want to be with this woman just as she is, not as you hope she will be or become."

The stooped man beside her gives a solemn nod. "Too many people marry someone because of what they think they can turn them into," he tells Max. "It's a waste of time and effort. Marry them for who they are, and then grow old together. That's what we did." He kisses the woman on the cheek.

"Sixty-six years," the woman smiles and says, "That's how long we've been married. But this conversation you two are having right now may be the most important you've ever had. Get it right, or you'll live only half a life, a life filled with frustration and disappointment."

"Come on," the man tells his wife as he pulls on her elbow, "I've got to find a bathroom."

"You always need a bathroom," she complains as they amble off.

Megan and Max slowly turn back to face each other.

She reads the disappointment and sadness in his downturned eyes and slack cheeks. "It's okay, Max," she tells him. "You'll find someone else."

"Well, I kind of already have, but I wanted to be sure there was nothing left between us that might get in the way of things. And I wanted to apologize to you for how I behaved after your accident."

Megan folds her arms across her chest and stares at him. "You know what, Max? You're a real ass. I bet your therapist hasn't told you that, has she? Just ask her and see if she'll be honest with you."

"Why are you mad?"

"Uh, let's see, I got up early this morning and drove two hours, thinking you and I were going to see if we wanted to repair our marriage when you're already lined up with and interested in someone else. All you really wanted out of this meeting was for me to forgive you so you could feel better about yourself. Look up the term 'narcissist,' Max. I think you'll find your picture beside it."

Storming past him, she heads toward the mall exit.

CHAPTER FORTY-SIX

Leaning on the handle of his shovel, Cross pauses to catch his breath from planting cherry oak trees in a customer's yard.

Buck approaches him, pushing a wheelbarrow full of mulch. "You know, we're not in a race here."

Cross ignores the comment and checks his phone to see if he's missed a notification of a new text message or missed call.

"And what's with you and your phone today?" Buck asks. "I've never seen you look at it so much."

Gripping the handle of the shovel with both hands, Cross positions the tip of the blade on the ground and then slams his boot onto it. Through gritted teeth, he says, "This is the hardest ground I've ever seen. It's ridiculous! It'd be a lot easier with a backhoe."

"True, but I think that'd be a little overkill for planting young saplings like these. The hole would be huge. Let me dig for a while, and you haul the mulch."

Cross jerks the handle out of the reach of his friend and says, "I'll get it done."

Holding his hands in the air, Buck says, "Okay, okay. I wish you'd tell me what's going on with you today. I figured you'd be in a great mood after the day we had on the lake yesterday. It looked to me and Betty like you and Megan had a lot of fun and got along great. Did something go sideways between y'all when you took her home?"

Dropping the shovel to the ground, Cross wipes the sweat from his forehead. "I'm all twisted up in my head and was awake all night, trying to sort it out. When I went to bed, I started thinking about Heather, and it made me feel guilty for having enjoyed spending time with Megan. I felt like I'd cheated on her. What kind of way is that for me to honor her memory by acting like I don't even care about her anymore, or that what we had between us wasn't special? And what would Claire think if she knew I spent time with a woman besides her mother? Can either of them see what's happening here on Earth from wherever they are? How do they feel about what I'm doing? What I did yesterday, Buck, it's not right; that's not the life I deserve. That was just me being selfish and pretending the past didn't happen."

Without warning, Buck gives him a hard shove. "You know what I'm tired of? I'm sick and tired of you using Heather and Claire as an excuse for staying miserable. You use their memory like a cross you've crucified yourself on and you're this martyr everyone should feel sorry for and admire for being so loyal to the memory of them."

Cross hits Buck in the chest with his open palms, knocking him back a step. "You can't talk to me like that!"

Red-faced, Buck jumps forward until his face is inches from Cross's. Poking him in the chest with his index finger, he says, "That's where you're wrong. I'm the only one who *can* talk to you like this, because I know you better than anyone else, and I love you like nobody else does."

Cross slaps away his hand. "You better stop."

Buck chest bumps him. "Who's going to make me?"

Clenching his fists, Cross says, "I'm warning you, Buck."

"Go ahead. You want to hit me? Then come ahead and do it." He holds his arms out to the side. "Take a shot."

Tears sting Cross's eyes. "Leave me alone!" he roars.

"I will not!" Buck shouts back. "I refuse to, and you can't make me."

Using both hands, Cross grabs the front of Buck's shirt and shakes him. "What do you expect me to do? What do you want from me?"

"It's simple, Cross. I just want you to live. You've been doing nothing but sleepwalking ever since the wreck. Sure, you go about your job and go to your meetings and play music sometimes, but there's no spark in your eye that tells me your heart is in anything you do."

Letting go of his friend's shirt, Cross takes a step back and shoves his hands in his back pockets. "What you're saying is true, isn't it?"

"Yes, Cross. I've been wanting to say it for a while but kept thinking you'd finally realize it yourself and snap out of it. I'd just about decided that part of you was dead and never coming back, but then Megan entered the picture. Yesterday, I saw that spark in your eye—real, heartfelt happiness about the day."

"But you know I don't believe I deserve a second chance."

Folding his arms across his chest, Buck stares at him and says nothing.

"What?" Cross asks.

"Let me ask you a question: How can a card-carrying, one-hundred-percent-committed member of Alcoholics Anonymous say someone doesn't deserve a second chance?"

Cross cocks his head to one side. "Uh, we don't carry cards, Buck."

"Whatever. You know what I mean. I thought the whole idea behind A.A. was based on believing people deserve a second chance. And before you say it, there's nothing special about you that makes you an exception."

Cross falls silent underneath the weight of Buck's message.

"What are you thinking about?" Buck asks him.

"What would Heather tell me to do? That's what I'm thinking about."

"I know what she would say. Do you?"

Nodding, Cross says, "Yes. She would tell me to move on with my life."

"That's exactly what she would say," Buck agrees. "Don't forget, I knew her, too."

Cross smiles at him, and Buck winks.

"You and Betty, and Heather and I had some fun times back in the day, didn't we?"

"Lord, yes! Do you remember that trip to North Carolina when we decided to spend the night in a motel and looked around until we found the cheapest one we could find?"

Laughing, Cross says, "Yes. When Heather looked in the bathroom of our room and saw a two-foot-wide hole in the wall around the faucets of the bathtub and you could see into the bathroom of the room beside us, she looked at me with daggers in her eyes and said, 'The only way I'm sleeping in this room is if I'm standing up.'"

They both howl with laughter.

"That was the maddest I believe I ever saw her," Buck cries. "And you went to the lobby to get our money back and made up some stupid lie about us being from a different time zone and we were going to try driving farther down the road."

Shrugging, Cross says, "Hey, money was hard to come by back then. I did what I had to do."

Buck wipes away tears from laughing so hard. "Those were good times. But that can't be the end, can it? There are more memories to make, whatever they might look like. And you and Megan will—"

Cross stops him. "Here's the thing about that. Megan's ex-husband got in touch with her and said he wants to try and repair their marriage. She's in Nashville right now, meeting with him."

"Why is she doing that? I thought the jerk deserted her when she got hurt?"

"She wants to see if maybe he's changed. Plus, I told her she should meet with him."

Looking toward the sky, Buck says, "Lord, how could this man be so smart and so stupid at the same time?" Turning his eyes on Cross, he asks, "I know I'm not going to like the answer, but why in the world did you tell her to go? Isn't that the same thing as telling her you're not interested in her and to go on back to her ex?"

“I didn’t want to tell her that, but I didn’t want her to have regrets later and wish she’d at least tried. I know if I was somehow given a second chance with Heather, I’d be a different kind of husband. This guy, Max, may be carrying a truckload of regret about deserting her and is wanting to make amends. I know what it’s like to eat, drink, and sleep with regret. It eats at you like a cancer. It’s not something I’d wish on my worst enemy. So, if Megan going to see Max does nothing more than let him unburden himself of that guilt, then it’s worth it.”

Tapping the side of his head with his fingers, Buck says, “That’s why you keep checking your phone, isn’t it? You’re wanting to hear from her how it’s going.”

Nodding, Cross answers, “Yeah, even though she didn’t say she’d call. I just thought maybe…”

Just then his phone vibrates, making him jump. Whipping it out of his pocket, he sees there’s a text message.

MEGAN: HEADING BACK HOME NOW. THINGS DIDN’T WORK OUT.

“Is it from Megan?” Buck asks.

“Yeah.”

“Well, what did she say?”

Cross reads him the short message, then types a reply and sends it.

“What did you tell her?”

“‘Thanks for letting me know.’”

“That’s it?”

“Well, I can’t tell from her text whether she’s happy or disappointed it didn’t work out. That’s why I hate texting. You don’t know what the person’s facial expression or tone of voice is. Megan might be smiling, or she might be crying.”

“Call her,” Buck urges him.

“If she wanted to talk about it, she would have called me. No, I’ll just wait until I see her next time. Hey, she may not want to talk to me about it. You’re looking at the situation like she and I have been seeing each other for six months. Look, we’ve had less than a handful of serious conversations.” He smiles. “Right now, we’re just friends, so you can hold off making wedding plans for us.”

CHAPTER FORTY-SEVEN

Sitting with Harlon and eating a corn dog at Sonic, Grace smiles at the message on her phone.

"Good news?" he asks her.

"Yes, good news. Megan's headed back home from her trip to Nashville to meet Max. She says things didn't work out. I never did like him anyway. He was too much like a peacock, wanting everyone to notice him."

"Did she say if she was happy or sad about things not working out?"

"No, just that they didn't, but I bet she's happy. She told me she's grown to love living here, even though she never thought she would." She takes a bite of her corn dog. "Sonic has the best corn dogs, don't they?"

Finishing off his corn dog, Harlon says, "Absolutely! They're even better than the ones they have at the fair."

"You know, I think getting to know Cross has helped Megan enjoy living here, even though she might not admit that. You've raised a good boy. He's polite and thoughtful and hardworking."

"I'd say most of the credit for that goes to his mother. When he was growing up, I spent too much time hunting and fishing with friends. I should have been taking him with me. Once he was grown, I made a promise to myself I'd take my grandchildren hunting and fishing." Shrugging his shoulders, he adds, "But that didn't quite work out like I hoped."

"I understand," Grace replies. "I think when parents get to a certain age, they dream of making up for all their bad parenting through their grandchildren. Unfortunately, that's not going to happen for me either."

Harlon puts the leftover napkins, corn dog sticks, and mustard packets in the Sonic sack. As he does so, he asks, "Have you told Megan?"

Grace knows what he's talking about without asking. It's the subject that's waiting around every corner, that keeps her awake at night. "No, I haven't," she answers him.

"Grace…"

"I know, I know. I'm eventually going to have to tell her. I just don't want her to get all upset and worried and afraid. And I especially don't want her to put her life on hold until I die. She's so excited about this new store she's getting ready to open for Cross and Buck. It's fun to see her this way after the long year she's had of recovering from her fall. I'll tell her, but later."

Cranking the truck, Harlon says, "How about let's drive over to Britton Ford?"

"That'd be nice. I wonder if our tree is still there, the one with the rope swing?"

Harlon pulls out of the parking lot and says, "You still remember that?"

"Of course I do. Don't you?"

"I don't think there's the tiniest thing I've forgotten about that time in my life. But I'll tell you, the tree you're talking about has probably died by now. No telling how old it was back then, and it's been several decades since we were last there."

"You make us sound ancient."

He smiles. "Well…"

"Oh, hush! I know how old we are. What's funny, though, is, when we're together like this, I feel just like I did all those years ago. It's like a magical spell that lets me travel back through time. Do you feel that way?"

"It's the same with me. I can't explain it exactly. I tried to tell Cross about it, but I don't think he understood."

Grace watches out the window as he turns off Highway 79 onto Oak Grove Road.

As they pass by the Sulphur Well Church of Christ, Harlon asks, "Didn't you go to church there when you were growing up?"

"Yes, but that building is three times the size of the one that used to be sitting there. The church must have really grown through the years."

"You don't attend there now?"

"No, I really haven't gotten involved in any church since I moved back, though I have visited a few. Church wasn't something my husband believed in, so I quit going altogether after we'd been married a couple of years. I kind of regret that now, especially for Megan. What about you? Do you go to church?"

"I lost my religion in Viet Nam, just like I lost a lot of other things, like respect for our elected officials and the whole red-white-and-blue patriot thing. I just feel like our government uses the military to advance its political agenda, but they make it sound like it's about saving people from oppression. Just like this cluster you-know-what that's been going on in the Middle East for years now. All that's about is oil and making politicians rich. If there is a God, how can He let all that happen, thousands of young people get killed?"

"You sound jaded, Harlon."

"That's because I am. I don't like seeing things the way I do, but I've not seen any evidence to convince me I'm wrong. But let's change the subject. Have you ever been to that Tennessee National Wildlife Refuge Visitor Center they built a few years ago?"

"No, I haven't."

"We'll stop there. It's a cool place with an interpretive and educational center, plus some hiking trails. We'll see some ospreys nesting, but we might also see a bald eagle or two. They've become a lot more common around here."

"I would love that! I want to do and see as much of life as I can while I still have time. That's one thing having this cancer has done for me; it's heightened my focus on what's important. I've spent too much of my life stressing and worrying over things that really didn't matter."

"So, what's the most important thing in life?"

"Relationships and spending time doing things with those you love."

The road they're on narrows and enters a virtual tunnel made of giant oak and poplar trees.

Harlon slows as he drives underneath the heavy canopy that lets in only filtered light from the sun.

"It's like an enchanted forest," Grace says as she rolls down her window.

Cool, damp air washes her face with the loamy smell of decaying leaves on the forest floor. A large bird zips across the one-lane road.

"What was that?" she exclaims.

"I'm pretty sure it was a wood duck," Harlon replies. "They're different from most ducks because they nest in trees."

Holding out her hand to him, Grace says, "I'm glad I was with you when I saw my first one."

He takes her hand and weaves his fingers between hers. "You and I have had a number of firsts together, haven't we?"

"For sure. You're the first boy I went skinny dipping with."

"You're the first girlfriend I ever had."

"You're the first boy I kissed on a merry-go-round."

"You're the first girl I ever had sex with."

They smile at each other.

Harlon stops the truck and puts it in park. He leans toward her, his eyes focused on her lips.

Her heart skips a beat, and she bends toward him.

Their lips touch, tentatively at first, then passionately.

When they separate, Grace gasps for breath. "That was…that was…my gosh, you're still a good kisser!" She kisses him again and whispers, "We were good together, weren't we?"

Putting the truck in drive, Harlon eases out of the canopy into bright sunlight. "We were more than just good—we were perfect."

Pointing up ahead, she asks, "Is that the interpretive center?"

"Yes."

An hour later, they exit the center and climb back into Harlon's truck.

"I'm glad you brought us here," Grace says. "It was so interesting. I actually learned a lot."

"I wasn't sure you would enjoy it, but I'm glad you did. Do you feel like taking one of the hikes they told us about?"

"I know you'd like to, but I think we should come back and do it another time. Is that okay?"

Pulling out of the parking lot, Harlon answers, "Of course it is. We'll definitely do it some other time."

"What I want to do now is see if our tree is still standing. If I'm remembering correctly, it should be close by somewhere."

"Your memory is correct. It's just a few miles from here."

"I wonder if it'll be as big as I remember it being. When I became an adult, I noticed things weren't as big as I remembered. Like the steps to my great-aunt Ollie's house. I remember them being so steep, I had to go up them on my all-fours. But when I revisited there after I was grown, I was shocked at how easy they were to climb."

"That's interesting. I noticed the same thing about the church my uncle in Kentucky went to. The ceiling looked impossibly high when I was a kid. But like you, when I went back for a visit years later, I couldn't believe how low the ceiling was. It was maybe twenty feet high. Age gives you a different perspective on things, doesn't it?"

Grace's mind drifts backward and picks out things she used to stress and worry about when she was younger. She silently shakes her head.

Harlon interrupts her musings by asking, "You don't think it does?"

"What? What does?"

"You don't think age gives you a different perspective?"

"Oh, goodness no, I mean yes, it does. Your question triggered scores of memories from the past, when I wasted my time stressing and worrying about things that don't matter in the big scheme of things."

“Wasn’t it George Bernard Shaw who said youth is wasted on the young?”

Grace looks at him with wide eyes. “You remember that from Mrs. Shanklin’s Senior English class? I’m very impressed, and she would be, too.”

Harlon strikes a pose. “I’m not just another pretty face.” Pointing to his head, he says, “I have things going on up here.”

She laughs out loud.

Just then, he turns off the gravel road and onto a dirt path that’s embraced on both sides by a thick mixture of switch grass, cord grass, and sage grass dotted with the purple blooms of towering ironweed.

“Oh, Harlon,” Grace sighs, “this looks exactly like it used to.” Rolling down her window and taking a deep breath through her nose, she says, “And I can smell the lake.”

They ease ahead another forty yards and enter a small clearing.

Grace grabs Harlon’s arm with one hand and points with the other. “There it is, Harlon! It’s still here!”

A thick, towering beech tree stands like a sentinel on the bank, providing shade to all within its reach.

“I really didn’t think it would be here,” Harlon says. “It’s amazing lightning hasn’t struck it and at least blown the top out of it.”

Exiting the truck, they hold hands as they approach the tree like they might approach a DaVinci painting in a museum.

“Look,” Harlon says as he points toward a lower limb suspended over the water. “People still tie ropes on it to swing and jump into the lake.”

“I remember the first time I did it,” Grace replies. “I was scared to death. And look at how many people have carved their names in the trunk.”

“But ours was the first.”

“I wonder if we can find it?”

Moving in opposite directions, they slowly circle the tree.

Grace comments, “Think about how many memories this tree holds.”

From the other side of the tree, Harlon says, “I found it!”

She hurries to him and finds him tracing their initials with his index finger. She imitates his movements while saying, “H D plus G C.” Looking up at the tree canopy, she says, “Think of all the stories this tree could tell.”

“And all the secrets,” he adds.

“Oh my, yes, the secrets.”

“Grace.”

The serious tone in his voice causes her breath to catch. Furrowing her brow, she looks at him and sees tears welling in his eyes. “Harlon, are you okay?”

“No, not really. My life is incomplete, Grace.”

“What do you mean?”

He takes her in his arms and pulls her close. “I want to marry you, Grace. Whatever time I have left to live, I want to spend it with you.”

Putting her hand on the side of his face, she replies, “Oh Harlon, you make me feel young again. But this cancer is going to take me in a few months, and I don’t want you to lose me again and feel the same pain I caused you years ago.”

“Well, it’s too late to save me from that. I feel like my heart has awakened from a deep sleep and losing you again will crush it whether you marry me or not. But here’s the deal, I could die before you do. I could have a wreck or a heart attack and die. Life’s just that fragile, and you know it.”

He bends his head toward her and kisses her.

Warmth spreads through Grace’s body like she’s sitting under the sun on a summer day. After a moment, she turns her face from him and gasps for breath. “Oh, my.”

“I love you, Grace.”

Looking him in the eye, she says, “And I love you, too.”

“Then there’s no reason for us not to marry.”

“But what about Megan? If you and I marry, what will she do? I really need to talk to her first, don’t you think?”

“If you do, you need to tell her about your cancer, too. She deserves to know, Grace.”

“That’s going to be so hard.”

“Yes, it is. But you can do it.”

Closing her eyes, Grace nods and says, “Okay, I’ll do it.”

CHAPTER FORTY-EIGHT

Instead of driving straight home after her meeting with Max, Megan decides to stop by the nursery first and see if any new items have arrived for the gift shop. Getting out of the car, she stands and stretches her back and legs, then notices several boxes sitting in front of the gift shop door.

A surge of excitement washes away the fatigue from her trip, and she walks quickly to carry the boxes inside.

After a while, she's sitting on her knees in the middle of empty boxes and bubble wrap and gazes admiringly at the flowerpots, windchimes, and an iron birdbath with a solar-powered water pump.

Getting to her feet, she slowly turns in a circle and takes in the entire gift shop. Her feelings of pride and satisfaction are just one reason she knows she made the right decision regarding Max.

This is not the dog-eat-dog world selling insurance can sometimes be. With this, people will come to me, and they'll leave feeling happy. It's just that simple. And I like simple.

Just then, she hears the door opening. Turning her head, she sees Cross.

"Come see what just came in," she says, with a smile.

"Oh, wow," he says. "Those pots are beautiful." Touching the birdbath, he asks, "What's this made out of?"

"Iron."

"Man, that'll last forever. It'll become some family's heirloom that can be passed down for generations. I like that."

Even though his words express pleasure, Megan can tell his face is shadowed by worry lines. "Is everything okay?" she asks.

"Well, that's really my question to you. I got your text about the meeting with Max, but I don't know how you feel about how things went. Are you disappointed or hurt?"

"Oh, my goodness, no, not at all. I'm relieved and happy. Just being with him a short time reminded me of the kind of person I used to be, and the kind of life I was living." A thought strikes her. "You know what I've just realized?"

"What's that?"

"My fall and injury was the worst thing and best thing that ever happened to me. It was devastating and cost me so much, but if not for it, I never would have gotten off the merry-go-round my life was. All those months of learning how to walk again gave me time to think and take stock. And moving here to live with Mother was a devastating blow to my ego. I mean, what grown person wants to have to go back and live with their parents? But now we've grown so close, I can't imagine not living with her."

Cross's eyes grow red, and he turns his face away from her.

Megan moves closer to him and puts her hand on his arm. "Cross?"

Turning back to look at her, he says, "Megan…there's something…I need to…" His voice trails off.

Furrowing her brow, she says, "What's going on, Cross? What are you not telling me?"

He shakes his head and smiles at her. "Oh, it's nothing. I just want you to know how glad I am Buck and I didn't lose you. This store is going to be amazing, I'm sure. I don't think anyone could have done such a good job as you have in putting it together from scratch."

Pulling back from him, she says, "Well, I'm glad of that, too, but I would have thought you'd be happy for our friendship as well. I guess, maybe, I misjudged or misunderstood where we stood with each other." As she turns and starts picking up bubble wrap and stuffing it in the boxes, she adds, "But that's okay. It just stung a little. I'll get over it."

"No, no, wait," Cross says as he grabs her arm and turns her toward him.

Worry creases the corners of his eyes, and his face is red.

"I *am* glad you're not moving away and we can keep our friendship going. Really, I am."

“Then why didn’t you say that? Why talk about your store? Is it because you’re excited about the money it’s going to make for you two? Is that what’s most important to you? Because if it is, then—”

He puts his hand over her mouth. “Don’t say that, because it’s not true.”

He takes his hand away and stares at her.

Megan feels herself getting lost in his blue eyes, and her knees grow weak.

“Listen to me,” Cross tells her, “Buck will tell you I’ve been mean and in a surly mood all day. And do you want to know why? It’s because I was afraid you were going to go back to Max and move away. And how I felt had absolutely nothing to do with this store. You hear me? Nothing! It was about not having you in my life anymore. It wasn’t until there was a chance you might move away that I realized how much you mean to me.”

Megan can’t believe her ears. She feels as if someone has opened her mouth and poured sunlight into her, filling every cell in her body. Her chest grows warm as her throat grows tight.

“Our friendship scares me, Megan,” Cross continues. “I don’t want either of us to get hurt again. We’ve both experienced enough of that. But Buck tells me I’ve been sleepwalking through life ever since I came back home from prison. That is, until you and I met. I didn’t want to believe him at first, but he’s right. I feel more alive when I’m around you.”

“You know what I feel like doing right now?” Megan whispers. “I feel like kissing you, but I don’t know if I should. I don’t know if it’ll change things between us. I don’t know if you want to kiss me and will pull away from me. Because if that happens, it’ll change things. We’ll feel awkward around each other because I stepped across a line we both agreed we wouldn’t.”

Suddenly, he covers her mouth with his and gently unlocks hers with his tongue. When she presses her body against his, he walks her backward three or four steps until her back is against a wall, then he lifts her off the floor, and she puts her legs around his waist and squeezes.

Just as she slips her hands under his T-shirt, the door to the store opens, and Buck calls out, "You in here, Cross?"

In an instant, Megan and Cross untangle themselves and turn to face him as he comes around a corner.

Buck looks from one of them to the other and grins. "Par-don me for in-ter-rupting. But y'all need to learn to lock the door." Winking at them, he says, "I'll just go back outside and wait."

"No, that's okay," Cross says.

Megan says, "We were just…"

"Yeah, I want to hear the end of that sentence," Buck tells her as he folds his arms across his chest and waits while still grinning.

"Enjoying yourself, aren't you?" Cross says to him.

"Im-mensely," Buck replies.

"What were you wanting me for?"

"A delivery truck from that nursery in McMinnville, Tennessee, is outside, needing to be unloaded." Holding up his hands toward them, he continues. "But hey, I'll do it myself. You two carry on with whatever it was you were doing."

Giving him a playful shove, Cross says, "Wipe that stupid grin off your face. Pop would say you look like a mule eating briars. Let's go outside and unload the truck."

As they head out the door together, Megan hears Buck tease, "What grin? I wasn't grinning." Then he breaks into a hearty laugh.

She puts her back against the wall and slides down to the floor. Lightly tracing her finger around her lips, she closes her eyes and relives the feelings of passion that raced through her just before Buck interrupted her and Cross.

Hugging her knees to her chest, she thinks, *How far would I have gone? How far would he have wanted to go? The next time we see each other, how will we act? Will we talk about what just happened, or pretend it didn't? I don't think I can pretend. I think I've turned a corner in my feelings for him, and I don't want to go back. But how does he feel? What's he thinking right now? Is he talking to Buck about it?*

Just then, her phone buzzes with the notification of a message. Standing up, she pulls her phone out of her back pocket and unlocks the screen.

MOTHER: I'M BACK FROM BEING OUT WITH HARLON. ARE YOU ABOUT READY TO COME HOME? I THOUGHT I'D START PUTTING TOGETHER A CHEF SALAD FOR US IF YOU ARE.

MEGAN: YES, I'LL BE LEAVING THE STORE IN A FEW MINUTES AFTER I STRAIGHTEN A FEW THINGS UP. SALAD SOUNDS GOOD.

MOTHER: GREAT. I'VE GOT SOMETHING I WANT TO TALK TO YOU ABOUT.

MEGAN: WHAT?

MOTHER: WE'LL TALK ABOUT IT WHEN YOU GET HOME. LOVE YOU.

MEGAN: LOVE YOU, TOO.

Megan stares at the screen, wondering what's on her mother's mind.

CHAPTER FORTY-NINE

When Megan arrives home, she scoops Lacy off the floor.

Instead of greeting Megan with kisses, Lacy sniffs her face, neck, and the front of her shirt.

"You don't miss a thing, do you?" Megan asks. "Yes, I've been with Cross. Is that okay with you?"

"Is that you?" Grace calls from the kitchen.

Setting Lacy on the floor, Megan heads toward the kitchen. "Yes, it's me, Mother."

"I've just finished making the salads," she tells her as she enters. "If you'll fix us some tea, we'll be ready to eat."

Taking two glasses out of the cabinet, Megan puts ice and tea in them and follows her mother to the table. As they sit down, she asks, "Did you and Harlon have a good time?"

"Oh, it was perfect, Megan. We found the tree he carved our initials on when we were dating. And people still tie rope swings on the same limb we used when we would swing out over the lake and jump in."

"Oh my gosh, that must have been so cool to find!"

"It was!"

They take a few bites of salad before Grace says, "And things didn't work out between you and Max?"

"No. Being with him really showed me how much I've changed since moving here, and it was obvious to him, too. And he didn't like it. I thought maybe he'd changed some, too, but turns out, he's still narcissistic. He's actually already seeing someone else."

"What? Then why did he even want to meet?"

"I think it was so he could feel better about himself by apologizing for deserting me. That's twisted up, isn't it, when you apologize so you'll feel better?" Shaking her head, she says, "No, I don't want my old life back. I like my life here. You know how angry I was about having to move in with you. But now I'm so glad I did. We might get on each other's nerves sometimes, but I still wouldn't trade the time we've had together for anything."

She reaches her hand across the table to her, and Grace takes it. For a moment, they look at each other smiling, then they return to eating.

"So, what was it you wanted to talk to me about?" Megan asks.

Laying down her fork, Grace says, "Well, there are a couple of things on my mind."

Her mother's tone stops Megan, and she sets her fork on the table. "I'm listening."

"I've already told you what a perfect day Harlon and I had. It was so perfect, he asked me to marry him."

Megan's mouth drops open. "Marry?"

"Yes. He was the sweetest thing about it, really romantic, and caught me by surprise. I knew we both had feelings for each other, but I thought that was as far as it would go."

"Do you love him, Mother?"

"Yes, I do, Megan."

"So, what did you tell him?"

"I told him I wanted to talk to you first."

Megan jerks back. "Talk to me? Why?"

Waving her hand at the room, Grace says, "This, this is our life, you and me, and I've loved every second of it. If I marry Harlon, this will change. The last thing in the world I want is for you and I to become distant from each other. The closeness we have now is something I always longed for but decided would never come to pass. This will sound strange to say, but it's kind of like the worst thing that could happen, your horrible injuries from the fall, turned out to be the best thing for us. I mean, I'm not saying I'm glad you got hurt, but look what happened because of it. Does that make sense?"

Smiling, Megan tells her about her conversation with Cross and how she said the exact same thing.

Grace says, "You've changed in so many ways. I've always loved you, but I like you more than I used to, and I'm glad I don't have to put up with Max. I never did like him."

A shadow of sadness passes across Megan's heart, and she looks around the kitchen. "If you and Harlon get married, I'll need to get my own place."

"See there?" Grace says. "That's what I'm talking about. It'll change things. I don't know where we'll live if we marry. Here, or in his house? We didn't get into any of that. I'm not going to let anything happen that'll disturb your happiness. That's more important than anything. If you have any objections to me marrying Harlon, or if you think it's not a good idea, then I won't do it."

"And your happiness is more important to me than anything, including my own," Megan replies. "I want *you* to be happy, Mother. And if you believe you'll be happy with Harlon, then by all means please marry him, because you being happy will make me happy. I'll adjust and do whatever I need to do. I mean it. The more I think about it, the more excited I get for you. You and Harlon are good for each other. You'll be much more content with him than you were with Father. I know he wasn't always easy to live with."

"I loved your father, Megan."

"I know you did. And I loved him, too, but boy, wouldn't life have been a lot more fun if it had been Harlon we were with?"

Chuckling, Grace says, "Oh, I've got to remember to tell Harlon that one. He'll get a kick out of you saying it."

Resting her forearms on the table, Megan says, “You’re going to tell him yes, aren’t you?”

“If you’re okay with it, yes, I am.”

Megan moves to the other side of the table and gives her mother a hug and kisses her cheek. “I’m so, so happy for you. And now I’m going to tell you something that’ll make you happy.”

“What’s that?”

“Cross and I kissed today.”

“No!” Grace cries, with excitement.

“Yes, we did! And it was no little peck on the cheek. I mean, we *kissed*.”

Clapping her hands, her mother says, “I knew it, I knew it, I knew it! I knew you two would finally find your way to each other. Oh, Megan, I’m so excited! So, what does it mean, this kiss? Where’s it going to lead?”

“Those are the same questions I’ve asked myself since then, and I really don’t know the answers to them. Buck barged in while we were kissing and blew the whole thing up. Cross and I didn’t get to talk after that, so I’m not sure what he’s thinking.”

Megan moves back to her chair and takes a long drink of tea. “It’s been a good day for both of us, hasn’t it?”

“Yes, it has.”

“Wait a minute. There was something else you wanted to talk to me about. What is it?”

Grace looks down for a moment, then lifts her eyes. The mirth that was in them has disappeared and been replaced with sorrow and dread.

A chill runs up Megan’s spine, and a lump is in her throat. Whatever her mother’s about to say to her, she doesn’t want to hear it, because she knows it’s going to crush her. She feels like putting her hands over her ears or running out of the kitchen. Instead, she braces herself.

“There’s no easy way to say this,” Grace begins, “so I’ll just put it out there. I have cancer, pancreatic cancer, and I only have a few months to live.”

Her mother’s words are like a vacuum, sucking all the life out of Megan and leaving her devoid of thought or emotion. She stares blankly at Grace.

“So, if Harlon and I are to marry, we’ll need to do it soon.”

“Does he know?” In her ears, her voice sounds hollow.

“Yes, we’ve talked about it, and he still wants to marry me.”

Megan’s feelings return with the force of a tsunami, nearly knocking her out of her chair. Shaking her head, she says, “This doesn’t make sense. You don’t even look sick.”

“Not yet, but you know I haven’t been feeling well lately. This cancer is very aggressive, and very soon I’ll begin a downward spiral.”

Standing up, Megan says, “No, that’s not going to happen. We’re going to go to Vanderbilt Hospital in Nashville and find an oncologist and start treating your cancer. People are cured of cancer every day. We’re not going to sit around and do nothing.”

“Megan, I’ve already seen an oncologist, and he’s said they can do radiation and chemo, but it’ll only give me a few extra months. That’s not how I want to die, with all my hair falling out and the nausea and vomiting that goes along with that kind of treatment. My days are numbered; I accept that. Please don’t fight me on this. I don’t want us to get sideways over it and ruin whatever time we have left with each other.”

Rushing to her mother’s side, Megan goes down on her knees, wraps her arms around her, and buries her face in her chest. A floodgate opens, and tears gush through.

“No, no, no!” she wails. “This can’t be happening!”

CHAPTER FIFTY

That night, Harlon and Cross settle onto their couch and recliner after supper to watch TV. Roxy joins them and lays next to Cross.

Stroking her head, he asks, "You want to watch the Braves game?"

"Have you ever known me to miss a game?" Harlon replies.

"No, not really."

As the TV comes on, Harlon says, "I just wish ol' Skip Carey was still around, calling their games. He made it fun, and funny, too." Just then, his phone rings.

Cross chuckles. "Probably a spam caller wanting to sell you an extended warranty on your truck."

Harlon looks at the screen, then answers the call. "Hello, Grace."

Seeing his father's face turn serious, Cross points the remote toward the TV and mutes it.

After a few moments, Harlon says, "How did she take it?" He nods as he listens. "I'm not surprised. Are you okay?" His face relaxes. "That's good. I know you're tired. Why don't you go to bed, and we'll talk more tomorrow?" Smiling, he says, "I love you, too." He ends the call and looks at Cross. "She told Megan about her cancer."

"Good. I've had to force myself not to tell her. I know it was awful to hear, but she needed to know. How did she take it?"

"Grace said she got really upset."

Nodding, Cross says, "I'm not surprised. The two of them are really close."

"Uh…yeah, they are. There's something else she told her I need to talk to you about."

"What's that?"

"I asked Grace to marry me."

Cross drops the remote control onto the floor, and the back of it pops off, sending the batteries rolling under the couch. "You did what?"

“I asked Grace to marry me.”

“But Pop, she’s going to…you know, the cancer.”

“Yeah, I know she’s going to die, but so am I, and so are you, and so is everybody. Either one of us could get killed in a car wreck tomorrow, couldn’t we?”

“Well, sure, but…”

“There’s no ‘but’ to add to that. Life’s uncertain, but death is sure. The older you get, you’ll see what I mean. I just can’t think of any reasons not to marry her. I love her, and she loves me. Besides that, we really enjoy being with each other. Why shouldn’t we spend whatever time we have left being with each other?”

Cross relaxes his face and smiles. “You’re right, Pop. I’m happy for you. So, it sounds like I need to be looking for a place of my own, doesn’t it?”

“You know, she and I haven’t talked about where we want to live, whether here or at her place. Either way doesn’t matter to me. If it’s here, I don’t want you to feel like I’m kicking you out. As a matter of fact, it’s fine with me if you continue to live here. I just don’t know what Grace would think about that.”

They fall silent and stare at the images on the muted TV, but their minds are elsewhere.

After a minute, Harlon says, “I hope you don’t feel like I’m deserting the memory of your mother. I never thought I’d marry again. I was thankful for having had a good wife and content living out my life as a bachelor. But I’ll tell you, Cross, sometimes love comes looking for you when you least expect it.”

“I’m glad you’re going to be with Grace. It’s going to be hard on you, with her having cancer, I hope you’ve thought about that.”

“I have. And you’re right; it’s going to be hard. But that’s more reason to marry her, so I can be there for her.”

“Don’t you think Megan’s going to want to do that? She might not want you interfering.”

Folding his hands in his lap, Harlon replies, “I hadn’t thought about that. Guess that’s something we’ll have to talk about.”

Cross slaps his hands on his knees and stands up. "I'm sure y'all will work it out. I think I need to go see Megan, give her a chance to talk about all this."

Harlon raises his eyebrows. "Aren't you going to call or text her first?"

"No, I'm just going to go."

"You don't want to watch the ball game?"

"Nah, I've got too much on my mind. I'll have my phone with me. Call me if you need something."

"I'll be fine. You run along."

Looking over his shoulder as he walks to the door, Cross says, "Roxy, you stay here and keep an eye on Pop."

The big retriever flops her tail against the couch where she's lying.

Harlon says, "Us old dogs'll help take care of each other."

The night air is heavy and smells of rain as Cross walks outside and heads toward his truck. He turns his head at a rumble of thunder from off in the west. High in the treetops, limbs shake their leaves like a cheerleader shaking her pom poms as the wind picks up.

A good rain would be nice. It'd help everyone's yard grow.

On the drive over to Megan's, thoughts and memories ricochet off each other; memories of his mother, thoughts about how he'd feel if his Pop was the one with cancer, imagining how Megan is feeling right now, and in the background his father's words, "Sometimes love comes looking for you," keep ringing in his ears.

In the distance, lightning pulsates in a cloud, revealing an ominous-looking front headed his way. At the same time, heavy raindrops dart across the light from his headlights and plop against the windshield.

Just as he reaches her house, a heavy gust of wind rocks his truck and brings with it a torrent of rain.

Jumping out of the truck, he races up the sidewalk but still gets soaked by the time he makes it to the porch. Using his index finger like a squeegee, he removes the rain from his bald head, then tries to shake some of it off his shirt.

The timer that keeps his headlights on after stopping the truck suddenly goes off, plunging everything into darkness. It's then he notices no light is coming through the living room windows, only the faint glow of light from somewhere deeper in the house.

Maybe I should have called her first. They might've already gone to bed.

Suddenly, the porch light comes on, nearly blinding him. The front door opens, and Megan stands in the opening.

"Cross?" she calls to him through the thunderous rain. "What are you doing here?"

He recognizes the signs of her grief: her blotchy, red face, and her swollen eyes. With a raised voice, he replies, "I thought you might need somebody to talk to."

Without a word, she waves him inside and closes the door behind him as a crash of thunder rattles the windows.

Silhouetted by what he guesses is the kitchen light, Megan tells him, "Let me turn a lamp on."

"That's okay, why don't we just sit in the dark?"

"At least let me go get you a towel. I know you're soaked."

In a moment, she returns with a bath towel and wipes his face and the front of his shirt with it. "Turn around," she says, and she wipes off his back.

Turning back around, he takes the towel from her and dries the top of his head.

A tiny smile pulls at the corner of her mouth. "At least your hair didn't get wet."

He returns her smile. "That's just one advantage in having a shaved head. I also never have to worry about how my hair looks."

"Maybe I should shave my head, too."

Turning serious, he reaches and strokes her hair. "Let's not get carried away."

She leans her cheek against his hand and closes her eyes. In the next instant, they pop open. "Why are you here?"

"Like I said, I thought you might want to talk."

"About what?"

"Your mother called Pop and told him she finally told you about her cancer."

She stares at him for a moment. "Did you already know about it?"

Nodding, he explains how he learned about it from Harlon but was sworn to secrecy.

"That's why you've been upset lately, isn't it? I could tell something was going on."

"Don't be mad at me."

Taking him by the hand, she leads him to the couch while saying, "I want to be mad at you, but what's the point in that? Sit down here with me."

They sink into the couch, his arm around her shoulders and her head on his chest.

"It's all too much, Cross," she says.

"Yes, it is."

"I don't want to lose her."

Her shoulders tremble as a new wave of sorrows strikes her, and she begins to cry.

Cross thinks about consoling her with words, but his throat is so choked with emotions, nothing comes out, so he tenderly rubs her back.

After a bit, Megan sits up and wipes her face. Sniffling, she asks, "And do you know they're planning on getting married?"

"Yep. Pop and I talked about it. At first I didn't understand, but when he explained it, it makes perfect sense. You know what he said?"

"What?"

"He said, 'Sometimes love comes looking for you.' I'm going to be honest with you, Megan, I think that's what's happened to me and how I feel about you. I mean, we've talked about how we've lived alone and decided that's what we deserve and we'll just be good friends to each other. But when there was a chance you might be going back to your ex-husband, it surprised me how bad it shook me. At first, I told myself it was because I didn't want to lose you as a friend, and that's true, but that's not the whole picture. The whole picture includes me never wanting you out of my life; it includes the truth that I love you. You hear me? I love you, Megan."

Pulling away from him, she covers her face with her hands, then runs her fingers through her hair. "Oh, Cross, if you'd told me this before I went to Nashville, I never would have gone to meet Max, because being with you is what I really want. But now, after learning of Mother's cancer? I just don't know how much of myself I can give you. I don't know how much assistance she's going to need, but I can promise you this: whatever she needs, I'm going to be here to give it to her." She stops, and her eyes grow wide. "And the store! The grand opening is just two weeks away. I don't know if I can give it the commitment and attention it needs. But I promised you and Buck I would. And we've got to plan a wedding!" Shaking her head, she says, "See what I mean? It's just all too much. What am I going to do?"

Taking her hands in his, he tells her, "This is not 'What am *I* going to do?' This is 'What are *we* going to do?' From now on, it's you and me."

"But relationships take work, Cross, and I don't want to have to focus on working on us, not right now at least. Do you understand?"

"Yes, I understand. You and I aren't going to work on *us*. We're going to focus on doing what we need to do to help each other with your mother and with her and my Pop getting married—that's all. Okay? We're not going to put pressure on each other and try and figure out our future. There's going to be enough to deal with from day to day to keep us occupied. And as far as the store is concerned, I want you to sleep on it. You've had a lot hit you today, and you need some time to sort through it all. If in the morning you want to bow out of our agreement, then that'll be fine. We'll wait until fall or next spring to open it. Don't worry about it. Okay?"

She sighs, and her body relaxes. Smiling at him, she says, "Thank you. That sounds like a good plan. I love how calm and level-headed you are."

Throwing one leg over his, she moves onto his lap and puts her hands on his face. "Now, how about doing me a favor and helping me forget about everything for a little bit?" She presses her body against his and kisses him.

Without warning, a giant flash of lightning strikes outside, immediately followed by an explosive *crack* and thunderous clap of thunder, and darkness swallows the house.

CHAPTER FIFTY-ONE

The next morning, while standing at the toaster waiting for her bagel to pop up, Megan smiles at the memory of sitting on Cross's lap and kissing him.

If the power hadn't gone off and woke Mother up and she walked in on us with a flashlight, what would have happened? First it's Buck interrupting us, then Mother; the stars just can't seem to get lined up for us.

The sound of her mother shuffling into the kitchen turns her around.

Does she look more tired than normal? Or is it just because of the storm interfering with her sleep? Or is it my imagination?

Smiling, she says, "Good morning, Mother. I'm fixing me a bagel with some cream cheese. You want one?"

"I'm not really hungry this morning. I think I'll just have coffee."

Warning bells go off in Megan's head. For as long as she can remember, her mother *always* eats breakfast. "It's the most important meal of the day," her mother would say. "Eat breakfast like a king, lunch like a prince, and supper like a pauper."

While waiting for the Keurig to finish brewing her coffee, Grace says, "I want to apologize again for walking in on you and Cross last night. I feel bad about it."

Megan laughs. "I told you last night it wasn't a big deal, and it still isn't. Actually, you probably owed me it because of that time I walked in on you and Father."

"Oh my gosh, you still remember that?"

"Uh, of course I do! It scarred me for life. At least Cross and I still had all our clothes on."

Grace laughs. "I don't think your father made love to me for a month, he was so afraid you'd walk in on us again."

"Well, you should have kept your door locked."

When the Keurig finishes dripping, Grace carries her cup of coffee and finds a seat at the table.

Megan joins her and spreads cream cheese on her bagel.

"What's the weather like outside?" Grace asks.

"It's perfect. It's in the upper sixties and not a cloud in the sky. It's going to be a beautiful day. What would you like to do today?"

Frowning, Grace asks, "What do you mean?"

"I thought you and I could spend the day together doing whatever you'd like to do. Wouldn't that be nice?"

"You've got to go to work today. Have you completely forgotten about the grand opening coming up?"

Megan averts her eyes. "Well, I've talked with Cross about it, and I think we're just going to wait until fall or next spring to open up the business. That way, you and I can spend more time together."

Grace sets her cup down on the table so hard, some of the coffee splashes out. "Young lady, you listen to me right now. You are not going to put your life on hold just because I have cancer. What are we going to do, sit and stare at each other all day, every day? I don't know about you, but that doesn't sound very enjoyable to me. We're going to go right on living life like we always have. I've heard people say you should live every day like it's your last, but that's not a very practical way to live, because no one would ever go to work or pay their bills or clean their house or mow their yard. You see what I mean? What you and I will do is treasure each moment more and fill our hearts with memories of the simple things, like this moment right here, us sitting at the table together and enjoying being together."

Tears well up in Megan's eyes. "But I don't want to miss an important moment."

"Honey, you're always going to miss important moments, because you don't realize how important they are until they pass. If you're not careful, you'll let your worry about missing moments cause you to do the very thing you fear. Worry is a thief; don't let it rob you of the present." She reaches over and pats Megan's hand. "You tell Cross you'll be in to work this morning, and you'll have that store ready for the grand opening."

Blowing her nose on a napkin, Megan replies, “I’ll try. I’ll do my best. But you must promise me if you ever need something, you’ll call me, no matter what. Okay?”

Nodding, Grace says, “I promise.”

Megan turns back to eating her bagel, and after a minute she says, “Two things you and Harlon need to decide: When and where are you getting married, and where are you going to live?”

“I believe that’s three things,” Grace retorts. “But you’re right, we need to get that settled. I’ll get with him today, and we’ll make some decisions, then I’ll let you know.”

Picking up her phone, Megan texts Cross. Almost immediately, he replies with a row of “heart” emojis, plus an exclamation point.

“Is that Cross?” Grace asks.

“Yeah. I told him I’m coming to work today and looking forward to the grand opening.”

“What did he say back?”

Turning her phone around, she shows her mother the screen.

“Mmhmm, little hearts. Wonder what that means?” Grace says, with a wink. “Sounds like there needs to be a little cupid emoji in there somewhere.”

“Let me help you rest your mind on that one, Mother. Cross and I have both told each other we love each other.”

A broad smile spreads across Grace’s face, and she closes her eyes. “That’s music to my ears. When are you going to get married?”

“You just don’t quit, do you? Look, I think we know we’re going to get married someday, but we’re in no hurry.”

“Why not? What reason is there to delay?”

Megan tries to look her in the eye but can’t.

“Wait a minute!” Grace says sharply. “It’s me again, isn’t it? You want to wait until I’m dead before you get married, don’t you?”

“Don’t say that! That sounds awful!”

“You can say it any way you want to. You can say you want to process your grief before you marry. You can say you don’t want to be distracted by your marriage plans because you want to be taking care of me. But the truth is, once I’m gone, you and Cross will be married. Why would you two deprive me of witnessing the one thing I’ve been wishing for, and the one thing Harlon’s been wishing for?”

Cocking her head to one side, Megan says, “I really hadn’t thought about it that way. But right now my head is so full, I think it’s going to burst. It’s just a lot to take in. I promise you, though, I’ll think about it. Will that satisfy you?”

Grace nods. “That’s okay. Just don’t take too long. Sometimes you overthink things.”

CHAPTER FIFTY-TWO

After Megan leaves for work, Grace calls Harlon.

"Good morning, dear."

"Good morning," he replies. "Did y'all's power go off last night during that storm?"

"Yes! That was a bad storm. I think lightning may have hit one of the trees in our yard."

"Have you gone outside to look around?

"Not yet."

"Is it okay if I come take a look?

Grace chuckles. "We're practically married, Harlon. You really don't have to ask permission."

He laughs. "I guess you're right. I'll be right there."

Ending the call, she goes to her bedroom and gets dressed, then goes to the bathroom to put on her makeup. But when she looks at herself in the mirror, she pauses.

Why should I put makeup on? Harlon needs to see what he'll be waking up to every morning.

A little bit later, she hears his footsteps on the porch and for a second feels panicky about her decision not to put on makeup.

Taking a deep breath, she opens the door and says, "Good morning. I thought it only fair to let you see me without makeup, so you'd know what I really look like."

Harlon smiles and gives her a kiss on the lips. “Good morning, love. Neither of us looks like we used to, but you and I, we earned our wrinkles. I guess I’m different when it comes to wrinkles; I find them fascinating, because each one tells a story.” Using his finger, he traces over the laugh lines at the edge of her eyes. “These tell me how much you like to laugh and smile. The ones on your cheeks here tell me you’ve known your share of sorrow and have a big heart. I especially like these on your forehead, because they let me know when you’re worried or mad. Besides all that, if we had a contest to see who has the most wrinkles, I think I’d easily win.”

She touches her finger to his lips. “I just wish society viewed wrinkles on a woman the same way you do. It’s okay for men to have wrinkles, but women are supposed to fix or hide theirs with surgery or Botox or makeup. It’s really not fair.”

“I totally agree. It makes me mad when I watch movies that have an older male star paired with a woman half his age or young enough to be his daughter. I think it makes the man look shallow, and in a subtle way it degrades older women.”

A smile breaks out on her face, and she kisses him. “I just keep finding new reasons to love you.”

Taking her by the hand, he says, “Come on outside here, and let’s see what the storm did to your trees.”

They don’t walk far before Harlon points at the ground and says, “Look at all that tree bark. Lightning blew it off one of these trees.” Looking around, he says, “But I don’t see any limbs or treetops on the ground. Usually that’s what happens, the lightning blows them off like a cannon would and often sets the tree on fire. Do you see any streaks around where the grass looks wilted? Sometimes the lightning will run down the tree and follow the shallow roots.”

“I had no idea about any of that,” Grace marvels.

“You probably don’t know lightning is actually good for grass and pastures, because it puts nitrogen in the air.”

“Who are you? Bill Nye the Science Guy?”

Harlon chuckles as he continues to look at the trees. Suddenly, he gestures off to their right. “There it is.”

Grace follows him to a towering willow oak tree.

"See there?" he tells her. "It's cracked from the top to the bottom. It's not split in two, like I've seen some, but it's for sure going to die."

"How does lightning do that?"

"It basically boils the sap."

Putting her hand on the tree trunk, Grace says, "It's kind of sad. This tree has been here a long, long time and seen so much. Is there anything we should do with it?"

"I've got an Amish neighbor who would love to cut it into firewood, if you want me to ask him about it."

"That'd be great. At least it'll get put to good use instead of slowly rotting away." Slipping her arm through his, she says, "Let's go sit on the porch."

As they walk in that direction, Harlon says, "What you said about that tree back there, I think the one thing most people our age don't want to do is slowly rot away. We want to be as vibrant as we can be, and then one day suddenly die, like the tree being hit by a bolt of lightning. But sadly, we don't get to choose how we exit this life, do we?"

Shaking her head, Grace says, "No, we don't. What you're talking about, though, is why I don't want to do radiation and chemo for my cancer. If there was a good chance it would cure me, that'd be different. To me, going that route would be like rotting away. And like you said, no one wants to go that way."

When he doesn't reply, she looks at him and sees his eyes are red and chin is trembling. Hugging him, she says, "I'm sorry this is so painful for you. Hurting you is the last thing in the world I want to do. You know, if we hadn't gotten back together and fallen in love, you could have avoided all this pain and sadness."

In a voice thick with emotion, Harlon says, "The only reason this hurts so bad is because I love you so much. It's like love's a double-edged sword. But to be able to spend the rest of our days together loving each other is worth whatever pain I have to bear." Putting his hand on his chest, he continues. "I just never thought my old heart could ever love someone as much as I love you."

Raising the back of his hand to her lips and kissing it, Grace replies, "Oh Harlon, stop it. You're going to make me cry."

Drawing out his red bandana, he blows his nose. "I think we need to accept that we're going to be sharing lots of love, and we're going to be sharing lots of tears."

They arrive at the porch and take a seat in the swing.

Grace says, "I suppose you're right. There's no way to avoid tears, is there?"

"Not for me. I'm just a big crybaby sometimes."

"Well, let's change the direction of our conversation and talk about our wedding. When are we going to get married?"

Harlon makes a move like he's going to stand up and says, "Let's go right now, as far as I'm concerned. We'll find us a judge in the courthouse who'll do it."

Laughing, Grace pulls him back and says, "I don't think Megan would be very happy if we did it that way. Not that we need to have a big wedding, because I don't want one. Do you?"

"Heck, no. Let's keep it simple and easy. Where do you want the wedding held?"

"I've been thinking about that. Why don't we do it outside underneath our tree at Britton Ford? I think it'd be sweet to do it there. What do you think?"

Clapping his hands together, he answers, "I think that'd be perfect! It'll be another memory to add to all the others we have from that old tree."

"Okay, that settles the where. Next is, who are we going to get to do the ceremony? Do you have somebody in mind?"

"I guess I haven't given that much thought. What about you?"

"I wonder if the preacher who was at the Sulphur Well Church of Christ when I was growing up is still around. I always thought he was such a down-to-earth, humble person, and he didn't use lots of big words and flowery speech when he was preaching. His sermons were easy to understand."

"Are you talking about Stephen Randle?"

"Yes! Do you know him?"

"I think most everybody around here knows Stephen, and you describe him perfectly. If you want me to, I'll get in touch with him and see if he's willing to do it, and when he's available."

Patting him on the leg, Grace says, "That'd be great."

Harlon puts his hand on top of hers. "I've been thinking about where we're going to live after we're married, and I think we need to live here. When you start getting really sick, it'll be helpful for you to be around familiar things; you'll be more comfortable. Don't you think so?"

A chill runs up her back, and her body shudders. In a quiet voice, she says, "You know I'm going to need you to help me be brave, don't you?"

He puts his arm around her shoulders and hugs her. "Don't you worry. I'll be whatever you need me to be."

Lifting her head to look at him, she says, "Kiss me."

His warm lips meet hers, and all her fears scatter like a flock of startled starlings. "Thank you," she whispers.

"It's going to be okay," he tells her. "I'm not for sure how, but we'll make it through this leg of our journey together."

"What'll make it easier is having you with me," she replies as tears blur her vision. "I'm so glad we found each other again."

Placing his rough hand on the side of her face, he kisses her again.

CHAPTER FIFTY-THREE

Unlocking the front door to the gift store, Megan steps inside just as the sound of a vehicle coming from behind startles her. Looking over her shoulder, she sees it's Cross. She stands in the doorway and smiles at him as he gets out and walks toward her, grinning.

"Hey there," she says.

Ignoring her greeting, he lifts her off the floor with a hug and spins her around as the door closes behind them.

Megan cries out in surprise. "Cross!"

Setting her down, he says, "You've really made me happy by agreeing to go ahead and open the store. I don't think you'll regret your decision. And I'll be around to help if you need it, and I'm confident Buck and Betty will, too. What made you change your mind?"

"Let me just say my mother is a force to be reckoned with. Everyone thinks she's this nice, sweet lady—and she is—but when she makes up her mind about something, there's no changing her."

Cross's eyebrows squeeze together. "What do you mean? What did she say?"

"Basically, we're going to keep living our daily lives like we always have. She's not going to have me sitting around holding her hand every day, even though that's what I want to do."

"I can see why you'd feel that way. But one thing I learned from my time in prison is to take things one day at a time. In there, it's easy to think and worry about what's going to happen tomorrow or next week, because there's so much uncertainty there. I mean, I saw men get stabbed to death or beaten half to death over something as simple as a pack of cigarettes. It was insane. I decided if it was going to happen to me, it was going to happen; there was nothing I could do about it. That's when I decided just to focus on one day at a time; actually, one moment at a time. I think that's what you need to do with your mom, and maybe that's what she was trying to tell you."

Reaching for his face, Megan runs her finger down the side of his nose, to the corner of his mouth, and stops at his chin. “Sometimes you’re really smart, aren’t you?”

He leans his head down and catches her finger between his lips and squeezes it for a second, then he lets go and says, “Who do you think is the brains behind this nursery business? You know it’s not Buck.”

She laughs.

They stand there, looking at each other, their arms resting easy on each other’s waist.

Hungry feelings run through Megan as her heart beats faster and breath grows warmer.
“Does Buck have a key to this building?”

“I don’t think so, why?”

Reaching over, she locks the door, then takes him by the hand and leads him to the shadowy storage room in the back. When he reaches for the light switch, she stops his hand and says, “We’re not going to need any light for what’s about to happen.”

~~~~~~~~~~~~~~~~

Sometime later, Megan stands up and pulls her jeans on, while Cross is fastening his. She pushes back her hair that’s sticking to her damp face.

“Now you’ve gone and mussed me up,” she jokes.

“Hey, don’t blame me. I believe this was your idea.”

“Well, I don’t think I noticed any resistance from you, did I?”

Sitting down on a stack of bags of potting soil, Cross pats it and says, “Come sit down.”

“I’m going to get me a bottle of water out of the little refrigerator back here. You want one?”

“Sure.”

After turning on the lights and retrieving two bottles, Megan joins him and takes a long drink. “Oh, that feels good going down.”

Cross joins and gives a satisfied “Ahh” after his drink.
~~~~~~~~~~~~~~~~

“Now that we have that out of the way,” she begins, “we need to talk.”

A sly smile dances across his face. “Got what out of the way? Taking a drink of water?”

Slapping his shoulder, she says, “Don’t be stupid; you know what I’m talking about.”

He gives her a quick kiss on the cheek. “Yes, I do. What’s on your mind?”

“Do you want to marry me?”

“Whoa, where did that come from?”

“Just answer the question. Do you want to marry me?”

“Yes, yes, I do, but do you want to marry me?”

Pointing to the spot where they just made love, she says, “What do you think?”

“I’ll be honest. Sex nowadays has become so casual; it hardly means what it used to. But that’s not the way it is for me. If I share that part of me with someone, it means something. It’s a way of showing how much I care.”

Megan feels her ire rising. “Well, what do you think it means for me? Do you think I spread my legs just for the fun of it?”

“I’m not trying to hurt your feelings. I know you don’t run around having sex with whoever. But I don’t know everything there is to know about you. I just need to know if it means something to you, too.”

Taking a slow breath, Megan relaxes and says, “Well, let me assure you it means something. Honestly, I fantasized about having sex with you before I hardly knew you. I mean, you’re a good looking man, Cross, and I’ve got desires just like anyone else. And I’ll also admit, I’ve had sex in the past just for the fun of it, but that’s not who I am anymore. Sometime during the past year, I concluded I probably wouldn’t ever have sex again, because I wasn’t ever going to be in a relationship again. And I was okay with that. Then you and those cobalt blue eyes came along, and the next thing I know, I’m wrestling with you on the floor of a dark warehouse.”

Laughter erupts between them and ricochets off the concrete floor and cinder block walls.

When their laughter dies down, Cross says, “So, I think we’ve established we both want to get married, am I right?”

Nodding, Megan replies, “You are correct. And my idea about getting married was to wait until after Mother passes away and I’ve had time to grieve before we do it.”

“I’m good with that, too. It would be too much to try and do it any other way.”

She tells him about her mother’s wishes and how them marrying would make her so happy.

Standing up, Cross rubs his hand across his scalp. “Wow, I didn’t expect that.”

Quickly, Megan says, “We don’t have to do it that way, if it’s too fast for you. I’ll just explain—”

He silences her by holding up his hand. “No, no. It just caught me off guard. If you’re ready to get married, so am I.”

Jumping off the bags, she exclaims, “Really?! You’d really do it? I mean, you really want us to marry soon?”

Looking at the spot where they made love, he replies, “If it means we get to do that on a bed rather than on concrete, then I’m all for it. I don’t think my elbows and knees could hold up to that again.”

She gives him a playful slap on the arm. “Oh, hush up! You’d do it again right now if I agreed to let you.”

He raises his eyebrows and starts to unfasten his jeans. “Is that an invitation?”

“See?” she replies. “You make my point for me.”

Stepping closer to her, he lifts her off the floor.

In a husky voice, he says, “You better get used to this, because I think I could make love to you all day long. I love you, Megan Charles.” He covers her mouth with his, and their tongues dance together.

Heat fills Megan's body, and she breaks off the kiss, gasping for breath. "And I love you, Cross Daniels. But we'll never get our work done if we keep doing this. Let's save it for our wedding night, okay?"

"If you say so. But it won't be easy."

"You know," she says, "we need Buck and Betty to be at the wedding as best man and maid of honor, don't we?"

"That's a great idea! So, who's getting married first, us, or your mom and Pop? And who do you and I need to get to do our ceremony?"

"I haven't even thought about that. I think you and I need to sit down with Mother and your dad and iron out some details."

They stand and stare at each other for a moment. Then they smile and say at the same time, "We're getting married."

CHAPTER FIFTY-FOUR

<u>*Six days later*</u>

On a warm morning in late June, underneath a hard blue sky, with her mother at her side and Stephen Randle behind them, Megan faces Cross, Harlon, Buck, Randy, and Glynn as the final refrain of "I'll Love Nobody But You" hangs in the air. They're all dressed in blue jeans and white long-sleeved shirts, as are Megan, Grace, and Betty.

Harlon says, "We'll play one more the boys and me picked out. It says exactly how me and Cross feel about you two."

Grace squeezes Megan's hand, and Megan smiles at her.

"A Good Woman's Love." Cross announces the song loud enough for a chapel full of people to hear, even though there's no more than this handful of people present.

By the time the song is finished, the women are dabbing their tears with tissue. Then Cross and Harlon hand their instruments to Glynn and Randy and take their places beside their brides-to-be.

Everyone turns to face the preacher, Stephen Randle, who is head and shoulders taller than anyone there. His face beams as he says, "I've performed an untold number of weddings in my life, but this ceremony holds a lot of firsts for me. It's the first that features bluegrass music, takes place on the shore of Kentucky Lake, and the first double-ring ceremony with parents *and* their children. The fact that Grace used to come to the church where I preached when she was a teenager gives you some inkling of how old I am, but the oldest member of this wedding party is this massive beech tree under which we stand. Grace and Harlon have told me their story that's connected to this tree and why they wanted it to be a witness to their marriage." Gazing upward, he says, "You know, if this tree could talk, it would reveal some secrets about my wife and I, too, we'd prefer to be kept private."

Everyone chuckles.

“To me,” Stephen continues, “this wedding is about second chance love. Everyone who has experienced the hurt, sadness, and disappointment of a love lost wonders if they’re doomed to be alone for the rest of their lives. Questions keep them awake at night: Is there something wrong with me? Will anyone ever love me the way I want to be loved? Can my brokenness be made whole again? Will I get a second chance? Do I *deserve* a second chance?”

Harlon and Grace, and Cross and Megan, look at each other.

“The answer to all those questions stands before me. This—this is what second chance love looks like. It has a warmth that comes from understanding, trust that comes from knowing, joy that comes from an appreciation of what each other brings to the table. Second chance love says, ‘This, this is what I’ve been looking for.’ It says, ‘Where have you been?’

“Matthew chapter six and verse eight says, ‘your Father knows exactly what you need even before you ask Him.’ One version of the Bible interprets it this way, ‘your Father knows better than you what you need.’ I like that, don’t you?

“What we wish is that God would make sirens, bells, and whistles go off to show us which choice to make. Instead, He probably sighs and shakes his head as we stumble along, making bad choices. This choice, though,” he points at each couple, “this just feels right, doesn’t it?”

“Amen!” Harlon exclaims.

Stephen grins and nods at Harlon. “Thank you,” he tells him. “Now, I want you all to face each other.”

As they do so, he reaches into his pocket and retrieves the rings.

“Each of these rings is a perfect circle with no beginning or end. They symbolize a never-ending love that needs to be a hallmark of your marriages. These rings didn’t happen accidentally; they required craftsmen. Let these rings remind you that lasting love doesn’t happen accidentally. It takes work, but it’s a labor of love.”

Handing the rings to Cross and Harlon, he says, “Place these on your bride’s ring finger, and repeat after me. I give you this ring…as a sign of my devotion…I will always love you…cherish you…and honor you…until death we do part.”

When Harlon says the last phrase, there's a catch in his voice.

Megan wants to turn around and see if he's okay, but Cross gives her hand a squeeze and keeps her focused on him.

Stephen then hands rings to Megan and Grace and has them repeat the same phrases.

Megan is surprised by how strong and even her mother's voice sounds, and she wishes she could keep her own from trembling.

If only I could stop time and keep this perfect moment from fading and hold off Death's sickle from cutting Mother away from us.

Stephen's voice interrupts her thoughts by saying, "Now, because of your vows, and by the authority of your license, I pronounce you man and wife. You men may kiss your brides."

As Cross leans down, Megan closes her eyes and hears nature all around them—the cooing of a mourning dove, cicadas in the trees, and grasshoppers and katydids in the grasses. Cross's face radiates heat, and she tastes the bead of sweat above his upper lip.

"May the LORD bless you and keep you," Stephen says in a loud voice, "may He make His face shine upon you, and be gracious to you; may the Lord lift up His countenance upon you and give you peace."

Buck, Betty, Glynn, and Randy break out with applause and hoots of celebration. Megan turns to her mother and gives her a hug, and Cross and Harlon do the same with each other.

Grace says to Megan, "Thank you for doing this for me. It makes my heart easy knowing you'll be happy after I'm gone."

Megan's vision blurs for a moment, and a lump forms in her throat. "Thank you for giving me a reason to go ahead and marry Cross now instead of waiting till who knows when." Winking at her, she adds, "You always seem to get your way, don't you?"

With a cunning smile, Grace answers, "Yes, I do. That's the way I like it."

Buck appears at their side and says, "I'm here to kiss the brides! Two for the price of one!"

Before either of them can respond, he gives each of them a hard kiss on the cheek.

Pushing him out of the way, Betty says, "You'll have to excuse him. I only let him out of his cage occasionally, and when I do, I always regret it." She hugs each of them in turn. "You both look radiant." To Megan, she says, "Welcome to this family, because that's what all of us here are—family. We'll always be here for you, no matter what, and we expect you to do the same for us."

"You can count on it," Megan tells her. "I've never had a sister. I'm counting on you being one."

"Aw, you're sweet. That sounds great to me."

"Well, I'm going to be on my way," Stephen announces to them. "Thank you all for letting me be a part of this special day. Remember, God's always close by, even if you don't acknowledge Him. There may come a day when you need Him. If that day comes, don't be afraid to hold His hand."

Megan feels as if a brief and sudden solar eclipse just took place, and it leaves her a little unsettled. Walking to Cross, she takes hold of his hand.

Looking down at her, he asks, "Are you okay?"

"I just had a funny feeling pass through me, but I'm okay now." Laying her head against his shoulder, she says, "Anytime I'm with you, I'm okay."

"And now I get to take you home with me, don't I?"

"Yes, you do. I'm telling you, I can't believe we got all my stuff moved into your house and all your dad's moved into Mother's."

"Okay, everybody," Harlon says to the group, "let's go celebrate at Blues Landing."

"All right!" Buck says. "Let's go!"

Everyone scatters to their vehicles and heads to the restaurant.

Inside, the band Twenty-Four Seven is finishing a final soundcheck, then starts playing "Unchained Melody."

Instead of making their way to a table, Cross and Harlon lead Megan and Grace onto the dance floor. As they begin to dance, everyone in the restaurant applauds.

"Why are they clapping?" Megan asks Cross.

"They all know we've just been married. They're friends and customers we invited to the reception."

Like a magic potion, the strains of the song build and push everything around Megan into a fog, so the only thing she sees and feels is Cross holding her in his arms as they slowly move around the dance floor.

"I love you," she tells him.

"And I love you," he replies.

"I don't want this moment to ever end."

"Neither do I."

Once the song concludes, the band starts playing "Any Way You Want It," and other couples descend onto the dance floor and begin dancing energetically.

A few hours later, Megan and Cross exit the restaurant and are embraced by a heavy night air. Holding hands, they walk across the parking lot and get into his truck.

"You're going to think I'm crazy," Megan says, "but do you know what I want to do?"

"Whatever it is, as long as it involves us taking our clothes off, I'm all for it," Cross replies.

Megan laughs. "Well, then, you're going to like this. I want to go skinny dipping in Kentucky Lake. I've never been skinny dipping."

Cross's eyes open wide. "You're kidding."

"About which part?"

"Both parts."

"Nope. Both are true."

"You want to go skinny dipping on our wedding night. You're just full of surprises, aren't you? Just know this: I won't be responsible for what happens once we're both naked."

She sends him an air kiss. "Don't you worry about me, honey, I can handle whatever you've got."

"Whoa, now." He roars with laughter and puts the truck in gear. "You're mighty bold and brave sitting here in the truck. Let's see if you change your tune when the time comes."

A thrill of excitement runs through Megan as they head out of the parking lot. "Where will we do it?" she asks.

"The best place is where we got married, underneath that old beech tree. The bottom of the lake isn't as muddy there as in other places. I think they might have quarried stone there before the land was flooded to make the lake."

"This is what I want our marriage to be like," Megan tells him, "making memories together, doing the unexpected, the out of the ordinary. We'll never forget this, will we?"

"Even if you chicken out when we get there, I'll still never forget you asking me to take you skinny dipping on our wedding night."

"Chicken out? What makes you think I'm going to chicken out?"

"Because you've never stood naked in front of God and the world and then gotten in water that looks black because there's no light. You can't see if there's anything in the water waiting on you or not."

"What do you mean by that? What would be waiting on us?"

"Snakes mainly. But they say alligators are slowly making their way north. Some have been spotted around Memphis already. Plus, there's catfish in this lake as big as a small car."

A finger of fear touches the back of Megan's neck, sending a shudder through her body. "You're just making that up. I know you. You'd like nothing better than to tease me about chickening out. Well, you can forget about that. I'm doing it!"

Pulling off the main road and onto a side road, Cross smiles and says, "Okay. Whatever you say."

"You are so cocky. I hope you're the one who chickens out. I promise if you do, I'll tell everybody you know what a chicken you are."

"I've got nothing to say. We'll see what happens when we get to the water."

A few minutes later, Cross pulls to a stop underneath the tree, cuts off the engine, and turns off his headlights. Like the giant fish that swallowed Jonah, darkness envelopes them.

For a moment, Megan can't see anything, then her eyes adjust and she sees the outline of the tree. "Wow, it's really dark, isn't it?"

"It is indeed," Cross answers her. "You still want to do this?"

"Honestly, I'm so excited, I can't sit still, and I'm so afraid, I can't move. This is so cool!"

Cross opens his door, and the interior lights blind Megan.

She gets out on her side, closes her door, and meets him at the front of the truck. "Listen to all the sounds. One of them is a Whip-poor-will, isn't it?"

"Yes, it is. Behind us, I hear a bard owl."

She turns to listen. "Yes, I hear it, too."

"And, of course, all the frogs are croaking."

"I like how they have different pitches. There's the deep, low tones from the bullfrogs and spring peepers singing soprano."

"I never thought of it that way," Cross says, "but you're right. It's like a symphony, isn't it?"

"What's that sound in the distance? I don't know that one."

"That's a loon."

"It's kind of a sad sound."

"Yeah, it is."

She finds his hand and says, "Okay, lead us to the water."

They slowly make their way to the edge of the water, where little waves are lapping on the shore.

Megan looks around. "You don't think there's anyone else out here, do you?"

"That's the risky thing about doing this. You can't really know. There could be some guys sitting out there in a boat right now, trying to see what we're doing."

"Really?"

"Really."

Reaching for the buttons on her shirt, Megan says, "Well, I don't care. I hope they enjoy the show if they're there."

"We need to undress fast and get in the water," Cross says, "or the mosquitos will eat us up."

Megan laughs. "And there are places on my body I really don't want to get a mosquito bite."

Cross laughs with her. "Me either!"

Once they're naked, Cross takes her hand and says, "Here we go."

The water's colder than Megan expects it to be, and her whole body becomes one giant goosebump. She wonders if it's affected Cross the same way it affected George Constanza in an episode of Seinfeld she saw one time when he blamed his penis shrinkage on the cold water.

"Come on," Cross says, "we need to get in deeper water."

Several steps later, the water is chest high, and Cross dips underneath and comes back up. "Whew, that's refreshing!"

"But it's so cold." She floats on her back and swims around him. "It really feels good to swim without any clothes on, doesn't it?"

"I don't know about that, but the scenery sure is a lot more interesting."

"Oh, shut up. It's too dark to see anything."

"Then what are those two water balloons I see floating in the water around me?"

"You can't see that good." The next thing Megan knows, a hand grasps one of her breasts, and she screams in surprise.

“I’m sorry,” Cross says, “I thought that was a water balloon.”

She grabs for him and dunks him under the water. When he comes up for air, he bear hugs her to him, and she immediately realizes the shrinkage factor doesn’t apply to Cross. “Hey, big guy,” she says, “is that a banana in your pocket, or are you happy to see me?”

He kisses her and massages one of her breasts. “I’ll show you how happy I am to see you, but not here in this dirty water. Can we go home now? You’ve gotten your wish to skinny dip. It’s time for me to have my wish.”

She kisses him back. “Just do one more thing for me, then we can go. Carve our initials in the tree.”

CHAPTER FIFTY-FIVE

Meanwhile, Harlon stands behind Grace, waiting for her to unlock the front door of her house.

"I need to get a key made for you," she tells him.

"We can do that tomorrow."

As they walk inside, his heart rate increases, not because he's eager to go to bed with her, but because he's nervous about it. He reaches inside his pants pocket and feels his bottle of Viagra.

I've got to time it just right when I take it. If I take it too soon, its effect will wear off. Taking it immediately before we go to bed won't give it enough time to work. Does she want to go straight to bed, or does she want to sit and talk for a while first?

"We've had a big day, haven't we?" she asks.

"A very big day," he agrees.

"I'm ready to get out of these clothes and into something more comfortable, what about you?"

"Uh, sure, that sounds good."

So, it's not straight to bed. I'll just wait.

He follows her into the bedroom where she turns to face him. "You know, we really haven't talked about what happens in here." She waves her hand, indicating the bedroom. "I'm embarrassed for you to see me without my clothes on. Father Time and gravity have taken over my body and done a number on it. It's not very pretty to look at. I know you've been pretty active sexually since your wife died, but I haven't had sex at all since my husband died. I'm afraid I won't live up to your expectations."

Her concerns and worries wash away all of Harlon's anxiety, and he takes her in his arms. "I love how honest you can be with me. As for Father Time and gravity, they've tied a rope around my feet and drug me down a gravel road behind a pickup truck."

Grace laughs at his description.

"There's an old Randy Travis song, 'Forever and Ever, Amen,' where he sings about how time changes a person's body, making brown hair turn grey. Then he says he doesn't care if the woman's hair all falls out, because he's not in love with her hair. I'm in love with *you*, Grace, with who you are, the person you are. That's what makes you beautiful to me; it's what makes you perfect. Even if I was given the power to, I wouldn't change one thing about you—not one thing."

Tears pool in her eyes, and she says, "You're so sweet, it makes my heart ache. But what about sex? Evidently, you're still awfully…uh, virile?"

Harlon fishes the Viagra bottle out of his pocket. Giving it a little shake, he says, "Not without this, I'm not. Mr. Johnson's get-up-and-go got-up-and-went a number of years ago."

Grace looks confused. "What's that?"

"It's Viagra, Grace—the little blue pill."

"You mean?"

"Yep. I can't get an erection without it. It's embarrassing to admit, but you and I are going to be honest about everything, aren't we?"

Taking the medicine bottle out of his hand, Grace marches into the bathroom.

When she comes back out empty-handed, Harlon asks, "What did you do?"

"I threw it in the trash. You're not using it anymore; not as long as you're with me. I don't think we need it to please each other sexually. I want us to feel free to tell each other what makes us feel good, to try things naturally, without medication or those stupid sex toys I hear about. I'll tell you what I'm looking forward to the most about being in bed with you. I'm looking forward to you holding my body next to yours and letting me feel its warmth. It makes me melt just thinking about it."

"There's no reason to be nervous about it, is there? You make it sound so easy."

"That's because it's going to be easy. I don't want either of us to feel pressure to be or do anything other than just be ourselves. We don't have any trouble talking to each other, do we?"

Smiling, he answers, "Not at all. Talking with you is the easiest thing in the world to do. I like that."

"Well, I think what we do in bed will just be another way of communicating with each other, except we'll use touch instead of words."

He puts his arms around her and pulls her close. "I just love you. Sex shouldn't be about performance, should it? It should be about me showing you how much I love you by doing things that make you feel pleasure. Am I right?"

"You're exactly right," she answers.

"So, are you ready to go to bed now, or do you want to stay up a while and talk or watch television?"

"Since we've talked about it, why don't we go ahead and cross that bridge now and see how things go in bed?"

"That sounds good."

Sitting down on opposite sides of the bed, they peel off their clothes and slip under the covers.

Grace turns off her bedside lamp, then Harlon does his, leaving only the faint light from the living room shining through the doorway.

~~~~~~~~~~

The next morning, Harlon is startled awake but unsure why. Looking beside him, he sees Grace isn't there. Then he hears the sounds of her retching in the bathroom.

Throwing off the covers, he gets out of bed, puts on his boxer shorts, and walks to the bathroom door. Tapping on it, he says, "Grace, can I come in?"

The only sound he hears is more retching, so he opens the door and finds her kneeling beside the toilet, looking pale.

"Grace! What can I do?"
~~~~~~~~~~

“I’ll be okay in a minute,” she says weakly. “I don’t know why I woke up feeling so nauseated.”

Dampening a washcloth with cold water, Harlon gets on the floor beside her and gently rubs her face and mouth while at the same time flushing the toilet.

“That feels good,” she says. “Thank you. I just feel washed out this morning. I think I want to go back to bed.”

“Sure thing. Let me stand up first, and then I’ll help you up.”

“I can get up.”

“No, let me help you.” Grunting, he gets to his feet and puts his hands under her arms. “Ready?”

She nods, and he lifts her to her feet.

“You may be old,” she tells him, “but you’re still strong as an ox.”

“And don’t I look sexy in my boxer shorts?”

“Don’t make me answer that. Remember, you said we’re going to be honest with each other.”

He laughs as he helps her into the bed. “Yes, don’t answer that. Now, do you want some pillows behind your back so you can sit up, or do you just want to lie on your back?”

“I think I want to try and go back to sleep.”

Sitting on the edge of the bed as she lies down, he takes her hand and holds it between his. “Can I tell you something before you go to sleep?”

She turns her head toward him. “Sure.”

“I don’t think I’ve ever enjoyed sex as much as I did last night. It was beautiful, and sweet, and tender, and thrilling. I just wanted you to know that.”

Smiling up at him, she says, “I couldn’t have asked it to be more perfect. You were a beautiful lover.” She kisses his hand. “Now, you go on about your day. I’m just going to rest and get up later. I love you.”

“I love you, too.”

He walks to the dresser and gets out a shirt and socks and pair of overalls and heads out of the bedroom into the living room, closing the door behind him.

As he gets dressed, uneasy thoughts run through his mind.

Is it her cancer making her sick? Has it already reached that stage? Surely, it's too soon for that. Do I need to take her to the doctor? Would she go if I asked her? Should I call Megan and tell her, or would that make Grace mad? I know one thing; I'm not leaving this house until I can see she's feeling better.

CHAPTER FIFTY-SIX

One week later, Grace carries a dust rag and walks slowly in the gift store, dusting each item. She sees Megan approaching her and says, "This is your big day, isn't it? The Grand Opening!"

"Yes, it is, but I'm worried about you helping out. Are you sure you're up to it? It's only been a week since you had that bad spell Harlon told me about."

"He shouldn't have worried you with it, and I told him so. I was just nauseated that morning, that's all. I'm feeling fine today."

Betty appears at the end of the aisle and joins them. "Is this a private conversation?" she asks.

"No," Grace answers her. "I'm just dealing with my worrywart daughter here. Will you tell her to quit worrying about me?"

"It would be easier to tell the sun not to shine," Betty replies. "We always worry about the people we love; that's just the way it is. To be honest with you, I intend to keep watch on you today, because *I'm* worried about you."

"Aren't you worried, Mother?" Megan asks.

"About what?"

"You know…about the cancer and…" She doesn't finish her sentence.

"You mean about dying? Like, when am I going to die, and what's it going to be like when I do? Not really. I'm just happy I'm here with you two beautiful, strong women, and I'm excited about us helping open the gift store. That's the only thing happening at this moment—that's it, nothing else is going on. How about let's enjoy the day?"

Megan and Betty look at each other.

Betty says, "I've got no comeback for that. Do you?"

"Nothing I can think of," Megan replies.

Clapping her hands together, Grace says, "Good, then! It's almost time to open the door. Let's get ready."

Buck, Cross, and Harlon come 'round the corner.

"There y'all are," Buck says. He opens the lid to a rectangular white box he's holding and says, "We got doughnuts, bear claws, and apple fritters. You all want one?"

Betty says, "Of course, my Buck would be the one to think of food."

The women laugh.

Harlon walks up to Grace and gives her a quick kiss.

Reaching for the corner of his mouth, she wipes off some glaze with her thumb. "I think that's the first time I've had a doughnut-flavored kiss."

"Well, someone had to test the food to make sure it was safe for you ladies to eat it," Harlon replies.

Looking inside the box, Megan says, "It looks like you all had to eat a generous portion before you were convinced it was safe."

Cross grins and says, "You can't be too careful."

"Oh, whatever." Megan takes the box from Buck and offers it to Betty and Grace.

Grace lifts out an apple fritter and takes a bite. She closes her eyes as her taste buds explode in reaction to the cinnamon, sugar, ginger, and apple flavors. "Oh my, this is delicious! It tastes so good, it's making my knees weak."

Immediately, Harlon takes hold of her arm. "Are you okay? Let me go find a chair. Is there a chair in here, Megan?"

Megan makes a start toward the storage area, and Grace says, "Hold up, don't go do that. I'm fine. I was just making an exaggeration about how good this apple fritter is. There's nothing to panic over."

Megan puts her hand on her chest. "You scared me to death, Mother."

"I was afraid you were going to faint again," Harlon tells her.

“Stop it!” Grace says firmly. “Everyone, stop treating me like I’m dying! I can’t enjoy being alive, because with every breath I take, one of you reacts like it’s my last. Right now, at this moment, I’m standing here, eating an apple fritter and am ready to help customers who come today. Okay?”

She looks at each of them, and they give a nod of assent. “Thank you. Now, isn’t it time to open the door and let people in?”

Megan looks at her Fitbit. “Yes, it is.”

“Where do you want us men?” Cross asks.

“Maybe the storage area? Just be ready when someone needs help loading some of the heavier items or if they decide to buy some mulch or soil or fertilizer outside.”

“Got it.”

The men move off, and Grace follows Megan toward the front of the store.

“I’m just going to stay around here in case anyone needs help finding something,” Betty says.

“That’s a good idea,” Megan calls back to her. “Thanks.”

Looking toward the glass front door, Grace says, “Look at the cars out there! I’m so excited for you.”

“I’m nervous and excited, too,” Megan says. “Give me a hug.”

They embrace.

Pulling open the door, Megan announces, “Welcome! Come right in!”

For the next several hours, the store is a beehive of activity.

During the middle of it, though, sharp pains shoot through Grace’s abdomen, and she hurries to the bathroom, where she throws up. The pains move to her back, shoving her to the floor.

“Dear God,” she prays silently, “it’s too soon to be this sick. I knew this was going to be part of it, but won’t You please give me just a little more time?”

Suddenly, the locked doorknob on the bathroom door rattles as someone tries to come in.

Pushing herself off the floor, Grace stands and splashes some cold water on her face. When she opens the door, Harlon is standing there, wearing a mask of concern.

"Come on, we're going home," he tells her. "I can tell you're not feeling well."

"I'm okay. I don't want to leave. Megan needs our help," Grace replies. But a sudden wave of fatigue hits her, and all she wants to do is lie in her bed and rest. "Okay," she relents, "take me home. But we're not going to tell Megan I got sick. I don't want her to worry."

"Then let's leave out through the back."

They're able to depart without being seen by anyone, and Grace leans her head against the headrest. "I'm just so tired."

Patting her hand as he drives off, Harlon says, "We'll be home in just a minute, and you can rest. One thing I've got to tell you, though. You've got to quit thinking any of us are going to stop worrying about you, because we're not; we're just not. So there's no point in you getting upset about it."

"But I don't want to be a burden to anyone and weigh them down with this."

"It's not a burden, Grace. It's a privilege to love someone so much, it just hurts to know you're going to lose them. Weren't you that way when you lost your husband?"

She hesitates a moment, then says, "I'm going to tell you something I've never uttered, because it makes me sound so coldhearted. There was a big part of me that was relieved when he died. Being married to him wasn't easy. Our personalities never meshed, and I had to tiptoe around him to keep from setting him off on an angry tirade."

"Did he hit you?"

"No, nothing like that. He was just so critical of everything; not a happy person at all. That's why the love I have for you is so different. You're easy to be around. What about you and your wife? You've never told me what it was like losing her."

“Honestly, it was hard. I really loved her, or I thought I did. I never doubted my love for her until you and I got back together. It’s made me decide there have to be levels of love, or different kinds of love, because the love I have for you isn’t like any love I’ve ever felt.”

Grace looks over at him and sees a solitary tear reluctantly slipping down his cheek. Reaching over, she erases the tear with her fingertip. “Don’t cry.”

In a voice choked with emotion, he says, “I can’t help it. I love you so much, it hurts my heart.”

She blinks, and tears splash onto her sleeve.

CHAPTER FIFTY-SEVEN

Being careful not to wake Cross, Megan slips out of bed, makes her way outside the house, and sits down on the edge of the porch.

Lacy, who snuck out with her, nudges her elbow with her nose, then crawls onto Megan's lap.

"What's the matter?" Megan asks her. "You couldn't sleep either."

Lacy's nose twitches as she sniffs the night air.

Stroking her pet's back, Megan says, "As far as I can see, your life is perfect. You sleep sixteen hours a day, have all you want to eat and drink, get to go outside and pee and poop anywhere you want to. Yeah, I'd say you've got it made, little girl.

Lacy's ears rotate back and forth like radar dishes searching for sounds from deep space as she tries to listen to Megan and the night sounds at the same time. Finally, she turns around and faces Megan.

"It's Mother, that's what it is," Megan tells her. "Her cancer is moving faster than I thought it would. I'm afraid she doesn't have much time left. It makes me so sad. Honestly, I wish I hadn't left the house and come here to live with Cross. I want to be with Mother every chance I get, but I don't want to say anything to Cross about it, because it might hurt his feelings; he might not understand."

Stretching her neck forward, Lacy sniffs her face.

"Do sadness and grief have a smell? Can you tell what's wrong with me?"

Lacy cocks her head to one side and gives Megan a quick lick on the lips.

Hugging her to her chest, Megan says, "You are the sweetest, kindest thing! Do you think I should talk to Cross about what I said?"

"I think you should."

Cross's voice startles her. "How long have you been standing there?"

"I just got here. I woke up, and you were gone." He sits beside her. "What are you doing out here?"

"I couldn't sleep."

"It's about your mother, isn't it?"

"How did you know?"

"How could you not be worried or thinking about her all the time? I know I am. It's awful how fast the cancer is progressing. I hate it for her, and for you, too. It's just not fair. She's a good woman, never has a bad thing to say about anyone, willing to help anyone, and she has to be the one to die instead of someone bent on doing evil. She even believes in God, for all the good it does her."

"Cross!"

"I'm sorry. That's just how I feel. If God wants someone to die, why doesn't He take some of the scum I was in prison with? The world would be better off without them. All they're doing is taking up space and costing us taxpayers money."

Megan doesn't know what to say, so she sits quietly.

After a moment of silence, Cross says, "What were you talking with Lacy about? What did it have to do with me?"

At the sound of her name, Lacy turns her attention to Cross and sniffs one of his bare arms.

Taking a deep breath, Megan says, "I wish I could spend more time with Mother."

"Do you want to close the store? Because if you do, Buck and I are okay with it. We've already talked about it."

"That's sweet of you both to be thinking about the situation, but I don't want to do that. Mother would be upset if I did."

"What do you want to do?"

"You're going to think this is crazy, but I want you and I to move in with her and your dad until…you know. I know that's stupid. We've just gotten married and are enjoying having sex again and having our privacy. I'm stuck between the proverbial rock and a hard place. I don't want to miss out on any time with my mother, but I don't want to miss out on any time with you either."

"I don't think your idea is stupid at all. I think it's exactly what we should do. That way, you can see your mother every morning and every night, and you'll know for certain how she's doing without having to rely on a phone call to find out. And we won't miss out on time with each other, because we'll be doing this together. I love your mother, too, you know."

"Are you serious?! You'd be willing to do that?"

He turns her face to look at him. "Look here, for the rest of our life together, I'm willing to do whatever makes you happy. All you have to do is tell me, because I'm not a mind reader."

She kisses him, then says, "That's what makes you so sexy and attractive. But what do you think your dad will say about us moving in?"

"He'll say whatever your mother says, because, like me, he'll do anything she wants. Once we Daniels men commit to something, we're all in, one hundred percent."

"Should we go over there now and ask them?"

Cross laughs. "You've forgotten what time it is."

Megan looks at the dark and chuckles. "Yeah, I guess we should at least wait until the sun comes up."

The sound of the screen door opening draws their attention, and Roxy pushes her way onto the porch. Yawning, she does a cat stretch, then moseys to Cross's side.

"I think she wants us to go back to bed," Cross says.

"Let's try to slip in a nap before the alarm goes off," Megan suggests.

Sliding his hand between her thighs, he says, "Or I might slip something else in before sunrise."

Taking ahold of his hand, she pulls it to her crotch. "I like that idea even better."

~~~~~~~~~~
~~~~~~~~~~

When Megan awakes, she's lying crossways in the bed, her head hanging halfway off and her legs tangled with Cross's, who lies with his head at the foot and feet at the head of the bed. She smiles and closes her eyes at the memory of why they ended up in this position a few hours ago.

Extricating her legs from his, she sits on the edge of the bed and checks the time on her phone. "Hey," she says, "it's seven o'clock. I'm going to take a quick shower, then let's head over to talk to Mother and your dad."

Groaning, Cross rolls onto his side and opens one eye as she walks past him to the bathroom.

"Don't go back to sleep," she tells him.

The smell of coffee greets her when she finishes drying off and enters the bedroom. "That smells wonderful!" she calls to him as she dresses.

"Which flavor creamer do you want this morning?" he asks.

"Pumpkin spice latte."

"Is there anything pumpkin-flavored you don't like?"

"No."

"I can't stand it."

Entering the kitchen as she tucks in her T-shirt, Megan says, "If you don't like pumpkin flavor, I'm not sure we can still be friends."

Turning to her with a travel coffee mug in each hand, Cross says, "I don't recall that bothering you a few hours ago."

She takes the mug he offers her and sips it. "Well, that situation was different."

"Oh, I see how it is," he says, with a laugh. "You ready to go? I texted Pop and told him we'd be heading their way."

"Yeah, I'm ready."

~~~~~~~~~~

When they arrive, Harlon stands at the door, waiting. All the creases in his face look deeper, and the bags under his eyes heavier.
~~~~~~~~~~

Before Megan can ask what's wrong, he says, "We had a bad night last night. The pain kept her awake, and she threw up twice. She's asleep right now, so I didn't wake her to tell her you were coming. I'll let you decide if you want to or not."

Megan's heart sinks, and for a moment she can't catch her breath. Moving past Harlon, she says, "I've got to see her."

Grace's back is turned toward Megan when she enters the bedroom with its blinds pulled shut. Walking to the other side of the bed, she looks at her mother's face. Sleep has wiped away the pained expression her face must have borne last night and replaced it with a peaceful, relaxed look. If it weren't for Megan knowing how sick her mother is, she'd never be able to tell. That's why, sometimes, knowledge is a painful thing to endure.

She kneels on both knees beside the bed. With a touch as soft as a butterfly alighting, she traces her mother's cheekbone and jawbone while whispering, "Sleep on, Mother. Dream pleasant dreams. Leave your body here, and go to far off places."

Grace's eyes flutter open. Lying still, she blinks a couple times, then focuses on Megan. In a thin voice, she says, "My beautiful daughter. Where am I?"

"You're in Harlon's house, Mother."

"Harlon's?"

"Yes, you're married now."

A smile lifts one corner of her mouth, and she closes her eyes. "Oh yes, I remember now." Opening her eyes, she asks, "So the dream I was just dreaming is real, isn't it?"

Kissing her mother's forehead, Megan answers, "Yes, it is. And I'm married to Cross."

Grace's arm appears from under the covers, and she takes ahold of Megan's hand. "Help me sit up on the side of the bed."

Megan starts to argue with her but chooses to let her have her way and pulls her to a sitting position.

"Who would have thought?" Grace says. "The two of us getting married again, at the same time. What a wonderful miracle. Are you happy with Cross?"

Nodding, Megan answers, “Happier than I’ve ever been.”

“Me, too.” Suddenly, she looks at Megan with questions in her eyes. “Why are you here? Isn’t it morning? What time is it? What day is it? Shouldn’t you be getting ready for work?”

Moving to sit beside her, Megan says, “Everything’s okay. It’s Tuesday morning, and Cross and I came by to talk to you and Harlon about an idea we have. Do you feel like getting up?”

“Sure, sure I do. Just help me get dressed first.”

“You don’t have to get dressed. Let me get your robe for you.”

Grace protests, but Megan ignores her and lifts the robe off the bedpost. “Stand up here,” she tells her and helps thread her arms through the sleeves.

“Please excuse the way I look,” Grace tells Cross as they enter the living room. “Grace wouldn’t let me get dressed.”

Walking to her, Cross kisses her cheek and says, “You look fine, don’t worry about it.”

“So, what’s on you two’s minds?” Harlon asks.

Megan opens her mouth to answer, but Cross speaks first.

“We want to move in with you guys and stay in Megan’s old bedroom. We’ll have competitions for which couple can make the most noise while lovemaking, and you two women can finally settle the argument as to which of us two men snores the loudest. Megan and I think it’ll be fun.”

His effort to keep her worries and insecurities from being the reason for the idea and presenting it in such a lighthearted way moves Megan deeply.

What other man would think to do that?

Harlon and Grace look at each other, then Grace looks at Megan. “I know what this is about, because I know my daughter. You want to be here when I pass, don’t you?”

"It's not just that," Megan answers. "I just want to see you every day, to see how you're doing. That way, I don't have to worry, or at least I can worry less. And before you say anything, I don't intend to sit around with you all day. I'll still go to work every day, just like I am now. But I'll see you before I leave and when I get home." She looks at Harlon. "I know it's a lot to ask. You all have only been married a month, and I don't like being the needy, clingy daughter-in-law, but—"

Harlon holds up his hand for her to stop. "Listen. We four are family now. You're my daughter, and Cross is Grace's son. I think having y'all here would be great, don't you, Grace?"

Looking at him with a smile, Grace says, "Do you remember that movie when we were teens, *Love Story*, starring Ryan O'Neal and Ali MacGraw?"

Harlon hesitates for a second, then says, "Oh, yeah, I remember it."

"In it, the roommates in college would hang a necktie on the doorknob or their room to let it be known they didn't want to be disturbed because they were having sex with their girlfriend."

The other three stare at her blankly.

"Don't you all get it? That's what we'll have to do when you all move in, so we don't accidentally walk in on a scene we really don't want to see."

There's a beat of silence, then everyone starts laughing.

CHAPTER FIFTY-EIGHT

One morning in late August, Harlon stands on the porch with Cross and Megan.

"Promise you'll call me if she gets worse," Megan tells him.

"I promise. Maybe she'll rally and feel better by the time you all get home from work."

"That's what I'll pray for," Cross says.

Megan looks at him. "You'll pray? But I thought…"

"Yeah, I know what I've said in the past. But this situation with your mother has really tested me and left me with questions I can't answer. I remember something Stephen Randle told us on our wedding day. He said, 'Remember, God's always close by, even if you don't acknowledge Him. There may come a day when you need Him. If that day comes, don't be afraid to hold His hand.' I'm trying to hold His hand, because I don't know what else to do."

"How come you haven't talked about it?" Megan asks.

"I really didn't know how to put it into words."

Putting his hands on each of their shoulders, Harlon says, "Right now, prayer is all we've got left. So let's all keep praying." He hugs Cross and gives Megan a kiss. "You guys have a good day at work. And keep your eye on that lazy, no-account Buck."

They laugh at his description, then head down the sidewalk.

Harlon watches until their vehicles disappear, then he goes back inside the house, where he's startled by the sight of Grace walking toward him.

"What are you doing out of bed?" he asks.

"Have Megan and Cross already left?"

Walking to her, he holds her arm and guides her to a chair. He's struck by how thin she feels. "Yes, they just drove off."

“Aww, I wanted to tell them ’bye.” Turning sideways toward him, she says, “Look at my stomach. It looks like I’m nine months pregnant.”

As he eases her into the chair, he says, “You know, the doctor said they can draw that fluid out if you want them to.”

“I know. But it’ll just come back again, so what’s the point?”

“You want a cup of coffee or something to eat this morning?”

Grace sighs. “I’ll try to drink some coffee. I’m just not interested in eating anymore.”

“You really need to try. It’ll help you keep your strength up. I’ll be back in a second with your coffee.”

His hands tremble as he lifts the filled cup from the Keurig, so much so, some spills on the floor.

Damn it!

He empties the cup then pulls some paper towels off the roll and cleans up the mess.

This time when the Keurig finishes, he takes the cup with two hands and holds it against his chest.

Grace’s eyes are closed and her face slack with what he hopes is sleep. Very carefully, he sets the coffee on the table beside her and, with a grunt, sits down on the couch.

Without opening her eyes, Grace says, “You sound like an old man.”

He smiles. “That’s because I am. Your coffee’s there beside you.”

She opens her eyes and reaches for the coffee. “It smells good.” After taking a small sip, she says, “It’s one of my favorite smells, along with honeysuckle and the way a puppy smells.”

“I like the way a hayfield smells after it’s cut and lays there for a day. And I like the way a yard smells after it’s mowed.”

“I like those, too,” Grace says. “Thinking about smells makes me smile and puts me in a good mood.”

“They also trigger memories,” Harlon comments. “Honeysuckle makes me think of us being at the lake and making out. When I was with you, I always felt like the world was set right and everything was going to be okay. You were like a drug, I guess. I could forget about all my troubles.”

They sit quietly for a few minutes as Grace takes another sip of coffee.

Harlon breaks the silence. “You know, here I am again, in the same place I was fifty years ago. I’m with you, and everything is perfect. But you’re going to leave me again.” His throat squeezes shut anything else he might have said.

“Yes, I am,” Grace says. “And I’m going to leave sooner than I thought I would. This cancer is almost finished with me. My only regret about dying is that I’m hurting you again. That breaks my heart. I’m so sorry, Harlon.”

Overcome with emotion, he begins to sob.

“Come here,” she beckons him. Patting her lap, she says, “Lay your head here.”

Rolling off the couch onto his knees, he walks on them the short distance to her and lays his head on her lap.

Stroking his hair, Grace says, “Your heart is going to be broken, but you’re going to be okay. You’re going to remember this brief time we had together, and you’re going to treasure it. You’ve got to be here for Megan, too. I know she’ll have Cross, but she loves you so much and thinks the world of you. You’ll be able to comfort her in a way Cross can’t.”

Harlon’s breath catches as he tries to speak. Coughing to clear his throat, he says, “I’m not ready to let you go.”

She leans down and kisses his temple. “I know. I have a feeling, though, just a feeling it won’t be long now. Don’t forget to do what I told you to do about my funeral, okay?”

Nodding, Harlon says, “I promise, I will.”

“Is it too hot to sit outside this morning?”

“It’s warm, but the humidity hasn’t kicked in yet. You want to go outside?”

“I want to sit in the porch swing with you.”

Harlon’s knees pop when he gets off the floor.

“There you go, making those old man sounds again,” Grace teases him.

Immediately, he starts buck dancing. “How’s this for an old man?”

“You better stop before you have a heart attack!”

Panting from the brief exertion, Harlon stops to catch his breath.

“See what I mean?” Grace asks. “Come on, let’s go outside and act our age.”

Slowly, they make their way outside, and Harlon eases her onto the swing before sitting beside her.

For several minutes, neither of them speaks as they absorb the sights, sounds, and feelings of the moment.

Patting his thigh, Grace says, “This moment right here with you, this is the memory I’ll have on my mind when I leave. It’s the most perfect moment I can imagine. Thank you for loving me like you do.”

CHAPTER FIFTY-NINE

During a quiet moment at the gift shop, Megan carries the sack from the drugstore into the bathroom and pulls out a box with an early result pregnancy test inside. She reads the instructions, then pulls down her pants and sits on the toilet.

It's silly to think it's even possible. I don't know whether to be nervous or excited. What in the world will Cross say if I'm pregnant? I don't even know how I'll feel if it's positive.

Holding the thumb grip, she pulls off the cap and pees on the absorbent tip. Then she sets it on the edge of the sink, washes her hands, and sets a timer on her phone for three minutes.

Mother will be over the moon excited if I'm pregnant. Maybe she'll even be willing to have treatments for her cancer, just so she can have a chance at holding the baby. She'd be a good grandmother. And Harlon would be an amazing grandfather.

But do I want to be a mother? In the past, it's never been a goal. Have I changed that much that I'd want to go through a pregnancy and give birth to a child? Will it make it harder on Cross and my marriage? I don't think he's the kind of person who'd want me to have an abortion, and I don't think I could either.

I'm probably not even pregnant anyway. Why worry about it? But if I'm not, then why am I feeling the way I am?

She checks the timer on her watch. Seven seconds left.

Megan holds her breath and counts down the time, then looks at the result window. In all caps, it reads "yes" with a plus sign beside it. She stares in disbelief until a feeling of exhilaration unlike she's ever felt surges through her, and she squeals with delight, "I'm going to have a baby!"

Rushing out of the bathroom, she checks to be certain no customers are in the store. Then she grabs her keys and exits the store, locking the door as she leaves. Just before she gets in her car, she retrieves her phone from her back pocket and calls Cross.

His phone rings several times before he answers, "Hey, sweetheart."

Megan practically yells, “Are you all still at the Patterson place?”

Anxiety tinges his answer. “Yes. What’s happened?”

“Stay right there. I’m coming!”

Without waiting for a reply or giving more of an explanation, she jumps in her car and speeds toward him.

Her phone rings, and she sees it’s him calling her back.

I don’t want to tell him over the phone. I want to see his face when I tell him, so I can tell for certain whether he’s excited or not.

She touches the screen on her vehicle and declines his call.

He tries several more times, but she continues to refuse to answer.

Fifteen minutes later, she careens up the driveway where Cross and Buck are working. As soon as she sees them, they start running toward her, so she skids to a stop and jumps out.

Both men have panic-stricken expressions on their faces.

Cross grabs both her arms and exclaims, “What the hell has happened, Megan?”

“I’m going to have a baby! I’m carrying a baby inside me! I’m going to have a baby!”

Cross stares at her and blinks his eyes. “A baby? You…you’re going to have a baby? How in the world…?”

Buck gives a triumphant yell and says, “You stupid boy, how do you think it happened? Congratulations!” He bear hugs Megan, lifting her off the ground and spinning her around. “I’m going to be an uncle or a godfather or something. Wait till Betty hears this!”

When he sets her down, she turns her full attention on Cross. Tears are running down his cheeks, and he falls to his knees. He opens his arms toward her, and she rushes into them, nearly knocking him over.

“Oh, Megan, Megan, Megan. A baby? We’re going to have a baby?”

“Yes, we are. I know we didn’t plan on it or talk about it. I mean, I didn’t think I could get pregnant. I’ve never taken birth control, never had to. I don’t understand how…are you happy about it?”

"I'm over the moon about it! You're going to be the best mother in the world, and I get a chance to be a better father than I was the first time." He looks at Buck, then back at her. "So, is this how God works?"

Buck joins them. "What do you mean?"

"I asked God to help it not hurt so bad when Grace dies. Is that what this baby is? God's gift to us, so we'll have something to focus on and keep grief from swallowing us up? It's like it's a miracle."

Megan looks down, wraps her arms around her abdomen, and whispers, "A miracle."

Putting his arms around them, Buck says, "Everything about you two is just one miracle after another. Both of you survived accidents that could have killed you. You both vowed never to love again, but you found each other. You never thought you'd be married again. And now you're going to have a baby. I'd say God's love came looking for you years ago; you just didn't know it."

Pushing Buck aside, Cross takes Megan's face in his hands and gives her a long kiss.

"Hey, look, boys and girls," Buck says, "you've already got one kid in the oven. Why don't you give things a break?"

They both laugh at their friend.

"I can't wait to tell Pop," Cross says.

"Me either," Megan agrees. "And Mother. Won't she be happy?"

CHAPTER SIXTY

On a September morning, when last night's fog lingers in low places and the sky is the color of nickel, three vehicles drive slowly through the grass-lined lane that leads to Harlon and Grace's beech tree by the lake.

Megan sits between Cross and Harlon as Cross eases along.

"Are Buck and Betty behind us?" she asks.

Cross glances in the rearview mirror and says, "Yes, and Glynn and Randy are behind them."

Patting the urn resting in his lap, Harlon says, "Our last ride together."

When they break through the grass and arrive at the clearing, Megan gasps. "Oh, no! Look what's happened to the tree!"

Cross stops the truck, and they stare in disbelief.

The top half of the tree is split down the middle, with one half hanging toward the ground. The exposed trunk has a black scar running through it, and all the leaves on the tree are brown. Tiny pieces of wood lie scattered on the ground beneath it.

"My gosh," Cross says, "lightning struck it. Must have been from that storm a few nights ago."

Megan's eyes grow misty, and she looks at Harlon. Leaning her head against his shoulder, she says, "Your tree. I'm so sorry."

"Nothing lasts forever, does it?" Harlon says. "It just didn't want to keep on living without Grace. I understand that feeling."

"But you've got to be here for this baby, don't you?" she tells him.

"Yes, you're right. I'm so glad Grace got to hear the news before she passed."

"Me, too. Now we've got several months to get over Mother's passing before the baby's born."

Cross lets off the brake and drives forward until he's underneath the tree.

Everyone gets out of their vehicles wearing the same white shirts and blue jeans they wore to the wedding.

A rope is tied to the tree and leads to Buck's pontoon boat that's beached on the shore.

Randy and Glynn hurry past everyone. Randy steps up on the front of the boat, while Glynn stays on the ground.

"Let us help you get onboard," Randy tells everyone.

After everyone is safely on, Glynn unties the boat from the tree, and he and Randy push it off the bank and into the lake before jumping onboard themselves.

The water's as smooth as glass.

Cross looks at the men and says, "Y'all ready?"

They all nod, and Harlon says, "Let's do this."

Cross hums a pitch, and they begin singing "Go Rest High On That Mountain."

Megan and Betty lock arms and cry together.

When the last strains of the song move across the water to some place on the opposite shore, Harlon empties the urn onto the water, then says, "This is where Grace wanted her remains to lie, at the spot on the lake beside which we shared so many good memories, especially underneath this tree. But as we've all just seen, the tree won't be here much longer. But the memories? The memories will last as long as we keep them alive by talking about them, laughing about them, and crying about them. And we need to do that for this baby Megan's carrying. I want it to grow up knowing Grace. We need to teach it the magic that comes with second chances."

THE END

Notes from the author:

I want to thank you for purchasing and reading Second Chance Love.

This book was very personal in that I was able to share many stories of things that have happened in my life and stories of friends who took a chance on second chance love. I want to especially thank these dear couples: the Kings, the McCadams, and the Mebanes. Together we have shared a rich association with fun-filled, soul-enriching, and heart-breaking experiences. My soul is richer for having known you.

And I want to thank God for giving me this gift of writing. He has blessed me beyond measure and much more than I deserve.

Self-publishing, without the support of a publishing house in promoting a book, is a daunting task. I'm relying on you readers to help me tell other people about Second Chance Love. It would mean a lot to me if you'd take the time to tell your friends about the book, post something on Facebook and/or Instagram, and especially post a review on Amazon. Those reviews are one of the main drivers of sales on Amazon.

Feel free to contact me via email davidjohnsonbooks@gmail.com or on my Facebook Author page. I'd also love to have you join my private Facebook Author group. If you're a member of a book club, I'm happy to join one of your meetings by way of the internet, or if you're in northwest Tennessee, I might be able to personally meet with you.

If you're a first-time reader of one of my books and enjoyed this one, you need to go to my author page on Amazon and check the other thirteen books I have published.

Made in United States
North Haven, CT
02 June 2024